Praise for the Inspector Bordelli novels:

'Over the course of his police procedurals, Vichi shows us ever more secret and dark sides to an otherwise sunny and open city. But his happiest creation, in my opinion, remains the character of Inspector Bordelli, a disillusioned anti-hero who is difficult to forget.'
Andrea Camilleri

'[Italian] writers are justifiably growing in popularity here: Marco Vichi deserves to be among them . . . [Bordelli] is stubborn, womanless, cynical and impatient, but strangely appealing.'
Marcel Berlins, *The Times*

'A real find for anyone who likes their crime novels atmospheric, discursive, humorous and thought-provoking.'
Guardian on *Death in Florence*

'Vichi's crime novels are enjoyable, mystifying and well worth reading.'
Literary Review

'Brilliantly evoking a society in crisis, Marco Vichi has given us a crime novel that is moving and memorable.'
Daily Mail on *Death in Florence*

'Once again [Vichi's] depiction of Italian history and culture is both fascinating and complex . . . As a portrait of a country struggling with its past, present and future, *Death in Sardinia* is a sharply observed slice of crime fiction with real depth.'
www.crimetime.co.uk

Also by Marco Vichi

Death in August
Death and the Olive Grove
Death in Sardinia
Death in Florence
Death in the Tuscan Hills

About the author

Marco Vichi was born in Florence in 1957. The author of twelve novels and two collections of short stories, he has also edited crime anthologies, written screenplays, music lyrics and for radio, written for Italian newspapers and magazines, and collaborated on and directed various projects for humanitarian causes.

There are six novels and two short stories featuring Inspector Bordelli. *Death in Florence (Morte a Firenze)* won the Scerbanenco, Rieti, Camaiore and Azzeccagarbugli prizes in Italy. Marco Vichi lives in the Chianti region of Tuscany.

You can find out more at www.marcovichi.it.

About the translators

Stephen Sartarelli is an award-winning translator. He is also the author of three books of poetry. He lives in France.

Oonagh Stransky has translated works by Pasolini, Lucarelli, Saviano and Pope Francis, among others. She lives in Italy.

MARCO VICHI

Ghosts of the Past

An
Inspector Bordelli
Mystery

Originally published in Italian as *Fantasmi del Passato*
Translated by Stephen Sartarelli and Oonagh Stransky

First published in Great Britain in 2018 by Hodder & Stoughton
An Hachette UK company

This paperback edition published in 2018

2

A CIP catalogue record for this title is available from the British Library

Paperback ISBN 978 1 473 61383 6
eBook ISBN 978 1 473 61381 2

Typeset in Plantin Light by
Palimpsest Book Production Ltd, Falkirk, Stirlingshire

Printed and bound in Great Britain by Clays Ltd, Elcograf S.p.A.

Hodder & Stoughton policy is to use papers that are natural, renewable and recyclable products and made from wood grown in sustainable forests. The logging and manufacturing processes are expected to conform to the environmental regulations of the country of origin.

Hodder & Stoughton Ltd
Carmelite House
50 Victoria Embankment
London EC4Y 0DZ

www.hodder.co.uk

Ghosts of the Past

Impruneta, December 1967

'Mamma . . .'

He raised his head from the pillow and opened his eyes. It was pitch black. He'd been dreaming, and he was sure he had spoken in his sleep. He lay back down and closed his eyes. He'd dreamt the phone was ringing in the night. He'd hopped out of bed and down the stairs, staggering, heart racing. When he picked up the phone, he heard his mother's voice.

'Franco, what have you done? How could you possibly do such a thing?'

At that moment he'd woken up.

'Mamma . . .' he repeated in a whisper. How long had it been since that name had crossed his lips? For many years now he'd had no reason to utter it. His mother's last days then came back to him, when she lay in the same bed in which she would soon lie in state for three days, exposed to all, in accordance with her wishes. He'd felt a great void after she died, the very same that sons had been feeling for centuries in those circumstances. And time had since done nothing but expand that void.

This was why he felt so disappointed. His mother's phone call had been just a dream. It would have been so nice to talk to her . . . Even nicer to see her, to be able to look her in the eye and squeeze her hands . . . To tell her all those things which . . .

'Franco, what have you done? How could you possibly do such a thing?'

It had only been a dream, and yet he'd heard those words clearly. He could not ignore them. It was his conscience, come to present him with the bill and speaking through his mother. He was guilty of having replaced the justice of the courts with his own personal justice. In his defence he could plead nobility of intention . . . He'd killed three men, three perverse murderers who'd raped and snuffed out little Giacomo Pellissari . . . and whom no human law would ever manage to convict. He'd followed his own path, challenging fate, and winning every bet. Only later had he started to feel the pangs of conscience, as though starting awake from a dream. He could perhaps have taken a different course, not let himself get carried away by the idea of being a sort of secular arm of fate . . .

'Franco, what have you done?'

'Mamma . . .' said Bordelli, perhaps only in his mind, hugging the pillow and letting himself slip away into distant memories, trying to recover a sense of peace . . . He was a little boy on the beach at Marina di Massa, with the waves breaking against the shore, one after the other, with an infernal din . . . His mother held him by the hand, and together they watched the spectacle in silence, faces stinging from a thousand droplets of salt water . . . That was all he remembered, the two of them at the edge of a rough sea, his hand in his mother's . . . Little by little he drifted off into other memories . . . Family episodes that had been recounted thousands of times around the table, dramatic or comical anecdotes about great-grandparents he'd never met, handed down and mythified by their descendants, secret moments never revealed to anyone . . . Until, at last, he was able to fall back asleep . . .

But the night still had plenty of dreams in store for him, and he woke up again softly caressing Eleonora . . . Beautiful young Eleonora, whom he was unable to forget . . . Just as he was unable to forget that whole terrible episode . . . He turned under the covers, still seeing her lovely face, smiling at him in the dream . . . Poor Eleonora. She'd been made the sacrificial victim in a matter that concerned only him, a police inspector who'd been unable to do his job . . . who'd failed . . . and who, after his defeat, had hoped to correct his own mistakes by avenging himself on the three unpunished murderers.

Every so often he would try in his mind to *push* those three murders back to the days of the war, in the hope of classing them among the Nazis he'd killed in combat . . . but they always came back. He would have to resign himself to bearing the weight of his guilt for the rest of his life. There was only one thing, one realisation that gave him some relief . . . He hadn't dragged anyone else into his morbid adventure; he'd confronted it alone, taken upon himself full responsibility for the path he had taken. For this reason, too, he would never tell anyone about it . . .

He'd dreamt of Eleanora, and he would carry those sweet moments around with him for the whole day. Opening one eye, he saw the dawn's first light filtering through the slats in the shutter. It must have been about seven o'clock. He put the pillow over his head, to return to the darkness, and tried to think of other things . . .

The summer had gone by peacefully, with only two murders, both solved by day's end. In October he'd taken almost a week to get a postal clerk to confess to killing a colleague for revenge, a sordid tale of frustration and vendetta spiced with a former rivalry in love . . .

All at once he thought he heard a dog barking, and immediately he imagined Blisk, the great white dog who had chosen to live in his house for a few months, until one day he went away. Bordelli got out of bed and went to peer through the shutter, but there was no dog. He put on a jumper, and after a visit to the loo went downstairs. He could barely see, but he couldn't stand electric light just after waking up. The air smelled of burnt wood, and a few embers were still smoking in the fireplace. Making his way through the penumbra, he prepared a pot of coffee, fascinated by the silence. He'd been living in the country for almost a year now, but the silence still amazed him. When he lived in Via del Leone, at that hour in his half-sleep he already used to hear the sounds of the neighbourhood coming to life. He missed San Frediano a little and sometimes imagined himself buying a small two-room flat so he could sleep in town every now and then.

He put the coffee pot on the burner, and as he waited his eye fell on the telephone. He imagined it ringing and him picking up and hearing his mother's voice . . . *Franco, what have you done?* But he would explain it all, he would defend himself, try to make her understand he'd had no choice . . . He would do it for her, to lessen her suffering. And in the end they would have said goodbye tenderly, and gone their separate ways . . .

Eleonora would never come looking for him, he was sure of that. If he ever wanted to see her again, he would have to make the first move himself, knowing it might prove useless. And yet he kept postponing it, sighing and putting it off. At times he felt like burying her memory forever, but then the next minute he would imagine himself phoning her or writing her a letter. He was behaving worse than an adolescent. Had Eleonora gone back to live in her little apartment in San Niccolò? Or had she moved back in with her parents? He looked up at his taciturn tenant, the human skull that for the past few months had reigned over the kitchen from its perch atop the cupboard. It had been a birthday present from Diotivede, the forensic pathologist and his friend. And a very fine skull it was, and rather expressive in its way, a now familiar presence which in no uncertain terms reminded mortals not to grow too fond of earthly matters. Its great antagonist was love, which spread its illusions of eternity all over the world.

He poured the coffee and went and sat down at the table, staring at the smoking embers. This was his first autumn since moving to the country. Nature's decomposition, the constant sound of drizzle, the grey sky, might seem sad to some people . . . Him, on the other hand, it made happy. He'd always liked autumn. In truth he liked all the seasons. You might even say he needed them. He could not have lived without them. To see nature die and then come back to life . . . He needed it. Not just now that he lived out in the country. He'd always needed it.

There were only a few days left till Christmas, and he thought back on his last Christmas dinner with his mother, at the house in Via Volta, just the two of them. After bringing the customary homemade *tortellini in brodo* to the table, his mother had said a prayer for her husband, and, as always happened, her eyes filled with tears.

He searched farther into his memory, to the last Christmas when his father was still alive. The afternoon dinner with relatives had been pleasant and noisy, and following the meal they'd all gone out for a walk, as was the tradition. For supper, on the other hand, it was just the three of them, and it had its share of melancholy moments. They'd started talking about the war, still so recent in their minds . . . The terrible months of the occupation, with the city of Florence still in the grip of the Germans and Fascists, the Allied bombings, the black market, the tortures at

Villa Triste . . .[1] At a certain point his mother had gone to get the letter he'd written on 9 September 1943, while sailing to Malta, which she'd kept framed on her bedside table. It was the last news she'd had of him at the time, followed by absolute silence until the end of the conflict . . . *I was sure you were dead, but I was also sure you would come back*, his mother had said, drying her eyes.

He finished his coffee as the daylight filtered into the kitchen. He went upstairs to his bedroom and opened the window wide. It was cold outside, but the sky was clear and the day promised sun even though a veil of fog still hung over the olive trees. Rather than trees they were large stumps with tufts of new leaves on top. The person who'd pruned them so severely was the farmer he'd hired to manage the grove, to rebuild the trees after their long period of neglect. The only advantage in this was the great quantity of wood now stacked in the cellar, but for at least two years he would have to buy his olive oil from the local peasants. Actually, he needed to remind himself to get some. In a few days the *olio novo* would be available, the kind that stings the tongue. For the past few days he'd been seeing the peasants atop their ladders, with great sheets of cloth or leftover wartime parachutes spread out on the ground below.

Before going out, with the easy movements of habit he stuffed firewood into the cast-iron stove he'd had installed upstairs. Living in a large country house was almost like running a ship; you had to be careful not to forget anything.

Driving slowly down to Florence, he forced himself not to smoke. Meanwhile he thought back on his dreams of the previous night while distractedly looking out at the landscape. Every so often the Beetle backfired, but it was perfectly healthy. That tank had come out of the great flood undamaged, a good wash having sufficed to erase all memory of the mud.

Not infrequently during the short drive from home to office he would let his thoughts coast on autopilot, imagining all kinds of nonsense, fantasising about unforgettable or crazy moments, bouncing blindly from memory to memory without any logical thread to guide him . . . It was a wonderful interlude of freedom, one that sometimes managed to lighten the burdens of life for at least half an hour.

Every time when passing through Mezzomonte he would turn to look at Dante Pedretti's big house, where he had spent whole evenings discussing everything under the sun and drinking grappa. He would give it just one long glance, without interrupting his journey through the void . . .

That morning he also remembered the Christmas of the year before, when Pope Paul VI had come to Florence to lend moral support to the wounded city, fifty-one days after the great flood. Before celebrating midnight mass in the Duomo, he'd made a stop in a very crowded Piazza Santa Croce and embraced the poor and elderly of Monte Domini, as symbols of the entire city's suffering . . . *Tonight, angels are flying through the sky*, he said, eyes turned upwards . . . Then a voice rose up from the piazza . . . '*At the moment a lot of Madonnas are flying* . . .'[2] The buzz from the chuckling crowd was mistaken by the pope as a shudder of faith, and he was deeply moved . . .

At Porta Romana Bordelli was forced to rouse himself. The traffic was moving in fits and starts, as children were dragged along the pavement to school. Every so often, while looking at children, it occurred to him that by natural law they would all survive him, and he would suddenly imagine the world in the year 2000. Would it be a more just world? Would people's lives be more peaceful, more comfortable? Or would World War III break out? Well, it could of course break out even before he exited the stage, considering the constant tension between the United States and the Soviet Union . . .

He slipped into Via Romana, which stank of automobile exhaust. Staying with the slow flow of cars and motorbikes, he reached Via Maggio and crossed the Ponte Santa Trinita at a walking pace. The shops had already been decked out in Christmas decorations for several days now, some of them gaudy, others more simple. He watched the groups of youngsters getting out of trolley-buses, and every time he noticed how different they were from the young people of his time. Not only because of the guys' long hair or the girls' tight slacks, and not only because of the political demonstrations of the past few months. It must be something in their way of being, of looking around, of walking. They were lighter, freer. The world was changing fast, and he feared he might not be able to keep up with it. He would try to understand, and even adapt; he had nothing against transformations, but personally felt too old to change . . . Even if, truth be told, he'd experienced more than his share of changes over his fifty-seven years of life.

At one intersection he sat spellbound watching a teenaged couple kissing, and didn't drive away until a horn honked in protest behind him. He couldn't help but think of Eleonora . . . When did they kiss for the first time? He could never remember . . .

A little more than a year had passed since the flood, and on the façades of many buildings in the centre of town a black line was still visible, a reminder of the level that the Arno had reached when it had swept through the city, devastating everything in its path. At times there was a hint in the air of the stench of oil and sewage. The shop windows dressed with Christmas decorations, coloured lights and long satin ribbons seemed almost to want to push that unpleasant memory away.

Entering the courtyard of the police headquarters he nodded a greeting to Mugnai, who had a thoughtful look on his face, perhaps due to an unsolvable crossword puzzle. He parked in his usual place and headed upstairs. He crossed paths with Lenzi, an inspector from Pistoia whom he had not seen in a long time.

'Chin up, Bordelli, someone will get killed today, just you wait,' Lenzi said. It was his favourite quip. Bordelli smiled and continued climbing the stairs, thinking of the bitterness in Lenzi's words. Unfortunately it was true: when someone was killed, there were others whose lives took on more palpable meaning.

He walked into his office and opened the window to let some air in. He went to his desk and sat down without taking off his coat. He signed some paperwork that he found there, an unlit cigarette in his mouth. He would light it later, maybe even after lunch if he managed to resist. His age-old struggle with tobacco was not over yet.

He stood up and closed the window, hung up his coat, and began to pace back and forth, still thinking of Eleonora. That morning he had not been able to get her out of his mind. He had lost other women, and it was never easy, but he had made room for them among his memories. Eleonora, on the other hand . . .

He had to find a way to talk to her, but the mere thought of ringing her made him upset. Writing her a brief letter was perhaps the least inopportune way of presenting himself, given the circumstances. Several months earlier he had tried this, but after a few attempts had thrown the paper into the fire . . . It was just too depressing to post a letter and then wait around for a reply that would surely never come , . . *Dear Eleonora* . . .

He shook his head and sat back down, smiling at himself. He chucked the still-unlit cigarette onto the desk. He was behaving worse than a boy in love with his cousin. He'd been on warships, on submarines, had volunteered to serve in the San Marco Battalion, had seen comrades die, and he himself had killed . . . And now, faced with a beautiful girl . . .

He began to write up a brief report for the investigating magistrate, something he'd neglected to do for a few days. He wrote slowly, without interrupting his train of thought. He could not deny that he felt different. Despite everything, for some time now he had felt more serene, practically docile. Or perhaps it was simply resignation. At his age he surely could not hope to start a family, or have children . . .

Only three more years and he would retire. And he was definitely not afraid of being bored. After quitting his job he'd spent six months without working, and never once had he been bored. There was always something to do in the country, and then there were books, the telly, dinners with friends, walks in the hills, and more than anything else, a forest of memories. He wasn't even afraid of feeling lonely. He had always enjoyed his long hours alone, even as a child . . .

The phone rang, and he waited to reply until he had finished the sentence he was writing.

'Hello?'

'Oh, pardon me, I must have dialled the wrong number, I was looking for Inspec . . .'

'Hi, Rosa, it's me,' Bordelli said, putting his pen down and leaning back in his chair. He was always happy to hear from her. Rosa was a marvellous woman, the living proof that working for more than twenty years in a brothel did not necessarily mean losing one's childlike innocence.

'*Mamma mia*, you sound so sad . . . I didn't even recognise you . . .' she said.

'I was lost in thought.'

'You can't fool me, Monkey . . . what's going on?'

'Nothing.'

'Hmm, I smell a woman . . .'

'Please, Rosa.'

'Don't tell me you've fallen in love yet again . . .'

'You know I'm a real man and never fall in love,' Bordelli said.

'When are you going to come and see me? I have a surprise for you to put under the tree.'

'How sweet.'

'You're going to love it. I can't wait to give it to you . . .' Rosa said with childlike glee.

'Rosa, I never thought I would hear you say such things.'

'What? Oh my goodness, what a pig . . . You only think of one thing . . .'

'It was a stupid joke, I admit it.'

'You're such a little pig.'

'Only when I'm with you, Rosa.'

'That's the way I like you . . . so, when are you coming to see me?'

'I don't know, maybe tonight.'

'Yes, do! That way I can give you your surprise . . . Briciola! Get down from there!'

'What's she doing?'

'She's on top of the vitrine, walking between my grandmother's glasses . . . Get down immediately, I said!'

Briciola was the black and white kitten that Bordelli had found behind some brambles just before the flood, when she was as small as a chick. Briciola could never have known it at the time, but without her desperate mewling, Bordelli would never have found Giacomo's killers, and would therefore never have killed them . . . In short, he could share the burden of his conscience with the kitten . . .

'Hey! Have you fallen asleep?' Rosa asked.

'Sorry . . . what were you saying?'

'I was saying goodbye. I have to get ready to go out.'

'Going into town to do some clothes shopping?'

'Clothes shopping?! Today I'm on phone duty at the Misericordia.'

'Since when?'

'More than a month, I told you. I like it, you know . . . It's nice to do something for others.'

'You've always done things for others, Rosa . . .'

'In bed! But it's not the same. And anyway, that's water under the bridge . . . Oh my goodness, it's late! I have to be there in an hour and I haven't even decided what to wear. Ciao ciao, kisses . . .' She hung up without giving him time to say a word.

Bordelli picked up his pen again, but had lost his train of thought. And just as he was recovering his train of thought, the internal line rang.

'Inspector, a lady just called . . . her brother has been killed . . .' said the police operator, with habitual calm.

'How did it happen?'

'I asked but she may not have heard me, and she hung up.'

'Give me the address.'

'Via Benedetto da Maiano 18/bis, near the intersection with Salviatino.'

'I know the area well. Notify Diotivede and the assistant prosecutor . . . But first find Piras, please. Tell him to wait for me in the courtyard.'

He hung up and stayed where he was, staring at the sky through the dirty windowpanes, thinking that he would like to spend a little time in Paris. He really needed to get organised, to free his mind of clutter. *Tabula rasa*, and start over again more carefree. He was burdened by too many thoughts, never had a moment's peace. Remorse, fantasies, regrets, memories, desires, hopes . . . Everything had randomly piled up, as in a dark old attic where no one had set foot for many years. The time had come to throw away the old trunks full of rubbish. A few weeks in Paris, bistro meals, reading on benches, museum visits, strolls along the Seine looking at women . . . He had been to Paris once, in December 1939. As soon as he had stepped off the train he had felt at home. He felt as though he had been born there. He spoke French poorly, but made himself understood. He had fallen in love with a girl he never saw again. The war had swept it all away.

He glanced at his watch and stood up with a sigh. He took down his coat and put it on as he was walking. He thought of Lenzi's quip as he went downstairs, and couldn't help but smile.

Young Piras was waiting for him in the courtyard, as immobile as a nuraghe.[3] Dark, small, and wooden. Although a beat cop, he was dressed, as usual, in street clothes. Bordelli had asked him not to wear the uniform, at least when they were together, to avoid being labelled for what they were, two cops. It was a sort of papal exemption that was accepted by everyone, even by Commissioner Inzipone.

They exchanged greetings and climbed into the Beetle. The Sardinian had joined the Florence police force five years earlier, fresh out of the Academy, when Bordelli had discovered by chance that he was the son of Gavino Piras, who had been his comrade in the San Marco Battalion. But that was not the only reason he had chosen him as his partner, nor was it because he enjoyed being with him. Piras was intelligent, sensitive, conscientious, never got tired and, on top of this, his intuition was superb. He would surely go far in law enforcement.

They reached Piazza San Gallo, made their way through the traffic, and turned onto Viale Don Minzoni.

'Do you know why I always bring you with me, Piras? So I don't give in to the demon of tobacco . . .' Bordelli said, knowing how much the younger man detested the smell of cigarettes.

'Good reason.'

'We're going up to Via Salviatino. There's been a murder.'

'I thought as much.'

'Everything all right at home?'

'Same as always.'

'Sardinians talk little but everything is so clear.'

'Florentines talk a lot but say little.'

'You're definitely not wrong about that . . .'

After Piazza delle Cure, they turned onto Viale Volta. Just before reaching Via della Piazzuola, the inspector slowed down ever so slightly to glance at the house where he had been born and raised. Nothing had changed, there were the same stains on the walls, the same trees, and the same shadows in the garden. A few melancholy seconds, as pleasant as ever.

'Are you free for dinner on Saturday, Inspector?'

'Well, to tell the truth, three or four women are waiting to hear back from me, but I would be happy to consider other offers.'

'Sonia asked me to invite you to dinner.'

'I know it isn't elegant to ask . . . but who else is invited?' Bordelli asked, worried about being the old man in a group of young people.

'No one else.'

'I would love to come. To hell with the women.'

'Good.'

'You never mentioned if your beautiful Sicilian ever finished her degree . . .'

'With honours. Now she is studying for the bar and in a few years she'll become a lawyer.'

'She'll be the most beautiful lawyer in Florence.'

'I know,' said Piras, sounding almost worried.

'Will you spend Christmas with your family?'

'I'm taking the ferry on the twenty-third. And you?'

'I have no plans yet. I might read a book in front of the fire.'

They drove on in silence, but with Piras even silence was like a conversation.

They reached Piazza Edison and turned right on to Viale Righi, where many years earlier Bordelli had seen an unforgettable woman . . . and in fact he remembered her well. It was summer, she moved along the pavement as if carried by the wind, wearing a light white dress, her gaze lost in infinity, far from the miseries of the world . . . She had light blond hair, and her red lips stood out against her fair skin. She was not just beautiful, she was a dream. Her eyes were those of an angel who had spent the night making love. He had stopped the Fiat 600 and got out, entranced. He had spent the following days scolding himself for not having had the courage to speak to her . . .

Exploring that memory, he came to the end of the Viale, drove across the small bridge over the Affrico and turned onto Via del Cantone. At the top of the street they turned left, on to Via da Maiano, which was lined with beautiful villas and ancient trees.

'They just can't stop killing,' Bordelli said. He was curious to see whether it would be an easy case, or whether once more he would find himself flailing about in a dark wood searching for the right path, hoping that a small flame might appear to lead him out of the darkness . . .

They continued driving up the deserted street. At number 18/bis they found an open gate, and the Beetle putt-putted its way into a well-tended but austere garden. They parked alongside a baby-blue Fiat 1100 in front of a fine, three-storey late nineteenth-century villa. The stone façade boasted an elevated entrance with a short staircase on either side. Above the balustrade they saw the motionless head of a woman with her hair pulled back. They got out of the car and went up to meet her. The woman awaited them with a wrinkled brow, standing as straight and dark as a cypress. She was elegant, no longer young, but rather beautiful. Climbing the stairs, Bordelli was quick to introduce himself.

'Good morning, signora . . . I am Inspector Bordelli, police . . .'

'Laura Borrani. I am Antonio's sister,' said the woman, voice slightly quavering, twisting her fingers nervously. Her eyes were red, her lips hardened with tension.

'And this is Piras, special agent.'

'My condolences . . .' the Sardinian muttered. The inspector was ready to kiss her hand, but the lady kept her hands folded over her chest.

'It was I who phoned . . . I'm still unable to . . .' She couldn't finish her sentence. It was clear she was quite upset, but good breeding forced her to master her emotions.

'You must be strong,' said the inspector, trying to be comfort her. If the woman hadn't kept her distance, he would have stroked her shoulder.

'Come . . .' she said. They followed her into the villa and found themselves in a large, dimly lit atrium. Sitting at the foot of a majestic staircase in *pietra serena*, a slender woman in an apron was weeping, face buried in her hands.

'This is Amalia. It was she who found him . . .' said the lady of the house, lightly stroking the woman's grey hair.

They all started up the stairs, watched from above by a large oil portrait of a man from another era in ceremonial dress. No one had opened any windows, and twilight reigned.

'I imagine Signora Amalia has the keys to the villa . . .' the inspector said softly.

'Of course,' the lady whispered, letting it be known that Amalia enjoyed her absolute trust.

'What was your brother's name?'

'Antonio Migliorini.'

'Did he live alone?'

'Yes. It's been more than ten years since his wife passed away. He never got over it.'

'Does he have any children?'

'Yes, two males, both grown up.'

'Have they been notified?'

'I tried to reach them at their office, but the secretary said they'd gone out on some appointments. She'll have them call me back at this number as soon as they return. I also tried calling both of them at home, but there was no answer.'

They'd reached the second floor, and Signora Borrani led them down a corridor in shadow. She stopped a few steps away from the only open door, from which a good amount of light was pouring in.

'My brother's study . . .' she said in a whisper.

'Has anyone touched anything?'

'No . . .' said the lady, voice cracking, barely able to hold back a sob. Covering her mouth with her hand, she walked away with her head down and shoulders heaving. Piras and Bordelli went into the victim's study and found themselves looking at a scene out of the theatre . . . In front of a sober desk, on a beautiful oriental carpet with blue motifs, a man of about fifty, in dressing gown and slippers, lay on his back, eyes wide open, a fencing foil stuck between his ribs, hands clutching the blade.

'He must have been a fascinating man,' Bordelli muttered, looking at the victim from up close. The foil shot up from his chest like a jet of water from a fountain.

They looked around. The study was warm and cosy, and furnished with precious antiques. Nothing looked out of place. There were no signs of a struggle. On the wall behind the desk was an open safe, and on the floor they saw the picture that had kept it hidden, a landscape in oils of flowering meadows and luxuriant shrubs. Missing from a large burgundy-coloured velvet panel hanging between two tightly packed bookcases was the murderous foil, whose ghost remained impressed in the velvet, below an ancient sword and a sabre of the *bersaglieri*.[4]

The inspector approached the safe, and inside he saw a grey folder tied shut with a ribbon. Pulling it out, he went and set it down on the desk beside a modern Olivetti typewriter, with Piras following behind. Untying the ribbon, he opened the folder, which was divided into compartments by sheets of thin cardboard . . . The deceased's passport, showing a variety of stamps, the most recent from Spain, from a few months prior. Bills of sale and rental contracts. Small sheets of paper with mysterious figures and letters on them. Banking documents, not only from Italy, giving the measure of Migliorini's wealth: account statements with dizzying balances, receipts for government bonds worth vast sums, similar papers for stocks and debentures. An old photograph of an attractive girl frowning, with the Eiffel Tower as background, slipped out, making Bordelli think again of Paris.

In sum, nothing of importance, except, perhaps, one detail . . .

'The killer could not have been interested in this folder, since apparently he never even touched it,' said Bordelli.

'Maybe he made off with a box full of gold coins,' Piras muttered, walking away.

'Maybe . . .'

The inspector shut the folder and put it back in the safe.

'He was reading,' said Piras, stopping in one corner of the study. Lying on a large upholstered chair was an open book beside a pair of glasses. Bordelli went and glanced at the cover: *The Leopard*, by Giuseppe Tomasi di Lampedusa.

'Have you read it?' he asked the young man.

'Yes.'

'I think I've got it at home . . . Is it good?'

'Yes.'

'Blimey, Piras, you'd make one hell of a literary critic . . .' Bordelli sighed.

Beside the armchair, a bit in shadow, was a small, low, oval table with a bottle of cognac and an empty snifter. Everything led one to think that just before being murdered, Migliorini had settled comfortably into his armchair, in his dressing gown, to read a good novel while sipping cognac. It seemed unlikely he was expecting a visit.

As Piras kept moving about the room studying everything, Bordelli turned back to the corpse. His first questions were forming in his head, and, as usual, there were too many of them . . . Who opened the safe? The victim, before being run through? And how long before? And for what reason? And did he do it when still alone, or only when threatened by his killer? Or had the murderer opened it after killing him, and therefore knew the combination? But was the safe the real cause of the murder? The inspector had learnt not to be fooled by first impressions, which often risked influencing the direction of an investigation. He had to take every hypothesis into consideration, even the most farfetched. All too often in the past, he'd been thrown off by drawing the easy conclusions. And what if it had actually been a suicide? Of course, it was a rather unusual way to . . .

Hearing steps in the corridor, Bordelli roused himself. Appearing in the doorway was a large black bag, held by Dr Diotivede, the forensic pathologist, who just a few months earlier, at the tender age of seventy-four, had married a beautiful woman thirty years younger.

'May I?' the doctor asked with a chilly smile. His pure white hair seemed to shine with a light of its own.

'You're always welcome,' said the inspector.

'A foil . . .' Diotivede muttered to himself, entering the room.

'You may not have noticed, but the foil is actually stuck in a dead man,' said Bordelli.

The doctor ignored him, approached the corpse, and stood there, studying it for a few seconds. Then he set his old black bag down on a chair, took off his coat, and got down on his knees beside the body. He poked his fingertip into one the cheeks, and then pressed the back of his hand against it. Afterwards, he touched the body in a number of spots.

'Can you tell me more or less when he was killed?' Bordelli ventured to ask.

'Most certainly more than a minute ago.'

'I don't know what I would do without you . . .'

'I don't like this "more or less" stuff,' Diotivede said pedantically. Piras looked on, immobile, but his eyes seemed to indicate that he agreed with the doctor.

'I just thought maybe you'd already formed an idea,' the inspector said by way of justification.

'I can affirm that rigor mortis is already setting in. It starts three hours after death and can last for up to two days.'

'Well, it's a start.'

'Give me time to conduct a few tests in the lab, but don't expect me to tell you the exact moment of death.'

'So you're saying you have to cut him open and rifle around inside him first, the way you like . . .'

'You have no idea the sorts of wonderful things you can find in there.'

'They must always be the same.'

'The same, and yet different, just like noses and ears,' said Diotivede, bending forward to have a closer look at the dead man's elbow.

'I'd never thought of that,' said Bordelli under his breath. The doctor took a handkerchief out of his pocket to pick something up.

'A little surprise for you,' he said, holding up a shimmering object. Piras and the inspector both stepped forward to look.

'Beautiful . . .' said Bordelli.

It was a little gold ring, with a small sapphire set amidst a corolla of diamonds. The doctor stood up without a sound and went and put the ring down on the desk.

'From the thirties. It looks like an engagement ring,' he said, pulling his notebook out of his pocket.

'It think it'd look good on your Sicilian girlfriend,' Bordelli said to Piras.

'Everything looks good on Sonia,' the Sardinian muttered, unable to repress a half-smile. The doctor finished writing some notes and put his notebook away.

'I've finished here,' he said, putting his coat on.

'When will you let me know something?'

'How soon will I be getting the body?'

'In three hours, at the most.'

'Try calling me tomorrow morning.'

'Maybe I'll even drop in . . .'

'As you wish. Work well,' said Diotivede, who then picked up his black bag and, nodding goodbye, left.

'Was that goodbye for us or for the body?' Bordelli asked himself aloud, as the doctor could be heard walking away. The question hung in the air for a moment, as befitting a great enigma.

They carried on their search of the study, attentive to every detail, but found nothing of interest. Now it would be up to the forensics team. Photos, measurements, fingerprints. The inspector would find the report on his desk the following morning.

The time had come to talk to the two women. As he left the study, Bordelli slipped the thirties-style ring into his pocket, hoping the precious jewel might help him find the killer.

'Signora Amalia, I'm sorry to bother you. I can come back at a more convenient time,' Bordelli said as kindly as he could.

'No, no . . . Please, go ahead, ask me whatever you need . . .' mumbled Amalia, dabbing at her eyes with a handkerchief. The two of them were seated at the kitchen table, a pitcher of water and two glasses between them. The grand old kitchen was in perfect keeping with the rest of the elegant atmosphere that reigned over the villa. Amalia had opened the wooden shutters and, through the iron grille, Bordelli could see the dark green of a thick laurel hedge that ran along the wall of the garden.

'Do you recall what time it was when you arrived at the house?' Bordelli asked for the third time.

'It was seven o'clock, just like every day . . . except Sunday,' Amalia replied, holding back her tears.

'Signora Borrani mentioned you have keys to the villa.'

'I've had the keys for a long time; I've been with the Migliorini family for more than thirty years,' she said with a touch of pride.

'You must have been very young when you started . . .' Bordelli said.

'I was seventeen, it was before the war . . . Dottor Migliorini was such a good man, even when he was young. There was no one like him . . . He would always go out on a limb to help . . .' Amalia broke into tears. She was thin, of medium height, with large, curious eyes, a Dantesque nose, and a natural elegance of which she seemed to be completely unaware. Bordelli waited for her to catch her breath.

'May I go on?'

'At Christmas he always gave me a hundred thousand lire . . . he'd put the money in an envelope and leave it by the telephone . . .'

'Can you talk to me about this morning?'

'Yes . . . Yes.'

'Everything you remember, and take as much time as you need.'

'I remember it perfectly, as if it just happened . . . I arrived at seven . . . When I turned the key in the door I noticed that it had not been locked . . . He must have forgotten, I thought to myself. . . I went inside and started doing my chores . . . Usually Dottor Migliorini came down for breakfast around eight o'clock. He'd sit right here and we'd chat about this and that. We even talked about personal things, things you don't talk about with just anyone . . . He'd known me since I was a girl, and I know he cared for me . . . He'd ask about my life at home and sometimes he'd tell me about his things . . . Sometimes a whole hour would go by! And in the meantime, I'd be cleaning the kitchen . . . There were other times when he'd come down and ask me to prepare a breakfast tray. That's how I knew that a young lady had spent the night . . . Then, an hour later, he'd come down again, and tell me to stay in the kitchen so his lady friend could slip out . . . and that was fine! The less I knew, the better . . .'

'Did you ever see any cars parked out front?' Bordelli asked.

'Of course, many times.'

'Do you remember what kinds of cars?'

'Oh, they all look the same to me,' Amalia said with a shrug.

'Going back to this morning, what happened next?'

'Well, he didn't come down at his usual time. A half-hour went by, an hour . . . I thought, maybe he has a fever because he always comes down to the kitchen . . . So, finally, I decided to go to the bottom of the stairs and call up to him . . . no answer. I felt ill, I don't know why . . . Holy Mother of God, how my legs were shaking. Somehow I think I already knew . . . Oh my Lord, it's just too much . . .' She made the sign of the cross, held back a cry of anguish, and went on.

'I went upstairs, my heart thumping . . . I felt a cold draught as if a window had been left open . . . I got upstairs and knocked on the bedroom door, at first softly, then harder. No answer . . . maybe he's sick, I thought, so I got up the courage and opened the door. The bed was still made, just as I'd left it yesterday morning . . . So I went up to the second floor. The light in his study was on, I saw it from under the door . . . The hallway was freezing. I started shivering . . . I called out again . . . Finally I looked in . . . My legs gave out . . .' She stopped to blow her nose, her hands dropped into her lap, and she stared off into space.

Bordelli waited a minute, but Amalia remained silent.

'Then what did you do?' he asked, encouraging her to speak.

'What? . . . Oh, I'm sorry, Inspector . . . I was distracted . . .'

'You were saying that you looked into his study . . .' Bordelli tried to get her back on track. Amalia shook her head, twisting her handkerchief in her hands.

'My legs went weak . . . It didn't make sense . . . Yesterday morning I made him coffee . . . He was in a good mood, and we even started joking . . . And now he's been murdered . . . It's the work of the devil . . . There are too many bad people out there in the world . . .'

'Do you know of anyone who had a grudge against him?'

'No, no, impossible . . . Everyone liked him . . . But even Jesus was good, and they crucified him just the same . . .'

'The last time you saw him was yesterday morning?'

'Yes . . .'

'How did he seem?'

'He'd been in good form for a while, but it wasn't by chance . . . He told me he'd fallen in love with a beautiful woman, and that she loved him too . . . After all these years, he wanted to get married again . . . but he couldn't, at least for the time being . . .'

'Why not?'

'I don't know . . . I couldn't possibly ask . . .'

'Did he often talk to you about private matters?'

'Inspector, I've already told you, I'm like family.'

'So, Migliorini wanted to get married . . .'

'He couldn't wait, he said . . . I was happy for him . . . I mean, Signora Carla was a real lady, bless her soul . . . but Dottor Migliorini deserved to start his life over . . .'

'By Signora Carla, you mean Migliorini's wife?'

'Yes . . . may she rest in peace. She died in a riding accident.'

'Did Migliorini tell you the name of the woman he was in love with?'

'He told me she was beautiful and from an important family . . . but that they couldn't talk openly about their relations. They had to keep it secret. He made me swear I wouldn't tell anyone, and of course I never would have. Who would I tell, anyway?'

'Did he ever mention her name?'

'No, and I didn't ask.'

'Going back to this morning . . . did you touch anything in the study?'

'No . . . wait, hold on . . . That cold air I mentioned? The window of the study was wide open, and so I closed it . . . I had to walk by the body. I turned away . . . I couldn't bear to look at him, his eyes were wide open . . . Poor man.'

'Do you think Migliorini opened the window?' Bordelli asked.

'No, he couldn't stand the cold . . .'

'Did he smoke?'

'No, he never smoked . . . I think the murderer opened it . . .'

'Why, in your opinion?'

'Oh, that I really don't know . . .'

'What did you do afterwards?'

'I went downstairs to call someone . . . I didn't know where to look for his children's phone number, so I called Signora Laura . . . I know her number by heart . . . I went outside to wait for her, and when she arrived, we went back in together . . . We cried and hugged each other . . . Then Signora Laura called the police.'

'You didn't notice anything strange? Nothing out of place?'

'No, I can't think of anything,' mumbled Amalia, trying to remember.

'How do you get to the villa?'

'I leave my bicycle down at Salviatino and walk up.'

'That's quite a walk.'

'I'm used to it . . .' Amalia said. Somewhere in the house the phone rang. Eventually, it stopped. From his pocket, Bordelli took out the ring he had found next to the corpse.

'Do you recognise this?' he asked. Amalia looked at it for a few seconds.

'I've never seen it before.'

'What will you do now that Dottor Migliorini is dead?' Bordelli asked, slipping the ring back into his pocket.

'I'll keep doing what I've always done . . . there's no shortage of housekeeping work. I will find a new family . . .'

'Are you married?'

'I've been a widow for about six years now. My husband was a builder, and he fell from a scaffold.'

'Do you have children?'

'I have a twenty-one-year-old son who works as a night porter in a beautiful hotel in Turin. He only comes down at Easter and at Christmas,' she said, holding back her tears.

'Do you live alone?'

'No, I live with my cousin Adele, who is almost twenty years younger than me. We keep each other company. She's on her own now, too. After three years of marriage, one morning her husband went out and never came back. Luckily, she has no children.'

'What does she do?'

'She works in one of Dottor Migliorini's factories, and at night she sews for a tailor.'

'Thank you, Amalia. That will be all for now. But you'll need to come down to headquarters to give a deposition,' Bordelli said, getting to his feet.

'What do I have to do?' Amalia asked, unsure of what he meant.

'Since you're the one who discovered the body, you will simply have to repeat everything you told me to my colleagues, who will write it down. Then, you'll sign it. It'll only take about thirty minutes.'

'All right, then.'

'If you like, I can have someone give you a lift now.'

'No, no, please don't bother. I need to go home and straighten myself up, I can't go out in this state . . .'

'As you wish.' Bordelli bowed slightly in farewell, and as he was leaving the kitchen, he heard Amalia start to cry again. He closed the door behind him and walked down the dim hallway, an unlit cigarette in his mouth, promising himself he wouldn't smoke until after lunch. He thought about the open window in the study, and whether that particular detail might have some special importance for the investigation. If Amalia was right, and the murderer had opened the window, why would he have done so?

He heard Signora Borrani's anguished voice, and he walked towards it. He peered into a small sitting room where she sat in an armchair, alone, weakly illuminated by a table lamp. She was on the telephone. No one had opened the shutters in that room, either. When she realised he was standing in the doorway, she covered the mouthpiece with one hand.

'Do you need me, Inspector?' she whispered, furrowing her brow.

'Please, I don't want to interrupt . . .'

'It's Claretta,' Signora Borrani said, as if he knew who that was.

'I'll come back in a few minutes,' Bordelli said. As he walked away, he heard her start talking again.

'Claretta, please don't . . . You're making me cry again . . . Please, stop, I beg you . . . I know it's terrible . . .'

Bordelli looked out of the window and into the garden for Piras. He saw that the Fiat van from Forensics had arrived and was parked next to his VW Beetle. He went upstairs to the second floor. Mainardi and Rossi were in the study, immersed in their work. He knew them both well, young but competent men.

'Good morning, Inspector,' they said, almost in unison, standing more or less at command.

'At ease . . . how's it coming along?'

'It's going well. We'll have a report for you by tomorrow morning.'

'Will you make sure to call the ambulance?'

'We've already called the Misericordia, they'll be here in a bit,' Mainardi said. At that precise moment Rossi extracted the sword from the corpse.

'Any fingerprints?'

'None. Probably wiped with a handkerchief.'

'I would have guessed as much . . . check for prints on the handle of the window. It was found open.'

'Already checked. Nothing there.'

'Fine. I'm going back downstairs. Carry on.'

'Thank you, sir.' The two men returned to what they were doing. Bordelli went back downstairs, wondering where his Sardinian assistant had gone. Suddenly he appeared in front of him.

'Where did you go, Piras?'

'The villa is huge, Chief. I went into each of the rooms. There's even a billiards room.'

'Find anything of interest?'

'I checked the front and rear doors. The locks are new and

secure, there's no sign of forced entry. The windows on the ground floor all have iron grilles, the first-floor windows are secure, and the windows on the second floor can only be reached with a fire ladder.'

'So no crowbars, but lots of questions.'

'That's right, Inspector,' Piras said.

It was clear to both that nothing was clear. The victim could have opened the door to the killer because he knew him, or even if he didn't know him . . . for any number of reasons. Or maybe the killer had duplicates of the keys. Maybe he had made copies in secret. Or maybe the killer was an expert at breaking in, one of those people who can open any kind of lock without leaving a trace . . . like Ennio Bottarini, known as Botta, one of Bordelli's closest friends, a thief, counterfeiter and con man by necessity but also, in the final analysis, by vocation.

'Nothing else?'

'I checked out the garage, it's practically a hangar at the far end of the garden. He had five cars . . . a Jaguar, a Mercedes, a Maserati, a Mini Morris and a Fiat 600 . . .'

'Basically, an average chap.'

'I'd be happy with the Jag,' Piras said in a serious tone.

'Did you see the Prosecutor?'

'He stopped by for a few minutes, he was in a rush.'

'Amalia said she found the window open in the study . . . Why do you think that was? It's cold outside, Migliorini couldn't stand the cold, and he didn't smoke . . . Anything come to mind?' Bordelli asked. The Sardinian bit his lip.

'Let me mull it over.'

'Let's go and talk to Migliorini's sister.'

Signora Borrani was sitting in the same armchair in which Bordelli had left her, staring into space in the half-light, the telephone resting on her knees.

'Sorry to trouble you at such a moment . . .' said Bordelli, startling the woman.

'I beg your pardon . . . I was distracted . . .' she said, putting the telephone back in its place. She ran her fingers over one cheek to wipe away a tear, then delicately blew her nose.

'May I open a window?' asked the inspector, who felt the need for some daylight.

'As you wish . . .' the woman whispered. Bordelli thanked her and, feeling relieved, went and opened the inside shutters wide. He paused and looked up at the clear blue sky and, without wanting to, thought of Eleonora and her dark, glistening eyes . . . For a few moments he imagined he was walking along the Seine with her on a summer evening, far from all the murders and murderers, as a *bateau-mouche* full of tourists glided silently by under a bridge . . .

Sighing as he stepped away from the window, he returned to Signora Borrani. He sat down opposite her with Piras, on a handsome but rather uncomfortable antique sofa. The younger man already had a notebook in his hands.

'If you have no objection, I would like to ask you a few questions,' said Bordelli, wishing very much that he could smoke a cigarette.

'Please go ahead . . .'

She was sitting on the edge of her armchair, as though about to get up at any moment.

'Was Antonio your only sibling?'

'Yes . . .'

'When was the last time you saw him?'

'Two Sundays ago. Every so often he came to our house for lunch, usually on a Sunday.'

'Are you married?'

'Yes. My husband is in Cuneo today, for work. He doesn't know anything yet, and I've been unable to reach him. I don't keep up with his business, so I know very little.'

'Do you have children?'

'A boy of thirteen and a daughter who's now twenty and studying in the States.'

'What line of business is your husband in?'

'Anselmo owns a paint factory, which he inherited, but that's about all I can tell you.'

'To return to your brother . . . Did he tell you anything of interest that Sunday?'

'I don't think so . . . No . . .'

'Was he perhaps worried? Did he seem in any way different from the way he usually was?'

'He was his usual self. A bit gruff, but very nice. My children have always adored him.'

'I'm getting the impression you didn't see each other very often, aside from an occasional Sunday lunch,' said the inspector. The lady nodded.

'I would sometimes run into him when invited to dinner at the home of mutual friends, or at parties. But that was rather rare. Antonio didn't like to socialise much, especially after Carla's death.'

'Did you stay in touch by phone?'

'Yes, we spoke often, even when we had nothing to say.'

'When was the last time?'

'Yesterday afternoon . . . My God, that was only a few hours ago . . .' the lady said, mildly astonished.

'Was it a normal conversation?'

'Yes, quite normal . . .'

'May I ask what you talked about?'

'Nothing in particular . . . Gifts for our nieces and nephews, Christmas Eve dinner . . . Antonio was very generous . . . At Christmas the whole family comes together, and my brother always shows up with his arms full of presents . . . It's a real celebration . . .' she concluded, staring into space as if she had the sumptuously laid table before her eyes, and the children were running about, excitedly waiting to open the presents.

'Forgive me for insisting, but . . . lately, had he happened to have any kind of altercation or argument with anyone . . . ?'

'No . . . Anyway, it was hard to get into an argument with Antonio. He was a very peaceable sort,' she said, smiling with emotion, as Piras kept taking notes.

The inspector stood up and started pacing back and forth, remaining on the carpet to avoid making noise. He concentrated better when he was moving, something he'd learned from walking in the woods.

'You were saying your husband's wife died some ten years ago . . .'

'In the spring of '56.'

'What kind of woman was she?'

'Beautiful, intelligent, elegant, a bit melancholic . . . In any case, a very special woman . . .'

'Amalia told me she died when she fell off her horse.'

'Yes. A dreadful accident . . . She'd taken off at a gallop through the woods and bounced straight out of her saddle . . . Antonio watched it all unfold before his eyes . . . Carla's death was a terrible blow for him. I don't think he ever fully recovered from it.'

'Where did it happen?'

'On the estate Antonio used to have in Maremma. He sold it just a few months after the tragedy. He couldn't bear to go back there.'

'May I ask whether there was a woman in Antonio's current life? A girlfriend?'

'I really don't think so – at least nothing serious . . . At any rate my brother was very reserved. He certainly didn't go around telling people about his love affairs . . . He was a true gentleman . . .' said the lady, holding back tears.

Bordelli stopped pacing and waited patiently for her to calm down, every so often exchanging glances with Piras.

'Signora Amalia told me your brother had fallen in love . . .'

'Amalia sees love wherever she looks. It's an obsession of hers,' said Signora Borrani, stirring slightly in her armchair.

'Amalia says he told her himself that he was in love.'

'Oh, rubbish . . . Imagine Antonio ever . . . Don't misunderstand me, Inspector. Amalia is a good woman, deserving of the greatest trust. She grew up with us, in our home . . . But to think that Antonio would ever confide in her . . .' she said sceptically.

'Why would Amalia make up such a thing?'

'Poor Amalia, I really don't think she does it on purpose. She just sometimes interprets things in her own way and then thinks they're true . . .'

At that moment they heard steps in the corridor, and everyone turned towards the door. In the doorway appeared Amalia, puffy-eyed, in an oversized coat.

'I'm leaving, signora.'

'Goodbye, Amalia.'

'I left the keys on the kitchen table,' said Amalia and, after mumbling a goodbye, she went out.

'Be sure to come and see me . . .' Signora Borrani said loudly, with affection. Bordelli waited for Amalia's footsteps to die out at the end of the corridor, then began pacing on the carpet again.

'I'm sorry . . .' he said. 'Earlier, you were talking on the phone with a certain Claretta . . .'

'She's my sister-in-law's younger sister.'

'You mean the sister of Antonio's wife . . .'

'Yes . . . She'll be here, at the villa, shortly . . . She's very upset . . .'

'Where does she live?'

'In Viale Don Minzoni.'

'Is she married?' Bordelli asked, for no specific reason. At the moment he was groping in the dark.

'As far as I know, she's never even been engaged. She still lives with her mother . . .' said Signora Borrani, her gaze wandering about the room. Bordelli noted a hint of opprobrium in her words.

'And Claretta's father?'

'Gualtiero is no longer with us. He passed on a few years ago . . . Claretta adored him . . .'

'Do you have a good relationship with your sister-in-law?'

'We see each other only at Christmas, and we talk by phone at Easter. Claretta has remained something of a little girl . . . She's very different from her sister, Carla . . . Growing up in the same family means nothing . . .' she said.

'Did Claretta get on well with Antonio?'

'They were very fond of each other . . . She was always very sweet to my brother . . . Claretta isn't exactly brilliant, but she's not a bad person . . .' said the signora, feeling perhaps a little guilty about her tone of a moment ago.

'Does Claretta have any brothers or sisters?'

'No . . . She's alone now.'

'Did she and Carla get on well?'

'Yes, they were very close. Even after Carla got married, they would still see each other every day. In the family we would sometimes say jokingly that Antonio was jealous, and perhaps it was true to some extent . . .' she said with an affectionate smile, managing not to cry.

'Sorry to change the subject, Signora Borrani, but have you meanwhile been able to speak with your nephews?' Bordelli asked, stopping his pacing in front of her.

'A little while ago I tried to reach them again at the office, but they hadn't returned yet. I'm waiting for them to call back.'

'What kind of work do they do?'

'A few years ago Antonio put them in charge of the family factories. They're two magnificent young men.'

'What kind of factories?'

'One is a shirt factory my father founded in the mid-twenties. The other makes Moplen objects.[5] It was Antonio who created it, in '57, a year after Carla died. At the time, my brother had thrown himself heart and soul into his work, just to keep his mind occupied.'

'Do you own any part of these concerns?'

'Thirty per cent of the shirts and fifteen of the Moplen,' the woman said hastily. The inspector resumed pacing, and looked at his watch. It was just twenty past twelve, but he felt as if a whole workday were weighing on his shoulders.

'How old was your brother?'

'He would have turned fifty-five in January.'

'So he retired early . . .' Bordelli observed.

'He felt that he needed to rest, but if he hadn't had two sons of such calibre, I'm sure he would have stayed put.'

'What sort of life did he lead?'

'I can't claim to know much about that . . . Antonio often used to tell me how much he liked to be alone, reading novels and history books . . . He would tell me about his long walks in the woods . . . And every so often he would allow himself a journey abroad . . .'

'Did he leave a will, to your knowledge?'

'I imagine he did. I've made one myself, many years ago, in fact. Our father always used to advise us not to wait too long, and to do it properly, with a lawyer.'

'When the time comes, if there really is a will, I beg you please to let me know what your brother's last wishes were.'

'To what end?'

'Nothing specific. It's just that I'd like, for now, to leave no stone unturned . . .'

'I have no doubt that Antonio divided his estate equally between his two sons. He was a very precise man, and would never have done anything unjust,' the woman said emotionally. Bordelli observed a respectful silence for a few seconds, then walked over to the woman and showed her the ring he'd found near the body.

'Are you familiar with this?'

'Of course . . .' she said, incredulous, taking the ring and studying it with emotion.

'Can you tell me to whom it belonged?'

'It's the engagement ring Antonio gave to Carla, one year before they got married . . . Where did you find it?' She seemed sincerely shocked.

'It was on the carpet, beside the . . . Beside your brother.'

'Antonio absolutely loved this ring. He'd ordered it in Paris from an important jeweller.'

'Did he keep other jewellery in the house?'

'Yes, but not just his own. He had a casket in the safe containing the family jewels . . .'

'We didn't find any casket.'

'As I said, it's locked in the safe . . .'

'Well, you must have seen for yourself that the safe was open,' said Bordelli.

'What do you mean, *open*?' said the woman, opening her eyes wide.

'You hadn't noticed?'

'Absolutely not . . . I didn't . . . So they stole the jewels? Then it was a robber . . .'

'There's no way of knowing just yet,' said Bordelli.

'Good God above . . . It's nothing compared to Antonio's death, but those jewels are immeasurably valuable . . . Nobody could ever compensate for the loss . . .'

'If we arrest the killer, perhaps we'll find the jewels as well,' said the inspector.

'I would give all the gold in the world to have my Antonio back,' the woman murmured disconsolately, collapsing into her armchair.

'I'm sorry to keep bothering you . . . but could you please describe the jewel-casket to me?' Bordelli asked.

'It's a small, mother-of-pearl chest – quite beautiful, actually – with the initials of one of our ancestors in relief on the cover: AS, for Adalgisa Sirtori, our great-great-grandmother . . . Her father was one of Garibaldi's Thousand . . .'[6] she said, unable to hide the pride she felt at having the Unification of Italy in her blood, and at being able to retrace her distant forebears back in time, just like the nobility . . .

'I must ask you please to let me keep the ring for now. It may prove useful in the investigation,' said Bordelli, adding a proper note of drama.

'Please be very careful with it, Inspector . . .' the lady whispered, and after a last loving glance at the ring, she gave it back to him.

'No need to worry, signora, I shall look after it with the utmost care,' the inspector said, nodding to her by way of thanks and putting the ring back into the inside pocket of his jacket. Signora Borrani leaned back into her chair with a long sigh and ran her fingers over her forehead, as though trying to understand something.

'Poor Antonio . . .' she couldn't help but say.

Bordelli had a great many more questions to ask, and after a few seconds of silence he turned to the woman again.

'All I found in the safe was a folder, which I took the liberty of opening. Among other things I saw a photo of a pretty girl in Paris . . .'

'Yes, that's Carla. I know that picture well; it was Antonio's favourite. They'd gone to Paris to celebrate their tenth anniversary, in '49 . . .' she said.

At that moment, one of the two lads from Forensics appeared in the doorway.

'I'm sorry, Inspector, I just wanted to let you know that the ambulance is here, and they're already upstairs. We're leaving.'

'Fine, I'll expect your report tomorrow morning.'

'Never fear, sir . . . Goodbye,' the technician said to all present, then left.

Signora Borrani looked at Bordelli.

'Are they taking Antonio away?'

'Yes . . . Would you like to see him?'

'No, not now, not now . . . Where are they taking him?'

'To Forensic Medicine. There's no getting round it, in such a case.'

'I don't want to think about it . . .'

'It'll be for just a day, two at the most.'

'Of course . . .' said the lady, massaging her temples.

'If you're tired we can resume another time.'

'No, don't worry . . . Actually, talking helps me . . .'

'May I ask whether you have any cousins?'

'My father was an only child, and my mother's sister died a spinster. I have some distant cousins, I don't know how far removed, but I've hardly ever seen them. They live in Argentina.'

'Do you know who your brother associated with?'

'Antonio knew many people, though deep down he always remained a loner.'

'I imagine he had many friends . . .'

'No, not many, as far as I know . . .'

'Do you know any?'

'A few, but only superficially. We'd always led two very different lives. On top of that, after Carla passed away, we saw each other a lot less often, and when we did Antonio was almost always alone.'

'Could you give me any names?'

'His dearest friend is Gilberto. They met at university and have remained close ever since.'

'What is his surname?'

'Giordanelli. He's Calabrian.'

'What line of work is he in?'

'He owns a number of hotels in the centre of Florence. A few are rather posh, but he's also got some boarding houses. He's the one I know best. He used to come to the house to study with Antonio when I was a girl . . . He liked to tease me and make me blush . . .' the woman said, lost in her distant memories. There was no escaping the long-buried images running through her head, called forth not in some moment of pleasant self-abandon, but by the questions of a police inspector trying to discover who killed her brother.

'Can you remember anyone else?' Bordelli continued, feeling a little guilty for prying.

'There was one called Olinto, whom I happened to meet. He seemed rather nice. Antonio would talk about him sometimes. I think I recall that he's an engineer, but I don't know his surname. And there's another who's named Ciro, but I only saw him in passing . . . I'm sorry, but that's all I can think of. I really know almost nothing about my brother's private life, especially these last few years. But I'm sure Gilberto can tell you much more . . .'

'Do you know where he lives?'

'He lives in San Domenico, but I don't know the exact address,' said the signora. Piras stopped writing in his notebook and intervened for the first time in the dialogue.

'I beg your pardon, but could you tell me who tends your garden?' he asked politely.

'A very fine young man does. And he not only tends the garden, he can do a great many other things, even cook. Antonio took him on almost ten years ago – or, as he liked to say, he *enrolled* him.'

'Did he not come to work today?' Piras continued, as Bordelli looked on in silence.

'Wednesday is his day off. Besides, he doesn't work only here, at the villa, and comes only when there's work to be done. Antonio paid him a regular salary just the same, and a rather generous one. He was very fond of the lad. I think they used to go hunting together sometimes . . .'

'Do you know him well?'

'Of course. He works sometimes at my house as well. I usually call on him when I have a lot of guests, and he helps out in the kitchen and waiting at table. But he also does things like repainting rooms or odd jobs around the house, or washing the car. He's a bit surly, but a sweet boy.'

'What is his name?'

'Oberto . . . I don't remember his surname . . .'

'Do you know where he lives?'

At that moment they heard the sound of footsteps coming from the entranceway and someone talking. All three sat in silence, listening. The orderlies from the Misericordia were taking away the body of Antonio Migliorini with the ease of habit. Signora Borrani held her breath, as though awaiting a catastrophe. Then there were two soft thuds, the ambulance doors shutting, then the muffled rumble of the motor, and the sound of the manoeuvres to drive through the gate . . .

And then away to Diotivede's butcher's block.

Signora Borrani stood up, a forlorn expression on her face. She staggered towards the window and looked outside, at the garden's fading autumn colours. Bordelli watched her suffer, thinking that hers was a privileged suffering. She could experience it in elegantly outfitted rooms, wipe away her tears with embroidered handkerchiefs, and continue her suffering at night in large, comfortable beds, between scented sheets in a magnificent, well-heated bedroom . . .

'I beg your pardon, signora . . . Do you know where he lives?' asked Piras, breaking the silence and repeating the question.

'I'm sorry . . . What?' she said, without turning round.

'Oberto . . . Do you know where he lives?'

'Ah, yes . . . in the Sant'Ambrogio quarter, I think. I'm sure Amalia will know . . .'

'Thank you,' said Piras and, casting a glance at Bordelli, he let him have the floor again. But the signora turned round, said she needed to absent herself for a moment and then left the room in a hurry. Bordelli plopped down on the sofa, next to his assistant.

'What do you make of all this?' he asked him softly. But it wasn't a real question.

'We have to talk to all of these people,' said Piras, which wasn't a real answer, either.

They sat there in silence, thinking. They had no leads. It would take a great deal of patience before they could find one, and they couldn't afford to let any details escape their notice. Something might pop up at any moment, though for now they were surrounded by fog . . .

The telephone rang. Not seeing the signora return, Bordelli picked up on the fifth ring.

'Hello?'

'I must have the wrong number,' said the voice of a man who sounded rather young.

'Wait . . . Are you Signor Migliorini?'

'Yes, but who—'

'I'm Inspector Bordelli of Florence police.'

'I don't understand . . .'

'I'm afraid I have some unpleasant news for you.'

'What is it? What's happened?'

'It's your father.'

'Don't tell me you've arrested him . . .'

'Unfortunately not.'

'What does that mean?'

'Your father . . . was murdered . . .'

'What are you saying?'

'I'm sorry . . .'

'That's absurd . . . Where is Zia Laura?'

'She's busy, at the moment . . . Ah, wait. She'll be with you presently,' said Bordelli, hearing her footsteps in the corridor. Piras stood up, as if it were disrespectful to remain seated. When the lady appeared, the inspector covered the receiver with his hand.

'It's your nephew,' he said. 'I took the liberty of telling him what happened . . .'

He handed her the phone, and the signora practically snatched it out of his hands.

'Hello? Guglielmo . . . My God . . . Yes, it's true . . . Please, come at once . . . Is Rolando with you? I don't know . . . I don't know . . . I'll tell you later . . . No . . . No . . . Come here now, I beg you . . . Yes . . . All right . . . Yes . . . Goodbye, dear . . . Goodbye . . .'

She sat down in the armchair and slowly set the telephone down on the table. She looked around as though lost, as if she'd just seen her brother lying on the floor. Bordelli realised it was best to stop for now, and exchanged a glance with Piras.

'Signora, please forgive us for pestering you . . .'

'What?' she said, rousing herself.

'That'll be all for now.'

'Yes . . .'

'Would you like us to wait for your nephews to arrive?'

'No, thank you, that won't be necessary . . . I'd rather be alone for a bit . . .'

But her wish was not fulfilled. In the hallway they heard the sound of high heels.

'Laura! Where are you?' shouted a shrill voice.

'It's Claretta,' said the signora, getting up and going towards the doorway, repeating, 'I'm here! I'm here! . . .'

She went out into the corridor as the sharp sound of the footfalls drew closer. Piras and Bordelli followed behind her and saw them embrace. Claretta was crying softly, her head on her sister-in-law's shoulder, giving off a strong scent of perfume. She was younger than Signora Borrani, and a little shorter. Tufts of black hair stuck out from under her hat, as her sister-in-law started kissing her forehead and whispering something.

'We'll be going now,' the inspector muttered, but a nod from Signora Borrani was the only reply he got. He headed down the corridor with Piras next to him. Outside he began to feel better, and as he was descending the staircase he looked up at the sky. A small white cloud was suspended beside the sun, soft and compact, like whipped cream.

'She looked like a pretty woman, that Claretta . . .'

'I didn't get a good look at her,' said the Sardinian.

They got in the car and, after a few manoeuvres, drove out through the gate. Coasting down the avenue, they looked around. Aside from the tall stone walls guarding the villas only the roofs and the treetops were visible. Every gate concealed a world unto itself. Migliorini's villa was isolated, the closest house a good hundred yards away. There was no point in wasting time talking to the local inhabitants. Even if they'd heard a car that night, what good would that do?

Bordelli drove along unhurried, thinking that this murder looked as if it would be a very tough nut to crack.

When they reached the Salviatino intersection they turned onto Viale Righi. The Beetle puttered along at a leisurely pace, as German as ever. A young officer from Bonarcado and an inspector on the threshold of retirement fighting the desire to light up a cigarette. They sat there in silence, but if thoughts made noise, people would be turning round to look.

When Bordelli pulled into his parking space at headquarters, it was almost half past one. Antonio Migliorini's body was probably already in Diotivede's hands. During the drive down, Piras had jotted down some notes and then put the pad away. They sat in the car for a minute as a blue Alfa Romeo Pantera peeled out of the car park. The inspector rubbed his face with fatigue. Only three years to go until retirement.

'If feels like we were up there for a week.'

'And this is only the beginning,' the Sardinian replied.

'It's not going to be an easy case, Piras . . . I can sense it . . .' Bordelli said, feeling discouraged.

'Maybe not, but let's get started.'

'You talk to the press; I'm going to Totò's for a bite to eat.'

'All right.'

'See you later in my office.'

They got out of the car and Bordelli set off towards the street. On his way out, he peered into the guard booth to wave to Mugnai, stopping to chat with him about cranky wives and demanding mothers-in-law. With a pat on the back, Bordelli left him to the mysteries of the *Settimana Enigmistica* and headed off down Via Zara, reflecting on how dull life would be without women. Could it be that women felt the same way? He doubted it highly . . .

He thought of the sapphire ring in his pocket. It was probably worth a heap of money, maybe a whole year's salary. What would Eleonora have said if he had presented her with a gem like that? Would she have cried in pleasure or thrown it in his face? He wondered again whether she had gone back to her apartment in San Niccolò after the flood or was still living with her parents. Who knew whether she still worked at the boutique on Via Pacinotti; he hadn't had the courage to go and see. Already a year had gone by since that horrid November night. He remembered everything, every single word of every sentence, the way she had receded back into the doorway, his slow drive home through the flood-ravaged city . . .

As he was walking down Via Lupi, he crossed paths with two beautiful, giggling girls. He blushed to think they might be snickering at him . . . Maybe his hair was a mess or he was walking oddly or his clothes were ridiculous. Then, as he was crossing Viale Lavagnini, he realised that one of the girls resembled Susanna, a girl who had charmed him back when he was in the fourth form. Lots of women had charmed him over the years, and still did, even now, on the brink of retirement. Only three more years to go. Then there would be no more hunting down killers, no more sprinkling salt on their tails. He could imagine himself tackling cases of lost dogs and stolen chickens, unable to give up the thrill of investigation, with Detective Piras stepping in to offer his assistance in his free time, pretending to take his old boss seriously, now that he had been put out to pasture . . . Shed a few tears and the picture was perfect.

He shook his head and put aside his lofty existential reflections for later. He realised he had made it through the morning without smoking and this pleased him immensely. Piras was right: it was a stupid vice. But didn't stupidity rule the world?

Viale Lavagnini was crowded with cars and motorbikes, horns blew incessantly. He crossed over and slipped into Cesare's trattoria. All the tables in the front room were taken but that didn't matter. He was used to eating in the kitchen, had been doing it for years. He would take his place on the stool and chat with Totò, the cook from Puglia, who ran the kitchen single-handedly. He greeted Cesare, said hello to the waiters, and walked through to the kitchen.

'Hello, Totò.'

'Ah, Inspector, help yourself to some wine, I'll be right with you,' Totò commanded from the height of his four-foot-eleven frame as a dozen sausages sizzled in a skillet with some beans.

'No rush,' Bordelli replied, pulling up his stool to the place that had been set for him on the counter. As he was waiting he took a piece of bread and put it into his bowl, drizzled it with oil and sprinkled it with salt, content to nibble on something light in that place of perdition. But before he could even take a bite, the cook put a dish of pappardelle with boar sauce in front of him.

'You really gotta taste this, Inspector.'

'At your command.'

'And how about a nice fillet of beef afterwards?'

'If you insist . . .'

'Too bad we finished the porcini . . . How about I fry you some potatoes?'

'Only one or two . . .' Bordelli said, swearing to himself that the next day he'd start his diet, a promise he often made to himself in order to enjoy a meal.

The cook was already back at the stove, filling up plates with food and passing them through the hatch to the waiters. He had learned Tuscan cuisine but periodically prepared dishes from his native region, which always met with great success.

Bordelli immersed himself in the sin that was the plate of pappardelle, finding consolation every so often with a sip of wine. He ate in silence, staring at the wall, trying to put some order to what he knew about Antonio Migliorini. It was like straightening books on a shelf, with Eleonora always present at the back of his mind. He kneaded ideas together, giving shape to strange conjectures and then dissolving them, formulating absurd hypotheses as a way of sinking into the atmosphere of the crime. Was it a robbery? A crime of passion? Revenge? Perhaps an unexpected argument between friends? At first glance it didn't look like premeditated murder . . .

'You're pensive today, Chief . . . somebody get knocked off?' the cook asked, dumping two bags of penne into a large pot of boiling water.

'Don't get me started.'

'Aren't you tired of working on corpses?'

'You work on corpses too, Totò. The difference is that you cook them,' Bordelli said, raising a forkful of pappardelle in the air.

'Who died?'

'Not now, Totò.'

'Just tell me how he was killed.'

'He was skewered with a kind of sword,' Bordelli said, certain that this piece of information would set the cook to talking about some crime that had happened back in his region. And indeed . . .

'Where I'm from, Inspector, right after the war, they found a schoolteacher in the woods who had been nailed to a tree with a pitchfork, like Christ on the cross,' Totò said, all the while preparing dishes and passing them to the waiters.

'That must have taken superhuman strength . . .'

'And you know who did it? A woman. Her name was Rosina, she'd been a maid during Il Duce's time and her honour had been offended by the schoolteacher, who was a high-ranking member of the Fascist party. Everyone knew about it.'

'She meted out justice on her own,' Bordelli said, recalling with a flash his own experience as an avenger.

'What else could she have done?'

'There are laws, Totò.' Sacrosanct words, direct from an officer of the law.

'And what have laws ever done for poor folk?'

'That's true . . . to a degree . . .'

'And then, a few years back, in a town nearby, they found a man hanging from a butcher's hook in a stall on a farm, his arms tied behind his back . . .' the cook continued woefully, adding that they never discovered the killer. Then there was a woman who was cut up with a hatchet, the boy who was killed with a horseshoe, an old man whose throat was slit with a razor, someone murdered with a screwdriver, another with a brick, one with a hammer . . .

'Can't you tell me a nice love story instead?' Bordelli asked, pouring himself another glass of wine.

'Oh, we have those, too . . . did I ever tell you about Crazy Carmela?'

'I don't think so.'

'Listen to this one . . .' Crazy Carmela was a farm girl from his region who had been orphaned when she was a child, a great beauty of a girl. When the war was over, she was left waiting for Johnny, an American soldier who had got her pregnant. He'd sworn he would come back and marry her, and she'd chosen to believe him. Months went by and no American showed up. Carmela gave birth to a little girl with blue eyes and kept waiting, saying that sooner or later he'd be back . . . They called her crazy and said that nobody would return, that she should stop thinking about him. But no, she swore he'd return. Crazy Carmela they called her. One day when the baby was about six months old, an American came to town, a good-looking young man. He asked around about a certain 'seniorina' and showed people a tattered photo of a girl. That girl was Carmela . . .

'How do you want your fillet? Rare?' Totò asked, rooting around in the fridge.

'You decide . . . Keep telling the story,' Bordelli said.

'Hold your horses . . .' Anyway, the townspeople were stunned. They were also embarrassed by everything they'd thought and said about Carmela. They told the American to wait in the piazza and they went to fetch Carmela, saying that her man had returned . . . She ran to him as fast as she could, laughing and crying at the same time, but when she got to the piazza she stopped short in her tracks. It wasn't her American. It wasn't Johnny. In a fraction of a second, she understood, and she thought she would die. The American was Johnny's brother. Johnny had been killed in August 1944, on the Gothic Line. His diary had been sent back to his family many months later, together with other personal objects. The diary was full of loving words for his beautiful Carmela and on one of the final pages he had written a last will and testament. *If I die, someone from my family should go to Carmela and tell her that I would have returned to marry her but that God decided otherwise* . . . Carmela cried day and night for a week. The American stayed on in a small hotel in town. Then, one morning, Carmela woke up smiling. She seemed happy and everyone in town thought that she had gone crazy. She said she had had a dream. Johnny had spoken to her and had told her what to do. In less than a month, Carmela and Johnny's brother were married. His name was Nick and he had fallen in love with her immediately. She loved him, too. Actually, she loved him doubly, as if Nick had also been Johnny. After their wedding, they went to America with the baby . . .

'That's the kind of story I need to hear, Totò,' Bordelli said, mopping up the last of the sauce in his pasta bowl with a piece of bread.

'Now try this fillet, Inspector . . .'

Bordelli came out of the trattoria a little heavier but satisfied for having refused a slice of custard pie and the usual little glass of grappa. On the avenue the light had changed. Some tired clouds were starting to cover the sky, but there seemed to be no rain in the offing.

He didn't feel like going straight back to the station. He wanted to be alone for a moment, and so he headed down the pavement at a leisurely pace and then turned onto Via Poliziano. At last he could allow himself a cigarette. He started searching his pockets. In the end it hadn't been so hard to postpone the cigarette until now. But he couldn't find the packet. Maybe he'd left it at the office . . . But instead of looking for a tobacco shop, as he would have done up until the day before, he decided to take advantage of the situation and prolong his wait until after dinner. He wasn't sure he wouldn't fall into temptation, and to help himself not give in he made up a stupid little game, a sort of bet with fate: if he succeeded in not smoking until after dinner, Eleonora would come back to him . . .

He smiled, enjoying the illusion of thinking he could influence destiny. His friend Dante said that man's life was entirely ruled by the imagination, and even total awareness could do nothing about this . . . *What makes the world go round is the will, which is shaped by desire, which is in turn governed by the greatest force in existence, the imagination . . .*

He crossed the Mugnone bridge and walked slowly along the Via XX Settembre, parallel to the small torrent . . . An important date, 20 September, he thought, which maybe shouldn't be remembered for the annexation of the Papal States into the Italian Republic, but rather for the pope's triumphal entrance into the new state that had just been stitched together to the accompaniment of great promises and bloodshed. An old story, apparently . . .

Nowadays Italy was flying on the wings of progress, dreaming of prosperity and fun . . .

Every so often he would let himself be carried away by such visions from above, but in his work he was doing the exact opposite. He had to examine everything from up close, evaluate every detail, look for the needle in the haystack. And above all he had to trust his own instincts, appearances notwithstanding.

Before reaching the Ponte Rosso he crossed the street and, mumbling a song by Modugno, entered the Botanical Gardens. Despite the cold, dozens of small children were playing in groups, scattered here and there under trees, and the buzz of the chirruping voices reminded him of a beach in summer. Their mothers chatted on benches, never taking their eyes off the chicken coop.

He went and sat down at the back of the garden, near the great hothouse. He knew he had some trying days coming up, and wanted to tackle them with a cool head. The sun by now was behind the buildings, and for a few seconds it shone through a break in the clouds and lit up the sky.

Just a few yards away came the twitters of a gaggle of little girls, each with her doll in her arms. They were playing at being mummies, busy lining up pebbles along the ground. Bordelli watched them and recalled his own childhood games. A string, a rubber band, a clothespin . . . Anything could be turned into a toy.

Gazing at the treetops, he wished he could go for a nice long walk in the woods. Ever since he'd returned to his job, he'd had so much less time on his hands, even for reading, and he didn't like it. He would try not to give up after three or four pages before falling asleep, but sometimes he was just too tired even for that. He was reading Chekhov at the moment, on the advice of the young salesman at the Seeber bookshop. He loved the book; it was a sort of journey through human weaknesses. But at that pace it would take him forever to get to the end . . .

'Who are you?' a little voice behind him asked. He turned round. It was a tiny little girl, with two half-undone black braids.

'Hi,' said Bordelli.

'What's your name?'

'Franco. What's yours?'

'Mirella. But who are you?'

'Well . . . I'm Franco . . .'

'Yes, but who are you?' the little girl repeated.

'Do you really want to know?'

'Yes.'

'Really really?'

'Yes.'

'I'm a man sitting on a bench . . . But don't tell anyone. It's a secret . . .'

'No, you're not, you're Mr Roly Poly!' the girl screamed, and before he could open his mouth she ran away, laughing madly. She went back to her little friends, who were waiting for her, and they all burst out laughing . . .

Was it possible to blush over the joke of a little girl? He smiled, but felt hurt. From a young age women learned how to crucify men. *Mr Roly Poly* . . . Good God . . .

The girls ran over to their mothers, who'd been calling them. All around the garden people were getting ready to go home, and a few prams were already heading for the exit. Some overexcited children kept kicking a football around; they would certainly be the last to leave. The inspector watched them, remembering when he used to play, usually alone, in the little garden in front of his house, and his imagination was able to turn a hedge into a forest, a bush into a witch, making him forget for a moment that his father was off fighting at the front . . .

A small white puppy appeared out of nowhere and started biting his shoelaces, growling playfully, when from the back of the garden a young woman came running.

'Arturo! Leave the gentleman alone!' she shouted.

Bordelli let the little furball amuse himself with his shoes, and when he reached out to pat it, the dog recoiled a few steps, barking and wagging its tail.

'I'm sorry . . .' the girl said, mortified. She looked to be less than thirty years old. Rather pretty, with black hair cut in a bob like Caterina Caselli.

'Not at all,' Bordelli reassured her. 'The pleasure's all mine.'

'Arturo, that's no way to behave,' she said, picking the little dog up. Keeping her distance, she looked at the stranger's shoes to check the damage.

'I'm still alive,' said Bordelli, smiling.

'He's just a puppy and doesn't know what he's doing,' she said in her defence, caressing the animal. She was wearing tight, form-fitting slacks, black high-heeled boots, and a short, elegant coat. Looking at her, Bordelli hoped she was an angel sent by destiny to make him forget Eleonora . . .

'When I was a little boy I had a goldfish called Arturo,' he said, as though uttering a magical formula that might detain her. She smiled faintly, letting the puppy chew on her collar.

'My apologies again . . .' she muttered, taking a small step backwards, ready to walk away.

''Bye, Arturo, be a good dog,' said the inspector.

'Oh, he's a very good dog . . . Just a little mischievous . . . Goodbye . . .'

'Be seeing you,' said Bordelli, actually dreaming that he would see her again some time. The young woman treated him to one last smile and then whisked her charm away, swaying on her heels. She had the proud gait of someone who aspired to great things. After taking a few steps she put her little dog back on the ground, and Bordelli hoped in vain the little imp would come back to him and bite his shoes some more. The girl was getting farther and farther away, oblivious to him . . . He thought of following after her, catching up to her, and saying something amusing to her . . . She would laugh, and he would keep talking about this and that in a familiar tone . . . He would ask her whether she might do him the honour of joining him for dinner, and after a never-ending moment of reflection, she would accept . . . A little restaurant in the centre of town, with soft light, a bottle of good wine . . . After dinner, a stroll down the narrow old streets, their shoulders continually touching . . . Why couldn't it be so easy? He would discover that Eleonora was not invincible, that he could free himself of her ghost . . . and that, above all, he would be right to forget about her . . . She was never coming back . . . He had to get that through his head . . .

He got up from the bench, feeling somewhat at a loss, heart racing like a teenager's, and, huffing and puffing, he started walking in the girl's direction, as she continued to wander about the garden, trying to keep the unruly Arturo in check. Various mothers headed for the exits with their babies in their arms, still chatting. Who knew how many secrets, how many confessions, had been whispered over the years in that garden? And now the age-old trees were about to witness a painful scene . . .

Would he be able to say anything to her? Even something amusing? He felt like an ass, but really, what, in the end, could happen to him? At worst, he would make a fool of himself . . . Though he really wouldn't like coming over as a lecher. He was now just a few paces away from the girl, but she had her back to him and was unaware. Arturo was far away, chasing after some children's football.

'That's one indomitable puppy,' he said, pulling up beside her . . . Man, what a brilliant line. The girl turned to look at him, mildly surprised.

'Maybe he takes after me,' she said, slightly curling her lip. She had the self-confidence of the rich.

'May I make an observation?' he ventured.

'Go ahead . . .'

'You're very beautiful.'

'My boyfriend never tells me that,' she said, amused, and walked away at a leisurely pace towards the frenzied Arturo. The inspector stood there for a few seconds, looking at her, then headed for the exit with his tail between his legs. He felt hurt by the young woman's indifference, almost as much as by *Mr Roly Poly*, but that was not the real defeat . . . He'd realised that no woman could ever make him forget Eleonora, at least at the moment, not even the beautiful girl with the dog. Not even Adele had been able, beautiful Adele, who just a few months earlier had made him fall more than a little in love with her . . .

He was still thinking about the pretty girl with the dog when he returned to his office. He hung up his coat and settled into his chair. On the desk, near his cigarettes, he found a carbon copy of an immaculately typed report, with no corrections, clearly the product of Piras's meticulousness. There was a brief list of the seven names, their home addresses and phone numbers: the victim's two sons; his sister Laura; sister-in-law Claretta Biagiotti; maid Amalia Calosi; friend Gilberto Giordanelli, with the names of his hotels; and, finally, Oberto Nicolosi, Migliorini's young handyman. At the very end, under the young man's name, Piras had also included the address and phone number of his mother, Nilva Nicolosi.

It was time to get busy. He would start with Oberto. He took a deep breath, picked up the phone, and dialled the young man's number. No reply. He rang the mother's house and a woman answered in a monotone voice. There was the sound of either the radio or the television in the background. Bordelli introduced himself and asked for Oberto, ready to reassure the woman that he only wanted to ask him some questions, but she wasn't at all ruffled. She told him that her son didn't live with her . . . *It's been years since he moved to his place on Via dei Macci, next door to the grocery shop.* The inspector asked her what time he might find her son at home but she said she had no idea.

'Once in a while he comes to eat and brings me his laundry.'

'Thank you for your time and sorry for troubling you.'

'No trouble at all.' The woman mumbled a farewell and hung up. The inspector put the receiver back on the cradle and then buzzed the switchboard.

'Find me Piras, please.'

'Right away, sir.'

While he was waiting he started thinking about the open window in the study, the one that Amalia had closed. What did it mean? Had the killer acted impulsively and, then, shaken by his act, needed some fresh air? If so, why didn't he close it? Was it opened on purpose or was it an oversight?

There was no point in mulling over all these questions. Not now, anyway. He started to fiddle with his packet of cigarettes, challenging himself not to give in. How on earth had he become a slave to a simple roll of paper filled with tobacco? During wartime, smoking had been acceptable. Whether it had been the endless, fretful waiting or the calm after a night patrol, there had always been a reason for smoking, mainly because you didn't know whether you'd make it out alive. Quitting was the last thing on your mind.

He knocked a cigarette out of the packet and onto the desk and stared at it. Maybe it was its seemingly benign appearance that made the cigarette so powerful. There it sat, looking innocent, just waiting to be transformed into smoke.

'There's no point in you staring at me like that, I'm not going to light you,' he mumbled. He slipped the cigarette back into the Nazionale packet and dropped it into the bottom desk drawer. He was supposed to be solving a crime and here he was talking to a cigarette. It was because he was disoriented, he realised. Usually, when he arrived at a crime scene, Bordelli could perceive something about the nature of the killer . . . nothing precise, just an impression, and sometimes even a wrong one. It was like imagining the protagonist of a novel by only reading the last page. This time, though, he could see only the spine of a closed book . . .

Someone knocked on the door. It was Piras. He sniffed the air, surprised not to smell smoke. Bordelli pointed to the list of names.

'Let's divvy up the work. You talk to Migliorini's sons and his friend, Giordanelli. I'll take care of Oberto and Claretta. Let's see what we can find.'

'Fine.'

'Let's start now. Meet back here around eight thirty?'

'I'll do what I can.'

The Sardinian sketched a salute and left. Bordelli picked up the phone to call Claretta. The phone rang and rang, but no one answered. He looked up Antonio Migliorini's number in the phone book and tried to call there, too, thinking that maybe the two ladies were still at the villa. He let it ring almost fifteen times before hanging up. Four phone calls that led nowhere. This was not turning out to be a lucky day. But since Fate sometimes sent out mysterious messages, like Pythia the Oracle from her three-legged stool, he thought about trying his hand at the lottery. Maybe he'd win five out of five.

He got to his feet, folded the carbon copy report in four, and put it in his pocket. He left the office with his trench coat over his shoulder, leaving the cigarettes behind in the drawer. On his way downstairs, he started to choose his five numbers. They needed to have some meaning. The date was a classic strategy, but he wanted to do better.

He got into the Beetle, and as he was leaving headquarters, he continued to think about the numbers, making his way towards the Sant'Ambrogio neighbourhood. He had to include a date. In memory of the flood, he chose the current month, the eleventh. Then, driving across town, he thought of his car, and how far it had taken him over the years. The first and last digits of the license plate next to each other made 17. Now for a third number . . .

What a silly game, he thought, looking distractedly at the people on the pavement. But he knew well that he'd keep on. He had never quite given up his childish spirit, not during the war, not even during his mother's funeral. It helped him not to lose himself. Once, in 1943, when his battalion was advancing up the Italian peninsula, ferociously tailing the Germans . . .

All of a sudden he caught sight of a beautiful blond girl wrapped in a fur coat. She was walking as if in a daydream. She looked like the nymph of the forest who bedazzled Apollo; bored by her surroundings, she had come to earth for a stroll. Of course she gave herself airs. But she could get away with it because of her beauty. He noticed that the building behind her was number 87, and thus the third lottery number was decided.

When he reached the end of Via dei Pilastri it occurred to him to use the last two digits of Claretta's phone number as the fourth number in the series. He parked in Piazza Ghiberti, next to the covered Sant'Ambrogio market, and took out the list to see the number: 36. Fumbling through the glove compartment, he found a pen and wrote down the sequence on the blank space of a thousand-lira note, under Giuseppe Verdi's sad gaze: 11, 17, 87, 36. He needed just one more number.

He got out of the car, put on his overcoat, and set off down Via Mino as evening was falling. The lights were on in the shops and cafés. Through service entrances he saw cooks in trattoria kitchens starting to fuss over their pots and pans. He turned down Via dei Mazzi to look for the grocer, remembering that an old girlfriend had once lived nearby, at the top of Borgo La Croce. That must have been in '54 or '55. Their love story had ended in tears – her tears. She had fallen in love with someone else, she said, and couldn't do a thing about it. He noticed how beautiful she was as she told him. He had stroked her hair and, after wishing her all good things, he had left her weeping into her pillow. Getting to sleep that night had been difficult but the morning after he already felt better. A clean break was much less painful than the usual slow unravelling . . .

Absorbed in recalling the episode, he had reached the end of the street and had to turn back, ultimately finding the grocer near the intersection with Via dell'Agnolo. Bags of dried beans lined the entrance and a strong smell of salted anchovies filled the air. Next door was a small four-storey house, number 37A. It had six buzzers, none of which had a name on it. He pressed one randomly, and took a step back, looking up at the building. He waited but no one peered out from above. He tried the other buzzers, also with no result. In the meantime, however, he'd found the fifth number for his lottery ticket: 37.

He entered the grocery and waited patiently as a hunched, elderly lady finished her shopping. The shopkeeper was heavy and had a vaguely porcine look. He had a stub of a pencil tucked behind his ear and was fascinating in his own way. The old lady fished her coins out of a purse, counting them slowly, and after paying for her goods, left the shop, trailing her creaky trolley behind her.

'What'll it be?' asked the grocer. Bordelli pulled out his badge and presented it to him.

'Do you know a young man named Oberto Nicolosi?'

'Sure, he lives next door. Good kid . . . not in any trouble, is he?'

'No trouble, I just need to ask him a few questions.'

'They needed to ask Buccia a few questions, too, and then they threw him in Murate for three years,' said the grocer, crossing his wrists in front of him to indicate prison.

'Do you know where I might find him?'

'No, sorry . . . Ask Lapo, the carpenter across the street. They're friends.'

'Thank you . . . And since I'm here, do you have any cannellini beans?'

'Perfect timing – have a look at these beauties.' The grocer walked over to an enormous sack of white beans, dug the scoop in, and pulled it out, full, ready to give them all to the inspector.

'Not that many,' Bordelli said.

'How much do you need?'

'A half-kilo will do.'

'Let them soak overnight,' the grocer said, pouring some of the beans into a paper bag, and putting it on a scale. The needle stopped at precisely half a kilo.

'Do you always get it exactly right?' Bordelli asked, in admiration.

'It's not that hard. You get the hang of it,' the man said with a shrug.

'How much do I owe you?'

'Nothing. You can take care of it next time.'

'Thank you, but no, I want to pay . . .'

'I won't go out of business for a handful of beans,' the merchant said, leaving the bag on the counter and turning towards the back of the shop.

'Well, I hope to return the favour some day.'

Bordelli took the bag and left, slightly embarrassed at the special treatment he had received. He crossed to the other side of the street and went into the carpenter's shop. A thin young man was energetically planing an old bench, surrounded by shavings. There was a pleasant smell of cypress wood in the air. Bordelli showed his badge and the young man stopped his work.

'What can I do for you?' he grumbled, a concerned look on his face.

'Are you Lapo?'

'Yes . . .'

'I'm looking for Oberto Nicolosi; the grocer told me you two are friends.'

'Has something happened?' the man said nervously. Bordelli gestured for him to calm down.

'I just need to talk to him.'

'You had me scared. . .' the lad said, starting to breathe normally again.

'Do you see each other often?'

'Almost every day. He lives across the street.'

'Do you know where I might find him now?'

'Sometimes he plays billiards over at Vasco's bar, in Piazza dei Ciompi.'

'Thank you, I'll go and see if he's there,' Bordelli said. After saying goodbye, he left the shop, and turned down Via dell'Agnolo towards the centre of town, his bag of beans in his hand. At that time of day the neighbourhood was a flurry of activity.

On the opposite side of the narrow street he caught a glimpse of a young woman walking towards him. He was attracted to her immediately, and felt warmth surge through him. He stopped to watch her pass, ignoring hostile looks from other passers-by who had to walk around him. Truth be told, there was nothing particular about her. Lots of men probably wouldn't even look twice at her. She gave herself no airs, wasn't wearing a miniskirt, wasn't made up, wasn't walking like a diva . . . Still, there was something about her . . . she was simply beautiful.

He watched her walk by, hoping she would turn round, even just for a second, but she disappeared round the corner. He continued on, pleasantly surprised by the apparition. He immediately thought of Eleonora. Was he still in love with her? He wondered not because of the pretty girl who had taken his breath away (he had always enjoyed looking at women on the street, carried away by his fantasies, even when he was deeply in love) but because of what had happened to them. Had the bitterness of certain memories kept him connected to her? Things had ended badly, in the worst way possible, and then guilt entered the mix. Was that why he continued to think about her? Perhaps he would understand only when he saw her again. He reached into his pocket for his cigarettes, but happily remembered that he had left them back at the office. He slipped the bag of beans into the pocket of his overcoat. When he arrived in Piazza Ciompi it was already dark. Teenage boys with longish hair sat on their scooters outside Bar Vasco, chatting and smoking.

He walked in and ordered a coffee at the bar. The air was thick with the smell of smoke and wine. While the senior barman worked the coffee machine, Bordelli took a look around. A youngster was playing pinball, surrounded by cheering mates. In a corner, a middle-aged woman made up like a doll played solitaire, a bottle of Biancosarti Amaro her only company.

He drank his coffee, left sixty lire on the bar, and headed towards the back. A kind of tunnel led to the billiards room, where smoke hung in long sheets in the air. Two boys were playing pool and two others were watching and commenting among themselves. When he walked in, they glanced over at him, and Bordelli knew that they recognised him for the cop he was.

He walked over to the billiards table and stood with his hands behind his back. He watched in admiration as the player sank a ball slowly and easily into a pocket. Once upon a time, Bordelli had known how to play like that, and watching now made him want to try his hand at it again. In his head, he identified Oberto as the skilful player. With his dark hair and taciturn expression, he was different from the others. He was there as if by chance, as if he belonged to a different world. Age-wise, he looked about twenty-five. He was dressed simply but there was something elegant about him. It was his turn again, and as he chalked the tip of his cue, he studied the table.

'I'm looking for Oberto Nicolosi,' Bordelli said. Everyone turned to look at him.

'I'm Oberto Nicolosi . . . Who are you?' the young man asked calmly. He was good looking, tall and thin, and had intelligent eyes.

'Inspector Bordelli . . . Can we talk in private?' After a moment's hesitation, Oberto leaned his cue against the wall. He put on his coat and followed the inspector out of the bar. They crossed the street and stood under the loggia of the covered market, far from the passers-by. Oberto waited, more taciturn than ever.

'It's about Antonio Migliorini,' Bordelli said.

'What happened? Is he all right?' the young man asked with alarm.

'Unfortunately, I have some sad news . . .'

'Is he dead?'

'He was murdered last night,' Bordelli said. Oberto went pale and stared at him with incredulity.

'Who did it?' he asked gravely.

'I'm trying to figure that out,' Bordelli told him succinctly, and, in a low voice, explained what had happened. Oberto looked around in amazement. Every so often he rubbed his eyes, as if to hold back tears.

'It can't be true . . .' he mumbled.

'You worked with Migliorini as a gardener, is that correct?' the inspector asked.

'Yes, he hired me about ten years ago.'

'When was the last time you saw him?'

'Yesterday afternoon.'

'Up at the villa?'

'Yes, I wanted to do some work in the garden.' He was trying hard to answer but it was apparent that he was taking it badly and needed to be alone to digest the terrible news.

'Do you have keys to the main gate?' Bordelli continued.

'Yes.'

'To the villa, too?'

'The *dottore* gave me them in case of an emergency many years ago, but I've never used them.'

'Where do you keep them?'

'In a secret place at home.'

'Yesterday did you only see him, or did you speak to him as well?'

'We spoke.'

'May I ask what you spoke about?'

'Nothing special . . . where is he now? Can I see him?' the boy asked.

'His body is at the forensic pathology laboratory, and will probably be returned to the family tomorrow.'

'Shit . . .' whispered Oberto.

'Going back to yesterday . . . did you happen to notice anything strange? Did he seem worried?'

'We joked around the way we always did.'

'Signora Laura mentioned that you and he confided in each other.'

'He treated me like a son.'

'Were you on familiar terms?'

'It's what he wanted, but it was hard for me,' the boy said with a sad smile.

'And you had known each other for a long time, correct?'

'Since I was a child. When my father died, Antonio took care of my family.'

'Did he ever mention anyone who might have borne him a grudge?'

'No, I don't think so . . .'

'What time did you leave the villa?'

'As soon as it got dark.'

'As far as you know, did Migliorini have a lady friend?'

'I'm sorry, Inspector, but if you don't mind, I'd like to be alone for a bit,' Oberto said, taking a cigarette out of a packet and putting it in his mouth. He offered one to Bordelli, but the inspector managed to resist.

'Of course, I understand completely . . . If you can come to police headquarters tomorrow, I have a few more questions to ask you.'

'All right.'

'Ask for Inspector Bordelli. If I'm not there, tell them what time I can find you at home.'

'Fine, see you tomorrow,' Oberto said, shaking hands with the inspector and setting off towards the centre of town. It occurred to Bordelli that he could have a son Oberto's age. He instinctively felt sympathy for the young man; he had a good, firm handshake, the sign of an upright, sincere person.

Bordelli had no desire to return to the office immediately and so decided to take a stroll through the neighbourhood. It seemed that everyone was in a rush except for him. He kept his hands in his overcoat pockets as he walked, and thought about how many murderers he had met over the years who seemed clean and sincere. A few years back he had arrested a young woman who had killed her seventy-year-old husband in order to enjoy his money with her lover. It was a classic homicide, almost textbook. The young woman was beautiful, elegant and sweet, practically angelic. If he hadn't arrested her, he would surely have courted her.

His thoughts went back to Paris. He would leave immediately after they made an arrest. But what if they never found out who did it? Then, no Paris. That would be his punishment.

He needed more time before heading back to the office, so he walked down to Via del Proconsolo. He stopped in a few shops along the way to buy food for dinner. He even stopped to drink a freshly squeezed orange juice at a bar on Borgo Albizi. Flipping through a tattered copy of *La Nazione*, he read about a wave of burglaries and hold-ups, massacres in Algeria, a legal dispute between Celentano and Don Backy, the unearthing of a conspiracy that would have eliminated Churchill, Roosevelt and Stalin in one fell swoop in Tehran in November 1943 . . .

At twenty minutes to eight he headed back to his car, hands thrust even deeper in his pockets. A cold wind had picked up and stung his face. Turning into Piazza Ghiberti, he saw a betting shop across the street and recalled his lottery numbers. He took the thousand-lira bill out of his pocket: 11, 17, 87, 36 . . . He mentally added 37 and crossed to the other side. Before walking in he stopped for a fraction of a second in front of the window and, in that very instant, someone grabbed his arm.

'Franco!' a smiling face said. Bordelli searched his memory. Yes, he recognised the face, but who was it?

'Wait . . . let me think . . .' he said, with a furrowed brow.

'Come on, Fogna . . . Don't tell me you don't remember . . . it's me, Gugo . . . Guglielmo . . . Remember, target practice on Bighead?'[7]

'Oh my God . . . Gugo . . . You haven't changed at all.' A leap in time in the flash of an instant. Liceo Dante, his group of friends . . . target practice on Bighead . . . Of course he remembered.

'How are things?' Gugo said.

'Not bad, and you?'

'Can't complain . . . I'm married, I have three kids . . . I work in a bank . . .' With only a few phrases he had painted an entire existence.

'What happened to Manzo? What was his name?' Bordelli asked.

'Mario Andorlini . . . I bumped into him a few years ago. He has a pharmacy in Piazza Nobili . . . but tell me about yourself. Are you married?'

'Not yet,' Bordelli replied, forcing himself to smile. His words also described an existence.

'Good choice. If I could do it all again . . .' Guglielmo mumbled with an unhappy smile.

'No one ever makes the right choice,' Bordelli said while mentally repeating the numbers 11, 17, 87, 36, 37 . . . Just then Guglielmo tipped his head towards the betting shop.

'Sorry, you were probably on your way in . . .'

'Hell, no, I've never bet on anything,' Bordelli said with a shrug.

Why the lie? It was not as if the lottery was evil. Was he afraid of seeming like one of those poor devils who hoped to win a fortune?

'Did you hear about Vannetti?' Guglielmo said.

'No . . .'

'He died three years ago. He was driving through the Consuma Pass and went off a cliff.'

'Oh, how sad,' Bordelli said, noticing that the lights in the betting shop were turning off, one by one.

'He sold television valves.'

'I'm sorry . . .'

'What can you do? That's life . . .' Guglielmo said, shaking his head.

'True, true . . .' Bordelli sighed. The employee of the betting shop came out, pulled down the metal shutters, and walked off.

'Well, it was great seeing you . . . you should come over for dinner one evening.'

'I'd love to.'

'I'm in the phone book. Look me up. Ciao, Fogna . . . God bless . . .'

'Ciao,' Bordelli said, putting the thousand-lira bill back in his wallet. It was probably better this way: he had saved a thousand lire. For today.

Walking back to his car, he thought again of the nickname that he had been given in secondary school. They used to call him the Fogna, 'the drain', because every morning he used to finish off everybody else's unfinished elevenses snacks. He remembered how, one day, after they had been let out of school, but before returning home for lunch, he had made a bet with two of his friends to see who could eat more cream-filled *bomboloni*. He managed to eat thirty-nine of them, a good ten more than his friend. When he finally got home, he proceeded to eat a full lunch but refused dessert, prompting his mother to put her hand on his forehead to check for fever.

He climbed into the Beetle and placed the beans and his other purchases on the passenger's seat. Driving slowly through the centre of town, he continued to travel back through time and memory. For once it was not about the war, but an even more remote time, one that he recalled with pleasure. Target practice with Bighead . . . how could he forget? Manzo's father had been a Mussolini sympathizer, and in the living room of their villa they had a very large marble bust of the Duce. Its size was directly proportionate to the owner's devotion. Once in a while Bordelli and his friends would gather at Manzo's house, purportedly to study, but one of their favourite pastimes was filling rudimentary blowpipes with clay pellets and firing them non-stop at his big head. No ideology informed their actions; it was just the thrill of doing something 'unacceptable'.

Entering his office, he felt as if he was returning to his native land after a long journey. He hung up his coat and heaved a big sigh. It was just twenty past eight, but he felt as tired as if it had been two o'clock in the morning. Truth be told, it was a mental weariness, the kind you cure by reading a good novel. But the day was not over yet; he wanted to know what Piras had been up to. Sitting down, he cast a glance over at the drawer in which he'd put the cigarettes. He'd managed not to smoke for the entire day and had sworn to himself he would resist until after dinner. Of course, he didn't actually believe that winning his stupid bet with himself would serve Eleonora up to him on a silver platter; all the same, at the very least, he would have smoked less. Now, however, he had to get back down to serious business. He dialled a number on the inside line and asked for Piras.

'I spoke to him via radio a short while ago, sir. He's on his way back.'

'As soon as he returns, send him upstairs to me.'

'Will do, sir. Any other orders?'

'That'll be all, thanks,' he said, hanging up. Staring into space, he started drumming his fingers on the desk. Why was Antonio Migliorini killed? Ever since the beginning of time, the three main motives for murder had been money, power and the passions. A jilted woman? A jealous husband? A little chest full of jewels had disappeared . . . But what if they were stolen just to muddy the waters? Maybe the killer merely took advantage of the situation after murdering Migliorini for some other reason . . . What if, in fact, the whole thing had been premeditated, down to the finest details, just to steal the jewels? One hypothesis was as good as another . . .

Bordelli leaned back in his chair, folding his hands behind his head. In the past he'd been able, not infrequently, to intuit at once what had driven a murderer to kill, and he would get an early idea as to where he needed to search . . . But that wasn't the case this time.

He had no leads to follow, no clear motive to explore, nothing that might inspire even a little research, and, although he was still waiting for the results from Forensics and from Diotivede's tests, he felt somewhat discouraged. If something decisive didn't crop up, all he could do was overwhelm Migliorini's family and acquaintances with questions, hoping to coax forth some detail worthy of attention.

He took the list of names written by Piras out of his pocket. Claretta Biagiotti lived not far from the police station, in Viale Don Minzoni. Just a stone's throw away. He tried dialling the number, and after three rings, a woman with a deep voice answered.

'The Biagiotti residence . . .'

'Good evening, this is Inspector Bordelli, police. Am I speaking with Miss Biagiotti?'

'I'm the housekeeper. I'll go and see if Miss Biagiotti is at home.'

'Thank you . . .' At the other end he heard her footsteps walking away, and, after a long silence, some other footsteps approaching.

'Hello?'

'Miss Biagiotti?'

'This is she . . . I'm sorry, but Fidalma couldn't remember your name . . .'

'Inspector Bordelli . . . We met this morning, at your brother-in-law's house.'

'Yes, I remember.' She had a vaguely childlike voice, a bit shrill.

'My condolences.'

'Thank you . . .' Claretta whispered, overcome with emotion.

'I'm sorry to bother you. Were you eating dinner?'

'Not yet. What can I do for you?'

'I need to talk to you. When could we meet?'

'Not tonight, I beg you . . . I'm still quite upset . . .'

'I understand,' said Bordelli, who actually wasn't in such a rush to go to her house.

'I got back from Laura's just a little while ago . . . Antonio's sons were still there . . . The despair . . .'

'I'm sorry . . .'

'None of us has any idea who could have . . . And who knows whether they'll ever find the killer . . .'

'We're working on it.'

'Have you found anything out yet?'

'I'm not at liberty to say anything . . .' Bordelli said with a sigh, in the tone of someone already on the right track. He didn't want to give the impression of being the classic detective without a clue . . .

'Forgive me . . .' Claretta was quick to say.

'I can understand your haste.'

'I'm just silly, I'm sorry . . .' said the young woman, in a frank tone Bordelli found fascinating.

'At what time can I disturb you tomorrow?'

'I don't know . . . Call whenever you like.'

'Thank you . . . My condolences, again . . . Good evening, Signorina . . .'

'Good evening, Inspector.'

There was a brief moment of silence, as though neither of the two wanted to hang up first. And then Claretta rang off after an ever so faint sigh. Bordelli leaned back in his chair, trying to remember the woman's face. Was she really as beautiful as he had thought? Her perfume was unforgettable. An unusual scent, which recalled . . . A blend of water and golden wheat. Nothing like those unbearable perfumes that stung one's nostrils . . . Even if she probably used a bit too much of it. Judging by her voice, she seemed quite different from Laura. More emotional, and more fragile, too. Laura had something icy about her. He couldn't imagine her ever letting herself go.

He let his mind wander amid these apparently pointless thoughts, knowing, however, that any detail might eventually prove useful to the investigation. And he had to admit that, after the phone call, he was more than a little curious about Claretta. He'd felt a sort of desire to . . . save her. From what, he did not know. This wasn't the first time this had happened. There were women who, without knowing it, inspired in others a protective instinct. There seemed to be a cry for help in their every gesture, even when they smiled. As though an inextinguishable brush fire of desperation were burning inside them . . .

Eleonora was not like that. She was an independent, luminous woman, who when she fell in love took pleasure in abandoning herself to a man's embrace like a sacrificial lamb. But it was only a game suited to the moment. Her healthy sense of freedom was part of her charm. A sincere girl, she liked to let herself be discovered little by little. Unfortunately he hadn't managed in time to discover her more hidden aspects . . .

There was a knock, and a moment later the door opened. Piras appeared, looking weary. The inspector gestured for him to sit down, then got up and started pacing back and forth with his hands in his pockets.

'Tell me everything . . .'

'There isn't much to say.'

The young Sardinian had gone and talked to Migliorini's sons. The meeting took place in their office in Via Martelli, which was closed for mourning. The two young men were grief-stricken. One of them, Rolando, tried to keep a stiff upper lip, but it was clear he was the weaker of the two. The one running the family businesses was surely his brother Guglielmo, though he was the younger. Both were married with children. They'd last seen their father four days before, in that same office, to discuss business, as they used to do two or three times a month. The last to speak with him on the phone was Guglielmo. They'd talked on the very day of the murder, late in the afternoon, and had a normal conversation.

Piras had also succeeded in finding Giordanelli, Migliorini's friend, after a long series of phone calls. Giordanelli already knew of the murder, having been informed by Signora Laura. Piras asked whether they could meet, which they did at the Pensione Norma, in Borgo Santi Apostoli, one of the hotelier's properties. It was a rather elegant little *pensione*, in its way, perfect for clandestine trysts or ladies of the night. Giordanelli was a colossus with a gentle mien and an ogre's voice who hadn't lost any of his Calabrian accent. His eyes were red and he had trouble speaking. He invited Piras to follow him up to the building's medieval tower, which wasn't open to the public. It had almost eighty stairs. One always got to the top out of breath, but it was worth it. From the terrace roof one could see Florence all around, all the way to the hills surrounding the city. You could practically touch Palazzo Vecchio with your hand. A bit farther on was Brunelleschi's dome, and on the other side, in the distance, loomed the Forte di Belvedere and the basilica of San Miniato.

Giordanelli recalled the summer evenings spent on that ancient terrace with Antonio, drinking wine and chatting about things happy and sad. He'd seen Migliorini for the last time on Friday evening, for their customary game of bridge, at the house of a lawyer friend of theirs called Emanuele Scacciati. It was an evening like any other. Antonio was in good spirits; nothing seemed out of the ordinary. They'd spoken again on Sunday morning, and again perhaps on Monday. Giordanelli couldn't quite remember, since they spoke often, even if only to say hello. They'd made an appointment to go to the movies on Thursday, to see *Frank Costello*. They often went to the movies together, just the two of them, and afterwards would go and eat at a trattoria. Their paths were to cross again the following Saturday at a dinner among friends at the home of Olinto Marinari, at Barberino . . .

'Di Mugello?' asked the inspector, still pacing.

'Val d'Elsa.'

'Go on . . .'

'I asked him a few other things . . .' said Piras. Giordanelli didn't know whether his friend was in any sort of love relationship at that time. In such matters Migliorini was very much a gentleman; he never boasted about his conquests, hardly ever said anything at all, in fact. When he showed up at a dinner party with a woman at his side, everyone would discover that they had already been together for some time. But he'd had more than a few women, though more or less every time he'd fallen in love.

'There are men like that . . .' said Bordelli, thinking of himself.

'I asked Giordanelli if he knew of anyone who might have borne a grudge against Migliorini, and he replied that he couldn't possibly imagine how anyone could have hated him enough to kill him. He added that disagreements and quarrels are part of life, but it took a lot more than that to drive someone to murder.'

'Find out anything else?' Bordelli asked.

'I got Marinari's telephone number.'

'Well done . . .'

'He's an architect. A few years ago he moved to the country, to Barberino, to a large estate he'd inherited from an old aunt.'

'Have you tried ringing him?'

'Giordanelli said he's abroad for work, in Switzerland. He'd already tried ringing him in the afternoon and talked with his wife, who was trying to reach him. He'd also phoned other friends of his, some of whom already knew of the murder.'

'And did you talk with the lawyer Scacciati?'

'Yeah, but nothing of interest. He wasn't a close friend like Giordanelli. That's all for now,' Piras concluded.

'So, nothing,' said Bordelli, sitting down.

'Less than nothing . . .' said Piras, laying it on thicker.

'Think we'll manage?'

'I don't know,' said the Sardinian, who was usually an optimist.

'Leave me the phone number of the architect in Barberino.'

'Olinto Marinari,' said Piras, and then he dictated the number, reading from his notebook. Bordelli looked at the clock. Nine thirty-five.

'Go home and get some rest, Pietrino. See you tomorrow.'

'You seem pretty tired yourself, Inspector,' said Piras, standing up.

'Give my best to Sonia . . .'

'We'll expect you for dinner on Saturday.'

After bowing respectfully, Piras left the room. Bordelli couldn't help but smile, thinking that the young Sardinian was surely on his way to see his beautiful Sicilian girlfriend, the future lawyer. A very fine girl, Sonia. Who knew whether she would be able to make her way through courthouse halls peopled by men with no scruples.

He was hungry as a wolf, but before thinking about dinner he had one last thing to do. Picking up the phone, he rang Olinto Marinari at home, apologising for the late hour. His wife's voice sounded very sorrowful, almost dark. She'd managed to reach her husband and tell him the terrible news.

'He's leaving Lausanne early tomorrow morning, on the train. He should be home some time in the afternoon.'

'Could you please ask him to get in touch with me at police headquarters as soon as he gets back?'

'Of course, rest assured . . .'

'If I'm not there I'll call him back as soon as I can.'

'All right . . . Inspector Porcelli, is that right?'

'Bordelli . . .'

'Oh, I'm so sorry.'

'Not at all.'

'I'll certainly remember to tell him.'

'Thank you.'

They said goodbye, and Bordelli hung up. When he stood up he did not forget to put his Nazionale cigarettes in his pocket, already thinking about lighting his first cigarette of the day after dinner. It would be a first, and he couldn't help but feel a twinge of pride.

There was nobody in the stairway as he descended. He went into the courtyard and got into his Beetle. While turning the car around he realised he didn't feel much like going home and cooking up a dish of spaghetti, and so he decided to go and have a bite in Totò's kitchen.

The shortest cook in Europe moved like a ballerina between the fridge and the cooker amidst clouds of steam and smoke. Now and then he'd start singing some popular tune, deforming it in an almost surreal way. Bordelli knew how proud the cook was of what he believed to be his talent as a singer, and he had never risked teasing him about it.

'Now I shall decide what you will eat, Inspector.'

'I'm entirely at your mercy . . .' Bordelli said. He sat patiently on his stool, waiting to discover his destiny.

'Allow me to serve you.'

'How are things with Nina?'

'Not bad . . . it looks like we're going to get married.'

'Well, you certainly don't sound very excited about it.'

'How I sound isn't important.'

'When will it be?'

'Right after Epiphany, or maybe in the summer. We still haven't decided.'

'Am I invited?'

'If you're willing to come down to my town in the Salento region . . .'

'You're not going to get married in Florence?'

'Certain things ought to be done in your native village,' Totò declared, as if it was a commandment.

'One day, will you introduce me to your pretty Nina?'

'Didn't I ever show you her photograph?'

'No . . .'

'Look what a beauty she is,' the cook said, thrusting a photograph under the inspector's nose. She was very pretty, chubby, with big blue eyes.

'We have to celebrate . . .'

Lasagne, sausages, beans and red wine in abundance . . . despite the hour, Bordelli couldn't resist the temptation of Ciacco.[8] Perhaps it was because it had been a frustrating day and he hadn't got anywhere with the investigation. Or maybe it was Eleonora's fault. All excuses were acceptable. But he didn't give in without a small show of resistance, refusing the offer of a grappa with the determination of a sapper from the San Marco Battalion. He patted the cook on the shoulder by way of goodbye and swore that from that moment on . . .

As soon as he left the trattoria, he found a Nazionale cigarette between his lips. It hadn't been hard to win the bet, but who knew whether he'd ever get the trophy, the beautiful Eleonora. He lit the cigarette, and felt a pleasure surge through him that he had altogether forgotten. He crossed the road, which at that time of day was practically empty, and turned down Via Santa Caterina. Perhaps the truly depraved person was the one who knew how best to dose his vices to make them last longer. One cigarette a day, maybe two, at most three. The real mistake that smokers made was in believing that the more they smoked the more pleasure they had . . .

Bordelli had already finished the cigarette and thrown away the butt by the time he reached Piazza Indipendenza. He saw blinking coloured lights in some of the shop windows. Women in scanty clothes strolled through the park, looking chilled. Rosa had taken a different path.

'Want to come up to my room, honey?'

'Another time, thank you.'

He went back the way he'd come, crossing paths with a few men in overcoats. It was past midnight. Despite his fatigue, he was still not sleepy. He climbed into the Beetle and set off down Viale Lavagnini, knowing full well where he was headed.

Ten minutes later, he parked on Lungarno Serristori, near the medieval tower and gate, and started walking down dark and shadowy Via San Niccolo. After that big meal, a short walk wouldn't hurt. He crossed paths with a few drunks who were discussing important questions of life on which they agreed amicably. The thick black line of the flood water was visible along the façades of the buildings, but no one seemed to notice it anymore. Eventually, the line would fade and disappear, but the memories of those days for those that had lived through them would not be easily forgotten.

A few metres above the black line of mud was a stone plaque that marked an earlier flood, that of 3 November 1844, when Leopoldo II rushed back to Florence from his villa at Poggio a Caiano and threw open the doors of Palazzo Pitti to his struggling people. So many things had happened since then: *i carbonari*, Cavour, Garibaldi, the Unification of Italy, the Great War, the Spanish War, Mussolini, the Pact of Iron, 8 September, Piazzale Loreto, the May King, Togliatti, Bartali, the invention of the Vespa, the invention of the Fiat 500 – the pinwheel of history was always spinning. When would something epochal like Garibaldi or the Fiat 500 ever happen again?

He had almost arrived at the church, where the road widened, and he sought out Eleonora's windows. Thinking he saw light shining through the slats of the shutters, he felt a shiver go up the back of his neck. But when he got closer he realised that it was only a play of the light from a street lamp. He stood rooted to the spot, staring at the dark shutters, biting his lip, until he realised that an old woman was watching him from the top floor of an adjacent building.

Heading back to the car the same way he had come, he let his mind wander. Had Eleonora gone back there to live? Was she asleep? Was she alone? Had she gone to a party and not come back yet? Had she stayed over at a girlfriend's house to sleep? Or was she at her boyfriend's? Had she rediscovered the joy of living after that terrible night? Did she have a boyfriend now or did she stay away from men? Did she have a young fiancé or was he an older man, like him? The questions could go on endlessly, and they would only get more painful . . .

He climbed into his car, discouraged. As he approached the Ponte alle Grazie he was tempted to cross over to the other side of the Arno and go and see Rosa for a few moments of tenderness. But he stayed his course, knowing that, after such a long day, leaving Rosa's sofa afterwards would not be easy . . .

He passed in front of Palazzo Pitti and made his way towards Santo Spirito. Driving along the narrow streets of the San Frediano quarter, he thought back to his old flat in Via del Leone, where he had lived for almost twenty years. Suddenly he found himself in a forest of memories. He was glad to be living in the country now, but if he ever found a small flat a good price in that area . . . it was not a new idea, and he knew that sooner or later he would really do it.

At Porta Romana, he turned up the long hill towards Poggio Imperiale. He preferred this route, which went past Pozzolatico, even if it was curvier than Via di Bagnolo. He let himself be carried along by the road, gazing out at the olive orchards and the black outline of the distant hills in the dark night. He was tired. He smoked a second cigarette as he drove, looking forward to going to bed with his book of Chekhov stories.

Instead, when he reached Mezzomonte, he slowed down and turned into Dante Pedretti's driveway. Dante was surely awake: he'd probably be bustling around the spacious underground laboratory that he had built in the cellar of his villa.

He parked, got out of the car, and looked down at the valley below. He shivered; the *tramontana*, a northerly wind, was blowing. He could see Florence off in the distance, beautiful and cruel, like a witch from a fairy tale. No one could say that Florence lacked mystique, but she was definitely a dangerous woman . . .

He pushed open the front door, which was never locked. It was pitch black inside. He didn't bother looking for the light switch, having never even been in the upstairs portion of the house. Lighting a match, he found his way down the steep staircase to the basement. At the bottom of the stairs he opened another door and stepped into Dante's kingdom. It smelled of cigar smoke. Soft music floated through the warm air, a symphony he couldn't identify. Two candelabras shed their light on the far side of the laboratory. The walls were lined with antique bookcases holding old books. Dante sat in an armchair, his back to Bordelli, his white hair enveloped in thick smoke.

'I hope I'm not disturbing you . . .' Bordelli said, walking towards the light. Dante raised a hand in greeting without turning round. The counter where he worked was crowded with all kinds of things, in what looked like disorder. He waited for Bordelli to approach and then gestured for him to have a seat in the armchair across from him. He was wearing his old yellow lab coat, unbuttoned.

'Not at all, I was merely trying to figure out how to refute the theory of relativity,' he said with a smile.

'I thought it was irrefutable, though I confess I've never really understood it.'

'It's not that complicated; even a child can understand it.'

'Children are smart.'

'I could use the example of the ant on an orange that is travelling in a carriage . . .'

'Don't bother, it would just be a waste of your time,' Bordelli said.

'How about a grappa, Inspector?'

'Just one finger, thank you. Then it's off to bed.'

'Coming right up . . .' said Dante, getting to his feet. He went to his worktable, cigar in mouth, selected a bottle from among the many there, and uncorked and sniffed it. He put it down with a grimace; it must have been one of his chemicals. Picking up another bottle, he uncorked and smelled it likewise, and smiled broadly. This time he had chosen the right one. He filled two small glasses, brought one to Bordelli, and then sat back down in his armchair. They raised their glasses to each other from a distance and took a sip. It was brutal, home-made stuff. The music seemed to come out of the darkness around them. Bordelli concentrated and managed to recognise Schubert's *Unfinished.*

'Bruno Walter?'

'Obviously . . .'

They listened to the music without speaking. Dante looked up at the ceiling pensively, every so often taking a puff on his Tuscan cigar. He seemed to be following a remote thought or a particularly convoluted mathematic formula; perhaps he really was doing battle with Einstein's famous theory.

The inspector lit his third cigarette, being careful to keep the flame a safe distance from his grappa. He leaned back in his chair and let himself be transported by the moving, vigorous melodies of the unfinished symphony, which he knew by heart. At certain points it felt as if he could touch the essence of nostalgia as with no other piece of music. It was an epic form of nostalgia – for things he had never actually experienced – and it was at once painful and pleasurable.

He looked around as he listened. He had always felt at ease there, with Dante. Periodically he needed to spend time there, even if they didn't talk. It was like entering a parallel world, an indefinite time, where terrestrial concerns were remote . . . *and how sweet to me to founder in this sea . . . how sweet . . .*[9]

Floating along on the music he almost fell asleep. Taking his last sip of grappa, he put out his cigarette in the ashtray, and found the strength to get to his feet.

'My bed awaits,' he said, without hiding a yawn. Dante stood up and shook his hand in farewell.

'I've been wanting to ask you a question for some time now, Inspector.'

'I hope it's not a difficult one.'

'It's very simple: if you had to do your line of work on the inside of a body, would you arrest an antibody simply because it had killed a virus?'

'What?' asked Bordelli, caught off guard.

'I know, it seems absurd, but to my mind it's worth examining.'

'I'll think about it.'

'If there really is a God looking down on us, don't you think that in his eyes the entire world is like one big human body? That's a rhetorical question, of course.'

'So I don't have to answer . . .'

'Goodnight, Inspector.'

'I was thinking about organising a dinner at my house, before Christmas,' Bordelli said.

'With pleasure . . .'

'I'll let you know when in the coming days.'

'Sleep well.'

'I'll give it my best.' After a final handshake, the inspector walked towards the dark side of the lab, accompanied by the last notes of the unfinished symphony's finishing movement. Before departing, he turned around and saw that Dante had already sat back down. He climbed the stairs slowly and stepped back out into his usual world, where people killed one another and women came and went.

The *tramontana* penetrated through to his neck. Even the seats in the Beetle were cold, giving him no choice but to wake up.

Driving home to Impruneta, he thought about Dante's bizarre question. What was he hinting at, by mentioning God and viruses? The moon was large, almost full. By its light, the soil under the dark branches of the olive trees looked almost phosphorescent.

Five minutes later he was bumping slowly along the uneven dirt road to his house. He parked on the threshing floor and got out of the car with an unlit cigarette in his mouth. The light that hung over the doorway cast its flat glow on the house's stones and bricks. His gaze went automatically to the castle in the distance; its shape broke up the soft line of the hillside. When he first moved to the country, there had always been a light on in the castle, at all hours of the night, and he had always wondered why. Then he'd met the owner. Now, no one lived there anymore. Contessa Gori Roversi had moved back to Puglia with Isadora, her young handicapped daughter whom she showered with love.

One day in the future, a group of men in suits and ties would come to the castle, take some measurements, and put a price on it. Then people in town would know that the contessa had gone to the great beyond. And what would happen to poor Isadora? Would she have to live out the rest of her days in a mental hospital? For her sake, Bordelli hoped that she would die before her mother . . .

The wind continued to blow in long gusts. Bordelli was certain that he could smell the scent of ripe olives, cypress trees, and even rotting flowers from the nearby cemetery. How long had it been since he had gone to Soffiano to visit his mother's grave? He always sought to avoid going on the second of November.[10] Any other day was fine.

He went inside, to a cold house. He hadn't watched the news all day. Had there been more protests in the piazzas? Had a war broken out? Who knew whether Moro was still the prime minister.

He was about to put the beans to soak in a pot of water when he realised that he wouldn't be able to cook them until the following day, and so he left them out on the kitchen counter. It would be better to put them to soak in the morning before leaving the house, cook them in the evening when he got home, and eat them the day after, seeing that they had to simmer for at least two hours. Preparing beans was difficult but worth it. With tuna belly and raw onions they would be exquisite.

After fetching some wood from the cellar, he filled up the pot-bellied stove on the second floor, where it was a little warmer. He got under the covers, turned off the light, and wished Chekhov a goodnight. It almost felt as if he'd never got out of bed. His dream from the night before still danced vividly before his eyes . . .

He heard some rustling across the roof tiles, a mouse perhaps, or a nightbird. Maybe it was just the wind. He imagined the fields outside, the woods, and the animals that lived there. Rolling over on his side, he hugged his pillow. His thoughts began to overlap, and he knew he was falling asleep. He may already have been asleep when he realised that tears were rolling down his cheeks . . . he felt an infinite sweetness in his heart . . .

'Mamma,' he said softly, and smiled as if it were a game.

He kept obsessively going over and over the same dream, tossing and turning in bed before he finally managed to wake up. It wasn't a real dream, but rather an exhausting situation that kept repeating without respite. He had to climb a very long, steep staircase in an enormous glass building, without knowing where it would lead, and every time he was about to reach the top, he found himself back at the bottom . . . More or less like Sisyphus. This sort of thing used to happen to him often as a child when he had a fever.

Now that he was out of the dream, he felt drained. Through the slats in the shutter faintly filtered the first light of dawn. Little by little he became aware of a rhythmical noise coming from outside and, overcoming his momentary confusion, he realised that Botta was hoeing the garden. When he'd gone back to work for the police it soon became clear to him he would have no time to worry about planting and pruning, especially as he knew nothing about such matters, and so he'd passed the responsibility on to someone who knew a lot more about them. Ennio could come and go as he pleased, and they would share the proceeds. In fact it was a kind of sharecropping, agreed with a handshake over a glass of wine.

For Botta it was a passion. Ever since he'd swung a deal worthy of the name, he hadn't been hurting for cash. He'd bought himself a fire-red Alfa Romeo and no longer looked like a cheap hoodlum. Not that he dressed with any elegance, mind; that would have made him uncomfortable. Rather, one noticed that he no longer struggled to make ends meet. A major new novelty was that he'd finally had a phone installed in his home. He'd never had one before, and in order to reach him one had to ring Fosco's bar in Piazza Tasso.

But, truth be told, Botta didn't actually seem that pleased with his new situation. It was as though something precious was missing, perhaps that perpetual emergency condition that had been with him since birth . . .

The noise continued without cease . . . *Thump . . . thump . . . thump . . . thump . . . thump* . . . It was impossible to get back to sleep. Bordelli got out of bed without turning on the light and shuffled into the bathroom. After running the water, he stopped to look at himself in the half-light of the mirror. Not bad. But everyone was good looking in the dark.

All at once he was convinced that this was going to be a special day. He had no reason to think so. It was just a feeling. But it didn't last very long. Going downstairs he'd already forgotten about it.

He sent a greeting to the death's-head, thinking that it was time to give him a name . . . Maybe he could call him Arturo, like the pet goldfish of his childhood or the pretty girl's dog in the Botanical Gardens . . .

He filled the espresso pot and put it on the burner. Arturo the skull . . . Arturo . . . The name made him think of the two assistants of K., the land-surveyor, Arthur and Jeremiah . . . *The Castle*, another unfinished work . . . Or perhaps Yaweh had taken measures so that Kafka's novel would have the most 'finished' ending possible, an ellipsis . . .

Arturo. So he would call the skull Arturo . . . Or maybe not. That would just remind him of the pretty girl with the puppy, whom he would rather forget. Jeremiah was better. Yes, Jeremiah it would be.

'Hello, Jeremiah, how do you do?'

It was just a first step. Maybe in a little while he would spend whole evenings talking to him, the way some women did with cats or parakeets.

He put on his overcoat and went outside to the threshing floor, into the cold of the morning. His first glance was for the poor old contessa's castle, which looked a little less austere in the light of day. Parked alongside the Beetle was a white and rather dirty Fiat 500. Whatever happened to Ennio's beautiful Alfa Romeo? With this question in mind, Bordelli circled round behind the house. Botta was kneeling in the garden, his back to the inspector, busy removing snails and turning the earth around the cabbage plants.

'Ciao, Ennio.'

'Oh my God! You scared me, Inspector . . .' said Botta, one hand over his mouth.

'I heard you hoeing.'

'Even the earth needs to breathe, every now and then.' He got back to work, with expert movements.

'Feel like a coffee?'

'As long as it's not muddy water . . .'

'What's become of the Alfa?'

'I lent it to a friend . . . He met a girl and wanted to show her a good time.'

'Sounds only right.'

'We do what we can.'

Ennio came out of the garden, closing the rudimentary little gate behind him and glancing disdainfully at the rickety piece of architecture Bordelli had built with his own two hands many months earlier.

'Have you got something against my fence?'

'It's sort of painful to look at, all crooked like that, but it'll do for now.'

'You can make the next one, which is sure to make the art history books,' said Bordelli, heading back to the kitchen to make the coffee.

'You joke, Inspector, but when I was a kid they used to call me Little Filippo.'

'Meaning?'

'Brunelleschi . . .'

'Is there anything you don't know how to do, Ennio?'

'Only the useless things,' said Botta in all seriousness.

Once they were in the kitchen, Bordelli ran and turned off the burner under the coffeepot, which was boiling.

'We'll have to make a new pot,' he said, pouring the hot coffee down the drain.

'Fate has decreed that I should make it.'

'*Ubi maior* . . .'

'What?'

'Nothing, it's a Latin saying.'

'And what does it mean?' asked Botta, rinsing the espresso pot.

'Didn't you say you'd studied?'

'Yes, but I hardly remember everything.'

'It means . . . In the face of the better man, the lesser man gives way,' Bordelli translated roughly. Ennio approved, bobbing his head as he continued to devote his attentions to the coffee with the seriousness of a surgeon.

'Haven't you thrown away that death's-head yet?' he said suddenly, gesturing towards the skull.

'He's called Jeremiah. He's a friend.'

'Ah, I see . . . *Jeremy, the skull that keeps you company* . . .' Botta said with a sneer.

'He's very wise. He helps me put things into perspective.'

'We don't need Jeremiah to tell us that women are at the top of the list.'

'But Jeremiah will whisper it to you in a very convincing manner,' said the inspector, filling a pot with water. He'd just remembered the beans, and was finally putting them to soak. He would cook them that same evening, so he could eat them the following day.

'Let's talk about serious stuff, Inspector . . . When are we going to have another nice dinner party at your place?' asked Botta, perhaps inspired by the beans.

'I've been thinking about that lately. How about next week? Would you be available on Friday?'

'Friday's fine for me.'

'I'll talk to the others and let you know,' said Bordelli, going and sitting down.

'Shall I do the cooking, or will you do it all yourself, like you did for your birthday?'

'We can work together.'

'It's enough that we do things right. There should only be one person giving the orders in the kitchen. Everyone else can peel potatoes.'

'So I'll do the peeling.'

'Perfect. Now we must decide what to make.'

'Whatever suits your fancy.'

'Okay, I'll start giving it some thought,' said Botta, never taking his eye off the coffeepot.

'Tell me something, Ennio . . . What are you doing with all that money?'

'What do you mean?'

'I'm just curious. You don't have to answer.'

'Well . . . I have a nice car, I eat well . . . I looked at a three-room flat in Via del Campuccio, a stone's throw from where I live, and I may just be able to buy it.'

'Sounds like an excellent idea.'

'Every so often I also lend a little to friends in need.'

'Even though you know you'll never see any of it again . . .' commented Bordelli, pleased that Ennio was so generous.

'There are more important things,' said Botta, shrugging.

'If you ask me, you can't wait to spend it all, so you can go back to your former lifestyle.'

'That's even quite possible, Inspector. At times I feel like I've gone soft. I no longer have to struggle to put food on the table . . . I'm still not used to it, and I'm not sure it's good for me.'

'I have a solution.'

'Let's hear it . . .'

'All you have to do is pretend you've got nothing, and carry on as before.'

'Not a bad idea. It won't be easy, but I can try,' said Botta, turning the burner off.

'Just don't get into any trouble. I would never forgive myself.'

'I've already told you, Inspector. I'm not going back to jail. Better the cemetery.'

'Jeremiah sends his regards.'

'Let's drink this coffee,' said Botta, pouring it into the little cups, into which he'd put the sugar beforehand, knowing the inspector wanted only a half-spoonful.

'Let's taste Little Brunelleschi's masterpiece.'

'Stop making me laugh,' said Botta.

The inspector took a sip and raised his eyebrows. Ennio's coffee might not be exactly the Pazzi Chapel, but it was nevertheless a small masterpiece of its kind.

Heading back towards Florence, Bordelli promised himself that he wouldn't smoke until after dinner, just as he had done the day before. He'd done it once, he could do it again. He pushed himself farther: he would respect that rule forever . . . *in saecula saeculorum.*

He thought back to the presentiment he'd had while standing in front of the mirror in the bathroom . . . Might it turn out to be a special day, precisely because of the deal that he had made with himself? But he didn't want to connect this enormous sacrifice with Eleonora's return. There was no point in deceiving himself any longer. He preferred to think that not smoking would merely help him take longer walks. He so much wanted to be in the woods and couldn't wait until Sunday for his outing to the Panca. He would get up early and prepare his rucksack so that he could stay out as long as possible.

There weren't many cars out on the Imprunetana. His was one of the few descending towards the city. Every so often he came up behind a tractor or a three-wheeled Ape truck that put-putted along at twenty kilometres an hour, and he'd wait for the right moment to pass it.

It took him a good thirty minutes to cross the city to Careggi. He climbed the stairs that led to the forensic science lab and went inside. At the end of a long corridor he came to a doorway, and pushed it open. Diotivede was holding a piece of dark flesh in his hand and talking to a young man in a white lab coat.

'Can I get half a pound of kidneys?' Bordelli asked as he walked in. Diotivede sighed, shook his head, and put the flesh down on the marble table.

'I only have a minute, or I'll be here until midnight,' he said, removing his gloves. There were several stretchers lined up along the wall, but only two had bodies on them.

'For so few people?' asked the inspector, indicating the four feet sticking out from under the sheets.

'I have five others in the fridge.'

'Oh, how I envy you . . .'

'Let me introduce you to Anselmo,' Diotivede said, indicating the young man.

'Nice to meet you, I'm Inspector Bordelli.'

'Dr Magliabechi . . .' muttered the young man, shaking his hand. He was no more than thirty years old, small and thin, with a mousy face. Mumbling a few words, he stepped away, looked into a microscope, and entered into the marvellous world of bacteria.

'When I retire next year, he'll take my place,' Diotivede said.

'Retire?'

'Your memory is evidently failing. I told you two years ago I was retiring.'

'Isn't it a bit early, at seventy-five?'

'I have to travel round the world with my wife,' the doctor said, with a cheeky smile.

'I can take her myself if you like . . .'

'Marianna is a lady, she wouldn't know what to do with someone like you.'

'A few centuries ago I would have challenged you to a duel,' Bordelli said. The young doctor turned to observe them with a strange look on his face, but as soon as he made eye contact with Diotivede, he turned back to his microscope and started fiddling with the knobs.

'Let's get down to business,' the pathologist said.

'I'm all ears.'

'I warn you, there's nothing interesting. Death occurred between midnight and three in the morning. It was almost instantaneous and was caused by a perforation of the heart. There are no unusual bruises or wounds. There is a modest amount of alcohol in the bloodstream. End of story. This time, I'm not much help. You'll have to do all the work yourself.'

'I'll manage. I'm used to it.'

'You'll have a written report by the end of the day tomorrow.'

'And Migliorini's body?'

'It's been made available to the family. I've already told the people in charge . . . But now I have to run.'

'One last thing.'

'Only if it's brief,' Diotivede said, starting to put his gloves back on.

'Are you free a week from Friday?'

'For what?'

'Dinner with friends.'

'No women, I presume.'

'As always . . .'

'No objections here.'

'I'll talk to the others. If I don't call you back in two days, it means it's on.'

'Fine. I'm going back to work now.'

'Kiss Marianna for me.'

'When hell freezes over,' Diotivede replied. Bordelli nodded in farewell to Diotivede's successor and left, realising that he would have to deal with young Magliabechi for at least two years before he, too, could retire. People in law enforcement ought to be able to turn in their badges by the age of sixty. But he wasn't as worried about retirement as he used to be. During the months after he'd temporarily quit his job he'd lived more or less like a retiree, and although he'd occasionally missed the work, he'd had a good time of it.

As he got into the Beetle, he thought back to that period. The days had passed slowly and calmly. He'd read a lot, eaten well, and slept without interruption. He'd made fires, taken walks, and organised dinners for friends. He'd spent pleasant evenings on Rosa's sofa, her cats scurrying around her flat. Then destiny came knocking – and he fell for it. He came out of it feeling both defeated and victorious, a little like Italy after the war. One thing was certain: the burden of what he had done was rooted in a corner of his mind and he would take it with him to his grave . . .

A car behind him honked in anger; he had run a red light. A Fiat 600 pulled up beside him, engine revving, the driver gesticulating angrily, and then cut in front of him. Bordelli made a gesture of apology and let himself be carried along by the traffic, thinking back to how pleasant it had been to listen to music in Dante's laboratory. At home he hardly ever listened to music, and yet he owned a good turntable and had numerous records on his bookshelves. Mostly classical music, but some Celentano and Pavone too . . . How long had it been since he had sat in his armchair and listened to a symphony? It was all because of work and the television . . .

Suddenly he remembered what Dante had said to him about antibodies and viruses and realised what he'd meant. Dante had understood that Bordelli had killed the three men who had murdered that child, and with that metaphor had absolved him. Not explicitly, or gruffly, but elegantly. It was kind of him, but there was still his own conscience to deal with . . .

How had Dante understood? Had it been something Bordelli said? Dante might look like a dreamer with his head in the clouds, but apparently he didn't miss a thing. Maybe even Piras and Botta had sensed something, but it would remain in the realm of suspicion. It was a secret he would take with him to the grave . . .

Sitting down at his desk, he saw the report from Forensics in front of him and started reading it without much hope, translating the tedious technical jargon into plain speech. No fingerprints on the grip of the foil: either the killer had wiped it clean with a handkerchief or had worn gloves. On the window handle in the study, clear fingerprints of only one person, the same that were found everywhere else, along with those of the victim, on the studio doorknobs and on that of the main door of the villa. They must certainly belong to Amalia, who'd closed the window. No other details found. The killer was no fool.

Nothing, in short. All he had to go by was a corpse, a fencing foil and some stolen jewellery. He was nearly convinced that he wasn't looking at a robbery that ended in murder, but that was as far as he got. All he could do was keep meeting with Migliorini's family members and friends and be careful not to miss anything important.

He grabbed the list of telephone numbers, picked up the receiver and called Claretta's house. There was no answer, so he hung up. Then he rang Laura Borrani at home, and the housekeeper asked him to wait. After a minute or so Signora Borrani came to the phone and answered with a feeble voice.

'Good morning, Inspector.'

'Good morning . . . I'm sorry to disturb you . . .'

'Not at all. What can I do for you?'

'I was wondering whether anything had come back to you in the meantime – say, some detail of your brother's life, or some person . . .'

'No, I'm sorry. If anything like that happens I'll be sure to call you straight away.'

'Has your husband returned?'

'Yes, late last night.'

'Would it be possible to speak with him?'

'You'll find him at his office, even though it's closed for mourning. Let me give you the number . . .'

'You're very kind . . .' said Bordelli. He wrote the number at the bottom of Piras's list and said goodbye to the signora.

It was already ten o'clock, and he still hadn't made any progress. He immediately rang Borrani's office. Signor Borrani himself answered. The inspector introduced himself and, after dutifully expressing his condolences, asked him when they could meet.

'I was just on my way out to help Antonio's sons choose a coffin,' Borrani said lugubriously.

'Perhaps this afternoon?'

'I could be back here at the office by half three.'

'Perfect, thank you so much . . . And the address?

'Via Maggio, 6/bis. Then I'll see you later, Inspector.'

'Goodbye.'

Bordelli hung up and tried to picture Anselmo Borrani. Good looking, like his wife? Or short, bald and potbellied? His voice brought to mind an elegant man, but the inspector knew how easy it was to be surprised in these matters.

One more phone call, this one to Oberto. It was anyone's guess what police detectives did before telephones existed. After many rings, a sleepy voice answered. It was Oberto, who mumbled that he hadn't got to bed until dawn. Bordelli asked him as well when they could meet, and they arranged for seven o'clock at the usual bar in Piazza dei Ciompi, in the billiards room.

He tried Claretta's house again, but there was still no answer. Olinto Marinari would be coming home in the afternoon. All he could do was wait.

He looked at the clock, realising he had time to pay his parents a visit at the cemetery. Outside of rush hour, traffic was manageable. Carried along by his thoughts, he found himself at Soffiano and walked through the gate and into the *camposanto*, the 'holy field', as his mother used to call it. He liked the word 'cemetery', too, which evoked an image of a dormitory.

There was hardly anyone there at that hour. Strolling among the graves, he occasionally turned to look at the ovals with portraits inside, the extinguished candles, the dates of birth and death. To go by the inscriptions, the beyond was populated with saints. It would be comforting if, every so often, they said something different.

Here lies So-and-So, the biggest son of a bitch of the last two hundred years . . .

A prayer for the dirty soul of this blasphemer, who in life loved wine above all else . . .

An abysmal husband and even worse father, he steadfastly applied himself to squandering his family's estate . . .

He walked past a young woman weeping almost shyly at the foot of a grave, and with a pang in his heart he thought of how sweet it must be to be remembered by someone who loved you. Who knew whether any woman would come and weep in front of his picture after he died. He hadn't managed to get a good look at the girl's face, but he had the impression she was rather pretty. He did, however, succeed in getting a glimpse of the photo on the tombstone . . . Her late lamented was a bespectacled bloke, and his dates showed that he'd checked out at age thirty-seven. Her husband? Brother?

He spotted his parents' grave from a distance. They'd been buried one atop the other, a few years apart. As he approached he saw that someone had brought them flowers that by now had wilted. Probably Zia Camilla, his father's sister, had come for All Souls' Day, perhaps in the company of her son, Rodrigo. He hadn't seen or heard from Rodrigo for some time now. He may not even have told him he'd gone to live in Impruneta . . .

Stopping in front of their grave, he sought out his mother's eyes in the photo and found her looking more severe than he remembered. His father, on the other hand, had the same gentle, faintly smiling eyes as ever. The haircut and moustache made one think of the Unification of Italy.

'You've been a naughty boy,' said his mother, disappointed.

'Yes, Mamma.'

'There are certain things you mustn't do. Understand?'

'Yes . . .'

'Don't you ever do it again. You must promise me.'

'Yes . . .'

'You must say: *I promise never to do it again* . . .'

'I promise . . .'

'Now go and bury that poor lizard and say a little prayer for it.'

'Yes . . .'

It was the first time he'd ever killed a living creature. He was five years old. Every time he thought back on it, he felt the same remorse as then. And so he dug a little hole in the garden and eased the lizard, with its bloodied little head, down into it, filled it with dirt and then put a large stone on top of it. He'd even said a little prayer. That evening he cried, troubled by the thought of the lizard . . .

'We don't eat with our mouths open.'

'C'mon, Ma' . . .'

'Go to bed, you have school tomorrow.'

'But it's only nine o'clock.'

'He who reads in bed or at the table is sure to become unstable.'

'I'll turn off the light in a second.'

'Thank God I don't tell your father . . .'

Simple words, but they contained an entire world. A vanished world. He remembered sadly the feeling of protection, the warmth he'd felt and continued to feel even during the bewilderment of adolescence.

'Time to get up, it's getting late.'

'C'mon . . . Just another minute . . .'

'Wash your ears well, with soap, because I'm going to come and check . . .'

He parked his German tank of a car in Piazza Frescobaldi, wheels on the pavement, and walked up Via Maggio, his usual morning route to the office. The roads were livelier than usual with Christmas fast approaching. People were in a hurry to do their gift shopping and mothers struggled with children who stood mesmerised in front of shop windows.

He stopped in front of number 6/bis, an elegant sixteenth-century building with a coat of arms carved in stone over its doorway. He was a bit early but rang the bell marked *Cav. Borrani* all the same. He heard the bolt click, pushed the door open, and walked through an ample, semi-dark atrium towards a wide staircase. He reached the second floor without effort, and found Borrani waiting for him. About fifty years old, of average height, Borrani had a bushy head of dark hair and an air of authority. He shook hands firmly, clearly the kind of man who was used to making deals.

'Again, my condolences.'

'Thank you . . .'

The inspector followed Migliorini's brother-in-law through the foyer and down an austere hallway paved with old terracotta tiles and lined with paintings. Borrani welcomed Bordelli into his office, a large and orderly room with one wall entirely filled with filing cabinets. On the wall opposite was a lone work of art – a stunning painting from the same era as the building, a Madonna and Child. The view from the window was the same that Bordelli saw from home.

'What can I do for you, Inspector?'

'I'll only steal a few minutes of your time.'

'Go right ahead.'

'I'm trying to work out who your brother-in-law was, who he

spent time with, what he enjoyed doing . . . I'm hoping you can give me some ideas and put me on the right track . . .'

'Unfortunately, I won't be able to help you much, Inspector. I admired Antonio, but we rarely saw each other. I used to see him at religious holidays and at dinners with mutual friends . . . but I honestly didn't know him very well.'

'Would you happen to know whether he was romantically involved with someone?'

'Here, too, you catch me unprepared. I can tell you that he greatly appreciated the fair sex, everyone knew that. But don't get me wrong: he was no womaniser. I remember hearing that he always used to fall in love, like an adolescent . . . what's more, Antonio was very reserved. He definitely wasn't the kind of man who would boast about his conquests just to impress others.'

'Did you ever see him with a woman?'

'Yes, once or twice. But that was several years ago . . . A very elegant lady who worked in fashion . . .'

'You never heard about any unpleasant episodes? Quarrels, disagreements of any kind, bitterness? Some old resentment . . . ?' Bordelli said, feeling as if he was barking up the wrong tree again. Borrani took a second to think about it and then shook his head.

'Nothing comes to mind, I'm sorry. In any case, as far as I know, Antonio really disliked quarrels. He always tried to solve things amicably. Even with his children he was always very understanding.'

'I confess to you that I'm grasping at straws.'

'I wish I could help you more.'

'Have you already set the date for the funeral?'

'The mass will be on Saturday at eleven o'clock at San Domenico church.'

'Thank you for your time,' the inspector said, rising to his feet. Borrani accompanied him to the door, where they shook hands again.

'Please find Antonio's killer, Inspector.'

'I will do my very best,' Bordelli said with some discouragement. 'Goodbye.'

'If anything comes to mind, please let me know.'

'Of course.'

'Goodbye.'

The inspector went down the stairs slowly, biting his lip. He left the building and headed for his car, hands in his pockets.

He hoped to learn more from Oberto. Since the lad worked at the villa, maybe he had crossed paths with one of Migliorini's lady friends, maybe even the one that he had most recently fallen in love with, if she even existed . . . For now, only Amalia believed in the existence of such a woman, and she had never actually seen her in person. And Bordelli wanted to believe Amalia . . .

If this lady truly existed, and if she was as much in love with Antonio as he was with her, if they had even discussed getting married, why hadn't she come forward? Was it a clandestine relationship? Was she married? Was this why they couldn't get married? And what if she was the murderer? Or maybe there was another woman . . . maybe a former lover who had been slighted or abandoned?

Not having any other leads, he'd become obsessed with Migliorini's lovers, ladies whom no one ever talked about. He had to start somewhere. He had to stop twiddling his thumbs and staring at a blank wall.

Everyone spoke so highly of the victim . . . But what if Migliorini was really a son of a bitch? Maybe he had done something horrible to someone and they had taken revenge on him. Maybe it was a woman . . . He dug around in his pockets for a cigarette, then remembered his promise. Ah, to know you could count on willpower . . .

He got into his car, but instead of crossing the bridge and heading back to the office he went down the Lungarno and parked in Piazza del Cestello, near the archway that led to Borgo San Frediano. Every so often he liked going back to his old neighbourhood and saying hello to some of his old friends. He might even mention that he was looking for a small flat . . .

Some of the craftsmen in the area had never reopened their workshops after the flood. Others had been resurrected with great effort and hard work. The same thing went for the trattorias and shops. The Christmas decorations in the display windows here were simple, almost homemade. There were none of the bright lights and garlands he had seen in the centre of town. It was like the difference between a small country church and the Vatican.

Costantino, the picture-framer, had been too old to roll up his sleeves and save his shop, and so had sold his eight-square-metre studio and continued working from the basement of his home, but only for his oldest clients and friends. Moreno, the smith, had a similar story. He had found work in a factory in Scandicci, and rented out his workshop to a lampshade-maker.

Bordelli strolled up Via del Leone, stopping to talk briefly with Cecco, the rag-and-bone man, who had managed to get his workshop going again thanks to elbow grease and hard cash . . . *If you hear of anyone selling a small flat, two rooms, third floor or higher* . . . They said goodbye, and Bordelli continued down the street. The Sicilian barber, Santo Novaro, had disappeared. They used to call him the Undertaker because he never laughed, and now no one had any idea where he'd gone . . .

Passing in front of his old building, Bordelli was tempted to ring the bell and ask whether he could see his former home, but decided against it. He simply glanced up at the windows. The shutters were open, there were a few potted plants on the sill. That was where Eleonora . . . No, he didn't want to think about that. Lots of other things had taken place in those rooms, too. Nice things . . .

It had only been a year since he'd sold his flat, right after the flood, but it now felt like long ago. He remembered looking out of the window and seeing a river of mud rushing down the street, carrying animal carcasses and debris of every kind . . . If he hadn't seen it with his own eyes . . .

He greeted a few other neighbours in shops and along the pavement, spreading the news that he was looking for a flat. Every so often someone would tell him the latest from the neighbourhood: Tronco had fought with Cioni over a game of *boccette* . . . Lando's daughter had married an outsider, someone from Lucca . . . Giuliana was pregnant, again . . . Pigia was back in the Murate prison . . . Maria, the butcher lady on Via Camaldoli, had fallen down the stairs and broken an arm . . .

In Piazza Tasso, the mud had reached a height of one metre. Generally speaking, the damage there had been less than in other parts of the neighbourhood. But not for those who lived below ground level, like Botta, who had one of the last basement flats on

Via del Campuccio. His house filled up with mud. Twenty metres on, there was no damage at all.

He went into Fosco's for a coffee and waved hello to a few people. Nothing had changed.

'Well, look who's here . . . I thought we'd lost you, Inspector,' Fosco said. They shook hands over the bar.

'Sometimes I think I *am* lost . . . and how are you, Fosco?'

'Still chugging along, Inspector. How about you?'

'Same as always.'

'What's the word in Impruneta?'

'The *olio novo* will be ready in a few days.'

'I get mine in Monteriggioni from a cousin. I can't wait to make *fettunta*.'[11]

'You're telling me . . . And Ennio? How's he doing?'

'He was here about an hour ago. You want me to give him a message from you?'

'Just say hello . . . and the Undertaker? What's going on with him?'

'I haven't seen him since the flood. Some say he went to Prato, to work in the mills.'

'To eat Mattonella biscotti is more like it.'

'I could never work in the mills, with all those noisy machines . . . When you walk around in Prato, that's all you ever hear.'

'It's the sound of money, Fosco . . .' As they were talking, Bordelli managed to mention that he was looking for a small place in the neighbourhood, but only from the third floor on up, where the Arno hadn't reached. He finished his coffee, and paid for one for Botta.

'What are you doing for Christmas, Fosco?'

'I'm going to light a candle for Saint Cash and Saint Revenue, Inspector, as always.'

'Better days will come . . .'

'If we don't see each other before, have a happy Christmas.'

'Happy Christmas to you, Fosco.'

When he walked out of the bar, it was already dusk. At the corner of Via della Chiesa he bumped into Ezilda, a kindly old prostitute who had hung up her knickers several years earlier. Even so, she was still made up like a young woman and kept looking around as if searching for business.

'You're still a fine hunk of man, Franco,' she said, rubbing a hand across his chest.

'The older I get the more I appreciate lies.'

'So tell me I'm pretty . . .'

'You're beautiful.'

'There was a time when even young men used to tell me that,' Ezilda mumbled with a sad smile. Memories of the good old days kept her afloat, especially those from the time of the African campaign, when men used to queue up for her and she wore clothes from the best boutiques in town. They walked down Via della Chiesa together, talking about everything they had lost in the flood. At the intersection with Via dei Serragli they hugged goodbye. Ezilda continued along Via della Chiesa, but Bordelli turned left. He wasn't ready to go back inside. He had nothing to do at the office except wait for his appointment with Oberto. It was more enjoyable to stay outside and admire the ladies and daydream . . .

He reached the corner and turned down Via Sant'Agostino. It was practically dark, and the cars all had their lights on. He saw an old man sitting alone at a table in a wine shop, an empty glass in front of him on the table. It reminded him of the famous painting by Cézanne, the one with the card players. The man had the same dignified, desolate look . . . Suddenly he stopped short. He knew that old man, he was certain of it. He recognised the gaze. It had happened to him before, that he recognised people merely by the expression in their eyes, even if they had physically changed. He got all the way to Piazza Santo Spirito and then suddenly turned round and rushed back. He had to see that man again. He stopped in front of the window. The old man had an unkempt beard, his hair was long and uncombed, and he wore an old coat that was much too large. Where had he seen him before? Who the devil was he? The old man realised he was being watched and looked down angrily. Bordelli had to get to the bottom of it. He went into the shop and walked up to the old man, under the indifferent stare of the bartender and a couple of onlookers.

'Pardon me . . .' he said in a low voice, but the old man kept his head down. Was he deaf? An unpleasant odour rose up from him; he smelled of neglect. Bordelli touched his shoulder, and the old man looked up. Yes, he was certain he knew him . . . but who was he?

'What do you want from me?' the old man whispered.

'We know each other . . .'

'You've got me confused with someone else . . . please leave me alone.'

'But of course, you're . . .'

'Please!' the old man hissed, grabbing Bordelli's wrist and pulling him down to sit. Bordelli wondered how on earth Colonel Arcieri could have sunk to that level.

'How . . . What happened to you?'

'Let's get out of here,' Arcieri whispered. He left a coin on the table and got to his feet with some difficulty. They went out and walked down Via dei Serragli. Arcieri limped slightly and looked worn out.

'Are you all right?' Bordelli asked.

'I feel fine. Just don't tell anyone that you've seen me.'

'Can you tell me what's happened to you?'

'I think we ought to say goodbye. Farewell, Inspector.' He wavered unsteadily on his feet, and Bordelli reached out and took his arm to steady him, smelling the misery in his dirty clothes. They looked each other squarely in the eye.

'I can't leave you alone.'

'You mustn't worry about me.'

'Come to my place.'

'No . . .'

'I don't live in San Frediano anymore. I live in the country. Come and rest for a bit.'

'I don't think it's a good idea,' grunted Arcieri.

'Why on earth not?'

'I can't . . .'

'Colonel, listen to me. At my house you can relax. You can take all the time you need to pull yourself together,' Bordelli said with sincere concern.

'You have no idea what's going on, Inspector.'

'Please, just come with me. I've got my car parked nearby.' It pained him to see a man like Arcieri in that condition, and he felt obliged to help him. They had met in the late '50s and had often done favours for each other.

'I don't want to get you into trouble,' the colonel said with some uncertainty.

'If you have any bags, we'll go and get them,' Bordelli insisted.

'Everything I have is in my pockets.'

'Wait for me here. I'll go and get the car . . . but promise me you won't disappear,' Bordelli said, staring at him. Arcieri looked around like a trapped animal, and then nodded.

'You win . . .' he said resignedly.

'Good.'

'Will your wife be all right with it?'

'I live on my own.'

'I hope you won't regret it,' said Arcieri, darkly.

'Give me five minutes.' He patted Arcieri on the shoulder and hurried off, all the while wondering what could have happened to the colonel. The last time he had seen him was shortly after the flood, when the city was still covered with dirt and debris. One night Arcieri had knocked on the door of his house to ask him for a favour. Bordelli had obliged and, as destiny would have it, that favour proved to be vital for the investigation into that little boy's murder . . .

In all truth, they had met only a few times, and were far from being close friends. And yet ever since they had been introduced they had recognised something in each other . . . Despite being completely different, they knew they had something in common.

Bordelli got in the VW and a few minutes later pulled up in front of Arcieri on Via dei Serragli, triggering a chorus of honking horns from the cars behind him. He gestured out of the window in apology. The colonel climbed into the car with some difficulty and fell back against the seat in evident pain. Bordelli drove off, followed by a long line of cars and motorbikes. He had rolled up the window but was forced to open the vent because of the stench. Arcieri did the same. Neither of the two men uttered a word, but at that moment it seemed like the most natural thing in the world.

'And here's my manor . . .' said Bordelli, pulling up on the threshing floor. It was the first thing he'd said since they set out. He left the headlights on, knowing that the little lamp over the door gave barely enough light to prevent one from stumbling. He helped the colonel out of the car, opened the front door and led him into the kitchen. He offered him his armchair by the fire and then went back out to turn off the headlights. When he came in again, Arcieri was staring at the skull. Fondly, truth be told.

'He's called Jeremiah,' said Bordelli, to break the ice. The colonel smiled.

'He's very nice. Reminds me of an old friend from the war.'

It wasn't clear whether he was speaking seriously or making a bitter comment.

'Would you like something to eat?'

'Not right now, thank you.'

'Shall I run you a hot bath?' asked the inspector, figuring that the colonel would probably like nothing more. Arcieri looked up with two grave eyes full of pride.

'I'm sorry to put you out . . .'

'Please, Colonel. Let's establish some rules immediately. You must realise that you're at home here and can stay as long as you like. The only task I'm assigning you is to choose which room you want to sleep in, after which you can feel free to move about as you see fit.'

'You're too kind.'

'I'll go and run your bath. I'll have to return to Florence shortly,' said the inspector, seeing that it was already a quarter past six.

He went upstairs and opened the hot water tap over the tub. From a bundle beside the chest of drawers in his room he took two clean towels, which he'd retrieved a few days earlier from the laundry. From his wardrobe he extracted some clean clothes and laid everything out in the bathroom. Arcieri was a little shorter than him, and rather slender. He might have to roll up the cuffs on the trousers.

Bordelli went back down to the kitchen and then led Arcieri upstairs. The tub was already half full, and the steam-filled air made them look like two souls in purgatory.

'I'll light a fire for you, but then I have to go out. If you're hungry, there's stuff in the fridge, but I have to do some shopping. Here are some clean clothes I've put out for you; you can use mine for now, then maybe I'll buy you something. But you can go ahead and throw away what you've got on; if you want, you can burn them in the stove.'

'Thank you . . . thank you so much . . .' Arcieri mumbled, as though embarrassed. It was truly sad to see him reduced to such a state.

'I should be back for dinner, but I can't say when that will be.'

'No need to hurry. I'll be here waiting for you,' the colonel said with a smile.

'All I ask is one favour of you.'

'Ask me whatever you like . . .'

'There's a pot simmering on the stove, and you must remember to turn it off in a couple of hours . . . They're beans . . .'

'Yes, sir,' said Arcieri, sketching a military salute.

After a final wave goodbye, Bordelli went back downstairs to the kitchen, and in no time managed to light a nice hot fire. Watching the flames, he couldn't help but wish he could stay home and read by the fire. He drained the cannellini beans and refilled the pot with fresh water, then added a garlic clove, a clump of sage from the garden, and a teaspoon of coarse salt. He put the pot on the stove, over a low flame, and laid a lid on top, not covering it completely. The colonel must already have been in the tub, in the company of his secrets . . . Who knew what he had seen, in all those years with the Special Services . . .

Bordelli got into his Beetle and headed back down to Florence, a bit bewildered by his meeting with Arcieri. He opened a window to let out the last traces of the colonel's bad smell, increasingly curious to know what had happened to the man.

He didn't want to be late for his appointment with Oberto, and after the turn for San Gersolè he took the short cut to Le Cascine del Riccio. Along the very narrow incline to Monteripaldi, he was lucky enough not to encounter any other cars, and a few minutes later he arrived at Viale Galileo. Sailing down into the city, he finally parked in Borgo Allegri. When he entered Vasco's bar, it was two minutes past seven, and he slipped directly into the billiards room. Oberto was there alone, working on some shots while waiting. His face looked tired, and paler than the day before . . . Apparently he was taking Migliorini's death very hard.

'Feel like playing?' the inspector suggested.

'All right.'

'When I was a kid I used to like to play eight-ball.'

'Whatever you like,' said Oberto, setting down his cue stick. From a box on a chair he fished out the missing balls, put them on the table, and racked them up. Bordelli hadn't seen a pool table for ages, and the minute he grabbed a cue, he felt as if he were back in the thirties . . . He heard again Mussolini's voice croaking over the radio, the songs of the Trio Lescano on the gramophone, smelled the lovely scent of his mother's cooking as it began to fill the house around seven o'clock every evening . . .

Oberto let the challenger 'break', taking half a step back from the table. Bordelli aimed with care. A crisp shot, with the balls scattering until they came to a halt. After surveying the table for a few moments, he chose the 'solids'. With his first two shots, he sank two balls, then failed.

'Your surname is not from around here . . .'

'My father was Sicilian.'

'And your mother?'

'Florentine.'

Oberto sank four balls in a row, then barely missed a fifth. It almost seemed as if he'd missed the last one on purpose, to prolong the match. Bordelli studied the table for his next shot. Meanwhile he tried to imagine Oberto running Migliorini through with a fencing foil, motive unknown. A bit of luck helped him sink another ball, with the cue ball nearly falling in as well. Then he flubbed one. Oberto didn't miss another shot, and to conclude sent the eight-ball rolling ever so slowly, on purpose, into the corner pocket.

'Dottor Migliorini taught me how to play,' he said, laying the cue down on the edge of the table.

'Mind if I ask you some questions?'

'Go ahead . . .'

'As far as you know, was Migliorini in a relationship?'

'I don't know anything about that sort of thing,' the lad said curtly. Bordelli was sure he was lying.

'I know how you feel. I don't like talking about other people's affairs either,' he said, rolling the cue ball slowly into a corner pocket.

'There's nothing to tell,' Oberto lied again. He wasn't very good at faking.

'Are you keeping a promise?'

'And what if I was?' the young man couldn't help but say.

'Knowing about Migliorini's private life could help me find the killer.'

'Well, at any rate, I know nothing.'

'Amalia told me Migliorini had fallen in love with a beautiful woman.'

'Well, if she says so . . .'

'Apparently Migliorini himself told her.'

'I don't know anything,' the lad repeated.

'I'll leave you some time to think about it, but I'll be back,' said Bordelli, looking him straight in the eye. And, waving goodbye, he went out. He had to find a way to make Oberto open up. The lad might know more than anyone else. He was an unusual young man, if not downright strange. He seemed very sensitive.

The shops were still open, but by the time the inspector had finished shopping, they were closing up. He loaded everything into the Beetle and drove off, hungry as a wolf. He couldn't wait to sit down at the table.

He'd bought a great deal of stuff: salted meats, cheese, fresh pasta, steaks, sausages, bread, fruit, vegetables, salad, white-meat tuna, and a few onions. As well as three bottles of Chianti and one of *vin santo*. All that was missing were candles, and maybe a pretty girl . . . say, Eleonora. Who knew if she liked country living?

Instead he would be dining with an old colonel of the Carabinieri who'd been absorbed into the Special Services and then appeared out of nowhere in miserable condition, limping and suspicious of everyone . . . The inspector felt happy just the same. Clearly he was very curious to find out what had happened to Colonel Arcieri, but wasn't going to ask him anything.

Walking into the house with the shopping, he heard music playing softly and instantly recognised Beethoven's First Symphony. Arcieri was seated in an armchair in the kitchen in front of the fire, reading a book. All cleaned up, he looked like another person, even if the clothes were too big for him. He hadn't shaved his beard entirely, but had given it a neater shape.

'That was fast,' the colonel said.

'You shouldn't have . . .'

The table was set with care, with knives resting on folded napkins and Bordelli's best glasses at each place.

'I took the liberty of putting on some music, and I stole a book.'

'You did well,' Bordelli said as he started to put away the shopping.

'Jeremiah appreciates good music too. We've become friends; we have quite a bit in common.'

'Jeremiah has discerning tastes,' Bordelli said in agreement, glancing over at the skull.

'I threw my clothes in the fire, as you suggested.'

'As soon as I can, I'll go and buy you some clothes. When you have a minute, make me a list of everything you need,' the inspector said. Arcieri nodded distractedly, his mind on other matters.

'Quite frankly, I prefer this to the Ninth Symphony,' he declared, tapping two fingers on the arm of his chair.

'And I would have to agree with you.'

'For years, I only listened to the Fifth and Ninth, just like everyone else. Then I discovered the first two, and their freshness won me over.'

'I don't think I could find a better word to describe it . . . Freshness . . .'

'I used to have a collection of seventy-eights of magnificent recordings, directed by Toscanini, but they were all lost in the flood . . . You don't happen to have any jazz, do you?'

'No, I'm sorry. I have to admit that I don't know a thing about jazz,' the inspector said, glad that his guest was relaxing. They sat silently together, listening to Beethoven, as the fire snapped and crackled in the fireplace. The colonel heaved a big sigh.

'The beans are done . . .' he said with a melancholy air. Realising that the inspector was perplexed by his tone, he explained that the exact same phrase had been used as code during war, transmitted on Radio London in 1944, when he was an officer at the English Command. But he could no longer remember what it meant.

'Better beans than war,' said Bordelli.

'The beans are done . . .' the colonel repeated slowly, travelling through his memories. He too had made his way up Italy doing battle against the Germans, like Bordelli.

'How about some *penne al pomodoro*?'

'Whatever you prefer.'

'It will only take a few minutes . . . if you want to keep reading, please don't mind me . . .'

'I'll just finish the chapter.'

'What book did you choose?'

'A wonderful novel I read many years ago,' Arcieri replied, holding it up so Bordelli could see *The Cossacks*. Bordelli had never even opened it, but he had had it for a long time. It must have been one of the many books from his mother's house on Viale Volta.

While Arcieri read, Bordelli put some water on to boil and opened a can of tomatoes. He needed half an onion. It was pleasant to cook with music in the background – why hadn't he ever thought of it? He usually kept the television on. Moving between the cutting board and the cooker he tried to keep Botta's lessons in mind: it was important to be serious about even the simplest dishes because in actual fact they were never simple.

He poured the pasta into the boiling water and, after stirring it a few times, went up to his room. It was almost nine o'clock. He rang Claretta's number, and finally someone picked up. It was the housekeeper, who told him to wait; a minute or so later, Claretta came on the line.

'Good evening, Inspector.' She sounded slightly out of breath.

'Forgive me for disturbing you at this hour, but I couldn't call earlier.'

'Not a problem at all . . . How can I help you?'

'As I mentioned yesterday, I need to speak to you. When might I come and see you?'

'Would tomorrow morning be all right? Not at home, however . . . Let's meet outside.'

'As you wish.'

They decided to meet at noon at the café in Piazza San Gallo. When they said goodbye there was an element of embarrassment . . . But why?

The inspector went downstairs, and as he entered the kitchen he saw that Arcieri had dozed off with the book in his lap. The colonel no longer had that destitute air that he did when he met him in the bar; he was starting to look more like the man he knew. He was a loyal man, maybe a bit too stern, even in his countenance. In fact, sometimes he looked downright unpleasant. And here he was, having rolled up the sleeves of the sweater and the hems of the trousers, and not even the oversized clothes could lessen the dignity of his person.

The inspector opened the wine and put it on the table. He tasted the pasta. It was almost done. He wondered how he should wake up the colonel, but there was no need. A log tumbled in the fire, and Arcieri raised his head.

'Oh . . . I'm so sorry . . .'

'Please, come and sit down, it's almost ready.'

'I'm letting myself be treated like a prince,' the colonel mumbled, getting up slowly from his chair.

'May I help you?'

'Please don't bother, I can manage.' The colonel struggled to stand up, using the armrests to raise himself, and after limping over to the dinner table he sort of fell into a chair. Bordelli dashed to the sitting room to turn the record over, as it had finished in the meantime. He drained the pasta in a colander, put some in each of their bowls and spooned the tomato sauce over it. Finally, he sat down too.

'Add a little olive oil to it,' he said, filling their glasses with wine.

For the first few minutes no one talked. They were too hungry. The penne were not bad at all, and Arcieri ate with gusto. He even cleaned out the extra sauce in his bowl with a piece of bread, meticulous as only a high-ranking carabiniere could be. Bordelli took away the bowls and quickly prepared a platter with tuna, beans and raw onions.

'A feast fit for a king,' Arcieri said, taking another piece of bread. It had clearly been a long time since he'd had a decent meal.

During the dinner the inspector recounted the story of Migliorini's murder, confessing to being at a loss. He kept filling their glasses and waited patiently for Arcieri to tell him what had happened to him. Why was he hiding? And from whom?

They ended their dinner by sharing an apple. The record had finished while they were eating. Bordelli helped the colonel settle back into the armchair in front of the fire, and as he opened a bottle of *vin santo* he asked what he would like to listen to.

'I saw you have *The Dream* by Mendelssohn, directed by Klemperer . . .'

Bordelli gladly got up to put that record on. He liked it very much and it had been ages since he had heard it. He went back to the kitchen to the sound of the first notes and turned off the overhead light, leaving only the corner lamp lit. He filled two glasses with *vin santo* and sat down beside the colonel. They gestured a toast and took a sip.

They sat in silence, watching the fire. It was an ideal situation for sharing confidences . . . The fire, the wine, sublime music, and Jeremiah, gleaming white in the dark . . . Bordelli hoped the colonel might open up, but time passed and nothing happened. For a moment he thought he might tell the colonel about Eleonora, about the first time he saw her, their nights together, the rape, how she had gone away . . . and his desire to see her again. He didn't know the colonel well, but he felt he could trust him.

Arcieri was frowning, moving every so often with some effort, as if in pain. Bordelli saw that his glass was empty and filled it again. The music ended, leaving an absence. They could hear the wind blowing through the trees.

'Would you mind if I smoked?'

'Please do, it's your home . . . Actually, do you have one to spare?'

They lit their cigarettes. For Bordelli it was the first of the day, and it tasted as good as ever. He went into the sitting room and turned the record over, exhaling through his nose. On his way back to his chair, he saw that the fire needed wood, so he gave it a nice big log, the kind that lasts a long time, in the hope that . . . He poured himself a little more *vin santo* and sat back down next to the colonel.

'You can trust me . . .' he said in a low voice. The colonel nodded, with almost a paternal smile.

'I've never doubted that.'

'Thank you.'

'I do have something to tell you, dear Bordelli. After thinking it over, I have come to a decision. Your kindness towards an old man persecuted by his conscience deserves an explanation. So, if it's all right with you, I would like to tell you a story . . .'

'I ask for nothing more,' the inspector said with some emotion. His desire to know would finally be fulfilled. Arcieri threw his half-finished cigarette into the fire, tipped his head back and slowly blew out the smoke. He extended his glass to Bordelli for a refill, and after taking a little sip he began his story . . .

'In early August of this year, I had a bad accident. I still feel the effects of it, as you must surely have noticed. I'm sure you know the small, winding road that goes downhill from Sant'Anna di Stazzema . . . well, I drove straight off that road and off the side of the mountain. I was driving an Alfa Romeo Giulia, a car unfamiliar to me. It's a miracle I am alive. It wasn't because I'm a bad driver, believe me, nor was it because I had been drinking. I remember the precise moment when the brakes stopped working, and I understood right away that someone had tampered with them. During my long recovery in hospital, I asked that the car be examined, but no one did a thing. But maybe I should start at the beginning. . .'

Bruno Arcieri emerged from the accident along the road to Sant'Anna di Stazzema with his body completely shattered. He was taken to Tabaracci Hospital in Viareggio, beside the pine grove, where he remained unconscious for a fortnight. He was already well past his sixtieth birthday, and the doctors could only shake their heads.

When he came out of the coma he wasn't able to move even his hands. His arms and legs were in casts and hanging from steel cables. He felt as if he were imprisoned in a spider's web. A plaster bust encased his neck and half his thorax, and he couldn't turn his head. For the first time in his life he had to suffer bedpans, urinals, and having the nurses clean his body. He felt pain all over, even just breathing. They were constantly giving him shots, so many he'd lost count.

But the hardest thing to accept was not being able to express himself in words, with his voice. With the doctors he was supposed to answer their questions by moving his eyes. Yes or no. After a series of extensive tests, they determined he'd suffered no brain damage.

At times he pretended to be asleep and would overhear the nurses talking among themselves. They said he was a lucky man and that, given his age, it was a miracle he hadn't given up the ghost. He remembered his flight perfectly, when, suspended in air, he'd felt for a brief moment an absurd euphoria. Perhaps it was a defence mechanism of the psyche in such extreme circumstances, one that enabled the mind to remove itself from what was about to happen, and ultimately from death. But then he'd survived, and was now going through hell in that hospital. It would have been better to die. One thought alone kept him connected to life. During those days he'd had Elena beside him, the only woman he had ever loved. That sounded like a statement from a melodrama or a serial novel, but there were no other words for it . . . And it was perhaps the first time he'd ever been able to say them clearly to himself. The story of their love had not been a serene one. Almost thirty years earlier, right before the war, they'd been about to get married . . . Elena Contini Arcieri . . . It even had a nice sound to it . . . But owing to circumstances conspiring against their passion, Elena had gone away and married a big cheese in the Israeli secret services. Nowadays she lived abroad and had great responsibilities and perhaps wasn't even happy. How had she managed to get away from home? What kind of excuse had she given? She'd shown up one night while he was asleep, and had asked the head nurse if she could spend the night at his bedside. He hadn't seen her there until the next morning, and for a moment he'd thought he was dead. After that Elena came often to see him, at every hour of the day and night.

It was a ghastly time, and the only escape was sleep, often drug-induced. Sometimes he dreamt there was a crowd round his bed . . . Friends, former enemies, faces and shadows from thirty years in the Special Services, old exiles who had survived the Barcellona massacre, Comintern agents, British spies and German spies, victims of persecution, fleeting as the fog . . . And boys and girls from the thirties, friends from grammar school and the Academy . . . Old retired Carabinieri marshals who'd disappeared . . . Women at the window letting the breeze caress their hair in springtime . . . Ageing jazzmen, failed writers . . .

He often woke up in the middle of the night from the pain. But he was unable even to cry out. His voice was gone. The last time he'd heard the sound of his own voice had been when his Alfa plunged into the void. His last memory was the sea of Versilia, a bright blade gleaming on the horizon. He'd seen it flip, with the sky below and the sea above . . .

Elena would watch him suffer and pass a wet cloth over his lips. She would stroke his hair, which was still black and straight. He could smell the scent of her breath, the warmth of her face . . .

'You must forgive me . . . I got carried away by my memories . . .'

Overcome with emotion, he lowered his head. He seemed to be

finally opening up, but it cost him great effort. Bordelli said nothing, not wanting to risk interrupting the story. The record must have ended some time before, but neither had noticed. Silence was more fitting at such moments. The colonel turned towards the fire and at last resumed . . .

One morning, two weeks after he had finally regained consciousness, they freed the fingers of his right hand and brought him a notebook. He tried writing a few sentences with a pencil stub, but they came out completely illegible. It was a real torment. Not only because of the pain in his fingers, but mostly because he was unable to make himself understood. He had so many things to say . . . To Elena, to the doctors, to the nurses, to the few friends who came to see him. Sometimes his thoughts would get all confused, and he had to shut his eyes. Whenever he opened his mouth, Elena would lean over him, lightly touching his face. She would even kiss him sometimes, lightly touching her lips to his . . .

'There I go again . . . Take pity on an old man . . .' said Arcieri, smiling sadly. He seemed unaccustomed to talking about himself. It must have been an extraordinary occurrence for him. It was probably the first time he had searched through his memory to retrace that period, prompted by the decision to reveal to Bordelli why he was in his current condition, and as he followed the threads of the past he would inevitably get bogged down in overly personal matters. Taking a deep breath, he resumed his tale.

Little by little he learned to write comprehensible sentences in the notebook. He recounted a few things to the carabinieri and to a man from the Special Services, a young captain he'd never seen before. Though Arcieri had retired two years earlier, he'd maintained his contacts with the SID,[12] *since officers such as he never really quit. During the days of the great flood they'd put him temporarily back in service, and he'd conducted a very sensitive investigation right in Florence, a case that involved the highest levels of the state. Shortly thereafter, in Versilia, he'd let himself get involved in a rather sordid affair, this time as a private citizen. But his colleagues knew what sort of rot he was digging around in, and they'd kept communication channels open. They were very trustworthy people. Arcieri had never hesitated to ask them for help, even on an unofficial level . . . But this young captain was someone he really didn't know, and out of professional instinct he hadn't opened up much with him. He didn't say anything that the people in Rome didn't already know. The little that remained he kept to himself, at least for the time being.*

The days and nights went by, yet in spite of his great efforts he was still unable to speak. He would fill up sheets of paper which Elena collected every morning, practically weeping.

Two months after the accident they freed him from his plaster armour, cutting it with a small, circular saw. A great stench rose up from his body, but to him it felt as if he were emerging from a coffin. A male nurse, a colossus with a wrestler's physique, delicately washed him with a sponge and massaged his legs and arms.

Arcieri continued writing with his pencil, just a few lines at a time, as his wrist would immediately start to ache and his fingers would go numb. Sometimes Elena had a lot of trouble making out the meaning of his scribbles, and she would smile at him.

He received a visit from a woman psychologist, then another from a speech therapist. They concluded that his aphasia was a result of shock. They were convinced that sooner or later he would talk again, but couldn't predict when. Weeks, perhaps months. Elena didn't want to resign herself. She sent for a specialist from Rome, a man at least seventy years old who looked like a scientist and who addressed Arcieri as if he were dealing with a small child, or even a madman. The colonel trembled with irritation, and in the end he wrote a phrase in his notebook, in block capitals, the meaning of which was unmistakable: GO TO HELL. The professor left in a huff, even though he certainly would not have neglected to get paid. Arcieri was happy to be rid of the windbag, but Elena was resentful and didn't speak to him for an entire day.

Then the day came when he was allowed to get out of bed, but only to sit in a wheelchair. Elena pushed him down the corridors and out to the terrace, and Arcieri was able to see a bit of sea, beyond the pine grove of Viareggio.

There was a second bed in his hospital room that had remained empty all this time. One morning they brought in a young man, who was sleeping under the effect of sedatives. He had bruises on his face. He'd been severely beaten in Viareggio, outside a dance club by the sea. His friends had found him bleeding on the beach and took him to the hospital. The incident seemed to have something to do with politics. Maybe the lad was a communist and had been reduced to that state by neo-fascists, or else he was a fascist and had been roughed up by communists. Someone had even died in the scuffle. Somebody had fired a pistol, though there was still no precise information at this time. Later a little more was revealed on the latest edition of the television news, where they mentioned a student demonstration and clashes with the police.

The young man slept his drugged sleep and didn't even open his eyes for the first few days. His long straight hair fell in locks over his brow. When they cut off the sedatives he woke up but spent the whole day staring at the ceiling. Every so often Arcieri would make gestures at him to get his attention. The lad would look at him for a few seconds without expression, then turn his head away.

Arcieri could not help but feel sorry for him and, writing with his pencil stub, he kept asking for information about him. It was perhaps a way not to think about other things. Whenever Elena saw the colonel get upset, she would try in vain to calm him down.

With great effort, he was able to learn a few things. The lad's name was Andrea Viani, and he was from Florence. Haematomas all over his body, and a few fractures. But he was strong and healthy and would soon recover.

'You're probably wondering why I'm talking so much about this lad . . . I'll just say in advance that he's the crux of this story, and also the heaviest weight I have on my conscience . . .' said Arcieri, clenching a fist. His eyes turned into charred chestnuts.

One morning, as he was getting his thousandth shot, Arcieri uttered his first words: 'That's enough.' The nurse smiled happily and Elena was unable to hold back her tears. He was quite emotional himself, but was unable to say anything else for the rest of the day. It was like a first crack in a dam, and he succeeded in making great progress in a very short while. A week later he could express himself almost normally.

'Why doesn't the young man speak?' he asked the doctor, who was studying his patient's progress with clear satisfaction.

'His case is the opposite of yours, Colonel,' the doctor whispered, so as not to be heard.

'What do you mean?'

'You can't speak, or at least you couldn't . . . The lad, on the other hand, apparently does not want to speak. He won't even try . . .'

'Perhaps it's an injury . . .'

'We've run every kind of test, but there's no injury to the brain.' The doctor turned a small silver wheel and then emitted a long whistle. 'One-thirty over seventy . . . Like a twenty-year-old.'

'Has anyone come to see him?'

'So far, no.'

'Not even his parents?'

'We looked them up, and it turns out they're both deceased . . .' said the doctor, still in a soft voice. Arcieri turned to look at the lad. He was very thin, his face gaunt and pale.

'You don't know anything else about him?'

'A friend of mine, a marshal of the Carabinieri, told me a few things . . . He asked the city for information . . . The lad is twenty-two years old, is in his fifth year of engineering school, and supports himself and his studies with a small inheritance from his parents . . . Your wife isn't here today?' asked the doctor, putting the blood-pressure cuff back in his bag.

'She's not my wife.'

'I'm sorry . . .'

'She had to go abroad,' said Arcieri, unable to hide his sadness. The doctor pretended not to notice.

'You've been taking giant steps towards recovery,' he said. 'If

you keep it up, in a fortnight or so I'll be forced to show you the door . . .'

He got up, smiling, and, waving goodbye, left the room.

'The giant nurse was always forcing me to do physical exercises, to bring back some muscle tone, and after a few days of that I was able to stand unaided. I remember it well; it was truly exciting. It's not easy, at my age, to recover from an accident like that. My legs still hurt, but I'd shown myself I could do it.'

The young man recovered much faster than the colonel and was now routinely wandering about the ward. The doctors said they had to keep him there because they'd found some early-stage phlebitis, but the lad didn't look like he felt too bad. Every so often they would meet up in the telly room and watch the news report . . . Students were still occupying some of the universities in the north of the country, and students all over the world were never missing a single opportunity to demonstrate en masse in the streets . . . It was happening continuously during those months, whether over events occurring on the other side of the globe, such as the US bombing of Vietnam, or to protest the killing of Che Guevara . . . Arcieri would watch those clips with a sort of wonderment, feeling as if he was witnessing an epochal transformation. The young people seemed to have a great desire to change everything . . . Was the world about to get better? Arcieri didn't think so, and at the same time he felt old, precisely because he didn't think so.

The young man would watch the news report without saying a word, his gaze attentive. He had large blue eyes and black eyebrows. Every so often Arcieri would venture a comment, or even ask a question, but got no reply. To him the lad seemed afraid, and he wished he could help him. It was strange to see a person so healthy shuffling about in the hospital corridors.

One morning he approached the young man's bed, but his room-mate just kept on leafing through a magazine, not deigning so much as to glance at him. Those pages, too, told of long-haired students, clashes with law enforcement, and faraway wars . . .

'Hello, Andrea . . . They tell me you're perfectly capable of

speaking . . .' he said, studying the lad's reaction. He thought he'd seen his eyelashes flutter, but wasn't sure. For some mysterious reason he'd grown fond of the young man and wanted to protect him. He had to find something to shake him up, to convince him to break down the wall.

'Are you familiar with James Bond movies? I'm a secret agent myself, you know.'

He felt like an old pensioner in the public park, who after reading the newspaper cover to cover tries to start up a discussion with passers-by. Indifferent, the lad said nothing. In the hall outside could be heard the doctors and nurses coming and going.

'Do you know what the SID is?'

No reaction. What else could he come up with?

'I know why you obstinately refuse to speak . . .' he whispered. Andrea finally turned and looked at him, an expression of fear on his face. But he said nothing.

'Actually, it's not true, I don't know . . . But I want to help you . . .' said Arcieri. The young man barely shook his head and turned his eyes back to his magazine.

'I'm told you lost your parents . . .'

Andrea turned and looked at him again, and only moving his lips, he mimed two words: I'm afraid.

'Of whom? Of the people who beat you up? Who were they? Neo-fascists? Communists?' Arcieri pressed him, whispering. The lad sighed deeply and looked out of the window.

'Or maybe it's nothing to do with politics . . . Gambling debts, perhaps? A woman you should never have touched? Whatever it is, I would like to lend you a hand,' Arcieri said in all sincerity. Perhaps he saw in the lad the son he'd never had, as sometimes happened to certain men on the threshold of old age. The youngster's eyes had become hard as stones, but not a word came out of his mouth.

Arcieri wasn't ready to give up. It had become a kind of challenge, and he missed no opportunity to win Andrea's trust. At last one morning, as he was helping him tune in a short-wave radio . . .

'Well, you certainly can pick up a lot of channels on your radio,' said the colonel.

'That's nothing,' the lad let slip.

So he could talk after all. No mute, he. Arcieri felt as if he'd opened the breach at Porta Pia.[13] *Andrea looked around as though confused, then shook his head and, glancing over at the door as if making sure nobody was about to come in, he added in a whisper:*

'Nobody can help me . . .'

'You have to trust me,' Arcieri whispered.

'Trust a cop?'

'If you really think nobody can help you, what have you got to lose?'

'I don't know . . . I don't know anything anymore . . .' said Andrea, seeming desperate.

'Look, nobody can hear us in this room. Tell me what happened to you . . .'

In the silence one barely heard the hissing of the S's. Andrea kept on shaking his head 'no', but he seemed undecided. What the hell had happened to the kid? Arcieri could smell his fear, and understood it. He might have done the same in his place. And what if there were indeed microphones in the room? He turned on the small transistor radio the lad had on his nightstand, found a station where someone was talking, and turned up the volume. He leaned even closer to Andrea.

'Even if there were a microphone, we've now neutralised it with this,' he whispered very slowly.

'I have nothing to say . . . I know nothing . . . I saw nothing . . .' Andrea said, his voice a mere breath. Arcieri squeezed his arm.

'What can I do to convince you that you can trust me?' he said, fidgeting.

'Maybe you're one of them.'

'Who's them?'

'I don't know.'

'Look me in the eye . . . I swear to you that—'

'They want me dead,' Andrea interrupted him, as if taking a shot in the dark. He must have had a very great desire to confide.

'Who are they?'

'They're only waiting for me to get out of here . . .'
'Who are they?'
'I don't know, bloody hell,' said Andrea, exasperated.
'Go and talk to the Carabinieri, tell them what you know.'
'That might even be worse.'
'What do you mean?'
'I know nothing . . . I don't want to know anything . . .'

'That same afternoon, while making the rounds, the doctor informed the lad that he would be released the following morning, and Andrea pretended he hadn't heard. I didn't have much time left, and I didn't want to throw in the towel. To make a long story short, after a long battle I succeeded in getting him to tell me a few things . . .. There was some nebulous matter at the heart of it . . . He seemed to have got mixed up in a rather messy affair, and had good reason to be scared . . . I deluded myself into thinking I could help him. I was counting on my connections . . . But at the moment I can't tell you what it was all about . . . First I have to settle the matter, if it's the last thing I do in life . . .' said Arcieri, with a solemnity that seemed to herald something tragic. In his present condition, he seemed like a pathetic Don Quixote . . .

The following morning he exchanged a few more words with Andrea before the lad's departure. The young man seemed slightly relieved. But he said he would not be returning to his home in Florence. He hoped to hide out with some friends in Versilia, at least for a little while. Arcieri wrote his home phone number on a scrap of paper. Then he added another, with a Roman exchange and a name beside it.

'Call this number . . . Tell them Bruno Arcieri gave it to you . . . Talk to this person, and in the meanwhile I'll do whatever I can to—'

'Farewell, Colonel,' Andrea interrupted him, as a nurse entered the room.

'Don't hesitate to ring me,' Arcieri whispered

'Are you still here?' the woman said, smiling, as she started to strip the lad's bed.

'I was just leaving . . .'

A last handshake, and Andrea walked away, down the corridor. Arcieri went to the doorway, and as he watched him the thought flashed through his mind that he would never see him again.

He didn't have to wait long to find out that he'd been right. It was the nurse who told him, a few mornings later, as she was preparing the syringe.

'Poor boy . . . Have you heard?' she asked, gesturing at the empty bed.

'No . . . Has something happened?' asked Arcieri, sitting up in bed.

'He killed himself . . . Threw himself out the window of his flat, four storeys up . . . There's a short notice in the paper . . . What's wrong? Are you all right?'

'It's nothing . . .' He could hardly breathe, but he managed to smile.

'Please turn,' the woman ordered, administering yet another shot.

As soon as the nurse left, he buried his face in his hands. He wished he could cry, but nothing came. He felt responsible. He'd thought he could . . . Had Andrea called that number in Rome? What if that had been a mistake? Now he regretted telling him to call, compelled by his desire to make himself useful, to help a young man in danger . . . Even though he knew that sometimes, within the SID . . . He had to find out what had happened. He didn't believe the suicide story for a second. Almost out of pure instinct, he tried phoning his colleagues in Rome, to ask whether they knew anything, but they all seemed taken by surprise. So who killed Andrea?

Arcieri paused, still staring at the fire. Bright flames, and not only the reflection of those in the hearth, seemed to burn in his dark eyes. He looked very angry. The inspector told him he clearly remembered the story of the young man who fell from the window, but he hadn't handled the case.

'If I'm not mistaken, I believe the person sent to gather evidence was Detective Silvis, but nothing came out to make anyone think it was murder.'

'They were professionals . . .' Arcieri muttered, sighing heavily before resuming his tale.

The first thing to do was to get out of the hospital. He couldn't stand staying there twiddling his thumbs any longer. He sent for the doctor, who shook his head.

'In all honesty, you're still in no shape to be leaving the hospital.'

'That doesn't matter. I have to go.'

'You need specialised care, Colonel. Listen to me.'

'I appreciate your concern.'

'Think it over a little longer . . .'

'I've already decided. Do I have to sign some papers?'

'As you wish. We certainly can't keep you here against your will.'

'Let's make this quick.'

Half an hour later he was in a taxi. He looked around. It was already autumn, and he'd hardly noticed. He had himself driven to Viareggio station and took the first train to Rome. He wanted to talk face to face with the most trustworthy of his colleagues in the service, almost a friend, to work out whether they actually did know nothing about this affair. It took forever to get to the capital. He avoided going directly to SID headquarters and managed meet his 'quasi-friend' in a café opposite the Pantheon. He got nothing out of him, aside from a few overly vague hints.

'Don't go getting yourself into trouble, Bruno . . .'

'What's that supposed to mean?'

'Nothing . . . But think about it . . . You're retired now . . .'

'The conscience never retires,' Arcieri blurted out. He could never stand the intrigues and half-mysteries circulating in those offices, which he had frequented for so long. There was never any real cooperation between the various sections; that was the most unpleasant thing of all. In short, he went away in a bad mood, more convinced than ever that he had to get to the bottom of the affair.

'The next train to Florence?'

'You're lucky . . . It leaves in twelve minutes, track eight . . .'

He got on the train. He was going to Florence with no precise intentions, perhaps only because Andrea had been murdered in that city. He could stay there as long as he wanted. He had his own place Florence, in Via Ricasoli. He hadn't been back there for many months.

During the journey he had the feeling he was being spied upon, and he kept changing compartment. But maybe it was just his imagination. The slow train stopped at every station, like a coach, and it took more than four hours to reach his destination.

He got off at Santa Maria Novella and walked towards the station's lobby amidst the crowd of passengers. He'd always liked Michelucci's station, which was so modern it could have been built in the '50s. It wasn't even very cold in Florence . . . Then a tall man looking straight ahead of him a bit too indifferently pulled up beside him. Arcieri would not have been surprised to learn that he was with the Special Services. He kept an eye on him, and he was right to do so. Suddenly the man took his hand out of his pocket and tried to stab him in the side with a syringe. Arcieri dodged him instinctively, stepping aside just in time, and with an agility he didn't know he possessed plunged straight into the crowd, not giving a damn about his limp. He kept turning round, and every so often, amidst the bobbing heads, he caught a glimpse of the assassin, who was still following him with the absent gaze of a professional. How else might he try to kill him? In the lobby he saw two railway police officers walking towards him, and as soon as he caught up to them, the assassin slipped away in a hurry. Giving the excuse that he didn't feel well, Arcieri had the officers accompany him to the taxi stand.

'For now,' he said to the cab driver, 'just drive round the square, then I'll tell you where I want to go.'

The driver set off, shaking his head. The colonel turned round to look at the cars, to see whether anyone was following them. He realised he was drenched in sweat and still out of breath. The cab went all the way up to Piazzale Michelangelo, then continued along the tree-lined avenue.

For a few seconds he was able to see the beautiful façade of San Miniato, a masterpiece of geometry and devotion. Florence was the same as ever, fascinating and full of dangers . . .

What could he do? It was clear that there was now someone else who wanted him dead, and it surely had something to do with Andrea. Obviously his car was sabotaged at Sant'Anna by henchmen of the man he was investigating . . . A nasty affair with origins in the war . . . But the assassin in Florence had been sent by different people.

'Don't ask me why. Just trust my instincts as a cop and a spy. But I'm almost convinced that some of my ex-colleagues are involved in this,' Arcieri said, and before continuing he poured himself more wine.

In short, he could no longer even trust his 'friends' in the SID. He felt the need to put his thoughts in order, without having always to look over his shoulder. Perhaps it was best to disappear for a while, until calmer skies prevailed. Maybe whoever wanted him dead imagined he would immediately flee from Florence, and therefore the best way to hide might be to remain in the city. Clearly he mustn't go anywhere near his homes in Florence and Rome, nor even try to cash a cheque. He still had a little money on him; he would have to make it last. But he must never ring his friends in the service, or even Elena. He would leave no trail. Scorched earth. One could become invisible just by living in an environment where no one would think to look for you.

'Please drop me off in Piazza Tasso, thank you,' he said, as the taxi rolled down Viale Macchiavelli. When he got out of the car it was past ten o'clock. The air was cold, but he felt hot. He walked as far as Via della Chiesa . . .

'For a second I thought of knocking at your door. I remembered you lived near there. But I'd decided to disappear completely, and that's what I did. I went and asked if I could stay at the Hospice for the Poor, and as luck would have it, a vagabond had died that very morning. So, thanks to that poor bastard, I had a bed. I never saw so many bedbugs in all my life. When I'd spent all the money I had in my pocket, I started washing dishes in a few trattorias, in exchange for a hot meal and a little cash. I was invisible among the invisible. Nobody can tell one vagrant from another . . . It wasn't easy, but I got by thinking of that young man's death . . . Until you recognised me, by God . . . Well, that's pretty much it. I'm just waiting to get myself back in working order, thanks to your kindness, then I'll be on my way. I have to find out who killed Andrea, even if it means sifting through a mountain of refuse with my bare hands . . . My conscience depends on it . . .' Arcieri concluded, his face darkening. He stared at the fire, following the whims of the flames licking what remained of a log.

'None of it is your fault,' said Bordelli, firmly believing it.

'Sometimes one can be at fault simply for making a mistake . . .' the colonel muttered, unwilling to forgive himself. Despite his weak condition, he looked as if he was carved out of wood, as always.

'Another smidgen of wine?'

'Better not . . . If you don't mind, I think I need to lie down in a bed.'

'What room have you chosen?'

'The one farthest from yours. So we can snore to our heart's content.'

'A very wise choice,' said Bordelli, who knew he snored like a tractor.

He helped the colonel to his feet and accompanied him upstairs to the bathroom door. Then he went back down to the kitchen to clear the table, suppressing the desire to light another cigarette. How many had he smoked? Perhaps four; maybe just three.

He put the dishes and glasses in the sink and threw the empty bottles away. Then poured himself just a drop of *vin santo*, which he downed in one gulp. He was happy to be able to lend a hand to a man like Arcieri. He went into the living room to turn off the record player, and when he went back upstairs the bathroom was already free. It was a strange feeling to know that another person was sleeping under the same roof as him. He wasn't used to it. Ever since he'd left his parents' home, a few years after the war, he'd always lived alone.

He filled the stove with wood, brushed his teeth, and went to bed, where he started reading, laughing and suffering along with Chekhov. So much bitterness and beauty in those pages.

Half an hour later his eyelids began to droop. He put away the book and started staring at the wall in front of him. He was sleepy but didn't want to turn out the light just yet. He wanted to savour a little longer the sweet somnolence in which he had loved to bask ever since he was a boy . . .

He slowly drifted off through time and found himself back at Monte Cassino . . . 15 February 1944, the day the abbey was bombed. He was watching through binoculars from a few kilometres away as those ancient walls fell to pieces under the powerful bombs of the Allies. Beside him he heard the voice of Nicolino, a young Abbruzzese released from jail to enlist in the San Marco Battalion.

'They may be our friends, but they're tearing everything down.'

'They're doing it for our sake, Nicolino, to make us understand we've been naughty boys . . . Every bomb is a spank . . .'

'Our bum's going to get pretty red, Commander.'

'Mussolini already did that . . . Now they'll make it bleed.'

When Bordelli came downstairs to the kitchen the following morning, he found the colonel fumbling with the coffee machine under Jeremiah's watchful gaze. The clock on the wall read 7.25.

'Did you sleep well?'

'I feel like a new man . . .' Arcieri said. He truly looked in good form.

'You weren't cold?'

'No, I was quite comfortable.'

'I'll have to leave you here on your own all day,' Bordelli said, taking two cups out of the hutch for coffee.

'Let's hope the big bad wolf doesn't show up.'

'Are you sure you won't be bored?'

'I'll be living the life of a pasha with sublime music, great books, a fire in the hearth . . .'

'Now you're making me want to stay home!'

'And anyway, I'm not really on my own. Jeremiah's always good for a little chat,' Arcieri said seriously.

'True, true. I always forget. His manner is so reserved . . .'

They sat at the table and drank their coffee, talking about this and that, without ever mentioning the tragedy they'd discussed the night before. At eight o'clock, the inspector put on his overcoat. The colonel stood to say goodbye, moving with considerably greater ease than the day before.

'I wish you a pleasant day.'

'If you'd like to take a walk, the key is in that drawer. And that key,' Bordelli said, pointing to a large old key hanging from a hook on the side of the hutch, 'is for the back door.'

'Thank you, but I think I'll stay inside.'

'I forgot to mention that next Friday I am hosting a dinner for a few friends . . . but if it's a problem for you . . .'

'Who?' Arcieri asked in alarm.

'A forensic pathologist, a cook who's also a crook, a psychoanalyst, a half-crazy but extremely intelligent scientist, and a Sardinian, the son of a comrade from the San Marco Battalion who works with me . . . No one will recognise you, and there will be no women . . .'

'I'm sorry. Do forgive me . . . Here I am, an intruder, and I'm asking you . . .'

'No, please don't worry about it,' interrupted Bordelli.

'I want you to live your life without worrying about mine.'

'For now, just rest. I'll see you later.'

'Have a good day,' Arcieri said again, shaking Bordelli's hand. The inspector got in his Beetle and putt-putted his way down to the office. Seductress Nicotine tried to tempt him along the way but he resisted her beguiling ways.

When he walked into his office, he noticed that the room smelled less stale than usual. He sat down in his chair and crossed his arms on the desk in front of him, staring at the yellowing paint on the wall in front of him. As he waited for the appointment with Claretta, he went over every possible lead in his mind. Now and then he got up and paced back and forth in front of the window. The radiators were piping hot; he soon had to remove his jacket and roll up his sleeves.

He chatted a bit with Piras, who was also stumped. The Sardinian had started by looking through the archives, which were managed by a man named Porcinai, who was so overweight that it was difficult for him to get up from his extra-large, reinforced chair. His search had proved fruitless; he hadn't found anything connected to the family or friends of Migliorini, not even an unpaid ticket. He hadn't expected to find the solution, but it was certainly better than twiddling his thumbs.

'Are you free next Friday, Piras? I'm organising a dinner at my house. When do you take the ferry?'

'Saturday night.'

'So you can come.'

'Yes.'

'It'll just be us men, the same group as always, except for an old friend I bumped into a few days ago . . . tomorrow evening I'll apologise to Sonia for our men's club.'

'No need.'

'Ah, long live modern women,' Bordelli said with a glance at his watch. It was 11.45.

He took his leave of Piras and set out on foot for his appointment. He wondered whether Claretta would be as pretty as he remembered. When he was a kid and went out riding his bike, if he saw a pretty girl he'd circle around and stand up on the pedals to get a second look, to see if she was as pretty as the first time around. Usually it was a letdown. Not that the girls weren't pretty – they were – but they were never quite as beautiful as their first divine apparition. They became more human. He could even approach them, if he wished. Once he even found the courage to do so. A girl named Letizia. She was 'more mature' than other girls, as they used to say back then. The kind of girl who always had more than one beau . . .

He walked into the café in Piazza San Gallo at 11.59 and immediately caught sight of Claretta at the farthest table, off in the corner. She was the only customer, and the bartender couldn't stop looking at her. Bordelli approached her; she was very attractive indeed. She wore a red jacket with an elegant geometric pattern, and a red fur hat, her black curls peeking out from underneath. Bordelli sensed that she had put a lot of care into getting ready for their meeting. She had beautiful legs and wore very fancy shoes.

'Good morning, signorina . . .' Bordelli bowed to kiss her hand, and enquired what she would have to drink.

'Nothing, thank you . . . Oh well, maybe a Martini Rosso.' She seemed a little jumpy.

'One coffee and a Martini Rosso, please,' he said to the bartender. 'May I sit down?'

'Please do,' she replied.

She was around thirty-five, not a perfect beauty, not a doll or model by any standards, but there was something fascinating about her. Her eyes were an intense blue, her most stunning feature. Her porcelain skin created a pleasing contrast with her raven hair. Yes, she truly was quite beautiful. The only flaw that Bordelli could find was that she used too much perfume. It was a lovely scent, but it covered up her own natural one.

'Are you feeling a little better?' the inspector asked.

'I'm trying to adapt, but I feel so empty without Antonio.'

'I understand . . . do you think you can talk?'

'I can try.'

'I simply want to ask you a few questions.' The usual things: the last time she saw him, the last time they spoke on the phone, what they said to each other, if he had changed recently, if he had ever confided anything particular to her. Claretta replied in clipped sentences and seemed pained.

The bartender arrived with their order. The young lady took a sip of her Martini, then another, and then a third. Only then did she put her glass down. The inspector knocked back his espresso in a single gulp and began to fiddle with the empty cup, all the while asking questions. The customary stuff, though perhaps differently phrased. He observed her carefully as he talked. She grew more attractive with every passing minute. He even liked her somewhat childish manner. He just couldn't understand why she used so much perfume. He was tempted to remind her of the saying '*Champagne a bocce, profumo a gocce*'.[14]

He took the ring that he had found next to the body out of his pocket and placed it on the table. Claretta was visibly startled. She picked it up and said she knew it well.

'It was one of the first gifts that Antonio gave my sister. They weren't even married yet.'

'Do you know where we found it?'

'Where?'

'On the carpet, next to your brother-in-law's body.'

'Oh my . . .'

'Apparently an entire jewellery box has gone missing.'

'No! So it must have been a thief . . .'

'That's one possibility.'

'Isn't it obvious?'

'Often the most obvious things are the farthest from the truth.'

'Ah, I don't doubt it,' Claretta said, fidgeting in her chair.

'You can keep the ring if you like. I don't need it anymore. Just be sure to tell Signora Laura that I've given it to you.'

'Oh, Antonio . . .' Claretta said melancholically, as she slipped the ring on her finger.

'Is it true that your brother-in-law was in love with a beautiful woman? And that he was considering marriage?' Bordelli asked. She shrugged and smiled ever so slightly.

'Where did you hear that? I highly doubt it . . . Antonio would have told me, we were close. And after my sister died, we grew very close.'

'But might he have been in a liaison at the time of his death?'

'He did have a lot of women, none of whom were very important . . . sometimes he brought them home. I'm not shocked, I know that men need certain things . . .'

'Did he tell you about them?'

'Yes . . .'

'Did he introduce you to them?'

'Why would he do that? I never wanted to meet them. If I know certain things, it's because we talked about them, as I said.'

'Have you thought about who might have hated him enough to kill him?' Bordelli asked.

'No . . . or rather, yes, I have thought about it . . . I'm not sure . . . but have they told you about Oberto, the handyman?'

'Yes, I've already spoken to him.'

'Ah . . . and what did he say?' Claretta asked, looking up suddenly.

'Nothing important.'

'Do you know why Antonio was so attached to him?'

'No, I don't . . .'

'I must confess that I never liked Oberto. He's always so moody . . . he seems angry with the world . . .'

'He seemed rather nice to me,' Bordelli said in the young man's defence.

'He has a way of looking at me that sends shivers up my spine,' Claretta continued, looking somewhat impatiently at the empty glass.

'Would you care for another Martini?'

'Pardon? Oh, I'm not sure . . . well, all right . . .' Claretta said blithely. The inspector signalled to the bartender.

'Another Martini, please.'

'I don't usually drink so much, but at times like this . . .'

'Not to worry, I completely understand . . . you were saying about Oberto . . .?'

'Ah, yes . . . a sad story, really. No one ever mentions it. It probably has nothing to do with . . . but I think it's important that you know . . .'

'Please, go ahead.'

'Well, one night, fifteen years ago, Antonio . . .'

She stopped as the waiter appeared with her Martini. After he left she took a sip, holding the glass with both hands. People walked in and out of the bar, but Claretta and Bordelli paid no attention to them.

'You were saying?' the inspector whispered. Claretta finished her Martini and leaned forward slightly, batting her eyelashes.

'One night, fifteen years ago, Antonio was driving home and ran over Oberto's father, killing him . . . It wasn't entirely Antonio's fault. Oberto's father was drunk and came out of nowhere. There were witnesses. But Antonio always felt guilty about it, especially after seeing the conditions the widow and her two children lived in. On top of that, Oberto's sister was mentally ill . . .' Apparently, Antonio went to visit them to express his great sadness and, without thinking twice, decided to help the poor woman and her family. He rented them a larger apartment and convinced her to move. He made sure she had money, and every so often he went to see her to make sure that she wanted for nothing. Antonio supported Oberto as he went through school, and would have paid for him to go to university, but the boy didn't want to study. So he gave him a job at the Moplen factory, but that didn't last. Antonio then suggested that Oberto become his gardener, and he paid him a banker's salary. Over time Antonio grew very attached to Oberto and treated him like a son. They used to go hunting together, took long drives in the hills, and sometimes Antonio would invite Oberto over to play billiards or to stay for dinner . . .

'He made sure the boy had an easy life, that he never experienced any of the difficulties he would have known otherwise . . . Personally, I always had the impression that Oberto felt somewhat bitter towards the man who had killed his father. I also think that all that generosity embarrassed Oberto. He often said as much to Antonio, but Antonio would just laugh it off . . . I'm sure of it. You know, I feel certain things. I wouldn't be surprised if . . . no, I can't say it . . .'

'Please go on.'

'Forgive me, it's ridiculous. Pretend you didn't hear me . . .'

'As you wish,' Bordelli said, understanding what she was referring to. It felt like a scene out of *The Betrothed*; she was acting like Father Don Abbondio's housekeeper but wore enough perfume for ten harlots . . . And yet, Claretta was the only one so far who had given him something to go on . . .

'Is there anything else I can help you with, Inspector?'

'May I ask you a personal question?'

'If it's not indiscreet,' she said, blushing slightly.

'Why have you never married?'

'Oh my . . . It's so simple, really . . . the most basic reason in the world . . . I have never met the right person. But when least expecting, start suspecting, isn't that what they say?' she prattled. Bordelli would have liked to think she was flirting with him. He imagined what it would be like to invite her to dinner, and he felt a slight flutter in his gut. On all levels, Claretta was a fascinating woman, and worth exploring . . .

'Thank you for your patience . . .'

'Despite the circumstances, it was a pleasure,' the young lady said softly, picking up her handbag. They stood up, and while Claretta fixed her hat in the mirror the inspector went to pay for their drinks.

He held the door open for Claretta and they stepped out. Christmas was in the air, and the piazza was teeming with automobiles.

'May I accompany you?' he said, awkwardly.

'I'm not going far . . .' she replied. She hadn't said no, so the inspector stayed by her side. Claretta walked proudly and coquettishly. She might even have been a little tipsy. Her perfume seemed less aggressive outdoors. Actually, it was almost pleasant.

'I'm curious: does your lovely name stem from some political passion?' Bordelli asked, referring to Mussolini's mistress.

'Thank you for the compliment, but I was born quite a few years before Clara Petacci climbed into bed with the Duce.' She might appear shy, but Bordelli could tell that Claretta also had a bold streak.

'That's hard to believe,' Bordelli said, not recalling exactly when

Petacci had met Mussolini. In reality he was still absorbed in trying to work out what kind of woman Claretta was. He smiled delicately and let the matter drop.

'Have you ever not found someone's killer?' she asked candidly.

'Losing is part of life . . .' Bordelli said with the gravitas of a Hollywood actor. Looking at the two of them, nobody would ever be able to guess why they were together.

'Well, here we are,' she sighed, stopping in front of a large wooden door.

'I wish you a very pleasant afternoon,' Bordelli said, bowing to kiss her hand and simultaneously noticing out of the corner of his eye that two young girls passing by were giggling at his gesture. He blushed.

'Goodbye, Inspector,' Claretta said, recovering some of her aplomb for the moment of leave-taking. She felt around in her handbag for her keys, seeming distracted, then disappeared through the doorway without looking back. Her perfume vanished, quickly replaced by the smell of car exhaust. Bordelli looked up at the four-storey neoclassical building; there were only three buzzers, and the one at the top said Biagiotti.

He walked back towards Piazza San Gallo, remembering how the two girls had snickered at his archaic gesture of kissing Claretta's hand. They were right: it was passé. The world was moving forward fast. You only had to look around to realise this. You could see it in what people wore, how they combed their hair, how they spoke, or what was in the news. The protests at the universities, the marches against Vietnam . . . the world was not becoming a better or fairer place, but at least things were evolving.

When he came out of Totò's kitchen it was just two o'clock. Normally at that hour he was still sitting with a flask of wine in front of him. But when he'd left Claretta it was already past one, and there'd been no point in going back to the office for just half an hour.

When he got to headquarters, he stuck his head inside the guard's booth and saw Mugnai in deep concentration.

'You're just the man I've been waiting for, Inspector. Number twelve down's got me completely stumped . . . Listen up . . . "Ulysses, to Polyphemus", six letters . . . Who would ever know that?'

'Nobody.'

'Exactly. They shouldn't make them so hard.'

'No, I meant that's the answer: *Nobody*.'

'What do you mean?'

'That's what you should write: *Nobody*.'

'*Nobody*?' He wrote it down, looking doubtful. 'It fits. Seems right . . . But how did you know that?'

'I'll tell you another time . . .' said the inspector, patting the guard on the shoulder and leaving him to his epic labours. As he entered the courtyard he heard the rumble of a squad car returning, and out of habit he stopped to watch it park. Two officers came out, along with a young lad they'd just arrested, who looked around in terror. Bordelli recognised him. He was the elder son of Foresto, a poor bastard from the San Frediano quarter, a smuggler, distiller, counterfeiter and purse-snatcher . . . And a fine fellow, always ready to lend others a hand.

'What did he do?' Bordelli asked.

'He was riding a stolen motorbike.'

'Leave him with me, I'll talk to him,' said the inspector, gesturing to the others that they could leave. They exchanged glances, then got back in their car and drove away again.

'What is this nonsense?' Bordelli said, putting a hand on the boy's shoulder and shaking him gently.

'I was just taking it for a spin, I would have returned it.'

'Yes, of course . . . What's your name?'

'Matteo.'

He was tall, thin, and shy. Quite different from the other boys of his neighbourhood.

'How old are you?'

'Sixteen.'

'Are you in school?'

'Yes . . .' he barely whispered.

'Listen to me, Matteo . . . In a couple of hours, you could find yourself in the reformatory, but I want to let you go. I advise you not to throw away an opportunity like this. Think it over very carefully tonight.'

'Yes . . .' The lad couldn't believe his ears.

'You can go, but if you screw up again . . .'

'No . . .'

'Good, I want to believe that. Now go . . . And give my regards to your parents.'

'Yes . . .' He was about to start crying.

'What are you waiting for? You want me to change my mind?' Bordelli said gravely.

The kid shook his head, stuck his hands in his jacket pockets and started walking briskly towards the exit, head down. Who knew whether he would actually take a cop's advice . . . But locking him up in a cell would have made no sense.

As Bordelli climbed the stairs he thought Matteo seemed like a sensible boy who hadn't yet found the right path. There was something special, or something strange, about him. Perhaps if he'd been born into another family he might have become an artist or a writer . . .

The inspector entered his office and on the desk found a note written in ink: *Phone calls. Olinto Marinari: he's at home, waiting for your call. Signora Rosa: she'll call back later.* He immediately dialled Marinari's number, and someone picked up after the first ring. It was a grief-stricken Olinto. The inspector asked him when they could meet.

'We could meet right now, if you like. But please don't ask me to come into Florence. I'm a wreck.'

'No problem, I can come to you. What's the address?'

'When you get to Barberino, ask for the Balzini farm. Everybody knows it.'

'I'm on my way.'

'You'll see a black gate. Just honk your horn and I'll come and open it for you.'

'Thank you. See you in a bit . . .'

Bordelli hung up, thinking that with Olinto Marinari he would end the first round of people for questioning, unless somebody else popped up in the meantime. Thus far only Claretta had mentioned anything that might merit further investigation. He had to go and see Oberto again, to try to clear up a few matters. Before leaving the office, he tried ringing him, but there was no reply. He took the opportunity to call home, but after many rings he gave up. Perhaps the colonel had gone out or simply didn't feel like answering, for fear of being discovered.

Before going out he also rang Dr Fabiani, the psychoanalyst he always invited to his men-only dinner parties, but there was no answer. He put his coat back on and headed down the stairs, wondering whether Oberto had a girlfriend. He could imagine the lad with a luminous blonde full of life. Opposites attract, they always said.

He got into his car, glad to leave the city for a few hours. It was just past three o'clock, and there would still be light when he got to Barberino. He'd always liked driving on country roads, even if his real passion was now hiking through the woods. Who knew whether Arcieri would manage to keep up with him on Sunday. The colonel was recovering his strength, but still seemed in pretty bad shape.

Bordelli took the *viali* to avoid driving through the centre of town, which by that hour was surely already teeming with people looking for Christmas presents to buy. At Porta Romana he turned up Via Senese, drove through Il Galluzzo and after Tavernuzze continued on to the Via Cassia. At the fork at I Falciani he went up towards San Casciano, downshifting for the climb. At last he was able to see the dark horizon of hills. The sky was tending towards grey, the sun seemed immersed in milk. When he reached the town he continued on the state road, with its alternations of straight sections and tight curves. He drove slowly, looking out at the fields and woods. There were more than a few olive groves and vineyards in a state of abandon, with the grass so high it would have been hard to walk through them. But he also saw some well-tended ones, the handiwork of the last peasants, most of whom were now toiling so that their children could go to school. The desire for the city was consuming the young, like the giant demon in the Baptistry mosaic eating the sinners.

But not even the neglected fields could wreck the beauty of that sight. The open spaces of the farms stood out against the woods covering softly rolling hills dotted with occasional villas, castles, great barns and age-old cypresses. Nature had done her part, but man, too, had been busy, and the result was magnificent. It was the same background as in certain Renaissance paintings, which many foreigners believed the painters had invented to symbolise heaven on earth . . .

With one thought following upon the other, he got to Tavarnelle and continued on towards Barberino. He hadn't been out that way for ages. The last time was more or less in '52, right after he'd been made junior inspector. He vaguely remembered going for a drive in his Fiat 600 with his girlfriend at the time, Elda, a shy, pretty girl from Carrara who was studying medicine . . .

He saw the church up above, to the right, then the town walls. A bit farther on he spotted an open space and pulled over. There was nobody about, aside from an old peasant woman walking up towards the medieval gate. He got out of the car and, quickening his pace, caught up to her.

'Excuse me, I'm looking for I Balzini.'

'Do you know the area?' the woman asked, stopping. She had a floral-print handkerchief tightly bound round her face and was wearing a threadbare overcoat that hung all the way down to her hobnail boots.

'Not really. Is it far?'

'That depends . . . Are you on foot?'

'No, I have my car.'

'Good, otherwise it'd take a while.'

'How do I get there?'

'You have to keep going straight for a while, then make a left turn on the road to Pastine, keep going and at a certain point you'll see a path on the right. It's right there, you can't miss it . . .'

'Thank you,' said Bordelli, hoping he would find the way.

Getting back into the car, he tried to keep the old woman's vague directions clear in his mind. After a couple of kilometres he turned left onto an unpaved but rather broad road full of rocks and mud puddles that ran along a crest, cutting an olive grove in two. He crossed paths with a small truck with its flatbed full of olives, and after flashing his high beam he waved a hand out the window. The peasant stopped and rolled down his window.

'Everything all right?'

'Is this the right way to I Balzini?'

'It's just past here. Keep going for another kilometre, and you'll see a broad path on the right.'

'Thank you . . .'

'They make good wine there,' said the man, who, after waving goodbye, went on his way, bouncing through the potholes. Bordelli continued along the dirt road, trying to avoid the puddles. The sun was high over the horizon, the sky still full of light. There was probably at least an hour left before sunset.

After a few bends he found the famous broad path and turned onto it. Some fifty metres ahead he saw a wooden sign nailed to a post, with the words PODERE I BALZINI painted in red. Through the trees could be glimpsed a house beside a barn. Parking in an open area, he noticed a thin, wizened man in a large black hat watching him from behind the gate. Getting out of his car, he went up to him.

'Good evening.'

'You looking for someone?' the man grumbled suspiciously.

'I have an appointment with the architect. He told me just to honk the horn, but then I saw you here and . . .'

'Who sent you?'

'I'm with Florence police . . . Inspector Bordelli's the name . . .'

'Something bad happen?'

'I spoke with the architect about an hour ago. He's expecting me.'

'Please wait here a minute.'

'I'm not going anywhere,' said Bordelli, raising his hands. The peasant stood there looking at him for a few seconds, then vanished behind the barn, muttering to himself.

Moments later Marinari came and opened the gate and, shaking Bordelli's hand, apologised for the peasant's rudeness.

'Beppe's a little wild, but he's a good man.'

'It's not a problem.'

'Do you mind if we stay outside? I feel the need for some fresh air . . .' Olinto was tall and stout with little hair, and although he was in rustic dress, he looked elegant.

'What a beautiful place,' said Bordelli, looking around.

'Come, I'll show you the vineyard.'

They went slowly down a broad, unpaved path in silence. Under a car port was an old army Campagnola[15] with flat tyres, which must have covered a lot of road in its day. They reached the edge of the embankment, which looked out over a gully covered with vineyards. Farther ahead rose a small wooded hill that at that hour seemed veiled in a violet light.

'This is my great love,' said Marinari, looking out on his domain. They sat down on a wooden bench to contemplate the view. Speaking softly, Olinto told how for years he had ignored the property, which he'd inherited from an old aunt of his mother's. When his daughter got married in '57, one year after his son, the following morning he'd come out to I Balzini by himself, for no precise reason. When he'd looked out over the valley, the sight of the abandoned vineyards made his heart ache. He'd gone into the house, where nobody had lived for years. The walls were covered in mildew, and there was no electricity. He'd sat down in a wicker chair in front of the cold hearth and immediately fallen asleep. And he'd had a dream: he was flying over the abandoned vineyard, and as he passed over it the vines filled with ripe grapes. When he woke up an hour later, he'd already made a decision, almost without realising it: he wanted to live in that house, and he would make wine. He'd felt as excited as a teenage boy in love for the first time, convinced it was the most important, and perhaps the best, decision of his life. When he told Giovanna, his wife, about it without much beating about the bush, she'd started laughing, thinking he was just joking. When she realised that he was in fact serious, she got worried. She didn't want to hear about living in a secluded spot at the top of a hill. Nevertheless he had the house restored with great care and then suggested to Giovanna that she accept a trial period, which she did, so as not to dampen his enthusiasm.

'Nowadays my wife is as attached to this land as if she was born here,' Marinari said, smiling. The sun was sinking before their eyes, off to the right, and the trees' dark boughs looked more violet than ever. They hadn't said a word yet about Antonio Migliorini, but the inspector didn't feel up to interrupting the architect's musings.

'Putting the vines back in working order was a Herculean task from all points of view. But no obstacle could make me change my mind. I paid for experts, I sought out the best craftsmen, bought the best, most modern machinery, dug out a cellar and then outfitted it. I'd already moved my studio out here to Pastine, but instead of working on my designs I closely followed all the work being done in the surrounding countryside. Nothing gave me more satisfaction. And three years later I could finally sell my first bottles. Don't take me for a madman, however. It was like watching your first child being born. I corked those first few hundred bottles myself, and my wife stuck the labels on them. I'd thought of calling the wine *Dolce Amore*, but Giovanna advised me to use the most proper name, *I Balzini*. The wine wasn't bad, and I knew how to make it better. In five years I think I can say I've reached a good level, thanks to my passion . . . Antonio also loved my wine . . . On summer evenings after dinner, we would sometimes sit out here, just the way we are now, and chat with a glass in hand . . .'

He smiled again, but in the twilight you could see his eyes glistening. He'd told that lovely story as a way to broach the subject of his friend, Antonio, to remember happy times in times of sorrow . . .

Bordelli didn't dare speak. Watching the approaching sunset, he was waiting for the right moment to ask his usual questions about Migliorini. But there was no need. After a pause, Marinari resumed speaking. He talked about how generous and loyal his friend was, about the last time he'd seen him, what they'd said to each other, and how at that moment Antonio had seemed serene, almost happy . . .

'One evening I asked him if there was a woman involved, and he smiled but said nothing. I didn't feel like insisting. I knew that it wasn't his style to talk about his conquests, but I got the impression that this time it was something very special. I'm sure I would have met the woman sooner or later. Antonio would have found the right moment to introduce her to me. He was a truly exceptional person. Try as I might, I simply cannot understand who could have killed him . . . It's especially hard to imagine a motive . . .' Marinari concluded, looking out on his vineyard, which was sinking into darkness.

'So you really can't tell me anything about this mystery woman?' asked Bordelli.

'No, I'm sorry . . . Antonio never talked about her with me . . .' Olinto said sadly.

They sat there in silence, like two old friends who don't always need to talk. By now it was almost night, and the gully beneath them had become a black void. Despite the cold Bordelli could have stayed there till dawn, contemplating infinity. He had no trouble imagining how pleasurable it would be to sit on that bench in summertime, in the company of a good bottle . . .

'I don't want to take any more of your time,' said the inspector, standing up. Marinari looked at him as if he'd just woken up.

'Well, you can't leave without having tasted my wine . . . And you should meet my wife,' he said, already on his feet. They walked through the garden and, after climbing a last stone staircase, came to the house. Signora Giovanna was reading a book in front of the fire. She stood up to meet the guest, and, smiling sorrowfully, extended a small, warm hand to the inspector. She was a tiny, pretty woman, who as a girl must have had decimated legions of suitors. Olinto kissed her lightly on the lips.

'Please sit down . . .' she said.

Marinari uncorked one of his bottles, and with priestly gestures poured the wine into three tulip glasses. Raising his in the air, he said:

'To Antonio's memory . . .'

'To Antonio,' his wife said softly.

Bordelli only raised his glass, so as not to intrude. The wine looked like dark blood. They all drank, just a sip, and the inspector felt a wave of pleasure pass over his tongue. Marinari was right. It was very good wine. It left a tart flavour in the mouth that invited the next sip. Bordelli would have gladly bought a few bottles, but in a situation like that he didn't have the courage to say it.

'What do you think of my plonk?' asked the architect.

'Magnificent.'

'No, not yet . . . But one day . . . I often used to talk about it with Antonio . . .' said Olinto.

It's now or never, thought Bordelli.

'I wouldn't want to seem improper, but I wouldn't mind buying a few cases of this wine.'

'It's our pleasure . . .' said Giovanna, exchanging a complicitous glance with her husband.

As it turned out, Marinari personally loaded eight boxes of six bottles into the Beetle and wouldn't hear of being paid. They shook hands, and again Bordelli felt a sort of familiarity with this good man, who was in love with his wife and his vineyard. The architect had one more thing to say, in keeping with the seriousness of the occasion.

'I know this may sound silly, but please don't misunderstand me . . . If you find Antonio's killer, I'll give you three hundred bottles as a gift . . . Please don't say anything, I beg you . . . Goodbye, Inspector . . .'

At half past seven, Bordelli pulled up on the pavement in Via dei Neri, just below Rosa's house. He hardly ever went to see her at that time of day, but as he was returning from Barberino, he'd had an idea and needed to ask her a favour. He picked up a bottle of Balzini and rang the doorbell. A few minutes later the bolt clicked open. He took the stairs to the top floor but found the apartment door closed. He knocked softly. There was a clatter of heels approaching.

'Who's there?'

'It's me . . .' Bordelli said. Silence. After a few minutes the door opened a crack and Rosa peered out. She spoke in a whisper.

'I can't invite you in now. I have a friend over . . . Briciola, come back here . . .' The kitten had gone out on the landing and was looking around, growling like a dog.

'I brought you a bottle of wine,' whispered Bordelli.

'How sweet of you . . .' Rosa said, taking it from him.

'I also wanted to ask you a favour.'

'Not now, Monkey . . . Briciola, if you don't come here, I'll close the door on you!' She crouched down, reached out and grabbed the kitten, which wiggled uselessly.

'When can I ring you?' Bordelli asked.

'Are you jealous? It suits you . . .' giggled Rosa.

'I'll smash his face in,' he said, to please her. Just then, Rosa's other cat, a big white one, slipped out the door.

'Oh, now Gideon! What a pain, tonight you're both driving me crazy!'

'Go on, lovey, don't get your mother angry,' the inspector said, pushing the cat back inside.

'Ciao ciao,' Rosa said, shutting the door on Bordelli. The inspector headed downstairs, disappointed. He would have enjoyed talking to Rosa . . .

He drove back across the Arno and up Viale Michelangelo. He considered turning left after San Miniato and taking the short cut that led to the Cascine del Riccio, but he changed his mind at the last minute. That evening he wanted to go the usual way, like a horse. He turned onto the road to Impruneta, reflecting on Colonel Arcieri all alone in that big, lonely house. He wondered whether the colonel had ventured outside or had spent the whole day reading, listening to music, and chatting with the always entertaining Jeremiah.

On the winding roads past Pozzolatico he came up behind a three-wheeled Ape scooter-truck sputtering white smoke from its tailpipe. He had to follow it for a stretch until he could pass it. The driver was a gaunt old peasant with skin like wrinkled parchment; the emblem of fatigue. He was why young people were fleeing the countryside.

Switching on the radio, he turned the dial to look for something nice and stopped when he heard the melody of a song he liked, with the deep and warbly vibrato of Don Backy. '*Io sono sicuro cheeeeeeee . . .*' It was a sad and simple song that tugged at one's heartstrings. '*In questa grande immensità, qualcuno pensa un poco a meeeeeeee . . .*'[16] Words and music expressed one same feeling, while the tremulous voice conveyed endless sadness . . . He felt his heartbeat race and had to remind himself it was just a pop song. But it was one that expressed suffering just as well as an operatic aria could. He turned the radio off before the song ended. He wanted to bask in that melancholy, imagining that Eleonora was listening to the same song. It was as if they were looking at the same moon from different places. He imagined how she would have liked it, and how she would have started crying, and how she would decide to see him again . . .

'And they lived happily ever after,' he said with a smile. He liked dreaming. It cost nothing and it did no harm . . .

As he drove through Impruneta's main square, he noticed that the small grocery shop was still open. He bought some bread, two hundred grams of hand-sliced prosciutto, and a piece of pecorino cheese. He couldn't wait to get home and open a bottle of Balzini wine with Arcieri and spend the evening talking, without thinking of Eleonora.

He parked the Beetle in front of the house. He walked in and was immediately greeted by the scent of pork being grilled on an open fire. In fact, the colonel was cooking up a few sausages on an iron grill over some embers in the fireplace.

'Excellent idea,' Bordelli said, putting the shopping down on a chair. The table was set and a few potatoes were dancing around in boiling water on the stove.

'I couldn't resist,' the colonel confessed, flipping the sausages with a fork.

'It's perfect, I'm as hungry as a wolf.' Arcieri had done his dishes and it looked as if he had also washed the floor.

'Dinner will be ready in a few minutes,' the colonel said, with the savvy air of an experienced cook.

'I'll be right there. I was given some wine as a gift . . .'

He went back outside, followed by the scent of sausages, and brought the wine in. He left the open box in the kitchen and took the others down to the cellar, as if they were his treasure. The house went on and on. He had never really explored all of it in great depth, and who knew how many surprises it held. In one of the large rooms where farm machinery used to be stored there were a few trunks, half hidden behind a heap of junk and some old wine barrels. Sooner or later he'd find the time and patience to open them and see what was inside. Maybe they were filled with gold coins . . .

'I just need to make a phone call and I'll be right there . . .'

'Take as much time as you need, I'll keep everything warm,' Arcieri said.

Bordelli went upstairs, and dialled Rosa's number. After numerous rings, she picked up.

'Stracuzzi residence, who's calling, please?'

'Rosa, it's me . . . I just need a minute of your time. I have to ask you a favour . . .'

'How can I help you, Inspector?' she said, bursting into laughter. 'Are you drunk?'

'Your wine was delicious – we've already finished it.'

'I can tell.'

'We've moved on to champagne.' In the background he could hear a man's voice calling out to her.

'Rosa, listen, just for a second . . .'

'At your command, Inspector.'

'I need your help finding girls – but upscale ones – who had a client by the name of Antonio Migliorini, who was a very wealthy businessman.'

'Oh my goodness gracious . . .' she said, bursting into peals of laughter again.

'What's so funny?'

'Nothing . . .' she said, still laughing.

'Could you please ask around for me? This man, Antonio Migliorini, has been killed . . . it's important . . .'

'I know sex is important . . .' There was more laughter, even the man was laughing now.

'Rosa, will you do it for me? Remember the name: Antonio Migliorini.'

'Yes, fine.'

'Don't forget.'

'What goes around, comes around . . . and everything always goes to seed anyway . . . *Du du du du dufour* . . .' she sang, imitating the jingle for a popular candy.

'Okay, Rosa, fine, I'll call you tomorrow. Have fun . . .' Bordelli said, and while Rosa and her friend were still laughing, he hung up. Yes, sure, he was a little jealous. She'd never shut the door on him that way before. Who on earth was that other man? He hoped that Rosa hadn't found a proper boyfriend. That would be dreadful, the end of an era. He'd no longer be able to go knocking on her door at midnight and get a little tenderness. But he was an officer of the San Marco Battalion, and therefore he was always ready to face adversities with courage.

Smiling at his silliness, he went back to the kitchen. He opened a bottle of the Balzini, and took a seat at the table. Arcieri moved about even more easily than the day before, and his colour was healthy. Potatoes and grilled sausage: a dish for kings, and the red wine went perfectly with it.

'A truly noble wine,' the colonel commented.

'This afternoon I tried to ring you.'

'I chose not to answer.'

'I understand, but what if I have to tell you something? We had better find a system. If I need to talk to you, I'll let the phone ring once, hang up, and then call back a few seconds later.'

'All right,' Arcieri said with some hesitation.

After dinner they moved over to the armchairs by the fireplace, but not before Bordelli threw some fresh logs on the fire. It was just like the evening before, only they kept the light in the corner on. They had brought their glasses over, as well as a second bottle of the Balzini, which was already half finished. Not that they were drunk or anything; Bordelli just felt a bit light headed.

'All we need is music,' he said.

'I had the Bach Suites on the gramophone earlier,' Arcieri said, using the archaic term instead of record player, which was now more in vogue.

'Even Jeremiah likes the Suites.' Bordelli went to put the record back on and after a short, crackling sound the house filled with the deep sounds of the cello, and its warm, magical geometry. The inspector sat down and picked up his glass. They sat together in silence, revelling in the spiritual, earthy music, following its contours delicately as if through the brain's own pathways, as though on a search for oneself. The fresh log sat atop the hot embers, the bark smoking, ready to burst into flames. The first movement ended, leaving a profound emptiness, but then the music started again. Bordelli felt himself relax: the wine, the fireplace, the cello, just like the evening before. It was the ideal situation for listening to a story, or for telling one.

'Have you ever had a dog?' Bordelli asked, hoping to jog his guest's memory. He smiled and set down his empty glass so it could be refilled.

'If you have time, I can tell you all about the charmed life of Asta, my wonderful, white mongrel.'

'Who could ask for more?' the inspector said, getting comfortable in his armchair. Arcieri sat back, and in that very moment the log caught fire, as if by magic.

'I was about thirty years old and living on the outskirts of Milan. My German shepherd, Bella, had died a year earlier. I never even dreamed of getting another dog. Back then, I used to play billiards in a bar two blocks from my rented house. One day, as I was walking to the bar, I saw my friends peering under a truck. They told me that a little puppy was hiding under it. We managed to pull it out, and suddenly I found myself with a small scruffy white mutt in my arms. It was terribly frightened, trembling like a leaf, and yet, at the same time, it kept licking my face. Someone had obviously abandoned the animal. Everyone knew right off that I would keep him. I led him home using a piece of string as a lead, trying to come up with a name. The puppy adopted me without hesitation, and I was able to experience the warmth of that kind of quiet and unconditional friendship, a relationship that I had almost forgotten. I named him Asta, like the terrier in Nick and Nora, the American film series about the two amateur detectives. How he pulled on his lead when we went out! Like a dog pulling a sled. It was impossible to get him to change his mind.

'Asta had only one dream: to escape. There was no way to stop him . . . but he always came back. I had a large garden, with hundred-year-old trees. It was walled in on three sides and at the back there was a chain-link fence. Asta always managed to dig his way out, and he ran away constantly. I kept inspecting the perimeter, but I was never able to find his secret passage. Asta would run off and get to know all the female dogs in the neighbourhood and even more remote areas. He often got into trouble with much bigger rivals of superior breed and would come home looking like a wounded soldier, all covered in blood, with a torn ear or limping. But passion always won out. He'd escape, get into fights, hump all the females he could, and return with a victorious air, showing me his battle wounds. Veterinary care back then was a luxury, and I ended up spending a large part of my negligible salary as an officer on an animal doctor in Corso Buenos Aires. During one of our many emergency visits, the doctor took some X-rays. He discovered that Asta was older than he seemed and had an oversized, hypertrophic heart. I believed it, based on his temperament alone. The vet said that Asta was a freak of nature, and that he'd always end up giving me problems, but this only added to my deep affection for the pup. We were profoundly different, he and I. In him I saw things that I would never become. Still, I tried to train him, if for no other reason than to save his life. For a while he obeyed me, then started spending his time with a little female dog who lived down the street. They used to run off together at almost the same time each day and he always made it back in time for dinner. The owners of the little female dog had a garden that was bigger than mine; they often rang me to say that Asta was at their house. This went on for years, without many surprises. Asta was unruly but he loved me. When we went out, he would trot ahead of me, often without a lead. But nothing lasts forever . . .'

Arcieri took a deep breath, in preparation for the dramatic part of the story, while the sombre notes of the cello continued to float about the house. Bordelli waited in silence, eager to hear what would happen next.

'One summer evening, Asta didn't come home. Dinner time came and went. I waited for him at the gate. Apologising for the late hour, I rang the neighbours, but they hadn't seen him. I walked around the neighbourhood, looking for him, calling his name. I was worried. I was afraid he had resumed his former errant ways. I hoped to find him back at home, but no luck. I waited up late for him, I had a book, but I couldn't focus on it. I could only imagine the worst. Around midnight I suddenly heard whining and ran out to the garden. There, in the moonlight, I saw Asta's shadow. He was moving strangely. I walked over to him, saying his name. He whined in a strange way that didn't sound good. When I bent down over him, I realised that his head was hanging to one side. He had broken his neck. I picked him up delicately and brought him into the house. He looked up at me, his eyes wide open, full of pride. I tried to imagine what he was trying to say. He had met with a rival that was much, much bigger and stronger, and still he had chosen to fight. I wrapped him in a blanket and placed him in the back of the car. I went to the vet's house and rang the bell; he lived above his office. When the doctor examined Asta, he told me he would never make it. Actually, he said it was surprising that he was still alive. His neck was broken, which is usually enough to kill a dog. He had probably been bitten by a bulldog or some other breed with powerful jaws. Asta listened to the conversation with resigned calm. He had lived like a hero and conquered all the female dogs in the area. I asked the doctor if I had to put him down; if it absolutely had to be done, I wanted to do it immediately. I didn't want Asta to suffer. The doctor ran a finger across Asta's neck, and was surprised when he wagged his tail and even tried to shake his head.

'"Let's see what tomorrow brings," he said.

'"So there's hope?"

'"It's hard to know, but he seems full of life. I wouldn't put him down now. Let's see how he is tomorrow."

'"At home I prepared some food for him, in the hope that he would eat. He lay on the ground, waiting for me, sniffing the air. As soon as I put down the bowl he rushed over, head dangling to one side. He managed to drink some water. I spent a sleepless night while he slept blissfully. I decided not to go to the office the next morning, I didn't care about law enforcement that day. Instead I was at the vet's clinic even before it opened. As soon as somebody appeared, I knocked. The vet opened up for me. He examined Asta properly, and smiled.

'"I bet he ate . . ."

'"He even drank."

'"He doesn't need to be put down," the vet said.

'"How can I help get him back to the way he was?"

'"Unfortunately, it's impossible to fix a broken neck. His head will always dangle like that. I still think it is going to be hard for him to live, but I have to believe in the evidence. This little dog can eat and drink, and he seems to be in good shape. In other words, for him, dying is not an option."

'I looked at Asta and his dangling head with great compassion. He looked back at me, as if to say that he would make it. The vet accompanied me to the door. He felt it was his duty to inform me that Asta would live for a year or even less.

'"From now on, keep him inside, and don't give him any brothy soups."

'He shook my hand, and didn't want to be paid. I took Asta home and set him up on the most elegant chair in the living room, the one that he was never allowed to sit on. He ate well, slept well, and whenever he needed to go out he would let me know so that I could open the door for him. I'd follow him out into the garden step by step, never leaving him alone. It was painful to look at his dangling head, but eventually I got used to it. Then, one day, I forgot to close the door, and Asta managed to escape. When I realised, I ran out to look for him. I was angry and upset. Asta came back several hours later, as if nothing had happened, with his head hanging to one side. Maybe he had just gone for a walk, or maybe other dogs had taken pity on him and chosen not to attack him. I scolded him, but he just wagged his tail. He ran off again several more times, always for just a few hours, and always came back unharmed. He must have found a female nearby . . .'

Arcieri smiled and took a long sip of wine.

'Asta got better. He was in better shape than ever. It even looked like he'd started carrying his head higher . . . I had to be wrong. The vet had been very clear. But I was right. Asta slowly managed to straighten his head. The months passed, and by summer's end Asta could hold his head almost perfectly straight. I took him to the clinic. The vet couldn't believe his eyes. He shook his head in disbelief. He took some X-rays, and didn't make me pay for them. He wanted to find out how it had been possible. With great pleasure I imagined him talking about Asta at some scientific conference. Anyway, my little mutt went back to being just like before, living for three more years. He went back to fighting over females, kept getting bitten, and kept bleeding for it. It was as if nothing had ever happened.

'One night I noticed that Asta was having difficulty breathing. It might have been the bad weather: it was five degrees below zero and there was dense fog. At eleven, I called him to bed, but he didn't want to get up. I had to carry him upstairs. I rested his head on the carpet and he looked a little better. I started to read my book. Every so often I looked over at Asta, who was sleeping peacefully, but breathing heavily.

'I must have fallen asleep; then I heard a short, pained whine that seemed to come from downstairs. I turned on the light. Asta wasn't there. I went downstairs in a hurry and found him lying on the ground in front of the door as if he wanted to go out. He was dead. I felt so empty, but I found strength in thinking about his adventures. The next morning, I buried him in the garden. Despite the cold, I worked up a good sweat. I even remember the smell of the earth as I dug.'

So ended the story of Asta. And only then did they realise that the music had ended, too. Bordelli got up to turn the record over, as if following an unwritten command. When he came back he opened a third bottle of Balzini. He filled their glasses and sat back down, letting the music's coils enfold him. A few minutes went by in silence in memory of Asta, and then Bordelli told his story about Blisk. The first Blisk: the huge German shepherd belonging to the SS that he had found at the bottom of a deep mortar crater a few months before the end of the war. Blisk was seriously wounded and in pain; if someone went up to him he would growl and bare his teeth. All the same, Commander Bordelli wanted to try to save him. With the help of some fellow soldiers, Bordelli managed to tie Blisk up like a salami. The dog wriggled but the sailor's knots were too difficult to undo. They put him on a military lorry and took him to the camp, tying him up to a stake planted deep in the ground.

The dog had lost a lot of blood and was weak. Whenever someone went up to him, he would bare his fangs. Every day they would throw him something to eat from a safe distance. For a week the dog didn't eat, and they couldn't examine his wounds. One morning Bordelli saw that the German shepherd had eaten everything around him. He seemed calm. Bordelli carefully made a muzzle out of rope and eventually he was able to dress Blisk's wound. They knew he was called Blisk because he wore a collar with a steel nameplate on it. After a few days, Bordelli and Blisk became great friends. At the end of the war, he took him to his family's home on Via Volta, and one year later, when he moved to San Frediano, his mother sighed in relief. She had always been afraid of him; he used to jump up on her, put his paws on her shoulders, and lick her face, practically knocking her over . . .

Bordelli went on to tell a few more stories about Blisk, while the log on the fire spat flames. Once, at the station in Bologna . . . Then there was that night when Blisk pulled the covers off him to let him know that someone had broken in . . . Then there was the time Blisk brought a kitten home, carrying it with his teeth without hurting him . . .

When Bordelli walked down the street with Blisk, people would part to either side like the Red Sea. Eventually, after many years, Blisk started to get tired. Bordelli stopped taking him everywhere, so as not to tire him out. One evening, when he came home, he found him lying on the floor next to the door, dying.

'Like Asta . . .' Arcieri whispered.

'He died shortly after. I stroked his muzzle and looked into his eyes; he had waited for me to come home, so he could say goodbye.'

That same night Bordelli took him to his family home, dug a big hole, and buried him in the garden.

They met back in the kitchen early the following morning, and after coffee Bordelli suggested they take a short walk in the area to stretch their legs. Bringing the colonel an overcoat and proper shoes, he led him out the back door. They headed through the olive grove, under a sky almost white. All the wine they'd drunk late into the night had left no hangover, as was usually the case with good wine. The colonel looked great. He seemed to have been transformed in just two days and was scarcely recognisable. He stood up straight and had a good colour. He ambled over the clods of earth with assurance, though the oversized clothes make him look a little like Stenterello.[17]

'I'd forgotten this kind of peace existed . . .' he said under his breath, listening to the roosters crowing from one farm to the next, one hill to the next. When they got to Hare's Ditch, which one could cross simply by lengthening one's stride, they headed into the vast pine forest. The underbrush was rather dense, full of broom and other scrubby evergreens. Only here and there did one see a few splotches of yellow and brown. They followed a barely visible footpath, dodging puddles along the way. At moments they could no longer walk side by side but had to proceed in single file. Every so often they heard the rustle of a fleeing animal and tried to spot it before it was gone.

A distant rifle shot reminded Bordelli of the blast with which he had killed Panerai, one of the little boy's murderers, and to avoid thinking about it he told the colonel how the name Impruneta came from the early medieval Latin, *inter pruneta*, or something like that, meaning *in the middle of the pine grove*, as was immediately obvious . . . It was a town famous for its terracotta, known as *collo dell'Impruneta*, very durable stuff, thanks to the iron ore in the clay. To bake it required many long hours in the kiln at extremely high temperatures, but to break an Impruneta pot you had to work very hard with a mason's hammer . . . He also told him about the Peposo, also called the Antica Fornacina, a lean beef stew cooked in pepper, invented by the workers of the kilns many centuries ago, which they would cook in their terracotta kilns . . .

They continued making small talk, jumping from one subject to the next, but also falling silent for long moments, listening only to the sounds of their footfalls. The wood in December was rather quiet, the silence broken only occasionally by the odd birdcall. The sun was rising, the colours of the vegetation changing with it. A few rifle shots echoed through the valley, and in the distance they heard dogs barking. After a short while they stopped in a clearing to contemplate the hills.

'Do you not have a woman?' the colonel asked out of the blue and, seeing Bordelli's embarrassment, excused himself with a wave of the hand.

'No need to apologise . . . The fact is . . . In short, it's a painful subject . . .' said the inspector.

'That was indiscreet, I'm sorry.'

'Please . . . Maybe this is the right time to talk about it . . .' said Bordelli, feeling a little strange. With the colonel he felt he could be sincere. And yet they hardly knew each other, and only in a professional capacity. He certainly wouldn't tell him about his exploits as an 'avenger' – that was a separate matter. It was a weight he would have to carry on his shoulders alone, and not hope to lighten the burden with an outburst or confession. Nobody must know, and if any of his friends had sensed something strange . . . well, too bad . . .

'I need to rest for a minute,' said Arcieri, sitting down on a large rock.

Bordelli stuck his hands in his pockets and, in a few broken phrases, began finally to talk about Eleonora. He mentioned the first time he'd seen her, 'on exhibit' in the shop display window, the time he'd run into her by chance on the day after the Great Flood, the fact that she was so much younger than him, their love affair . . . But it was the last part he'd wanted to tell about . . . The night of the rape . . . It was a warning to him, stemming from the bloody investigation he was conducting, forcing him to step on the toes of some powerful people . . . And so Eleonora had left . . . He'd felt responsible for it, and hadn't even tried to stop her. And he'd never stopped thinking about her, wanting her, but had never got up the courage to look for her . . .

'I'm still just a boy in these matters,' he said, to downplay the whole thing.

'Well, you're right just the same. It's a very sad story.'

'Every so often I try to write her a letter, but I always give up.'

'Who are these powerful people anyway?' asked Arcieri, with the curiosity of a carabiniere.

'Freemasons, as far as I could gather.'

'Are you sure about that?'

'Well, I have to admit I haven't given it much thought since then. I was too upset . . . I just connected the dots.'

'Let me start by saying I'm not a freemason myself, but I do know a bit about it. Freemasonry is founded on noble, humanist principles, and its adepts have to follow a specific path of enlightenment. Aside from that, it seems very odd to me that a brutal rape of a defenceless girl would have anything to do with masonic principles. It sounds more like the work of some lowlifes paid by someone higher up. But it's also true that the world has got a thousand surprises up its sleeve. Like anything else, freemasonry can have a few bad apples who will use their network of connections and power for ignoble purposes. Man has always been a great alchemist capable of transforming gold into shit, as happened even with Jesus Christ, and with the great utopia of justice that was communism.'

'I can't help but agree,' said Bordelli, distracted by a concern of his own. He was trying to make sense of what Arcieri was saying. At the time he'd taken for granted that Eleonora's rape had been ordered by Monsignor Sercambi, who'd used his power within the masonic brotherhood. A masonic prelate seemed almost a contradiction in terms, at least in appearance, even though the world was full of such contradictions. That aside, might not the colonel be right? Maybe it was only a couple of 'bravos', like those of Don Rodrigo in *The Betrothed*, who'd been hired by any one of the three killers, or perhaps all three together. But the upshot was the same in the end . . . Eleonora had been subjected to an ignoble violation and had gone away. At the time, after something so disgusting and painful, he hadn't bothered either to reflect on or dig deeper into the question. He'd only tried to forget – to leave it all behind. He'd never been one to engage in empty accusations, but this time, he had to admit, he'd fallen prey to them. Unfortunately it was too late to change things now. Destiny had already dealt its blows, and there was no turning back. It was better not think about it . . .

'If I were in your shoes, I would play my best card – the card of clarity,' said the colonel.

'In what sense?'

'I was referring to Eleonora.'

'Ah, yes, of course . . .'

'Clarity has one great merit: no matter how things go, it lets you always feel at peace with yourself . . . Sorry to burden you with my cheap wisdom . . . it sometimes gets the better of me . . .' said Arcieri, getting up.

They started heading back, and Bordelli glanced at his watch. Almost half past nine. He wanted to go to Antonio Migliorini's funeral, which began at eleven in the church of San Domenico. He had no precise reason for going, but didn't want to leave any path unexplored.

'I almost forgot . . . I have a dinner engagement this evening at the home of some friends, but only if that's not a problem for you . . .'

'Of course it's a problem. I demand you come home for dinner,' said Arcieri, smiling. He seemed a little more light hearted now, even though there still seemed to be a shadow of apprehension in his eyes.

'I'll probably be home a little late, I'll try not to wake you . . .'

'Don't worry about me. Pretend I'm not even there . . .'

They got to the ditch, crossed over to the other side, and five minutes later were inside the house. Arcieri asked whether he could light a fire and immediately got busy crumpling up some newspaper. Bordelli went upstairs to change his shoes, and when he came down again he could already hear the smaller branches crackling in the fire. He put a bottle of wine in a small bag, to take to the dinner.

'See you in the morning.'

'Have a good day,' said the colonel.

'Don't forget the code. If I want to call you, I'll first let it ring once, then call back.'

'Yes, sir, Commander.'

Finding a parking spot near San Domenico church was impossible. There were cars everywhere, even double parked . . . Alfa Romeos, Ferraris, Lancias, Mercedes, Porsches. A few drivers in livery stood together on the pavement, chatting. Bordelli looked over at those bundles of millions of lira on wheels and thought that his flood-damaged Beetle was better than all of them. It could stand up to any test, just like some women he knew, who were so full of life they were comparable to any Paris model. He left the car in the square in front of the Badia Fiesolana, and walked back up the steep hill to the basilica.

Pushing open the door of the church, he discovered that the mass had begun some time earlier. The church was filled with so many elegant ladies and gentlemen that people had to stand. Bordelli remained near the entrance. He positioned himself next to a blonde in a fur coat, who glanced over at him from time to time with curiosity, probably wondering who on earth he was. He certainly was not dressed to the nines as they all were. The old Dominican friar was in the middle of his homily, his smooth voice droning on about terrestrial death and eternal life. The usual comforting message.

In one of the last rows, two people started chatting, whispering in each other's ears. The inspector looked around, imagining that the killer might be hiding in plain sight. From afar he saw Amalia, in her best get-up, head bowed in prayer, pressed up against a column, as if she was afraid to bother someone. Bordelli scanned the crowd for Oberto but couldn't see him; he kept an eye out for him until the end of the mass.

Ite, missa est . . . A few seconds after the final words, the crowd began to make for the exit. The inspector was the first to feel the sunshine on his face again, and he quickly stepped to the side, near a column in the loggia, to watch the fashion show. There was haute couture, much elegance, not much jewellery, but all worn with great discretion. There were members of noble families whom Bordelli recognised by sight. He observed the faces of the people coming out of the church, imagining that he could guess from their expressions what they were thinking. In reality he had no idea why he'd come to the funeral. What on earth did he hope to discover? He supposed it was just a way for him to remain active, not to feel powerless. He decided to stay on a little longer; he wanted to observe these ladies and gentlemen carefully. He saw how they hesitated for a few minutes outside the church, looking like survivors, how they shook each other's hands and spoke in soft tones, breath delicately rising visibly from their mouths like little clouds. Some of them smiled wanly.

A long black hearse drove up and stopped in front of the church, in the middle of the crowd. The church doors were thrown open and moments later four men came out carrying the coffin. Bordelli recognised Olinto Marinari. The two young men must have been sons of the deceased. The fourth man was probably Giordanelli, if he recalled Piras's description correctly. The last people to exit the church were other family members, including some children, and ladies with reddened eyes clutching hankies. Laura held hands with a beautiful child, who smiled at everyone. Claretta had donned a large pair of sunglasses which were better suited to the beach than a funeral, and as always she left a trail of perfume in her wake. She turned towards the inspector for an instant, then carried on without even a hint of a greeting, as if she had not even seen him.

Traffic stopped behind the hearse while the coffin was placed inside. The driver closed the back door and got behind the wheel. Pulling slowly away, he immediately turned into an open area to let the traffic pass. The people who had attended the funeral hurried off to their cars, and in a few minutes there was a long, disorganised queue. The hearse left slowly in the direction of Florence, followed by the thrum of an entourage of dream cars. Bordelli watched those sheet-metal sculptures as they passed, reflecting that he hadn't seen Claretta again after that first time.

'Hello,' someone said behind him. It was Oberto. He was wearing a leather jacket and stood with his arms crossed over his chest.

'Ciao, I didn't see you inside,' the inspector said, shaking his hand.

'I didn't go inside.'

'I tried to ring you several times . . . do you have a minute?'

'I can't talk now.'

'Can I give you a lift into the city?'

'I have my car,' Oberto said.

'When can we meet?'

'I've already told you everything I know.'

'Don't be stubborn.'

'I have to go now.'

'I heard about your father's accident,' Bordelli said, in an attempt to keep his attention.

'Who told you?' Oberto asked bitterly.

'It doesn't matter . . . but I want to talk to you. And not only about that.'

'That has nothing to do with anything.'

'At this point in time, it's the only motive I've been able to come up with.'

'Well done . . .'

'We need to talk.'

'You're following the wrong lead, Inspector. For me, Migliorini was like a father.'

'Prisons are full of innocent people,' Bordelli said provocatively, trying to reason with him.

'That almost sounds like a threat.'

'I just want is to find out who killed Migliorini.'

'I'm devastated by his death. It's like I've been orphaned for a second time,' Oberto said, staring firmly at the inspector.

'Let's say for a minute that I believe you . . . do you want the killer to get away with it?'

'No.'

'Then you must tell me everything you know.'

'I'm not used to gossiping about other people's business.'

'This is not gossip. This is murder. Every seemingly minor detail could be helpful, even the most intimate ones,' Bordelli said in the most convincing tone he could muster. The young man bit his lip.

'I have to go now. My mother and sister are in the car.'

'Think about what I said . . . when will you be home?'

'I don't know. I come and go. Try giving me a ring,' Oberto said, and with a nod he walked off, hands deep in his pockets. Bordelli waited for him to disappear round the corner, and then followed him. He was curious to see what kind of car the young man drove.

A few steps from the corner, a Fiat 850 coupé moved out, Ferrari red. The inspector recognised Oberto's mother and sister; they had the same messy hair as Oberto, and the inspector felt terribly sorry for them. They had come to say goodbye to their benefactor, but they hadn't felt up to entering the church, with all those furs and camel-hair overcoats. The Fiat drove away at a brisk pace, and Bordelli set off towards the Badia to get his Beetle.

He had to speak to Oberto. He had to get him to talk. He wanted to hear about his father's tragic death, and needed to understand whether he felt any kind of bitterness towards Migliorini, as Claretta had suggested. He felt conflicted: on the one hand he treated Oberto as if he was a possible killer, on the other, as if he was a precious witness. So it wasn't just women who felt conflicted . . . What was it that sweet Teresa always used to say to him, in the most unlikely moments? *I hate you, but I love you* . . . Indeed, that little post-war fling hadn't lasted very long . . .

Sonia and Pietrino had made a variety of dishes, mounting a challenge between Sicily and Sardinia that had all the intensity of a boxing match. Bordelli was the sole arbiter, and for a few hours he didn't have to worry about murders and murderers. Napkin tucked into his shirt collar, he let himself be served. He would savour each dish without commenting, and would deliver his verdict after the pudding. They sat at a round table tastefully laid out in a large, cosy dining room.

Sonia was more beautiful than ever. A Norman Sicilian, blond with green eyes and fair skin. Next to the swarthy Pietrino she glowed like a lamp. She was wearing a tight little white dress with an olive-green pattern. Bordelli amused himself flirting with her – with the utmost delicacy, of course. He addressed her as *Dottoressa* Zarcone, never missing an opportunity to praise her charm, and she smiled at the flattery. Piras tolerated the game, pretending to be torn between jealousy and pride, but, truth be told, he was having a jolly good time. He was very different from his usual self, sleeves rolled up and speaking with pleasure. There was little wine left in their glasses, and Sonia was laughing ever more readily. She played the silly girl with a law degree quite splendidly. Piras and the inspector had also drunk a fair amount, but held their liquor better.

'It's not a bad job, being a judge,' said Bordelli, feeling like a fatted pig. Each new recipe was better than the last, and in order to evaluate them properly, he was forced to leave nothing on his plate. He consoled himself by resolving to take a long walk through the woods the following morning.

Jumping from subject to subject, they recalled the day in which the two young lovers had first met, three years before, through the 'unfortunate' agency of a very sad investigation into a maniac who was strangling little girls. For Piras it was as if he'd found a pearl in a pile of faeces. It wasn't a very cheerful thought, in short, but if those poor little girls had never been killed . . .

The subject changed again with the desserts, two of them Sardinian and two Sicilian, forcing Bordelli to sacrifice himself in order to judge them. Being a judge is a serious matter. Gavino Piras's vintage Sardinian *vernaccia* wasn't part of the challenge, but it certainly helped the inspector confront his difficult choice.

The moment to declare a winner had arrived, and the contestants awaited the verdict with bated breath. They were young and beautiful, and to see them together was a real pleasure. Bordelli pretended to be racked with doubt, but even before he'd tasted the first starters and taken his first sip of wine, he'd already decided. He couldn't very well give the victory to the man. It was a question of nobility of soul . . . And Dottoressa Zarcone was so beautiful . . .

'By a hair's breadth, Sicily wins,' he proclaimed, raising his glass in Sonia's direction. He felt truly chivalrous. She smiled, pleased with herself, and stood up to give him a kiss on the cheek, the way girls do with nice grandads. Pietrino hadn't batted an eyelash, but it was clear he was happy with the outcome, too. He would never have wanted to win.

They toasted Sicily with a little glass of Zibibbo,[18] and after a few more comments on the meal they ended up talking about how complicated love can get.

'May I ask an indiscreet question?' asked Bordelli, sincerely interested.

'Go ahead . . .' said Sonia, more curious than he.

'Don't you two ever quarrel?'

'Of course,' said Piras.

'I mean really quarrel, with plates flying,' the inspector insisted, refilling his glass.

'We quarrel just like anyone else,' said Sonia, smiling.

'I just can't imagine it,' Bordelli confessed.

'And we say the nastiest things to each other, we insult each other like a couple of sailors, but once the storm is past, there's nothing left behind. That's why we get on so well together.'

'You couldn't have expressed it any better, especially for a woman,' said Piras, happy with his own quip. Sonia pretended not to have heard, and kept on talking to the inspector.

'I don't think they're the kinds of things you can learn. You're either that way or you're not.'

She was right, thought Bordelli. There were couples who built up rancour with each new squabble and eventually poisoned their lives. They lacked the will to manage the conflict. The secret lay in a lucky chemistry. And what about him with Eleonora? When combined did they become a salve for pain or an explosive mix? They hadn't had time to find out, having broken up too soon . . . And not over a quarrel . . .

'Some grappa, Inspector?' asked Piras.

'No, thanks, I've had enough to drink . . .'

He'd turned melancholy, and carried away by his mood he was on the verge of starting to talk about the war. But he stopped himself in time and tried to recover a little good cheer.

'See this scar?' he said. 'It has nothing to do with the war. I cut myself when I was a little kid.'

And he rolled up one sleeve all the way to his shoulder and told about how he had stupidly scarred himself. Then, naturally, everyone showed his or her own wounds, down to the very smallest. Sonia said she had a little scar on one of her buttocks, and when she laughingly threatened to show it, Pietrino baulked.

'Just kidding,' she said, sitting back down.

They kept on telling family anecdotes, and not only amusing ones. Around 1 a.m. Bordelli noticed that Sonia was tired, and he thanked the two youngsters for a lovely evening.

'Next time you need a judge, you know where to find me,' he said, standing in the doorway. Then he kissed Sonia's hand and shook Pietrino's. Descending the stairs, he imagined the pleasant night the two would be spending together and felt a sweet pang of envy.

Going out the front door, he pulled his coat tight around him. He hadn't smoked a single cigarette, not wanting to disturb anyone, and now finally lit one up. The Beetle's seat was cold, but after all that wine he didn't mind at all. Driving up Via Trieste, he turned onto Via Bolognese and leaned forward to look at the dark façade of Villa Triste, where there had once been a torturer of partisans by the name of Carità, which meant 'charity', giving the lie to the famous saying, *nomen omen* . . .

After he reached Piazza San Gallo, steering with two fingers, he turned onto the avenues towards Piazzale Donatello. It was Saturday, and despite the cold there were still a great many cars in circulation. There was a yellowish halo round the street lamps, and the trees with their naked branches looked like monuments to suffering. He kept thinking about Sonia and Pietrino . . . *Quant'è bella giovinezza* . . . How true that old poem was . . .[19]

As always, the nocturnal drive home was a journey through the past. Bordelli wondered why remembrance was always so pleasant – even when the memories themselves were sad.

He parked in front of the house, trying to be as quiet as possible. The smell of burnt firewood and ash that filled the air had become familiar; it was the smell of home. The lamp on the table in the corner of the kitchen was on, and on the table was a note from Arcieri . . .

'*I had a beautiful day. Goodnight.*'

Smiling, he crumpled the paper and threw it into the fireplace, waiting for it to catch flame. He sat down in the armchair and allowed himself his second cigarette of the day. He smoked it while listening to the ticking of the wall clock . . . *Quant'è bella giovinezza* . . .

He threw the butt into the fireplace and, getting to his feet, felt the effect of all the wine he had drunk. But he didn't want to go straight to bed. He felt slightly euphoric and wanted to take advantage of this in some way.

There was one thing he could do, something he'd been thinking about for a long time. On the far side of the house, on the ground floor, there was a windowless room he had filled with boxes during the move. He started digging around in the dusty boxes, breathing with his mouth closed, and after a few attempts, he found what he was looking for. It was a shoe box he hadn't opened for ages, full of old photographs. He clutched it under his arm and went upstairs. He could hear Arcieri snoring in his bed down the hall. It was warm. He opened the door of the pot-bellied stove and saw that the colonel had already fed it some wood.

He went into his room, leaving the door open so the heat would come in. He walked gingerly over to the bedside table to light the lamp and checked to make sure there was some water left in the bottle. Ever since childhood he had to have water at his bedside or he couldn't sleep.

He took off his shoes, lay down on his side on the bed and opened the box of memories. He started to look through the photographs, one by one. Many he knew and remembered well, others he felt as if he had never seen before, even if he recognised the figures. It was a continuous hopscotching through time.

He saw grandparents, great-grandparents, his mother as a girl, a great-aunt who died of pneumonia at age ten, a newborn on a cushion, Great-grandmother Eugenia in her coffin. His father as a child, Aunt Matilde wearing a fez, his parents posing on their wedding day, one beside the other, wide eyed. Every so often there was a photo of him, at various stages in his life: in his San Marco uniform, in sailor suit and cap, or in Fascist Youth garb . . .

Amid the photos, there was a large piece of black paper folded in four. He opened it as if it was an ancient manuscript, and his eyes welled with tears. They were drawings done in coloured pencil . . . he would always remember that September afternoon at Marina di Massa beach, the storm, the never-ending rain . . . and Isabel, a Spanish lady, one of his mother's friends. She noticed how bored he was and offered to draw for him. . . . Whatever you want, tell me . . . And so he described in detail the frightening monsters that he had invented over the years and Isabel drew them for him, giving life to his imagination . . . There was the *Scorobò*, the ghost monster that chased him when he went pee-pee in the garden, its eyes as big as eggs . . . there was the *Vienula*, a white wolf as big as a refrigerator that could swallow you in one bite . . . and finally there were the *Ripoli*, the little red mice that crept up into your bed and nibbled on your feet. His mother had framed the drawings and hung them on the wall across from his bed; not long after, the monsters became his friends. He couldn't remember exactly when they were taken down, or by whom. He had forgotten that they even existed. He folded up the piece of paper and put it back in the box with the photographs, ignoring the desire to reframe it and hang it on the wall as when he was a child. Those drawings belonged to the mythologies of childhood, and he didn't want them to become part of the disillusioned world of adults. It was much nicer and wiser to leave them where they were, together with his most secret memories.

Warmed by these thoughts, he kept looking through the photographs, dusting off anecdotes he had lived through or heard about. But there were still more surprises. He found another piece of paper, this one open, with a typed poem on it: *Stars* . . .

So long
since I'd seen
the stars.
I'd forgotten
I was nothing.

He stopped for a minute to think about these lines, and then reread the poem several times, and even recited it out loud. It was simple and profound, and it moved him. Who had written it? And when? He looked through the pictures to see whether there were others, and found an envelope full of poems. His mother's name was written in pencil on the envelope. There were dozens of poems, some of them handwritten on graph paper, others typed on onion-skin paper . . . 'Libeccio' . . . 'Summer Rain' . . . 'Autumn in Tuscany' . . . 'Desert Rose' . . . He started reading them, his amazement growing by the minute. Each was more beautiful than the last, pure as snow, but capable of waking hidden emotions . . . After reading the final one, 'Vanitas', he lay back and stared at the beams on the ceiling . . . He had entered an unknown world . . . it had never occurred to him that his mother . . . he felt a little bewildered, light headed . . . No, when he thought back to his mother, he saw her as a different woman . . . *Dreams born in the morning, dead in the evening* . . . What kinds of thoughts had triggered those lines? And when? Before he was even born? Or perhaps during the war? *Content to wander timeless space, cradled by good mother earth* . . . He kept repeating certain lines in his head, memorising them with a smile. Why hadn't his mother ever let him read her poems? Did she think they were worthless? Was she afraid of being teased?

When he felt himself falling asleep, he sat up and put the poems back in the envelope, kissed it gently, and placed it on the bedside table, so it would be nearby. It was a little like having her next to him. He undressed quickly, got under the covers, and turned off the light . . . *Cradled by good mother earth* . . . He hugged the pillow and in his torpor kept thinking about his mother's verse . . . until at last he fell asleep.

It was a fine, sun-drenched morning, cold but windless. With the colonel in the passenger's seat, Bordelli took the Beetle to La Panca, but instead of stopping in the usual clearing beside the road, he continued driving up the dirt path and parked at the top of the hill. He didn't want Arcieri to overexert himself, even if he seemed to be in pretty good physical shape. The old 'geezer' had recovered fast, and a long walk could only do him good.

They set out on the trail in silence and headed into the woods, steam rising from their mouths. They were nicely bundled up, and on his head the colonel was wearing a snow cap with a pompom that Bordelli had found in a drawer.

Every so often they saw a ribbon of pale blue fog at the base of the trees. There was a smell of rotten leaves and sodden earth in the air, which the inspector breathed in with pleasure. When he looked at the stark-naked chestnuts, the expanse of black trunks always brought to mind a wartime cemetery.

They stopped under the majestic oak of Monte Scalari, which had lost every last one of its leaves. Its powerful boughs floated weightless aloft, sketching a complicated pattern against the blue sky. Bordelli started recounting how that beautiful tree had been used by the Germans to hang Italian 'traitors', including women and children. The little tabernacle at its feet had been built in memory of the dead. Arcieri listened intently and, staring up at the black tangle of branches, imagined the bodies of those poor innocents hanging there. He himself had seen similar scenes, sometimes worse. But he said nothing.

They resumed walking. They passed the time-worn gate to the ancient abbey, and at the fork of the Cappella dei Boschi, they turned right, towards Pian d'Albero. It was one of the inspector's favourite trails. By now he knew these hills quite well. The first time he'd come up here it was to unearth the dead body of little Giacomo, and since that day he had never stopped coming back. He'd seen the wood in every season. By this point he know where the rainwater streams cut athwart the paths, where the biggest puddles would form, forcing one to walk along the edge of the gully. He remembered where all the strangest trees were located, all the little plateaux where until fairly recently the coal merchants used to burn wood. And he certainly would never forget how Panerai the butcher 'committed suicide' in these woods . . .

'I feel indebted to you,' said Arcieri, breaking the silence.

'Why's that?'

'Yesterday morning you confided in me about your romantic distress.'

'It was a moment of weakness,' said the inspector, smiling.

'You treated me like a friend, and now it's my turn.'

'There's no obligation,' said Bordelli, as they walked along the edge of the gully to avoid a large mud puddle.

'If you don't mind, I'd like to tell you about Elena Contini . . .'

'Go right ahead . . .'

'It's probably all because it's such a beautiful day, and this is such a beautiful wood . . . But I feel as if I could talk about Elena without getting too sad, and without hiding behind a mask . . .'

'If that's what you feel like doing, I'm more than happy to listen.'

To their right, the land sloped steeply down for a good hundred metres, and on their left it rose up again. The sun filtering through the leafless trees almost seemed as if it could warm one's face, but it might have been an illusion.

'Since we've got the time, I'd like to start from the beginning,' said the colonel, walking as erect as a plank.

'All right . . .'

'It's the first time I'm allowing myself to talk to anyone about this. Strange, no? At the tender age of sixty-five, it's more than a little surprising. And I have to admit, it makes my heart race.'

'What would life be without surprises?'

'There are a few I would rather have lived without,' Arcieri said softly, smiling.

'Careful: it's slippery here.'

As soon as they were past another puddle even larger than the last, the colonel bent down to pick up a broken branch. He used it to break the bank of the puddle, and the turbid water began to flow down the slope.

'I couldn't resist,' said Arcieri.

They stood there watching, happy as two little boys. When the water stopped flowing downhill, they resumed walking.

'Look! Up there!' Bordelli whispered, taking the colonel by the arm. Some fifty yards ahead, two boar were running up the hillside, soundlessly, and in a flash they vanished down the other side, as if they'd never been there.

The two men continued along the path, side by side, constantly looking around in the hope of seeing other animals. The colonel took off his cap, put it in his pocket, and after a few more steps also undid a few buttons on his coat.

'Are you ready to listen to an old man's laments?'

In January of '37 Bruno Arcieri was detailed to Florence, with the Legion of Carabinieri, owing to a gunshot wound in his right leg. His superiors had thought they were doing him a favour by sending him back to his home town. He was already thirty-six and held the rank of captain. He, too, had been expecting a pleasant homecoming. He'd imagined himself coddled by the city he'd left in tears on the eve of the Great War, when his father was transferred to Milan. But he found none of the atmosphere of his childhood there. Even the railway station was not the same as the one from which he had departed. They'd built a new one, a very modern one. And he too had changed. All he could remember of his old schoolmates were their first names, and he had no idea how to find them.

He had an office job. A desk and a telephone, in a white room with two windows giving on to what at the time was called Via Foscari . . . It had been different in Milan; he'd worked in the investigative unit. He would never sit for more than half an hour at a time. He missed the active life more than he could have imagined.

His parents were no longer around, and he had no other relations. At the time it wasn't easy to make new friends, especially in a closed city like Florence. To say nothing of women.

Men unwilling to frequent bordellos had to find a good girl in a hurry and marry her. Arcieri had never been too keen on the idea of paying for a woman's favours; but neither would he ever have taken lightly the notion of marrying someone. If he wasn't in love, there was no point.

In his free time he would stroll through the streets of the city centre, seeking out the colours and smells of his childhood. He knew this was absurd, and that he couldn't wish that time had stopped. Everything was so different from back then . . . Women's dresses, the carriages, the automobiles, the bicycles . . . Even the way people acted and spoke had changed. Perhaps this, too, was why his loneliness seemed to eat away at him.

He started going to museums. There certainly was no lack of art in Florence. He would spend long stretches of time gazing at Botticelli's Primavera, *Michelangelo's* Doni Tondo, *and Bronzino's portraits. Looking at these masterpieces, he felt as if he regained a certain equilibrium, re-establishing within himself the concept of universal beauty. He was able, at least for a short while, to throw off the feeling of alienation that had been tormenting him. Who knew what the tourists thought when they saw the young carabiniere officer standing motionless like a sentinel in front of a painting. It certainly wasn't a good place for meeting new people. He almost never saw Florentines in the museums, except for the occasional groups of art history students chattering among themselves. It was a real surprise, then, when a beautiful blond girl stopped beside him and started talking to him . . .*

'I'd never believed in love at first sight. It had always seemed farfetched to me, pure myth. But then I had to revise my opinion. We introduced ourselves. Elena was full of life, but at the same time had a melancholy side that lent her an unusual charm. She looked at everything with gentle detachment, as if she'd always thought she was only passing through this world. Her manner seemed aristocratic, but that certainly wasn't what attracted me to her. She simply seemed like a very special woman to me.

'As we came out of the Uffizi, the most natural thing to do was to invite her to lunch, and she was pleased to accept. We kept talking, at times quite animatedly. We both felt keen to know each other better, to find out what the other was about. I think we were falling in love . . .' said the colonel, letting himself get momentarily carried away by the same light-headedness he'd felt back then. Bordelli recalled his first dinner with Eleonora, when they'd felt the same things, but his thoughts were interrupted by Arcieri's voice.

'The lunch wasn't even over, and I already knew a great many things about Elena. She was twenty-five years old, she was Jewish, and she belonged to a very wealthy family. Since childhood she had loved to read and listen to music . . . She'd lost her mother a few years earlier . . . Two of her uncles were important university professors . . . Her cousin had an adorable little dog called Gipo . . . We could talk about anything, but the important thing was to gaze into each other's eyes. Listening to her made me happier than I'd ever felt before. I didn't say much about myself . . . What could I have told her? That my father was a government clerk and my mother a housewife? And that after secondary school I'd joined the Carabinieri and done my duty as best I could? For the moment I preferred to listen.

'She'd had a boyfriend until a year before, when he'd left her without any explanation. I can still remember the pang of jealousy I'd felt. I tried my best not to let it show, but much later she admitted to me that she'd noticed and that it had pleased her very much.

'Elena also used to visit the museums often. Unlike me, though, she didn't want for human company, but she did tell me openly that the circles she frequented held no interest for her. She needed something completely different, she added, smiling.

'In the weeks that followed, whenever I had a few free hours, we would go together to the Uffizi or the Accademia museum. Even just standing in silence beside her, admiring a painting, made me feel good. One time I told her that the hollow pupils of the *David* were carved out in the shape of a heart, and she didn't want to believe me . . .'

'But is it true?' asked the inspector.

'So I was told, but I've never climbed up there to check.'

'Sorry, I interrupted you,' said Bordelli, and he waited for the colonel to resume his journey through the past.

'Then the day arrived when . . . Well, anyway . . . By late afternoon we were unable to separate. We walked side by side along the river, talking about everything imaginable. We went to dinner at a restaurant in Borgo San Jacopo, amidst a throng of rather drunken British and American tourists. I even managed to make her laugh. Watching her laugh was the best gift she could ever have given me.

'We headed back to her place on foot. I was walking slowly, in the illusory hope we'd never get there. Suddenly there we were, without my realising it. She lived alone, with a housekeeper, in a small art-nouveau house not far from the outer boulevards. Outside her gate I made as if to kiss her hand, like a good old-fashioned lad. Elena smiled sweetly, blond hair flowing. The moment had arrived. We exchanged an ever so delicate kiss, and she vanished into the house.

'The following evening we dined together again and, talking and talking, ended up drinking a whole bottle of wine. As we walked arm in arm down the narrow streets, Elena said something out of the blue . . . The following day her housekeeper would be sleeping at her mother's house, like every Saturday. There was no need to say anything else. Saturday evening we ate out again, at a restaurant within my means, and then we went to her place. Elena's refinement was visible even in the furnishings, which were more modern than anything I'd ever seen. I'd brought with me a few jazz records by some American big bands . . . Benny Goodman, Duke Ellington . . . As of that evening, it became the music of our nights together . . .

'We never said it to ourselves out loud – for us it was a kind of game – but it was clear that we were a couple. She introduced me to her family and some people from her milieu, determined to carry on with our relationship in the light of day. I felt like a fish out of water in that crowd. The first few times I went to posh parties I wore my uniform and felt everyone's eyes on me. That was the world Elena inhabited, and she didn't like it but wasn't strong enough to leave it. I was a foreign body, and her friends treated me with condescension. Oh, they were polite, mind you, but I could tell they didn't really like me. But it wasn't a big problem, in the end. We didn't go often to these high-society affairs, and as time went by, it happened less and less.

'By this point, we could understand each other with just a glance. We both felt out of place, and our love only kept growing. That spring I realised that the whole thing was making her unhappy, even though she never stopped being the luminous girl I knew. Out of respect, I never asked her about it. But she knew she couldn't hide her suffering from me, and so she left everything hanging.

'Some time later, in spite of myself, I discovered one of the reasons for her anguish. Her mother had been killed by Nazis, and when Hitler came on an official visit to Florence in '38, she'd actually got it in her head to assassinate him. A courageous plan, but she would never have come out of it alive. As fate would have it, I was actually the person in charge of security for the Führer's visit, and luckily I was able to stop her in time. I still wonder what would have happened if I had let her do what she had in mind, and she had succeeded. I was only doing my job, and by stopping her I saved her from getting massacred.'

'So, in short, you changed the course of history . . .' muttered Bordelli, though Arcieri seemed not to have heard, and merely continued recounting his memories.

'Our dreams of living together were swept away by those days in Florence, by the racial laws passed in September, and then by the war. Following the success of my operation I was asked to go to Rome for a colloquium with some gentlemen. The meeting was held in an anonymous flat in the middle of Rome. They invited me to join the Secret Service, which at the time was called the SIM, and I decided to accept. I thought I could do something for my country, in spite of Fascism. Whatever the case, I felt I was made for that kind of work. Ever since I was a little kid I'd felt an attraction for uncovering secrets, maybe because they made me uneasy, forced me to think . . .

'In September of '39 Hitler and Stalin invaded Poland, and I was sent abroad on a variety of missions. Elena's family was suffering terribly from the racial laws, and they all moved to Rome. I was also sent to Rome, in 1940, just after Mussolini joined the war. And so we were together again. We no longer wanted to be ever apart, and decided to get married. But we didn't want to do it during a war. It seemed too sad. We had no idea of the tragedy that was about to engulf Italy. After the armistice in '43 Elena miraculously made it back to Florence and hid at the home of a woman who had worked for her family. Even during those terrifying months we managed every now and then to see each other. I had to do impossible things to go and see her, and the kisses were never enough.

'When Florence was liberated and the front moved north, we started thinking about marriage again. Then the war ended, but we didn't want to get married amidst the rubble and suffering. We preferred to wait for better times. The months went by, and then the years, and for one reason or another we were continually forced to postpone the event. Finally, in August of '48, Elena suddenly vanished. I went a long time without any news of her, and was getting more and more worried, and then in '49 I received a letter . . . *Caro Bruno, I'm writing to you without my husband's knowledge, since he would never understand* . . . I had to sit down at once, before I recovered the strength to read the rest . . . She said she loved me very much . . . She'd moved to Israel . . . She'd made her travel plans without telling me; she said she would never have found the right words to explain her decision . . . She'd moved away some months before, with a powerful but loving man, who gave her a sense of security . . . I couldn't believe it . . . It couldn't be true . . . I could tell she was lying . . . I knew she was . . . She was hiding the truth from me for some unknown reason . . . But, in the end, was anything different? She was no longer around, that was true. But that was all that was true. I was already forty-seven years old, and this made me feel older than ever . . .'

The colonel paused for a long time, staring into the emptiness. Bordelli didn't breathe a word. Amidst the silence of the woods they could hear their own footsteps on the path, and every so often, a distant rifle shot.

'After that I only saw Elena very rarely, and every time I was overwhelmed by the past . . . I felt the same emotions that shook me in '37, in Florence . . . It was as if time had stopped and I was trying to immerse myself in the illusion that nothing had changed . . . Sorry if I'm sounding rhetorical, but there's no other way to put it . . . That woman is a part of me; I can't separate myself from her. And when I was immobilised in that hospital bed in Viareggio and she would wet my lips, I realised that it was the same for her. We are both aware of it, even if we have never ventured to talk about it. We could have got married and spent our lives together . . . But when the devil has a hand in things . . .'

'You're telling me,' Bordelli muttered.

'So now you know my torments,' said Arcieri, trying to snap out of his melancholy.

They continued walking at a leisurely pace, in silence, weighed down by their memories. They were survivors, of past love affairs as much as the war, and resigned to the fact that they would never forget. The wood around them pretended to be dead, but sooner or later spring would come to rouse it, and it would burst forth with life and colour and a thousand scents and animal calls . . . Until the leaves began to fall again . . . And so on forever and ever . . . Amen . . .

Bordelli bent down to pick up something that had been sticking out of the ground. He cleaned it off as best he could with his fingers. It was a piece of mortar shrapnel the size of a Prato *biscottino*. At the moment of explosion, it had been incandescent and deadly, but now it was just a gnarled scrap of iron. He handed it to the colonel, who weighed it in his hand, and almost without wanting to, they began recalling the days of the war . . .

After their long walk, they ate with gusto and enjoyed their good, red wine. The colonel insisted on washing the dishes and sweeping up, and then went to his room to rest. Bordelli phoned Fabiani with an invitation for Friday's dinner.

'Wonderful to hear from you, Inspector . . . thank you for thinking of me, but tomorrow morning I leave for Viterbo. I'm spending the holidays with a dear lady friend whom I just happened to meet again.'

'You sound very happy.'

'Well done, Watson. I confess she's an old flame from my university days. I actually never stopped thinking about her, even though I always loved my wife. She, too, lost her spouse. Who knows, maybe something will blossom between us . . . I feel like a teenager with a crush, it's ridiculous . . .'

'I'm so pleased for you and I wish you a romantic and ridiculous Christmas.'

'Happy Christmas to you, too, Inspector. Give my best wishes to the others. I'm off to pack my bags.' They said goodbye. Bordelli hung up and stood there for a minute, hand resting on the telephone. He thought of Fabiani's childish joy and felt a sense of affectionate envy.

Relinquishing his thoughts of Eleonora, he went and sat in one of the armchairs by the fire to read to the delicate music playing. It was a good feeling to lose oneself in a novel; it was like living another life, like being someone else. At that moment this was exactly what Bordelli needed. He was especially happy about the fact that it had become easy for him to delay his first cigarette until after dinner; it had become a new routine. He simply needed to be careful not to give in to temptation.

He reluctantly got up a couple of times to telephone Oberto, but both times he hung up after letting it ring and ring. He needed to talk to him, it was serious, he had a number of things to ask him. By now he was convinced that the young man knew Migliorini better than anyone, but first he wanted to hear about the death of the lad's father, so that he could observe his reactions. Was it true, as Claretta said, that he felt bitterness? Bordelli continued to read on, page after page, sinking deeper and deeper into the story . . . until he fell asleep with the book in his lap, without even realising it had grown dark.

When he opened his eyes, Arcieri was standing at the stove with his back to him. The clock on the wall said almost nine. The table was set, and a lovely scent of good food filled the air.

'I must have dozed off,' Bordelli mumbled, rubbing his hands over his eyes. Arcieri turned round and faced him.

'You snore like a tractor.'

'Usually I hear that from the fair sex.'

'I took the liberty of whipping up something for dinner,' the colonel said, stirring one pot and then another.

'The smell is enticing.'

'I can't promise you a masterpiece.'

'I'm sure it will be an excellent dinner.'

'This is one of my mother's recipes; she made it often, but this is my first try.'

'I appreciate your courage,' Bordelli said, getting up from his armchair with some effort. He wanted to contribute to the dinner. He yawned, stretched, and then opened a bottle of wine and poured out two glasses. Then he cut the bread and put it on the table.

Bordelli was usually rather bearlike and loved his solitude, but Arcieri's presence did not bother him at all. On the contrary, it was rather pleasant. Perhaps it was the colonel's politeness, or his old-fashioned, gentlemanly manners. Or perhaps it was because, despite appearances, they really did have a lot in common, aside from their stories of love lost. They were far more similar than either of them expected: not in the way they faced situations, or in their relationships, so much as in sharing a certain view of the world. The fact was that in the old carabiniere's company, Bordelli never felt ill at ease, not even during their long silences.

The roulades of meat that the colonel had prepared were not

bad at all. Inside each he had put a slice of prosciutto and a leaf of sage from the garden. As a side dish, sautéed potatoes and onions.

'I hope my mother is pleased.'

'I bet she's clapping her hands . . . Do you all cook like this at SID headquarters?' Bordelli asked. The colonel smiled.

'Let me tell you about something that happened once. Just before the war we were assigned to keep an eye on a man we suspected was a British spy. We set up three agents in a flat across the street from our suspect's flat. We hid a sixteen-millimetre movie camera behind a curtain. These were the early days of hidden microphones, and we had planted some in his home. It was all terribly American, but I had wanted to give it a try. I went to check on the men twice a day, and one evening I showed up and found them cooking. One of the three agents, a Sardinian with a degree in medicine, wanted to teach the others how to make risotto with squid ink. They were arguing furiously because the youngest one, who had done the shopping, had bought cleaned squid, so there was no ink for the risotto. I almost exploded. I started shouting at them that while they were thinking about risotto and squid, the potential spy in the building across the way was doing whatever he pleased. In the end I sat down to eat an inkless squid risotto with them . . . but the Sardinian taught me the recipe for the one with ink . . .'

'A very instructive investigation,' Bordelli commented.

'The potatoes didn't come out quite the way I wanted,' the colonel said, a little upset.

'They are delicious.'

'Still, they didn't come out the way I wanted them to.'

'You can try every day until you get them right,' Bordelli said, refilling their glasses.

'I would also like to try and make vegetable soup.'

'An excellent idea . . .'

'It sounds easy, but it isn't at all. My mother's vegetable soup was the best.'

They continued to chat about this and that, avoiding going down any melancholic paths. Arcieri relaxed a little and was happy to joke around, even if he still had that worried look in his eyes. After dinner they moved over to the armchairs, bringing their glasses with them, and as usual Bordelli fed a log to the fire.

'How does Bach sound to you?'

'Any time . . .' the colonel said, eyes half closed. Bordelli went to put on a record, and gradually the room filled with music. He lit a cigarette, the first of the day. He enjoyed the reward after the long wait.

As on other occasions, they started telling old stories. But this time they were droll stories, even humorous ones. Bordelli described the embarrassing moments and ridiculous scenes he had experienced with former girlfriends, and at moments he blushed almost as badly as back then. The colonel smiled and every so often exhumed an equally amusing story. But they also sat without talking, just listening to the music.

During those evenings together they had never once turned on the television, not even to watch the news. They didn't miss it. For the news, Bordelli flipped through *La Nazione*, which he found each morning in the bread bag outside his door. At the office he would leaf through the other papers and read the headlines, but rarely read an entire article. Evenings he would bring a newspaper home to light the fire. But before he wadded them up and committed them to the flames, he would pass the papers on to Arcieri.

'What do you think of all these young people and their protests?' the colonel asked, after a long period of silence. The music had ended some time before.

'Well, it seems to me they really want to be in control,' Bordelli said with a bemused smile.

'You may be right, but I admit that reading about these things brings up some strong feelings for me. When I was their age I was not allowed to protest. But it's not just that. When I think about how this generation is fighting for their freedoms, I realise that I never allowed myself the chance to fight against the part of me that is less free . . . I'm sorry, that must sound very confusing . . .'

'I think I understand.'

'I know how difficult it is for someone my age to change, but I don't want to throw in the towel just yet. I'd like to think that a great inner revolution can happen even *in articulo mortis* . . .'

'It's important how one dies,' Bordelli said. They were entering deeper waters. It was the wine's fault. The colonel had not yet finished his argument.

'We all have such firm opinions, we defend our ideas and notions tooth and nail, but we never stop to wonder where the principles we use to read the world come from, we never wonder whether they are healthy or sane. Sometimes we convince ourselves that something is true just because it soothes our frustrations – just to defend ourselves, in other words, to survive spiritually, but the result can be disastrous . . . In fact, not infrequently, there have been thinkers and philosophers who have attempted to elevate their personal intolerances to universal laws, in perfectly good faith . . . Do you know what I mean?'

'This is where my friend Dante would come in handy . . . Actually, one evening we should go and see him. He lives nearby.'

'In a *dark wood*?' the colonel asked, alluding to Dante's *Inferno*.

'More or less . . . but in any case, he'll be at the dinner on Friday night.'

'I can't wait to meet him.'

'Dante says that man is entirely governed by his imagination,' the inspector said, and from his tone it was easy to infer that he agreed. The colonel thought about this for a minute.

'That, effectively, is an excellent synthesis of what I was trying to say,' he said with some satisfaction.

'Another drop of wine?'

'Thank you . . .' Arcieri said, looking down at his empty glass.

After that digression they went back to talking about lighter things. They talked about how difficult it was to maintain a vegetable garden, and how much attention olive trees needed. It was decided that the colonel would help prepare Friday's dinner, but under Ennio's supervision. Who was Ennio? Well, it wasn't easy to describe him in a few words. At that point, Bordelli went over the guest list, trying to give the colonel a cursory idea of who the guests were, but he realised that none of them was easy to describe . . . and then they got lost again in complicated ideas and universal concepts . . .

When Arcieri went to his room it was almost one in the morning. The inspector remembered that he had not yet confirmed the dinner with Dante, and he went to call him.

'This is wonderful news,' Dante said.

'No Christmas presents, promise me.'

'It's a full moon tonight, and Leopardi is here with me.'

'What light reading . . .'

'*What, moon, are you doing in the sky? Tell me what you are doing, silent moon.*'

'I knew that one by heart, back in secondary school.'

'Goodnight, Inspector. I can hear that you are tired . . . *Are you not yet sated with travelling the same timeless roads . . . ?*'

And, while declaiming those sublime verses, Dante hung up. Bordelli smiled, thinking of his mother's sweet, melancholic poems. He would read some before he fell asleep. Mamma versus Giacomo Leopardi . . . Sorry, Mamma, but no one measures up to Giacomo . . . But second place isn't so bad . . .

'Please don't tease me, Franchino,' his mother said, laughing.

'I was only exaggerating a little, Mamma . . .'

'Don't be silly . . . I just put my words down on paper. They're worthless.'

'No, you're wrong . . .'

He wished he could carry on like this with his mother after reading her poems. Maybe one night she would appear to him as some kind of ghost. He wished she would. That big old lonely house was perfect for ghosts . . .

He was about to go upstairs when the phone rang. In the silence it sounded like a desperate scream. He rushed over to reply, certain that it was Dante.

'*And of time's silent, endless passing . . .*' he whispered into the phone.

'What? Who is this?' It was Rosa, and her voice was trembling.

'Rosa, it's me . . . what's going on?'

'I'm scared . . . there's a noise. It's as if someone . . . hold on . . . there, I heard it again . . . you have to come over right away.'

'Tell me what you hear.'

'Shhhhh . . . Hold on . . . Don't hang up, I'll call you back.' And she hung up. Bordelli stood there with the receiver in his hand and his fingers on the base, anxious to know where the noise was coming from. He heard something and turned around. Arcieri was at the top of the stairs in his pyjamas; his face looked worried.

'Everything all right?'

'It's a friend . . . she heard a noise in her flat . . . She's going to call me right back.'

'If you need me . . .'

'Thank you.'

'Goodnight.'

'Goodnight.' Minutes passed, and still Rosa hadn't called back. Finally he decided to call her himself.

'Hello?'

'Rosa, it's me. So . . . what was it?'

'Nothing . . .' she said calmly.

'What do you mean, nothing?'

'It was nothing . . . it was Briciola . . . she had got trapped in the closet and was scratching at the door.'

'You could have called me back . . . I was waiting . . .'

'But I said it was nothing . . .'

'I understand, but how was I to . . . Oh, never mind.'

'You know that you're strange sometimes?'

'Give Briciola a kiss, and Gideon, too. Goodnight.'

'Ciao ciao,' fluttered Rosa, hanging up.

'Ciao,' Bordelli said, too late.

As he climbed the stairs to his room, he found himself wishing that he was more like Rosa, as light as a feather.

That morning the Beetle rumbled down from the hills of Impruneta a bit more noisily than usual, and instead of heading for police headquarters, it turned and made its way towards Ponte del Pino. There was less than a week to go before Christmas, but at that hour there weren't many people out in search of presents to buy.

The inspector parked at the bottom of Via Pacinotti, took a deep breath, and got out of the car. He'd finally worked up the courage to do it. Sticking a cigarette between his lips, he strolled nonchalantly past the women's clothing shop where Eleonora worked, but without turning to look inside. He played it cool, proceeding along the pavement with a pensive air. After passing the display window he stopped, hoping she would come running out . . . preferably with tears in her eyes. What a silly fantasy. And yet there he waited, fighting the temptation to light the cigarette. He bit his lip. Wouldn't it be better to grab the bull by the horns? What, after all, could really happen? At worst, she would tell him to go away . . . It wouldn't be the first time that a woman . . . But maybe it was the dream itself he didn't want to give up, like some adolescent still wanting to believe in Santa Claus. Come on, old codger . . . You're a San Marco Battalion commander . . .

He took another deep breath and went back, stopped in front of the display window with his pulse beating in his temples, and looked into the shop . . . Instead of Eleonora he saw a blond girl, busy attending to a customer. She was as shapely as Gina Lollobrigida, but like so many girls wore her hair in a Caterina Caselli bob. The inspector pretended to be highly interested in the items featured in the window and patiently waited for the customer to leave. As soon as she came out, he pushed open the door and slipped inside.

'Good morning,' said the young woman, coming up to him with a salesgirlish smile.

'Good morning . . . Sorry to bother you, but does Signorina Eleonora no longer work here?'

'I'm sorry, I don't know who you're talking about,' said the blonde, perplexed.

'I was just passing by and thought I'd . . .'

'I'm afraid I can't help you.'

'The young lady worked in this shop about a year ago.'

'I don't know what to tell you . . .'

Now she was looking at him with an ironic grin, imagining the classic old man besotted with a pretty girl.

'And how long have you been working here?'

'Why do you want to know?' asked the girl, mildly irritated.

Bordelli thought for a moment of flashing his police badge, and even telling her Eleonora had been his girlfriend, but he knew he would later regret it.

'You're right, I'm sorry . . . I didn't mean to cause any trouble . . .' He gestured an awkward bow and exited the boutique feeling like a perfect idiot. He'd made an utter fool of himself, damn it all. Best forget this ridiculous scene as quickly as possible.

Heading towards his car, he happened to pass a men's clothing store and decided the moment had come to buy something decent for Colonel Arcieri. It could not be very pleasant for him to be wearing oversized clothes. He based his choice of garments on how he remembered the colonel used to dress before becoming a vagrant, hoping to get the size right. As the salesman was filling two large shopping bags with his purchases, the inspector had to pull out his cop's badge to get the man to accept a cheque.

To complete his shopping, he slipped into a shoe store and bought the colonel a pair of shoes. Black and shiny, fit for a carabiniere.

Deep down he was almost pleased he hadn't found Eleonora. Everything remained as before, and he could therefore keep on hoping, giving his fantasies free rein. She loves me, she loves me not, she loves me, she loves me not . . .

Walking past a bar, he saw a sign in the window announcing the latest Lotto results and stopped in his tracks. He read them over several times, almost convinced he recognised at least four of the numbers. Dropping the two shopping bags, he reached for his wallet and pulled out the thousand-lira note on which he'd written down his chosen numbers. He wouldn't have won a thing, but he'd saved a thousand lire. The only number he'd got wrong was the 11, which he'd chosen because the flood had occurred in November. In its place a 2 had come out. His birthday. Picking the bags back up, he reached his car, trying to think of other things. For example, he still had to buy a little Christmas present for Rosa. But no more gifts after that, to keep life simple.

There was already a good bit of traffic on the avenues, and it took him almost half an hour to get to headquarters.

As soon as he entered his office he dialled Oberto's number. Still no answer. He called up Migliorini's sister, to ask her for news of the will.

'It's going to be opened this afternoon, at four o'clock,' said Laura.

'Who's the lawyer?'

'Busotti Santi, a close family friend.'

'I know him pretty well myself. I'll give him a ring later this afternoon.'

'Excuse me for asking, but why are you so interested in Antonio's will?' the lady asked.

'No precise reason. But it might help me understand your brother a little better.'

'Are you going to catch the killer, Inspector?'

'There is no doubt in my mind,' Bordelli lied.

'I'm hoping with all my heart . . .' said Laura, a faint quaver in her voice. Bordelli allowed her a moment to recover, then said goodbye with the required delicacy.

He tried ringing Oberto again and gave up after ten rings. Fiddling with his pen, he tried to work out what needed to be done. Amid the silence, a large fly was hovering an inch or so below the ceiling and buzzing sadly.

Why did Oberto so stubbornly refuse to say anything about his benefactor's private life? Was it out of an excess of respect or was he hiding something? His affection for Migliorini seemed sincere. But what if this impression was mistaken, and Oberto was just a good actor? Claretta seemed convinced that the boy harboured resentment against the victim . . .

Tearing a blank page from his notebook, he started writing a message: *Dear Oberto, time to stop playing games* . . . He crumpled it up and tore out another page . . . *Oberto, I am quite shocked that you* . . . This also found its way into the wastebasket. How could this be so difficult? He wasn't writing to Eleonora, after all. In the end he wrote the simplest thing that came to mind . . .

> *Hello, Oberto, I absolutely must speak with you. Come and see me at police headquarters, and if I'm not in, leave word as to how and when I might get in touch with you. If I can't get hold of you by tomorrow, I will be forced to have you officially summoned as a murder suspect. Best wishes, Inspector Bordelli*

He folded the sheet in four, wrote *For Oberto* on the outside, stuck it in his pocket, put on his coat, and left the station on foot. With all the traffic about, it was best to forget about the car; a little stroll would do him some good. Saying goodbye to Mugnai, he turned down Via San Gallo. After crossing the overcrowded centre of town, he finally came to Sant'Ambrogio.

He randomly rang one of the six nameless buzzers, and after waiting about a minute he tried ringing another, and then another . . . Only on the fifth try did the latch click open. As he was going through the door, he heard a woman's voice calling:

'Who is it?'

'I'm sorry, I've made a mistake,' Bordelli shouted, then heard a door slam rudely by way of reply.

He looked at the mailboxes. Only one lacked a name. There was no Nicolosi.

He climbed the stairs in semi-darkness, and on the first floor read the names on the doors: *Letta* . . . *Bollani* . . . He kept climbing. On the second floor there were two more doors: *Bacci* . . . *Manetti* . . . On the third floor only one of the two doors had a name tag, this one handwritten: *Cavaciocchi* . . . That left only the nameless one. He brought his ear to the door, to see if he could tell whether anybody was at home. He thought he heard some light footsteps, rather like bare feet against a hard floor. When he knocked, the footsteps stopped. He knocked again, harder this time. Nobody came to the door. Taking the note out of his pocket, he slipped it under the door, so that only one corner stuck out. He went back down the stairs, trying to make as much noise as he could, and as soon as he got to the first floor, he turned round and came back up on tiptoe. The note was gone. Putting his ear to the door and holding his breath, he clearly heard the rustling of the paper being refolded.

'Oberto . . .' he said aloud, knocking. Then he heard an ever so faint groan on the other side of the door. He knocked again.

'Open the door, Oberto. It's me, Inspector Bordelli.'

Nothing.

'Come on, would you please open the door? I know you're in there.'

Silence.

'Did you read my note? Don't force me to become unpleasant.'

He waited a bit longer, but said no more. Then he heard some bolts slide and a key turn in a lock, and he saw the door handle move. The door opened less than an inch, held back by a chain, and in the crack he saw the tender face of a very young girl.

'Oberto's not here,' she said, a bit frightened.

'Please let me in. I'm a police detective.'

He showed her his badge, to let her know he wasn't lying. The girl shut the door for a moment to unhook the chain, then opened it and took a step back. Before him appeared a tiny, enchanting creature wrapped in a light blue silk dressing gown. She had black hair, a mole on her upper lip, and her porcelain face had something oriental about it.

'Oberto's not here,' she said again, keeping one step away. She certainly wasn't a common girl; she had the manner of someone who'd grown up in comfort. Bordelli left the door ajar and looked around. The apartment was clean, with modern furnishings that must have cost more than a little.

'Are you Oberto's girlfriend?'

'Yes . . .' She was still holding the folded note.

'What's your name?'

'Emma.'

'Where is Oberto?'

'I don't know. He never tells me anything.' But she didn't seem to mind.

'Well, he should be coming home sooner or later, no?'

'But I don't know when.'

'Listen to me, Emma . . . I need to talk to Oberto as soon as possible. As soon as you see him you must tell him to get in touch with me; he'll know what it's about. If you love him you'll tell him not to be a fool . . . Do you promise me you'll do that?'

'All right . . .'

'I just want to talk to him.'

'I'll tell him . . .' Emma muttered, as though intimidated, which made her seem even prettier.

'Thank you, Emma.'

He held out her hand to say goodbye, and she stepped forward and shook it. Her fingers were small and soft, and warm as bread just out of the oven.

'Goodbye . . .'

'Ciao,' said Bordelli, half smiling. He shut the door behind him on his way out and headed down the stairs. Why was it so pleasant to see a lovely creature like that? Was it even good for one's health? He had to remember to bring up the question with Dante one of these evenings, perhaps after a few nips of grappa. It might lead to an interesting discussion on the power of nature . . .

Exiting the building, he headed towards the centre of town, dodging people on the pavement. So pretty, Oberto's girl. As he was shaking her hand, he'd almost wanted to say: *You're so pretty* . . . Emma would surely have blushed, and uttered an ever so shy *Thank you* . . . Next, as the dream continued, she would have thrown her arms around him, whispering into his ear that he, too, was very handsome . . . And at that moment Eleonora would happen to be passing by and witness the scene, breathless in her jealousy . . .

A bit the way he used to make up little stories to himself as a boy before falling asleep, such as when, cheek sunk into his pillow, he would imagine saving his mother from an evil ogre . . . Even then he knew they were just fantasies, yet letting oneself go in dreams was a serious matter. It was more or less the same with novels. You knew that it wasn't you living out the story being told, and yet . . . Who could really say that the feelings one experienced while reading weren't real?

*

Arcieri was tempted to spend another afternoon at home, reading and listening to music, but in the end he felt he needed to see the sky. Leaving the house through the back door just after lunch, he followed a barely visible footpath, heading towards the woods. It had been quite a long time since he'd last taken a solitary walk in the country, in nature. All around him, the olive-tree stumps were full of leaves.

Crossing Hare's Ditch as though crossing a border, he entered the trees with great relish. The Dark Wood . . . Maybe it was inside us, not outside. He felt he should be honest with himself, and admitted he was afraid. Not because he feared for his life – that was another matter . . . This fear was different in nature, and had to do with loneliness . . .

He smiled, thinking of all the pitched battles he'd fought in, the ambushes he'd endured, the bombs that had fallen all around him. In war the thought of losing his life was ever present in his mind, but he'd never felt the kind of fear that takes your breath away. He'd always been able to summon his courage. But his life had always been accompanied by a kind of fear . . . A fear of letting himself go, of letting his emotions get the better of him. Every time he'd succeeded in overcoming this fear, life had given him a thrashing. His biggest fear now was loneliness . . .

He advanced through the wood at a slow pace, without limping too much, as a light breeze caressed his face. The path was hard to see and became very narrow in spots. In certain places he had to step on large, moss-covered stones jutting up from the ground . . . What if he were to fall? And injure himself? He could already see the headline in *La Nazione*: OLD MAN LOST IN IMPRUNETA WOODS . . . Then, below: *Found injured in the middle of the night. After being hospitalised, he tries to hide his real identity but is quickly identified as Bruno Arcieri, retired colonel of the Carabinieri.* He couldn't let himself slip. It would be like putting an ad in the papers: *Here I am, come and get me* . . . He had to take care where he put his feet. One slow step at a time . . .

Long ago he too used to go walking alone in the woods, like Bordelli. But that was back when he lived in Milan, and it was now a distant memory . . . His father, a railway clerk, was transferred there before the Great War. At the time, the countryside began just outside the city. The landscape was quite different from the Tuscan one. The horizon was an indistinct blur that vanished across the vast plain. On clearer days, the Alps marked an unreal boundary. But Milan was too different from Florence, and he'd felt as if something had broken inside him. There were plenty of wooded areas there too, and he had come to know them in solitude. But he'd never got over having had to leave Florence. Not that he'd ever had many friends there. He'd been a loner since childhood. He hadn't played in the street like the other boys, and so he'd never developed antibodies. Always alone, even when forced to be with others, such as at school. His thoughts would wander far away, to the worlds evoked in his father's illustrated magazines and in the novels of Verne and Salgari, to visions of fabulous places . . . Wherever he was, he would flee into a world all his own. Even now, as an old man, if he were to follow his heart . . .

He saw something move in the underbrush, and stopped. At first he thought they'd found him, then was relieved to discover it was just an animal . . . A hare? No, something bigger . . . Then he saw it quite clearly. A wild boar, with, just behind it, two, three, four more . . . a whole family . . . They cantered lightly, in silence, through the bushes, as though not touching the ground. It was strange to see an animal so primitive in appearance, with a bristly coat and tusks, move so delicately, without making a sound . . . But then the reason was obvious. To survive in the woods, one had to be quiet.

He, too, would have to be quiet in order to survive. And to hide out as best he could. He had no intention of getting himself killed. First he had to find out who had liquidated the young man from the hospital, and why. He felt his stomach twist up. It was all his fault, he kept repeating to himself. He'd promised the kid he could help him, but he'd been dead wrong. In the end he'd merely stirred up a hornet's nest. How disappointing that his old acquaintances from the Secret Services . . . It just went to show that he himself no longer mattered . . . Thrown away like an old shoe . . . Someone to sacrifice, even . . .

He kept on walking, unhurried, taking care not to stumble. At moments the sun managed to shine through the branches, flecking the underbrush with light . . . It reminded him of certain

Impressionist paintings he'd seen in '38, when he was in Paris on assignment . . . Then even more remote memories came forward, resurfacing from who-knew-where . . .

His father had very nearly started beating him the evening he'd announced he no longer wanted to continue grammar school. He couldn't believe it . . . A diploma wasn't some luxury item for the rich, as it had been in his day – he shouted – and even if it required sacrifice . . . In short, he couldn't understand how on earth his son, at age sixteen, would rather look for a menial job than study . . . But that same hard-headed son had actually gone through with it, driven by a desire for independence. He became an apprentice in a factory on the far outskirts of the city, beyond the canals, at Lambrate. There they were building the first Fiat lorries, the 18 BL, which had been through the Great War, and which the Fascists would later use for their 'punitive expeditions'.

His father was deeply disappointed and refused to speak to him at meals. His mother, on the other hand, coddled him and tried to defend him. Every so often she would break into tears. Bruno continued to follow his own path. But life at the factory was hard and eventually wore him out, and finally the day came when he was forced to admit defeat. He resigned, as he put it, with his tail between his legs. His father slapped him, reminding him that his stubbornness had cost him two years of schooling. Still, as soon it as it was possible, he wasted no time re-enrolling him at the grammar school, then at secondary school – indeed, at the Liceo Cesare Beccaria, frequented by the scions of the cosseted bourgeoisie, who made him feel uncomfortable. This was in 1918, the same year in which he met his first girlfriend, Antonietta. A very pretty, sweet girl, she believed in her Bruno to the point of surrendering herself entirely to him, a rather rare thing in those days. He, for his part, had not been entirely sincere. He had known from the start that their relationship would not last. He liked Antonietta, of course, but there was something which . . . In brief, he left her after just a few months, even while tormenting himself with guilt feelings. He had never been quite honest with her, and this ate away at him, along with so many other things. He who claimed he'd always behaved like a gentleman and never stooped to compromise himself with anyone, not even himself . . . Who knew where Antonietta was now, whether she was even still alive . . . Had she lived a happy life? Had she found a man to love her?

He, for his part, had met Elena Contini, the great love of his life . . . But she certainly hadn't been his only woman. He just didn't always fall in love. Sometimes he'd gone along with a situation just to have a little company, out of the plain and natural need to enter a woman's body. To avoid, in the final analysis, having to resort to bordellos . . .

There were other times, too, when he hadn't given his best, so to speak, and not only with women. As a Carabinieri officer in '33 he'd fabricated false evidence to help convict a man, a frail fifty-year-old who seemed like an honest man but was in reality a sordid character, a molester of little girls. And though the man was rather clumsy about it, he always managed to get off scot free. He was very clever, and whenever they found him alone with a little girl, he would start shouting that the maniac had just run off and he was trying to console the child. His harmless appearance fooled everyone. But Arcieri eventually found out that the maniac was none other than him, that same soft-spoken man. An informer for the Carabinieri had told him in the midst of talking about something else. At any rate, to entrap the pervert, Arcieri had planted a goodly amount of cocaine and a stolen handgun in the squalid hole in which the man lived. He received anything but a light sentence. At the time, certain weaknesses cost very dearly in the eyes of the law. The man ended up in San Vittore prison, amidst the veterans of the Milanese underworld. Arcieri had always heard that in prison everyone always came to know everything, even the most hidden things, and he had his proof on that occasion. After just one week at San Vittore, the man was found hanged from the bars of the bathroom, completely naked, sloppily emasculated with who-knew-what instruments. Nobody knew who had done it, of course, not even the warders . . .

The path now went uphill and was full of rocks and grooves carved out by the rains. He proceeded slowly, feeling slightly short of breath. It was best to turn back before it got dark. He just wanted to get to the top of the slope, to conquer the summit. He felt his heart racing, even in his temples . . . How many compromises had he stooped to, anyway, in his life? How many mistakes had he made because he took things too lightly? Right after the end of the war, in '45, he'd allowed a young man to be shot. A Fascist, of course, and friend of the Nazis. Twenty years old. He was called Gianfalco, a name impossible to forget. But he couldn't have been any worse than so many others of his ilk . . . Like certain *repubblichini*[20] who barely a year or two after the war had resumed their positions in various police departments and government offices around the country . . . To say nothing of those who actually entered politics . . . What was the name of that French writer who was put on trial and then shot for collaborating? Brasillach . . . Robert Brasillach . . . De Gaulle himself had denied him clemency. But there were so many like him, also in Italy . . . Writers, film-makers, actors who, despite their past, now went about their lives undisturbed. That twenty-year-old boy, in other words, did not deserve to die. It made no sense. But Arcieri hadn't lifted a finger, hadn't tried to stop that ragtag firing squad . . .

Reaching the top of the slope, he stopped for a few seconds to look at the horizon. Sunset was fast approaching. He had better head back. He could have walked for many hours more, recalling his most painful memories, summoning past faults back to the surface. He had never been so honest with himself before, so ruthless. But it pleased him in the end; he saw it as a kind of redemption.

Daylight was fading, and he quickened his pace, hoping to stay a step ahead of the darkness. The forest had set his memory going, and as he wandered through the fog of the past he relived the moments of his fall through the air at the Sant'Anna bend. He'd been airborne for several seconds, and his feeling was almost one of relief. When he reawakened in a hospital bed, all banged up, he wasn't exactly happy still to be alive. He felt like a man at the end of his rope, and not only because of the accident. He'd seen every sort of horror imaginable and could no longer stand to exist amidst such iniquities. Life had not been terribly kind to him. When young, people are incapable of understanding just how tired the elderly can feel at times, no longer wanting to go on. At times he even resented Elena, who looked after him so lovingly in his sickbed, even though having her there beside him was the most wonderful thing he could possibly wish for. Then fate, too, had intervened, introducing him to that frightened young man and giving him one last matter to take care of . . .

He felt a cold chill run through his body. Darkness was encroaching fast, and the temperature had fallen. But he couldn't be very far now from the ditch. He could no longer really see the path, and the trees seemed to come alive in the twilight. It was like being in an enchanted forest in a fairy tale, one peopled by witches and ghosts, and every rustle in the underbrush made him start . . . He remembered when his mother used to read him fairy stories to make him fall asleep. When he was sick with a fever, those adventures would come alive in his bedroom . . . It was fantastic, but also scary . . .

Reaching the ditch, he strode over it with relief. Coming out of the wood, he found a glimmer of remaining daylight and headed calmly up towards the olive grove. In the faint glow of sunset, he saw Bordelli's great farmhouse looming ahead, with the tips of the cypresses jutting above the roof. Arcieri smiled, thinking that it felt as if he were 'heading home'. Some good music and a novel to read by the fire . . . For how long could this peaceful life last? For how much longer could he take advantage of the inspector's hospitality? But he mustn't feel guilty. He was only trying to recover his strength before heading off again . . .

The afternoon seemed endless. A week had already passed since the murder, and he hadn't taken one step forward in the investigation. He sat there ruminating, trying to come up with some detail that would set him on the right path, doodling on a piece of paper all the while. Would Emma manage to persuade Oberto? What on earth was the young man trying to hide? He truly wanted to find out. It might not lead anywhere, but Bordelli needed to explore all options and he couldn't have any doubts.

As usual, he had lunched at Totò's restaurant but this time had managed not to stuff himself. Also as usual, the cook had fed him a string of gory stories from his town in the Salento. He told them well and with pleasure, all the while tending to the pots and skillets on the cooker. Here was another matter to discuss with Dante, he thought, over a good grappa: why did people love to talk about misfortune so much?

The phone rang, making him jump. Before answering he wadded up the paper he was doodling on and threw it away. It was Rosa, all excited.

'Try and guess . . .'

'I don't know . . . you won the lottery?' Bordelli asked, happy for the distraction.

'Ha! The lottery!'

'You're getting married?'

'Sure . . . to the pope!'

'Tell me, I give up.'

'I simply can't understand why they chose you to be chief inspector . . . Write down this phone number . . .' She couldn't wait to tell him.

'Yes, ma'am,' Bordelli said, picking up a pen. He wrote down the number on his pad. It started with 57, the exchange for Campo di Marte.

'Her name is Juliette . . . and guess what? The man who was killed was one of her clients!'

'Ah! You managed to find her . . . Thank you.'

'You're welcome. Now you owe me dinner at a restaurant.'

'Fair enough.'

'And if you arrest the killer thanks to me, you have to take me to Paris,' she said smugly.

'What? You mean you wouldn't be happy with just the bliss of a selfless gesture?'

'I'd rather go to Paris.'

'Why don't you go with your friend from the other evening?' Bordelli queried, eager to investigate.

'Which friend? Oh, that guy, you mean? Oh, please . . . I wouldn't even go to Compiobbi with him.'

'And yet the other evening it sounded like you had an enjoyable time together.'

'Well, you should know that I certainly didn't go to bed with him . . .'

'There's no law that says you have to tell me even if you did.'

'He's just a friend, an old client from the Villa days. We had some good laughs.'

'I noticed.'

'Be careful with Juliette. She's a first-class hooker.'

'I'll try not to pick my nose.'

'And brush your teeth before you go; you never know,' Rosa said with a giggle.

'Is Juliette French?'

'No, no, she's from Grosseto . . . Her real name is probably Giulia.'

'When should I ring her?'

'You can ring her right now, I just spoke to her. She's expecting your call. Prepare yourself: she has a lovely voice.'

'I'll call her right away.'

'You're not going to fall in love with her, are you? They say she's very beautiful.'

'I'll have to run that risk.'

'You like them all, anyway. Ciao, Monkey . . . and remember Paris.'

Rosa hung up brusquely, in her usual manner. The inspector smiled and immediately dialled Juliette's number.

'Hello . . .' It was true. She had a charming voice.

'Good evening, may I please speak to Signorina Juliette?'

'Speaking . . .'

'This is Inspector Bordelli, Rosa Stracuzzi's friend.'

'Yes, she called me a little while ago . . . How can I help you, Inspector?'

'Would it be possible to meet?'

'Well, actually, I am free today,' Juliette said in her warm, soft way.

'Would you be willing to meet with me now?'

'Yes, if you would like that . . .'

'Where can we meet?'

'Would you be willing to come to my apartment?'

'As you wish.'

'Via Baldesi 12/bis, fifth floor. I'll be waiting for you.'

'I'm on my way.'

'See you shortly, Inspector.' She hung up the phone ever so delicately.

Bordelli put on his coat and walked out into the courtyard. It was growing dark. He climbed into the Beetle and drove out of headquarters. The traffic in Piazza San Gallo was heavy and moved at a snail's pace. Once he got beyond it, he turned into Viale Don Minzoni. After the flyover at Le Cure, the traffic flowed a little more easily, and in a few minutes he turned onto Via Baldesi.

Looking up at the building numbers, he drove along until he reached the intersection with Via Cocchi. Number 12/bis was a large, late nineteenth-century building wedged between two other buildings of the same era. He parked outside the entrance and got out. It was dark now and he had to light a match to read the names on the doorbells. On the top right he saw her name: *Juliette*. He rang and a few seconds later heard the click of the door lock being released. He eschewed the elevator and climbed the stairs with a mountaineering spirit.

He reached the fifth floor without too much effort. She had left the door ajar. He knocked lightly and heard the sound of heels coming slowly towards him. Juliette appeared: she was wearing a tight, cream-coloured dress that had a black motif at the waist and a plunging neckline. She was truly beautiful, as well as elegant.

'That was fast,' she said, with a movie-star smile. She was like a statue of Venus. Her eyes were intensely green, and her long brown hair was gathered in a bun at the nape of her neck in a seemingly casual manner.

'Good evening,' Bordelli said awkwardly. Beauty always made him feel terribly embarrassed.

'Please, come in . . . sorry about the mess,' she said, closing the door behind him and turning down the hallway. The inspector followed her, admiring her elegant movements, which was to say her magnificent derrière and her call-of-the-forest legs. He wondered what 'mess' she was referring to . . . that book resting on the elegant table? Or the scarf? Even the lighting had been chosen with care. He wondered what Juliette would say if she saw his house in the country . . .

They walked into a cosy yet discreet sitting room decorated with modern furnishings. Three identical sofas arranged around a low glass table, a bookcase full of books, abstract paintings on the walls. From various corners of the room a soft light glowed from unusually shaped lamps. In the warm air he could smell Juliette's perfume; she was one who would never over-scent herself.

'Do take off your overcoat,' she ordered him gently.

'Thank you.' It was indeed quite warm, and he removed his coat with some relief. Juliette took it from him and rested it carefully on the back of an armchair.

'Please . . .' she said, inviting him to take a seat. The inspector relaxed into one of the sofas, wondering whether this was how she always welcomed her clients.

'You have a beautiful home . . .'

'May I offer you something to drink?' Juliette asked, still standing.

'I wouldn't want to bother you.'

'A cup of tea? Or would you prefer a glass of white wine?'

'Whatever you have is fine for me.'

'One minute, I'll be right back,' Juliette said, leaving the room with a delicate step.

The inspector looked around. He had never been in such a dwelling, and yet he felt entirely at ease. It was surely due in part to the pleasant, discreet lighting. On the wall next to the bookcase hung a reproduction of an odd painting consisting of splotches and squiggles, and it wasn't bad at all. A bronze nude stood on a clear pedestal, a hand behind her neck. A large, dark Persian carpet filled the centre of the room.

Juliette came back with a silver tray that she set down on the table: a bottle of white wine from the Trentino, a small dish with some savoury bites, two glasses, and a corkscrew.

'When there's a man around, it's up to him to open the bottle,' she said, sitting down across from Bordelli on one of the other sofas.

'At your command,' stuttered Bordelli, getting to work. While fussing with the bottle he tried not to look at Juliette's crossed legs, but it was impossible. One heel dangled in the air, and her skirt rode up a little too high.

He opened the wine and poured two glasses, offering one to Juliette. They had a sip, and she smiled. She had perfect teeth, with a charming gap between the two front ones. Her soft lips seemed created for kissing . . .

'I'm all yours, Inspector.'

'What? Yes, of course. Well . . . I simply wanted to ask you a few questions about Antonio Migliorini . . .'

'Poor Antonio, I was so saddened by his death.'

'Did you know him well?'

'He was one of my clients, but we were also friends.'

'Can you tell me a little about him?'

'What would you like to know?'

'Whatever comes to mind.' He was in no hurry.

'Oh, he was a fascinating man . . . on the evenings we met he would come and pick me up and we'd go to a lovely restaurant somewhere outside the city. He so enjoyed flirting with me during the meal. It was delightful. In his company I would forget what boredom was, and I assure you that in my profession it doesn't happen very often. We would talk about art and literature, he would tell me about his trips abroad or his children, how well they ran the factory, and almost every time we were together he also talked about his wife, who died ten years ago.'

'Yes, I heard . . .' mumbled Bordelli.

'After dinner we'd go back to his villa. We'd sit in the living room for an after-dinner drink, and keep talking . . . but not for long. At some point, Antonio would come over to me and kiss me. You can imagine the rest. I can only add that getting paid for those nights almost seemed like theft. We were like two adolescents in love. When he took me home in the morning, we'd kiss goodbye on the lips and go back to our separate worlds. We never talked about money but Antonio always managed to sneak an envelope into my bag with his gift . . . he was a true gentleman.'

Juliette was visibly moved, and to keep from crying she took a small sip of wine. Her teary eyes made her even more beautiful.

Bordelli sat in silence, out of respect. He found her fascinating. Looking at her legs, he tried to imagine what it would be like to spend the night with her. She was unquestionably intelligent, elegant, ironic, and worthy of being with a man like Migliorini. He was certain that, even in intimate moments, she was quite special.

'Did you see him often?'

'More or less once a month, but it wasn't fixed. When I read the news in the paper it had been some time since we'd seen each other.'

'When was the last time?'

'I think it was in the middle of October.'

'Did Migliorini ever talk about his love affairs?'

'Never. The only other woman he spoke about was his wife.'

'Did he ever mention whether he had any enemies, or anyone who might have been angry with him?'

'No . . .'

'Did you ever bump into anyone at the villa?'

'No, not really . . . once in a while I saw Oberto, the gardener . . . a nice-looking, dark-haired lad.'

'Yes, I've met him,' Bordelli said.

'I would sometimes chat with him. So intelligent. Antonio talked about him a lot.'

'What did he say?'

'He liked him very much, and he made sure that Oberto never wanted for anything . . . it's a long story . . .'

'Are you referring to the death of Oberto's father?'

'Yes, the accident . . . so you know?'

'Yes, I've been told.'

'Antonio never stopped feeling guilty about it, though there was no reason.'

'Did he ever mention whether he thought Oberto might harbour some bitterness towards him because of his father?'

'No, he trusted that boy entirely. And, for what it's worth, I never noticed any kind of bitterness myself. And I know a thing or two about men.'

'I imagine you do,' the inspector said a little awkwardly.

'Not only in that sense, believe me,' she said, seriously. Bordelli quickly changed the subject.

'Have you given any thought to who might have killed him?'

'I didn't know much about his private life. And yet, I believe it must have been a woman.'

'Why do you think that?'

'I just feel it,' Juliette said with conviction.

'Forgive the question – for now it's just a formality – but where were you on the night of the murder?' the inspector asked, in the tone of someone asking for directions. Juliette smiled.

'Are you asking whether I did it?'

'At this point I can't rule anyone out.'

'So it's just a tasteful way of saying you don't know which way to turn?' Juliette queried.

'A person's choice of words is very important,' mumbled Bordelli.

'Even more than the look in their eyes?' Juliette asked with feigned naivety, looking him straight in the eye.

'Perhaps not . . .' Bordelli felt himself blush. He didn't want to play games with her; he knew he could never compete. Juliette set her empty glass down on the crystal table to indicate that she wanted more wine, and Bordelli served her.

'Thank you . . .'

'You still haven't told me where you were on the night of the murder.'

'You're right, how silly. I was here at home with a client, but don't ask me who. It would be like asking a priest to tell you the sins of people whose confession he'd heard.'

'I understand.'

'Can I help you with anything else, Inspector?'

'For now, I would have to say no . . . Thank you for your patience,' Bordelli said. He took one last sip of wine and stood up, feeling a little sad to be leaving. It was like finishing a good book. Juliette accompanied him to the door and on the threshold shook his hand.

'I'm sorry I couldn't be of more help to you,' she said, with surprising sweetness. Her green eyes were somewhat dreamy, and she smelled of wheat fields in the sun, which made him want to bite her. Bordelli took a deep breath. It was now or never . . .

'Would you give me the pleasure of joining me for dinner?' he mumbled in an old-fashioned way, not knowing where to look. Juliette let him stew for a second and then, with an almost maternal smile, replied:

'Is half past eight all right?'

'Perfect,' the inspector said in great embarrassment. With a hint of a bow he left, his ears on fire. As he descended the stairs he wondered how he had managed to let the situation get so out of hand. Perhaps he just needed to spend some time in the company of a pretty woman, as a kind of pick-me-up. It was all Eleonora's fault. He climbed into the car and backed out of the space. He hoped that Juliette didn't get the wrong idea. It was only an invitation to dinner. There would be no sequel. He had never paid for that kind of thing, and he certainly wasn't going to start now.

Entering his office, he started pacing back and forth, thinking of Juliette. He'd invited her out to dinner, and she'd accepted. There were another two hours and more to go before their rendezvous. He stopped in front of the window, to look at his reflection in the glass. He didn't see himself as being so old, really. Dante, in short, was right: imagination ruled the world . . .

Suddenly remembering the will, he quickly phoned Busotti Santi, the solicitor. After exchanging greetings, he asked him for news on Migliorini's last will and testament, which became a public document after it had been read to the next of kin. The lawyer said there were more than a few surprises in it. A number of properties and large sums of money had been left to people outside the family.

'These heirs know nothing about it yet, because it wasn't indicated on the envelope of the will that they should be summoned for the reading. I'll seek them out tomorrow morning.'

'Could you please tell me their names?' asked Bordelli, pen in hand.

'Please wait while I get the file . . . Here were are . . . So . . . Amalia Colosi, Averardo Butelli, Giuliana Lorenzi, Nilva Nicolosi née Iacopozzi, Oberto Nicolosi . . . And that's it.'

'What did he leave to Oberto Nicolosi?'

'An apartment in Via dei Macci, a commercial space in Via Calzaioli, another apartment in Piazza del Cestello, twelve million in Treasury bonds . . .'

'He's become a rich man,' the inspector interjected.

'The others, too, as far as that goes.'

'Could you please do me a favour and make me a copy of the will? I just need to know the names and the bequests, of the family members as well.'

'How soon do you need it?'

'As soon as possible.'

'Would late tomorrow afternoon be all right?'

'That would be fine, thanks. Shall I send one of my men to your office round about seven to pick it up?'

'Perfect.'

They said goodbye, and Bordelli made a call on the internal line, asking for Piras. While waiting he reread the names of the lucky beneficiaries, which he'd written down. Two of them he'd never heard of before: Averardo Butelli and Giuliana Lorenzi. So he had two new people to talk to. Unless Giuliana was . . . Juliette. It wouldn't be hard to find out, that evening at dinner. As long as she kept her promise to go out with the inspector, that is.

There was a knock at the door, which then opened. It was Piras. Bordelli gestured to him to have a seat, then told him what he had in mind. It was a delicate task, one which might prove rather difficult.

'I want you to go and question Antonio's relatives and friends again, and ask them all where they were on the night of the murder. If anyone gets offended, just tell them you're following my orders.'

'Okay,' said the Sardinian, not batting an eye.

'Observe their reactions closely. I'm very interested to know them, too. But forget about Olinto Marinari, who was out of the country at the time. And don't bother with Oberto, either. I'll handle him myself,' the inspector concluded, as though thinking aloud.

'All right, then . . . Signora Laura Borrani, Antonio Migliorini's sons—'

'Talk to their wives, too.'

'Yes, I was thinking the same thing . . . Then there's Gilberto Giordanelli, Amalia Colosi, and Claretta Biagiotti . . .'

'Leave Claretta to me too,' said Bordelli, without explaining. It might be a good pretext for seeing her again, or at least talking to her. He couldn't hide from himself the fact that he liked her.

'All right,' Piras muttered, squeezing his chin between two fingers. Whenever he did that, it meant he felt discouraged.

'I'm also looking for a certain Averardo Butelli,' the inspector said, avoiding any mention of Giuliana Lorenzi.

'And who's he?' asked Piras, a little surprised.

'I don't know, at least not yet.'

The inspector told him about Migliorini's will and the beneficiaries outside the family.

'Generous man . . .' was the Sardinian's comment.

'Tomorrow evening I want you to drop in at the office of Busotti Santi, the probate lawyer, in Via del Corso. He'll give you a summary transcription of Migliorini's will. It may prove completely useless, but given the point we're at . . .'

'Something will turn up sooner or later.'

'I certainly hope so . . . Try and check everyone's alibi by tomorrow evening. I think we'll need to work by process of elimination. So far we haven't come up with anything.'

'I'm almost certain it was not premeditated murder,' said Piras, almost as a kind of encouragement.

'I'm also convinced it wasn't, but that doesn't get us very far, does it?' Bordelli sighed, looking at his watch. It was only 6.35. There was still a long time to go before dinner . . .

'I talked to my dad yesterday by phone, and he told me to send you his regards.'

'Thanks . . . How's Gavino doing?'

'Not bad. He also told me to ask you when you were coming to visit him in Bonarcado.'

'He's right, I really should go and see him one of these days. Your father is the only San Marco comrade I've kept in touch with.'

'Have you ever thought of writing your war memoirs?' asked Piras.

'Who on earth would be interested in that? Maybe four old codgers like myself who still can't stop thinking about what happened?'

'Sooner or later, "what happened" will be forgotten, if nobody writes it down.'

'Italians have short memories, there's nothing we can do about that.'

'Well, *I* would read a book like that,' said Piras, standing up.

'With the four old codgers, that makes five.'

'I'm going out to look for a present for Sonia . . .'

'What do you want to get her?'

'I don't know yet.'

'You up to entering the fray?'

'It'll only get worse in the coming days.'

'That's for sure . . . See you tomorrow, Piras.'

'Have a good evening, Inspector.'

The young man left the room, delicately closing the door behind him. Bordelli looked at his watch again, thinking of Juliette. Six thirty-nine.

He tried ringing Claretta, but her housekeeper said she wasn't at home and didn't know whether she would be coming home for dinner.

'When might I find her in?'

'Try again tomorrow, late morning.'

'Thank you so much . . .'

He hung up and ran his fingers over his eyes slowly, as though wanting to forget everything. There was still an eternity before his rendezvous with Juliette. Perhaps he should follow Piras's example and use the time to look for a present for Rosa. After all, the Migliorini case wasn't going to move forward even one millimetre that evening . . .

He put on his overcoat, descended the stairs and exited the station through a door that came out in Via San Gallo, under the arcade. As he approached the centre of town, the crowds grew denser and denser. In Via Ginori you could barely walk, and cars had trouble getting through. Bordelli merely ogled the pretty women of all ages, and tried to sniff their perfume amid the crowd.

Meanwhile he eyed the shop windows, trying to come up with an idea . . . Clothes . . . Shoes . . . Perfumes . . . Hairpins . . . Scarves . . . Never mind. He would never find the right thing amidst all the chaos, not even by a miracle . . . Chocolates . . . Rings . . . Miraculous skillets . . . What the hell . . . Nothing seemed right . . .

Finally, in the display window of a trinkets shop, he saw it. He'd found Rosa's present. It was sitting on a glass shelf, next to a Christmas-tree ornament . . . It was a funny little painted terracotta pig, with a slot on its back revealing its function as a piggy-bank. He entered the crowded store and steeled himself to await his turn, checking his watch. At last, after some thirty minutes, a salesgirl was able to fulfil his request, whereupon she carefully wrapped the little pig. It wasn't exactly cheap, in the end.

Now it was almost eight o'clock. He headed back towards the station with the present under his arm, taking some less busy streets to get there sooner. Giving Rosa that piggy-bank was not an invitation for her to save her money. It was, rather, a sort of medal for valour. Rosa had acted like the ant in the fable, and after years of hard work in the soft beds of bordellos she had bought herself a little flat overlooking the rooftops in Via dei Neri. She would never have taken to the streets, to compete with the breathtaking girls of twenty.

It was already ten past eight when he entered the courtyard at police headquarters. He promptly climbed into his Beetle and headed into the inferno of downtown traffic, hoping not to be late.

Creeping forward at five kilometres an hour, he was wondering where he should take the beautiful Juliette to dinner. To a posh restaurant or a simple trattoria? In town, maybe even in the centre? Or up in the hills, as Migliorini liked to do? He would play it by ear. It would also depend on how she was dressed.

He felt excited, there was no denying it. And maybe even a little worried. How would he feel, beside a woman like that? Like a bold youth or an old codger? He had to make her understand this was only an invitation to dinner. He couldn't see himself taking out a banknote for fifty thousand lire for a night of lovemaking.

At nineteen minutes past eight, he was still on the flyover at Le Cure, amidst clouds of exhaust smoke. He was hoping Juliette didn't stand him up. It would be just too depressing to go home with his tail between his legs.

'Bloody hell . . .' he muttered to himself. He had forgotten to tell Arcieri not to expect him home for dinner, and now it was too late. But in the end it was nothing serious. The colonel knew well that a law-enforcement officer did not have regular working hours. The biggest problem, at the moment, was something else entirely. To wit: where was he going to take Juliette for dinner? He suddenly imagined Eleonora walking into the same restaurant . . . Would she become jealous? Or would she just smile at him with unconcern? Actually in such a circumstance she would surely come accompanied, and he, for his part, would die of jealousy. In his fantasies he began to imagine unreal scenes . . . The two women scratching each other's faces and tearing out each other's hair over him, before the terrified eyes of Eleonora's beau . . . How silly, he thought, all the while continuing his game . . .

Traffic flowed a little better in Via Marconi, and by 8.29 he was pulling up outside Juliette's front door. Remaining seated in his Beetle, he began to count the seconds. At half past eight, it occurred to him it might seem inelegant to arrive perfectly punctual. So he started up the car and quickly turned right. There were no shops on that street, and very few cars. Proceeding slowly, he came to Piazza Fardella, biting his lip with impatience . . . What if she didn't come to the door?

He turned round, going back by way of Via Cento Stelle, and when he pulled up again outside Juliette's front door, it was 8.37. Taking a deep breath, he got out of the car. He hesitated for a few moments longer in front of the doorbell, then finally made up his mind and pressed it. In the building next door, he could hear a small child crying on the ground floor . . . How old could it be? Three, four years? It wouldn't be his age until about 2020 . . .

The seconds went by, and nothing happened. Should he ring again? No, it was better to wait. Eight thirty-nine. By now he was convinced Juliette wouldn't come. He felt older than ever, not to mention ugly and silly. He'd walked into the trap like a little boy, and there he was, outside in the cold, waiting for a woman who . . .

At that moment he thought he heard some footsteps inside the building. The front door opened, and Juliette appeared, a smile on her lips.

'Please don't say women are always late.'

She was wearing a short camel-hair coat gathered at the waist by a belt, and small boots with low heels. A real lady.

They got into the car and drove off. Bordelli excused himself for not owning a Porsche, imagining the luxury cars her clients must have. She, on the other hand, seemed to enjoy riding in that little German tank, which backfired every so often. The inspector felt light headed, and even handsome, truth be told. This hadn't happened for a long time.

'Would you rather stay in town, or shall we try our luck in the hills?'

'I imagine Juliette is not your real name . . .' the inspector said, pouring her a little more wine. She smiled but did not reply. Her turquoise dress had a neckline that was difficult to ignore. She was a very elegant lady; you could tell from her table manners. If someone had placed two books under her arms they wouldn't have fallen. He wouldn't have managed to hold even two dictionaries.

They had gone to a restaurant of her choice on Via Bolognese. They had to wait for half an hour before being seated but had chatted amicably, and time passed quickly.

Their table was positioned in front of a large window that looked out over the valley. In the distance were the lights of Florence. The food was excellent, the waiter was polite but not obsequious, and the wine that Juliette had chosen was truly excellent. Bordelli realised that people were staring at them, doubtlessly wondering what such a pretty girl was doing with an old man like him, and imagining the most vulgar motivations. Men were envious and the women tried to hide their jealousy. It was fun – he felt like Sean Connery in a 007 film. He was in a good mood and not even the thought of Eleonora could ruin his evening.

'If your name is Giuliana Lorenzi, I have a surprise for you.'

'Have you been investigating me? Yes, that's my name,' Juliette replied, amused.

'Then I can tell you: Migliorini named you as one of his heirs.'

'Don't be silly . . .' She was in shock, hands frozen over her plate, fork and knife in hand.

'It's true. The lawyer will be getting in touch with you tomorrow morning.'

'It all seems so . . . I don't know . . .'

'As far as I can tell, he left you quite a fortune.'

'That's absurd.' She still couldn't believe him.

'You'll have to accept it. In addition to being beautiful, I am afraid you will also be very rich.'

'Right now I am just confused,' Juliette said, going back to cutting her fillet of beef.

'May I ask you an indiscreet question?'

'Please do, I'm used to them.'

'Why did a woman like you choose this line of work?'

'If I don't reply will you be offended?'

'Fine, forget I mentioned it.'

'What do you mean by "a woman like me"?'

'I'm sure you understand what I mean.'

'I just wanted to give you an opportunity to list my qualities,' Juliette said with a smile.

'I would only be saying things you've probably already heard a thousand times.'

'Oh, but really, I don't think I'm all that pretty.'

'I may end up getting offended after all . . .'

'Why on earth would you get offended?'

'You're saying I don't understand what beauty is.'

'Or that you're a liar.'

'All right, then, I'll tell you: you're ugly, inelegant, unfriendly, and not at all intelligent,' Bordelli declared, eating her up with his eyes.

'You forgot the most important thing . . . I am a hooker,' whispered Juliette.

'No, that's just your job,' the inspector said, with more sincerity than ever. She looked at him with some surprise.

'You're not trying to make me fall in love with you?'

'Would I even stand a chance?'

'Who knows . . .'

'We'll need another bottle,' Bordelli said, pouring the last bit of wine into Juliette's glass.

'Your wisdom is comforting . . .' They continued teasing each other, ever more confidently. They didn't talk any further about Migliorini's will, as if it had already been forgotten.

For dessert, Juliette ordered chocolate cake, and the inspector kept her company with a glass of *vin santo*, one of the best he had ever tasted. Or perhaps it was those green eyes that made everything seem so special.

'Pardon me . . .' Bordelli said, getting up to go to the loo. After he'd finished, he looked at himself in the mirror. He didn't look so bad, really, despite the wrinkles. Was that because of Juliette? She was a fantastic woman, and would be hard to forget. Migliorini had chosen well. An evening with her was good for one's health. He shook his head and thought about kissing her. Just one kiss, to have something to remember, so he could dream that he had been loved by a woman like that. He walked out of the toilet like a cowboy, and when he sat down he saw a small silver plate on the table with the bill and some change.

'You didn't . . .'

'I'm an heiress now, am I not?'

'But *I* invited you to dinner,' Bordelli protested. This had never happened to him before, and he felt terribly flattered.

'I like being naughty,' Juliette said.

'You're not trying to make me fall in love with you, are you?'

'Would I even stand a chance?'

'Who knows . . .' Bordelli got up to retrieve their coats. The last guests in the restaurant had surely seen that Juliette had paid the bill, and they must have been a little surprised. The inspector motioned for his lady to lead the way, and he crossed the room as if walking on air. It took so very little to give meaning back to life . . .

They climbed into the Beetle and headed down towards Florence without saying a word. It was a pleasant silence, highly suggestive. The inspector drove slowly, wishing they might never get there. But actually time passed faster than usual, and in the blink of an eye they were in front of Juliette's building. He accompanied her to the door, and when they said goodbye she leaned in for a kiss, her mouth slightly open. They kissed without embracing, a long, delicate kiss that tasted of chocolate and wine.

'Farewell, Inspector . . .'

'Sweet dreams.'

'In another life, things might have been different,' said Juliette, and after one last smile she disappeared into the building. Bordelli stood there listening to the sweet clicking of her heels as she receded towards the far end of the lobby, the metallic sound of the closing door of the elevator, and then silence. He thought he could still smell her perfume in the air. How was it possible not to feel sad after a farewell like that?

He got into the car and headed down the dark street, which was poorly lit by a few old street lamps. It was ten minutes to midnight. 'Farewell' was the right word, as Juliette had said. They would never see each other again, if not by chance. She certainly hadn't killed Migliorini, of this he was certain. What motive would she have had? Why would she want to steal a jewellery case? No, he couldn't see her doing it. Jealousy? It would have been odd. But Juliette's gaze was clear and untroubled. Her beautiful green eyes expressed her sincere affection for Migliorini. And he had certainly felt the same way, as he had named her as one of his inheritors.

It was Tuesday, and there weren't many people out. Crossing Ponte San Niccolò he turned to look at the level of the Arno, the way everyone did. It was like a sleeping monster, lying there, quietly breathing. Turning onto Viale dei Colli, he gripped the steering wheel with his knees and lit the first cigarette of the day. It was far better than the twentieth could ever have been, or even the second, for that matter. He opened the window vent to let the smoke out. He kept on thinking of Juliette, but he would have much preferred forgetting her.

He took the Arcetri short cut, past Poggio Imperiale school and on down towards San Felice a Ema. The road was deserted. The Beetle started climbing the Imprunetana hill with its calm rumble, advancing like a horse returning to its stall.

At Mezzomonte he turned, as always, to look at Dante's villa, with its crenellated tower visible behind a row of cypress trees. One day he would go and visit Dante with the colonel, maybe after Christmas.

He turned towards the village and then continued on towards home, crossing paths with no one. He might not have made much progress in the investigation, but at least he had spent a pleasant evening. He drove up the dirt road to the threshing floor in front of the house. He left Rosa's little pig in the glove compartment and got out of the car, taking with him the two big bags full of new clothes for Arcieri. It was colder there than in the city, by at least five degrees. He hoped it would snow at Christmas, so the countryside would turn all white. While he was fumbling around for the keys, he looked up at the big, bright moon, and thought about how it observed the destiny of men with indifference. *Such, unblemished moon, is the mortal condition. / But mortal you're not, and to my few words indifferent.*

He walked in, trying to make as little noise as possible. Only silent, wise Jeremiah was in the kitchen. Everything was in perfect order, the floor had been swept, and there was not even one dirty plate in the sink. He went into the living room and placed the shopping bags on the floor next to the sofa. When he went back to the kitchen he saw a handwritten note: '*Tonight at eleven o'clock the phone rang for a long time. As you can imagine, I didn't answer. Goodnight.*' Who had called? Ennio? Piras? Or maybe Rosa? What if it had been Eleonora? Of course, to tell him that she couldn't live without him . . .

He wadded up the piece of paper and dropped it into the fire. He climbed the stairs, checked the stove, and saw that it had been filled with wood. Arcieri had become a perfect house-husband, he thought with a smile. He went to the bathroom to brush his teeth, but didn't want to look in the mirror. He was afraid that Juliette's magic had worn off.

His room was warm. He undressed, laid his clothes on a chair, and got under the covers. It had been a long day and he was tired. But before turning out the light he read one of his mother's poems, written on a typewriter. The final lines were impressive, and he couldn't go to sleep without repeating them in his head: *Not even a drop of seawater could you ever create. And you sing victory?*

'Sleep well?' Arcieri asked as the inspector came down the stairs, eyes glued shut with sleep.

'I dreamt I was playing cards with a high-ranking SS officer,' muttered Bordelli, pleased to see that the espresso pot was already on the stove.

'That would be a good way to wage war,' said the colonel, setting two demitasses down on the table, along with some toasted bread and a bottle of olive oil. Bordelli plopped down in a chair.

'He was a big fat German a lot like Göring, and every time he threw down a card, he said . . . *Kaputt* . . .'

'Sounds like fun.'

'Everyone gets the dreams he deserves,' said the inspector, wondering why he hadn't dreamt about Juliette. Arcieri brought the coffee pot to the table and sat down.

'How's your investigation coming along?'

'I'd rather talk about Göring.'

'Still nothing?'

'Forget about it.'

'I really do wish I could help you. I mean it.'

'Thank you for the thought.'

'But you mustn't get discouraged. I'm sure you'll nab the killer well before the New Year,' said the colonel, filling the demitasses.

'Let's hope you're a soothsayer.'

'You never eat anything in the morning?'

'A cup of coffee's enough for me.'

'Ever since I've been staying at your house, I've been waking up in the morning feeling very hungry,' said the colonel. He poured a little oil on the bread and began to eat with relish. Bordelli was happy to see the colonel so placid and hoped that he, for his part, managed before long to solve the riddle that had been so on his mind.

'I bought you some clothes. I put them in the room with the record player.'

'How kind of you.'

'I hope I got the size right. If you don't like them I can always exchange them for something else.'

'You must tell me how much you spent, so I can pay you back as soon as possible.'

'There's no hurry. Meanwhile try them on to see if they're all right . . . I also got you a pair of shoes, size forty-one . . .'

'Good guess,' said Arcieri, taking another bite of bread. The inspector gulped down his coffee, thinking he had to remember to buy a few more litres of the new oil for Friday's dinner party.

'How would you like me to introduce you at dinner on Friday?'

'Shall we say I'm an old comrade of yours from the war?'

'Excellent idea. I'll say we met at Cassino. Now you're a retired general.'

'Never quite attained that rank,' Arcieri said, smiling.

'If need be, we'll say you live in Milan. We ran into each other by chance in Florence, and I invited you to spend Christmas with me . . . What do you think?'

'Perfect.'

'Oh, I almost forgot . . . At this point we've established a custom for these occasions. After dinner everyone must tell a story, and so you'll be expected to do so as well.'

'I won't back down.'

'Have a good day,' said Bordelli, getting up.

'Until what time should I wait for you for supper?'

'I should be back this evening, but if by nine o'clock I haven't returned, go ahead without me.'

'Can I ask a big favour of you?'

'Let's hear it . . .'

'If you happen to pass any music shops . . . I would like to listen to a jazz record . . . Anything at all would do . . . To be added to my bill, of course.'

'I'll see what I can do.'

'Only if it's not a bother.'

They said goodbye, and Bordelli headed down to Florence accompanied, as usual, by a caravan of memories. Oppressive black clouds hung low in the sky, but above the horizon beamed a tongue of light that called to mind some unattainable paradise.

Often it was the dead that kept him company along the Imprunetana, emerging as though afraid of being forgotten. They would resurface almost shyly in his memory, and he would welcome them with a combination of sorrow and pleasure. It was a little like calling them back to life . . . He would see their faces again, hear their voices again, share again the sad and pleasant moments of the past . . .

Traffic in town moved much more slowly than usual, and the pavements were packed with pedestrians. There was less than a week to go before Christmas, and people were coming en masse from the provinces to buy presents. Parking in the police station courtyard was like entering the peace of a cloister.

He went upstairs to his office and collapsed in his chair. Would this be yet another useless day? Actually, the previous day hadn't been entirely useless; he'd spent a splendid evening with Juliette. Outside her door they'd exchanged their first and last kiss, and he would never forget it. He wondered again what it must be like to spend the night with her . . . Better not to think about it.

He picked up the phone and dialled Oberto's number, which by now he knew by heart, like a girlfriend's. Drumming his fingers on the desktop, he wondered what he should do next. Nothing. The only thing he could think of doing was having a good talk with Oberto. It was becoming a bee in his bonnet. Probably nothing would come of it, but who could say? Rather than sitting there twiddling his thumbs, he dialled the number again, and after a good ten rings, just as he was about to hang up . . .

'Hello . . .' It was Oberto, sounding gloomier than usual.

'Hello, Oberto, it's that pain-in-the-arse police inspector again.'

'Good morning.'

'Look, Oberto, my patience has run out. Don't leave your flat. I'll be there in half an hour. If you're not there, I'll be forced to have you arrested,' Bordelli said in an untroubled tone of voice. After a few seconds of silence, he heard a faint sigh through the receiver.

'Let's meet at the usual bar,' said Oberto.

'See you shortly.'

The inspector hung up, grabbed his overcoat, and put it on as he was descending the stairs. He left the station by way of the usual side door that gave onto Via San Gallo, and started walking down the pavement in the cold morning air. The sun was rising in a cloudless sky.

He crossed the centre of town, where the streets were full of elegant ladies and vivacious girls. He ogled them all, didn't miss a single one. Thinking back on Juliette's kiss made him feel more handsome. Of course there were also men out on the street, but compared to the women they looked like figures in black and white.

Arriving in Piazza dei Ciompi, he slipped into Vasco's bar, heading straight for the billiards room. Oberto was alone there, killing time by trying to sink a ball in a pocket with the most complicated of shots. Bordelli was in time to see a ball ricochet five times before it clipped another ball and sent it into the corner pocket.

'I guess some are born with a cue in their hand,' he said with admiration. He could never have pulled off a shot like that, not even when he used to play every day.

'It's not hard,' said Oberto. He then positioned two balls and strutted his stuff by executing a miraculous shot, something which, if you told it to others, they wouldn't believe . . . He struck a ball very low, and hard, making it spin in such a way that it remained stationary for a second, then hopped backwards and traced a ridiculous curve, struck the other ball, making it ricochet twice and sending it softly into the farthest pocket.

'Not bad,' muttered Bordelli, thinking that one could make one's living playing pool that way, fleecing fools and braggarts.

'All it takes is a little practice,' said Oberto, laying the cue down on the edge of the table. The inspector smiled, then heaved a big sigh and looked the lad in the eye.

'Don't try to hide things from me, Oberto. It's possible what you know is of no use to me, but for now I'm completely in the dark.'

'I really don't know anything so important.'

'I just want to ask you some questions. Maybe something useful will come out of it.'

'Didn't you say I was a suspect?'

'I said that your father's death is the only shred of a motive I've been able to find.'

'Isn't that the same thing?'

'No, I think not.'

'My father was a drunkard. Antonio just came across him there without warning,' said Oberto, as if to end the discussion. Bordelli couldn't stand being shut up inside those squalid, smoke-imbued walls any longer.

'It's sunny outside . . . Shall we go for a walk?'

'Okay,' said Oberto, shrugging his shoulders.

Coming out of the bar, they turned down Via dell'Agnolo in the direction of the avenues, walking along the narrow pavement crowded with bundled-up pedestrians.

They walked past the dark stones of the Murate prison, one of the saddest places in Florence, inhabited mostly by poor bastards who, to get by, had been forced to ignore the law. Even the phenomenon called Ennio had spent a few months in there, on several occasions, though he was one of the finest men in the world. On the other side of the street, as a kind of mirror, stood the Santa Verdiana women's prison. Men and women lived confined just a few yards distant, but could never even get a glimpse of one another.

They came out onto the Viale della Giovine Italia, which was jammed with traffic, and turned towards the Arno. The inspector gestured towards the very fine Fascist-style building on the other side of the boulevard, which over time had become the Cinema Cristallo.

'When I was a kid, there wasn't anything here.'

'That's not hard to imagine,' said Oberto, casting a quick glance at the large off-white building. Bordelli had seen it go up in the late 1930s, when it was inaugurated as the Italian Fascist Youth House, or, more simply, the Casa GIL, for Casa della Gioventù Italiana del Littorio. Then, after the war, it was turned into a movie theatre. It was a fine architectural specimen, there was no denying that. When one drove by in the car, one didn't pay much attention to it, but now that he was on foot, Bordelli could look at it at leisure. Against its pale façade, the black line of the flood almost looked painted on.

'You have a very pretty girlfriend . . .' said the inspector.

Oberto nodded, mildly irritated by this intrusion into his private affairs. They walked along in silence, accompanied by streams of cars advancing in fits and starts. When they reached the river they crossed the San Niccolò bridge. Traffic was slow even up on Viale Michelangelo. The plane trees were bare, the broad pavements nearly deserted. Bordelli and the lad walked side by side, unhurried, hands in their pockets.

'I remember my father well . . .' said Oberto, as though resuming a conversation that had just been interrupted.

'So you never felt any resentment towards Migliorini, not even as a little kid?'

'Oh, maybe for a little while, but then I realised he was not to blame.'

'Did your father always drink too much?'

'Not at first. He was always a hard worker. He started drinking when he got it into his head that my mother was seeing someone else.'

'So it wasn't true?'

'Mamma always swore it wasn't, but he didn't believe her and kept on tormenting her. I can still hear the crazy quarrels they used to have,' said Oberto, who seemed finally to be opening up.

'Jealousy can play some nasty tricks.'

'After my father died, our home life became peaceful again. When he was alive, it was hell, but I would rather have had hell and him alive. Papa was a good man, and even amidst the madness I could feel that he loved me. And my mother always loved me too. I grew up with a lot of affection, and nobody can ever take that away from me.'

They both fell silent, as though appreciating Oberto's words. They kept on walking slowly, with no precise destination. Bordelli thought about his own parents, feeling himself sink into nostalgia. He too had been showered with affection and knew how important it was. It remained like a concrete base under your feet for the rest of your life. Everything else could collapse around you, but you would never lose your balance.

They crossed paths with two girls, who looked over at the handsome Oberto more than once. The inspector felt a twinge of envy, but consoled himself by thinking that a man near sixty could never compete with a strapping youth. Still, in his day, he too . . .

'Did you ever talk about your father with Migliorini?'

'The subject would come up every now and then. And Antonio, in spite of everything, felt a little guilty. If destiny had used him to kill a man, there must be a reason, he used to say . . .'

'Destiny . . .' the inspector muttered to himself, or perhaps he only thought it. Indeed, they were just passing by the villa of Monsignor Sercambi, one of little Giacomo's killers, and Bordelli couldn't help but think back on that sordid affair.

'Have you ever failed to solve a murder case?' the young man asked, just as Claretta had done.

'Only once, a very long time ago.'

'Whoever killed Dottor Migliorini mustn't be allowed to get away with it,' said Oberto, his eyes flashing.

They'd come to the Assi bend, the long curve that skirted the sporting complex where Bordelli had sweated as a lad. He even remembered when those playing fields were used as a dumping site for construction refuse, more than twenty years before Oberto was born. But he said nothing, not wanting to keep seeming like an old man.

'Where were you on the night of the murder?' he asked instead. Oberto looked at him darkly, clenching his jaw. The inspector gave a hint of a smile.

'Don't worry, I know you didn't do it.'

'Since when?'

'I don't know. I think I've known all along.'

'Well, at any rate, I was having dinner with a friend until about half past ten, then I went to see my girlfriend and spent the night with her. You can verify all that, if you like.'

'No need.'

'Suit yourself.'

The lad was trying hard not to seem bitter.

'Is it true that Migliorini was in love with a beautiful woman?' the inspector continued, as though making small talk. That question, however, was what interested him most. Oberto bit his lip, still undecided.

'Do you really think these private matters are so important?'

'Whenever someone is murdered, it's normal to search through his intimate life. How else are we supposed to find the killer?'

'I understand . . .'

'I give you my word that whatever you tell me will remain between us, unless, of course, I need it to send the killer to jail,' said Bordelli, hoping to persuade the lad to talk. Oberto remained silent for a long time, staring into space, then finally nodded.

'Yes, it's true . . . He'd fallen in love . . .' he said, as though reluctantly.

'How do you know that?'

'He told me himself. I've never seen him so happy.'

He spoke of Migliorini as though he were still alive, and when he realised this he smiled sadly again.

'And who is the woman? Have you met her?'

'I saw her just once, from far away, as she was getting out of Migliorini's Mini Morris. That was just by chance. Normally in the winter I was hardly ever at the villa at that hour.'

'What time was it?'

'It must have been about half past four. I was running late because of a leaking spigot in the garden.'

'When was this?'

'About two weeks ago.'

'Think you could recognise the woman?'

'I sincerely doubt it. She was wearing a scarf on her head and sunglasses, even though the sun was already setting.'

'Do you remember what she was like?'

'Tall, well dressed . . . Blond, I think . . . That's about all I remember . . .'

'How old do you think she might be?'

'Antonio told me she was twenty years younger than him.'

'Did he talk about her often?'

'We used to talk about a lot of things.'

'What else did he tell you about her?'

'He asked me not to breathe a word about her to anyone, even though I'd barely caught a glimpse of her. Absolutely no one was to know that he was seeing her, at least for the time being.'

'And why not?' asked the inspector, recalling that Amalia had said the same thing.

'She's from a very important family, and got married to a Florentine nobleman barely a year ago.'

'I see . . . An inconvenient relationship . . .' Oberto seemed to know more about her than anyone else.

'Antonio told me they were very much in love, and that neither of them liked living like thieves, but they didn't want to create a pointless scandal. They preferred to take things one step at a time, since in any case everything had already been decided. They'd found each other, and they would never leave each other again. That's what he said.'

'And what had they decided?'

'She was afraid of her husband and the brouhaha that would follow, but sooner or later she was going to find the courage to demand an annulment from the Church. They wanted to get married in broad daylight and travel the world.'

'So Migliorini really told you everything.'

'Well, not everything, but he trusted me. He knew I was as silent as the grave . . . Even though, now . . .'

'You can talk. You're doing it for him.'

'I hope so.'

'Did you know his wife?' asked Bordelli, resuming his questioning.

'No, that was before my time. I was hired at the villa two years after the signora's accident.'

'Did Migliorini ever talk about her with you?'

'Sure, every now and then. He talked about how her death weighed on his conscience. Nobody knew what had really happened, but one night Antonio told me . . .'

'Mind letting me in on it too?'

'I may as well, at this point . . . Signora Carla was very jealous, and as they were going on horseback that day to their property in Maremma, she was besieging him with questions. In the end Antonio admitted to having had a few passing affairs, though nothing serious. She tried to strike him in the face with her riding whip but missed, and then took off at a gallop through the woods. He chased after her and saw her fall from her horse.'

They'd reached Piazzale Michelangelo. Propping their elbows on the stone parapet as though on a windowsill, they looked out and enjoyed the winter sun. Florence was truly beautiful, viewed from afar. She was like a high-society lady, full of life, but if you got to know her well she was merely an attractive nun who liked to eye you with the promise of forbidden pleasures, only to leave you alone with your desires.

'Had you ever seen other women at the villa?' Bordelli asked.

'Before this last one, I'd seen a few pass through, but none lasted very long. But don't get the wrong idea. Antonio wasn't a seducer. Every time he had a new woman, he was convinced he was in love.'

'That's also what everyone else says.'

'Because it's true.'

'Did you meet any of these women? Could you give me some names?'

'No, I only saw them from a distance. They all looked beautiful to me, but I can't tell you any more than that. Besides, I didn't pay them much attention. There was only one I managed to exchange a few words with. Antonio said she was a high-class prostitute.'

'Juliette?'

'I see you've already found out a few things on your own,' said Oberto.

'What did he tell you about her?'

'He said she had a much purer soul than a lot of high-society ladies.'

'I've no trouble believing that,' said the inspector, smiling.

'He had great admiration for Juliette.'

'I went and paid her a call. She's a very special woman.'

'I liked her a lot too,' Oberto mumbled, as though he could see her. Bordelli waited for Juliette's ghost to leave, then leaned with his back against the parapet.

'I hear you used to go hunting with Migliorini,' he said, changing the subject.

'It was just long walks in the woods more than anything else, with our rifles on our shoulders. We never fired a single shot.'

'Did you go out often?'

'A couple of times a month. Every so often we'd see a hare or a pheasant up ahead, but we would just keep talking. And when hunting season was over we would still go out for walks.'

'Always just the two of you?'

'No, sometimes Averardo would also come. He was an old friend of Antonio's from before the war. He has a hardware store near Le Cure.'

'His name is Butelli, isn't it?'

'Do you know him?'

'Just the name. He's also inherited something from Migliorini, though he doesn't know it yet,' said Bordelli.

'I'm not surprised. They were very fond of each other.'

'You don't know it either, but as far as I know, Migliorini apparently left you a fortune, too.'

'You can't be serious.'

'It's true. The lawyer will be notifying you.'

'That's insane . . .' said Oberto, turning aside to hide the fact that he was getting emotional.

'He also listed your mother and Signora Amalia among his heirs. I think you're all rich now.'

'Money's got nothing to do with it . . .' the lad muttered, gently shaking his head.

'May I please speak with Signorina Claretta?'

'One minute while I call her to the phone.'

'Thank you.'

Bordelli waited impatiently to hear the fascinating young woman's shrill voice. It was true he liked her, though he wasn't sure how much, or even why. She had something that was . . . how could he put it . . . Sometimes when he thought of her he imagined holding her and kissing her . . . maybe it was her mouth and those soft lips that never stopped moving, or the way she cocked her head, or her small, fluttering hands, her observant eyes, her porcelain ears, her ever so suggestive voice . . . but he mustn't forget that he was in the middle of a murder investigation, and therefore . . .

'Good morning, Inspector, how nice to hear from you.'

'Good morning Claretta . . . May I call you Claretta?'

'Of course, please do.'

'Sorry to bother you.'

'No bother at all. Do you have any news?'

'For the moment, no . . . I am calling you about something else . . .'

'Do tell.' She seemed quite excited.

'Well, I'd like to ask . . . please don't think any less of me . . .'

'For heaven's sake.' Claretta giggled. 'Don't keep me guessing . . .'

'Forgive me, I'll get straight to the point . . . I need to check the alibis of all the people who were close to Dr Migliorini, friends and relatives alike.'

'Ah . . .' she said, trying to hide her disappointment. He could only guess what she had imagined.

'Perhaps I should have asked sooner . . .'

'I really don't know how I can be of help to you,' Claretta said.

'I need you to tell me where you were on the night of the murder.'

'In what sense?' she asked, puzzled.

'I have to ask you just as I have asked everyone else . . . your brother-in-law's sons, Ms Laura, everyone. Consider it just a formality.'

'Well, if it's absolutely necessary . . .'

'Do you remember where you were on the night of the murder?'

'Of course . . . I was at home all evening.' She sounded somewhat offended.

'Can you tell me what you did that evening?'

'Nothing special . . . I made a few phone calls, watched a little television, and then went to bed and read until late.'

'Is the lady who answered the telephone also there at night?' He couldn't remember her name.

'Of course, Fidalma has been living with us for the past ten years. She takes care of my mother, mostly, who never leaves the house.'

'Does Signora Fidalma have a day off?'

'Of course she does – Saturday. She leaves after lunch and stays over at her sister's house in Galluzzo.'

'So, on the evening of the murder she was at home.'

'Yes, of course.'

'Can Signora Fidalma confirm that you were at home that night and never went out?'

'I doubt it. She sleeps in a room at the end of the hall and she goes to bed early,' Claretta said drily.

'Mightn't she have heard you?'

'I doubt it. She is a very heavy sleeper.'

'And your mother?'

'She also turns in very early; we only see each other in the morning.' Claretta was getting testy.

'Where is your mother's room?'

'Next to Fidalma's, far from mine. Just to be clear: our penthouse apartment has nine rooms. Get the picture?'

'Of course . . .'

'Any other questions, Inspector?'

'Well, in short, we can say you haven't got a proper alibi,' the inspector ventured to say, but in an almost joking tone of voice.

'I'm sorry, but I really didn't think I needed one,' Claretta said acidly.

'I didn't mean to offend you.'

'I'm not offended, on the contrary. It's quite a pleasure to be suspected of murder,' Claretta said, her voice breaking.

'Forgive me, Claretta. I wish you a pleasant afternoon.'

'Goodbye,' she said brusquely, and hung up somewhat emphatically.

He had succeeded in getting her angry, Bordelli thought, looking at his watch. Ten past one. He was hungry, tired, and even a little confused. Every so often he imagined Juliette's eyes, and sighed . . . Who knew where Eleonora was now, or what she was doing. He'd better take a break, maybe go and have a bite to eat at Totò's . . . now that Claretta hated him. Best not think about it . . .

The inspector entered his office and dropped into his chair like a sack of potatoes. He'd given in to the temptations of the diabolical angel, Totò, but it was also the fault of the hearty appetite he'd worked up on his long walk with Oberto. He swore to himself this would be the last time. From now on . . .

At last he had some peace and quiet in which to think things over. So the mystery woman did, after all, exist. She was probably very beautiful, and Antonio loved her very much. They had wanted to marry and travel the world . . . Okay, but how was he going to find her? And where should he start? Antonio had told Oberto very little about his secret mistress. Just that she came from a prominent family and had married a Florentine nobleman. In short, the mystery woman belonged to a world that Bordelli didn't know at all and didn't even know how to find, a gilded world in which the nobility and the wealthy joined in mutual admiration – more or less the way Arcieri had described his Elena's world, when speaking of the 1930s.

If only he had a name, a photograph, an address . . . It was like looking for a needle in a haystack, maybe even worse. Clearly Commissioner Inzipone would never let him start digging among those Olympian gods, for fear that he might ruffle the feathers of some high-ranking member of government. And never mind mouse-faced Ginzillo, the investigating magistrate, who started trembling like a leaf and talking like a castrato whenever he had to deal with powerful people. The man would rather swim in pig shit than do anything that might jeopardise his career.

Averardo Butelli, on the other hand, would be easy to track down. Bordelli opened the phone book and looked for a hardware store in the Cure district . . . There it was: *Ferramena mesticheria Butelli*, via Boccaccio 49/51. Migliorini had friends of all kinds, as was often the case with people who lived freely. He seemed to pay no mind to other people's social standing. It was humanity he sought. He himself belonged to the Florentine upper bourgeoisie, but was very fond of Oberto, Averardo, Juliette . . . To the point of including them among his heirs. But a man's life didn't end with his death. Oberto was right: money had nothing to do with it. In this case, money became just a form of affection, nothing more.

Before going out to the hardware store in Le Cure, he got the idea to ring his friend Agostinelli, a big cheese in the SID, the Italian secret service organisation, and an old friend from the days of the war. Dialling the number, the inspector wondered why he hadn't thought of this sooner. Perhaps there was something of interest on Migliorini in the SID's archives.

'Hello . . .'

'Ciao, Carnera,' said the inspector, calling him by his nickname.

'My God, Franco, did you know I was just about to call you?'

'How are you?'

'I can't complain. And yourself?'

'The usual stuff . . . I bet you've gained weight and no longer have a single hair on your head.'

'Not everyone grows old like you, dear Inspector. How is life among the chickens, anyway?'

'It's not very gentlemanly of you to talk about women that way.'

They carried on joking, as they always did, and even brought up a few old memories of when they were on the same ship.

'I need to ask a favour of you,' said the inspector, turning serious.

'Me too . . . But you go first . . .'

'I need all the information you have on a certain Antonio Migliorini.' He explained who Migliorini was, how old, and how he'd been killed.

'A rather original murder, I'd say,' commented Agostinelli.

'I've been unable to come up with anything so far, and I'm getting a little discouraged.'

'I'll send someone to dig through the archives and get back to you as soon as I can.'

'Thanks . . . And what did you want to tell me?'

'It's a rather delicate matter, and so I would ask that you not mention it to anyone.'

'Even rocks are more loquacious than I. What's it about?'

'We're looking for one of our own, a man who retired a few years ago. He's been in hiding and would seem to be presently in Florence.'

'And who was he?' asked Bordelli, adopting a playful tone.

'His name is Bruno Arcieri, perhaps you've met him . . .'

'The name is not unfamiliar to me . . .'

'He's a colonel in the Carabinieri, a fine, upright fellow, actually. But he's got himself into trouble, almost certainly without wanting to.'

'What kind of trouble?'

'Don't ask me anything, I'm not at liberty to answer. As I was saying, he is almost certainly hiding out in Florence.'

'Sorry to ask, but if he's one of your own, why doesn't he just get in touch with you?'

'It's a very complicated matter . . . And it's not even my section that's handling it . . . But anyway, if you were to run into him, I would ask you please to let me know . . .'

'Of course.'

'We want to protect him.'

'I'm sure you do,' said the inspector, unhappy to be forced to lie to a dear friend. But never could he have betrayed Arcieri's trust.

'Thank you, Franco. I'll ring as soon as I have anything on this Migliorini.'

'You can also call me at home if you like. I'm never in bed before midnight. Have you got the number?'

'You gave it to me last year, the one with five digits.'

'How come you're not trying to recruit me this time?' asked Bordelli, becoming playful again.

'Well, I confess that it's not quite the way it used to be around here. There are things I don't like, but luckily I'll be retiring in just a couple of months,' Agostinelli said in a serious tone.

'I've got another three years to go. It's not the end of the world, but I don't exactly feel like popping open a bottle of champagne either.'

'Come on, you enjoy it. Then you'll become a farmer and I'll buy my olive oil from you.'

'I'm too old to learn.'

'You could always become the Tom Ponzi of Tuscany.'[21]

'Oh, go on, I really can't see myself tailing the unfaithful wives of rich men.'

'Then you'll go round the world with a beautiful woman.'

'That's the first sensible thing I've heard you say.'

'But you've only got three years to find the right woman,' said Agostinelli, laughing.

'Well, with a little luck . . .'

'I've got to leave you now, I have a meeting lined up. I'll get in touch as soon as I know something.'

They said goodbye, and the inspector leaned back in his chair, feeling pensive. Carnera's last 'prophecy' stuck in his mind, and he imagined himself going round the world, perhaps with Eleonora . . . Or maybe Juliette, why not? First the capitals of Europe, then the Americas, faraway India, China, Africa, Australia . . . He might never come back. He would buy a cottage in Lapland, among the reindeer, or maybe in Marrakesh, or the Loire valley . . .

It was fun, as usual, to dream, but he knew well he would never do any of it. It would be too sad to give up Rosa's pamperings, Ennio's company, Piras's eloquent silences, Dante's prodigious arguments . . . and everything else. He loved walking in the woods, reading novels, having friends over to dinner . . . and he might even try in earnest to become a farmer. That was all it would take – just these few things – to fill up his life. As his mother had written in a poem:

Not much, but
nothing's really missing.
If you try, you can count
on both hands
the things you need to live.

He got up with effort, and, before going out, reread the address of Butelli's hardware store. The Cure district wasn't far away, and so he decided to go for another walk. Mostly he had no desire to get stuck in Christmas traffic.

As he crossed Piazza San Gallo, which was jammed with cars, the air stank worse than usual and people wouldn't stop honking their horns. On Viale Don Minzoni, he passed the building in which Claretta lived and instinctively raised his eyes to look at the top-floor windows. The woman had a special allure that was hard to define. He might even be able to fall in love with someone like that, who could say? And were he able to win her affections, after their first night of love he would ask her to stop using perfume as if it were water.

The thoughts kept coming as he walked. He'd kissed Juliette, was sensitive to Claretta's charm, and was spellbound watching the women in the street . . . Then why was he unable to forget Eleonora? Not that he wanted to, mind. Before closing that chapter he had to be sure that there was no longer any possibility. But he wasn't lifting a finger to find out whether this was the case, as if he would rather stew in doubt like an adolescent. Perhaps because there was still hope in uncertainty . . . He was a little confused, in short . . .

When he reached Piazza delle Cure, it was already getting dark. The pavements were almost as crowded as in the centre of town. He went down Via Boccaccio, looking at the street numbers of the shops. He knew the district well. He'd grown up not far away, and his head was filling with memories . . . As a boy he used to have his bicycle repaired by a mechanic everyone called Gobbetto, or 'Little Hunchback'. He'd never found out whether that was his surname or just a nickname. At any rate, the man was not the least bit hunchbacked; in fact he stood straight as a tree. He was bald except for an oily thicket that ran from ear to ear by way of the back of his head. He was often busy with a hammer and always had a bitter smile on his lips. *I'm a foolish man*, he started saying one day to those who came into his workshop, then laughed in that strange way of his . . . *Ergr . . . ergr . . . ergr* . . . It sounded like a saw trying to cut a piece of iron. He killed himself that same evening, hanging himself with the brake cord of a bicycle.

But there were more pleasant memories, too. Like the pretty girl with black hair who worked as a nursemaid in Via Brunetto Latini. For years he'd dreamed of kissing her . . . Her name was . . . Petronilla . . . Actually, she looked a bit like Eleonora, if one thought about it . . .

Butelli's hardware store was the last shop before the Ponte alle

Riffe. It was a rather big, chaotic space, like all hardware stores. Peering in through the window, he saw a short man behind the counter, with a simple air, a big mass of grey hair and eyeglasses on his nose. He was attending to a rather elegant-looking housewife.

Bordelli pushed open the door, which was attached to a little bell, and the man greeted him with a quick smile.

'This is a very fine paintbrush, signora. Trust me,' said the man. Despite his cordial manner, his eyes were full of sadness.

'How can I be sure the bristles won't start falling out?' the woman asked, looking at the paintbrush with suspicion.

'Signora, all paintbrushes lose a few bristles at first, it's perfectly normal. But if, after the first half-hour, it loses so much as a single bristle, bring it back to me and I'll return your money.'

He waited for a sign of assent, then wrapped the paintbrush as if it were a sausage and put it in a small bag along with two cans of paint. The woman paid without a second thought and left the shop, gesturing the vaguest of goodbyes. The shopowner shook his head, smiling.

'At Christmas time everyone's shop is packed, but mine is deserted. Nobody ever thinks of giving someone a nice screwdriver set for a present, or an electric drill, or even a spade.'

'I certainly would like that kind of present,' Bordelli said to console him, feeling an instinctive sympathy for the man.

'Pay no attention to my mutterings . . . What were you looking for?' He was trying to appear cheerful, but failed.

'Are you Averardo Butelli?'

'Yes . . .'

'I'm sorry to bother you, but I'm Inspector Bordelli, police, and I'm investigating the murder of Antonio Migliorini . . . I'm told you were good friends . . .'

'Excuse me for a minute,' the man muttered, his voice quavering. He came out from behind the counter and went and locked his shop. He stood for a few moments in front of the glass door without moving, then ran his hands through his hair and came back. Opening a curtain, he invited Bordelli to sit down in the back room, a small, clean space with a table and two chairs. As soon as they sat down, a flask of red wine appeared, and there was no way to refuse. It felt like being in an old country tavern.

'Do you feel up to talking about Migliorini?' the inspector asked.

'I still can't believe he's dead,' said Butelli, staring at his glass.

Somebody knocked at the front door, but Butelli only shrugged, as if to say it didn't matter. The inspector waited patiently for the customer to leave, then rested his elbows on the small table.

'When did you last see him?'

'He came here the evening before he died, just as I was closing the shop . . . Sitting right where you are now.'

'And did he seem untroubled?'

'We felt good together, as always.'

'Did you see each other often?'

'He used to come and see me at least once a week, at the end of the day. That last evening he couldn't stay, but we would usually go out to a restaurant after I closed up, and we might even play a game of *briscola* at the Casa del Popolo, afterwards.[22] Sometimes on Sundays we would pretend to go hunting. So in fact we didn't do anything out of the ordinary, but we always had a good time together. As Antonio used to say: *It doesn't matter what you do, but who you're with.*'

'When did you first meet?'

'We met during the Albanian campaign. He was an officer, and I was a simple soldier. But we immediately became friends. Antonio was an exceptional man, so generous it touched the heart.'

'Can you tell me anything about him?' asked the inspector, noticing that Butelli seemed to want very much to talk about his friend. Between one thing and another, something useful might emerge. Butelli took a deep breath and began.

'I'll tell you just one story, so you can see what kind of man he was. After the war my family found itself out on the street. We'd lost everything. Sometimes I couldn't even manage to put food on the table. Nobody likes the smell of poverty, and it wasn't easy finding some fool to give me a job. My wife would try to console me, saying that sooner or later things would get better. It can't stay this way forever, she would say over and over. Our son was seven years old at the time, and I used to try and make him laugh so he could forget he was hungry.

'One day I collapsed onto a bench in Piazza Indipendenza and buried my face in my hands. I was in despair. At that moment I heard someone call my name, and when I looked up I saw a well-dressed man. At first I didn't realise who it was . . . *Is that really you, Averardo?* When I recognised him I started crying like a baby, and we embraced. There was no need to tell him that I was in a bad way. He could see from the shape I was in, and it was written all over my face.

'Antonio immediately offered to help me, in a way that pleased me very much. He knew I was a proud man, and to avoid offending me he said it would just be a loan. *You'll pay it all back to me, down to the last lira*, he said with a smile. To make a long story short, he bought me this commercial property, and even put up the money to open a business. Every month I would pay him back what I could, trying to give him as much as possible. Two years ago we celebrated the end of my debt by going to a good restaurant, and Antonio paid for the dinner with the last ten thousand lire I'd brought him that same evening. I had quite a bit to drink that night, and as I thought about everything he'd done for my family, I got rather emotional. I avoided thanking him too openly, since I didn't want to embarrass him and I knew that in any case he wouldn't have liked that. But if our paths hadn't crossed that day twenty years ago, who knows how I would have ended up? I was destined to wallow in poverty, but instead I've been able to send my son to school . . . Nicola now has a university degree and has been working for the past five years at the firm of an important architect, in Via dei Servi.'

He raised his glass slightly, as though toasting the ghost of his deceased friend, and took a sip of wine. His eyes were moist, but he was smiling, and for a brief moment his chin trembled. He emptied his glass and then refilled it, squirming in his chair. Then he stood up, walked around the room, and sat back down. Taking another sip, he leaned back in his chair and started rubbing his eyes, pressing them hard. Bordelli waited silently for Averardo to regain his composure, patiently respecting the man's sincere grief and homage to friendship. A long minute, perhaps two, went by, and when Butelli finally reopened his eyes, they had the look of someone who had just been through a forest of memories.

'Is it all right if I ask you a few more questions?' asked the inspector.

'Forgive me . . . You can ask me whatever you like.'

'I've been told that Migliorini fell in love with a beautiful woman much younger than him . . .'

'Yes, he'd hinted at that with me as well. He was as happy as a lark. Normally he hardly told me anything about his women, but this one had really charmed him. It was the first time he'd fallen seriously in love since his wife's death.'

'Did he ever tell you the woman's name?'

'No, not even her first name. Actually, he said the whole business must remain a secret, at least until a certain thing happened. But he never told me what this thing was. And he only talked about her because he couldn't help himself. You should've seen him! His eyes sparkled! The times he was most willing to talk about her was when we were walking in the woods. We were sometimes joined by Oberto, the lad who worked as his gardener.'

'Yes, I know him.'

'He's a very fine young man. He was like a son to Antonio.'

'Do you know how Oberto's father died?' Bordelli asked.

'Of course. I know the story well. Antonio used to talk about it often.'

'Do you think Oberto might have harboured any resentment towards Migliorini because of it?' the inspector asked. Butelli looked at him as if he was mad.

'Not at all! I hope you're not thinking that the boy . . . For heaven's sake, Inspector, I'll swear on a stack of Bibles . . . Oberto loved and admired Antonio.'

'Did Migliorini ever mention to you anyone who might have hated him? For any reason . . . A quarrel, a woman . . . Or maybe something to do with his business . . .'

'I really don't think so . . . Well, except for an old story that dated back to the war . . .'

'Do you feel up to telling me about it?' asked the inspector, still hoping. More than once in the past he had been able to unearth some old and apparently time-buried resentment that had resurfaced to guide a killer's hand. Butelli knocked back another gulp of wine and started telling the story with relish . . .

When the Italian Social Republic[23] *was founded, Antonio Migliorini was thirty years old. In the north of the country the Fascists celebrated their survival with clamorous military parades, and Pavolini was giving birth to his most sinister creation, the Black Brigades.*

Antonio had fought in Albania and Greece, and after being wounded in the thigh he no longer had any military obligations to fulfil. In Florence he was known as a bigio *– that is, as an inactive antifascist. After the 8th of September he retired with his parents and wife to one of their farms in the Castellina area. His children had yet to be born. The whole family lived in one of the old farmhouses in less than pleasant conditions. The great lordly villa had been occupied by a command of the Wehrmacht. It wasn't a pretty sight. The Germans demanded that they be served and revered, and the peasants of the farm came running with flasks of wine, bottles of oil, salamis, and legs of prosciutto. The most zealous was a young peasant named Averino Buzzi, who every morning used to bring the German officers no fewer than three chickens and then pluck them before their eyes with a servile smile on his face. Nobody knew where he was getting the birds in that time of shortage. In spite of this he never missed a day.*

Migliorini had never been an impulsive man, but once he was unable to control himself. In March 1944, a unit of the Black Brigades filed into the centre of Poggibonsi, sleeves rolled up and machine guns in hand. He was there by chance, along with hundreds of others, resignedly watching the scene with heads down. At a certain point among the Fascists he recognised two lads he knew well, two dolts with less than clean records, and for reasons unknown the spectacle made him see red. All at once he raised his fist in the air and shouted:

'You're all slaves of the Nazis! Give your weapons to us and stop betraying the Italian people!'

As one might imagine, he was immediately arrested. Two police officers in civvies stuffed him into a black Fiat 1100 and took him straight to Florence. He was locked up in the Murate prison with all the common criminals, awaiting a trial that never came. For others who, like him, had been arrested for 'political reasons', prison was a very dangerous place. If there was an attack against the Germans or the Fascists on the outside, he would be one of the first to be shot by a firing squad in reprisal.

After three days of desperate searching, his parents finally managed to find out where he'd been imprisoned, and didn't hesitate to mobilise all their friends and acquaintances in the hope of getting him released. At last, after a fortnight in detention, the charges against Migliorini were conditionally revoked. He later told his wife that it had been a very instructive experience for him. And now that he was free, he even found it amusing.

A few months later, on 11 August, Florence was liberated. Kesselring moved the Gothic Line a bit farther to the north, committing atrocities along the way, to the point of upsetting even Mussolini. Meanwhile, in the newly liberated areas, partisan fighters were popping up like mushrooms and parading in the streets. Many of them had fought bravely, daily risking their lives, and breathing the effervescent air of new-found freedom with great excitement. Others emerged from the basements where they had holed up for almost a year and tied red bandanas round their necks opportunistically or, worse, out of self-interest. Migliorini scorned such cowards.

In October 1945, a 'people's tribunal' was instituted in Castellina with the blessing of the Allies and summoned Migliorini's father to appear and face a public trial. He was charged with having mistreated his own peasants – in other words, with being an oppressor of the working class. Antonio was disgusted by these calumnies and decided to show up in his father's place at the tribunal, which had been set up in the former Casa del Fascio. The atmosphere in the lecture hall was gloomy, a bit like a French tribunal at the time of the Terror. The local partisan chief sat half reclining in his chair. After a few formalities, the representative for the prosecution was called upon to speak. Migliorini was utterly dumbfounded to see before him none other than Averino Buzzi, the young peasant who used to come running to the Germans every day with chickens. Averino likewise recognised him, averting his eyes and starting to mumble the charges, which he'd clearly memorised. At that point, Antonio could no longer contain himself, and he approached the other with a wry expression on his face.

'Don't you remember? While I was in Murate prison for anti-Fascist activities, you were plucking chickens for the Germans . . . Have you told your comrades this?' he said, staring at him with scorn. There was a loud buzz of voices in the hall, but the partisan chief slammed the butt of his pistol on the table, and everyone stopped talking.

'Is what Migliorini says true?' he asked Buzzi. The young man seemed unable to answer, but among the crowd some people were nodding in agreement, while a number of others shouted that Migliorini was telling the truth. Still others saw things differently, or else wanted simply to speak ill of a rich man, and indeed more than a few insults were flying. But in the end the truth emerged. Terrified, the young accuser was casting hateful glances all around. With a single gesture, the partisan chief had him taken away, and as soon as things calmed down he asked Migliorini to tell everyone about his time at Murate. Antonio said the charge against him was there in black and white at the Florence courthouse. He had offended the honour of the Fascists, it said in writing.

In short, he felt proud of having been imprisoned. And in the end he was escorted, practically in triumph, back to his villa, while Averino Buzzi was put on trial for collaboration with the enemy and shut up in a cell for a while. Over the years Migliorini happened to cross paths with him several times, and every time the chicken-plucker was unable to conceal his bitterness towards him.

This was a new lead worth investigating, Bordelli thought while walking back to the office. An old grudge, resurfacing with venom . . . It could well constitute a motive. That old story was all he needed to get his imagination working overtime. And that, after all, was his job. To look into the past, imagine things, intuit leads, sniff out scents, hunt down prey . . .

It wasn't exactly fun, but essentially he enjoyed his line of work. When he was in secondary school he didn't know what he would be when he grew up, but he always had an image in his head . . . a warm, breezy summer night, the feeling of returning home after a day of work, exhausted, but with the pleasurable sensation of having done his job well.

It didn't look as if the stream of traffic had any intention of abating, and the air stank worse than ever. Averino Buzzi, chicken-plucker . . . Truth be told, he didn't really believe in the lead but it was worth looking into, seeing that he had nothing else to go on for now. If only he could find the 'mystery woman', as he had started calling her. Maybe she could put him on the right track? Clearly, it had been a meaningful love affair, the kind where one shares one's deepest secrets, and it was precisely among the secrets that Bordelli had to go looking.

No one really knew Antonio Migliorini: his dreams, fears, deepest feelings . . . Not his friends, his sister, not even Juliette. The three people who knew him best were the cleaning lady, a gardener and a hardware shopowner – but none of them knew the name of the mystery woman. How would he ever find her? Certainly not by ringing up the super-rich, aristocratic families of Florence . . . 'Pardon me, but I'm looking for Antonio Migliorini's mistress: a beautiful, married lady; might you know where I can find her?' It would set off a scandal and still he'd get nowhere. And yet, the idea of giving up was inconceivable.

Bordelli crossed Piazza San Gallo easily by walking between the blocked cars. Drivers beeped their horns at each other, as if that might somehow make the traffic go away. What a mess it would be on Christmas Eve . . . he didn't even want to think about it. He already had a gift for Rosa; to everyone else he would send his warmest holiday wishes, accompanied perhaps by a nice bottle of this year's olive oil. He made a mental note to remember to buy at least a dozen litres . . .

But as he was walking by a shop window, destiny stepped in, and he saw the perfect gift for his friend Diotivede. It was a silly trifle, so silly that . . . he couldn't resist. Giving gifts was like falling in love at first sight: it took a *coup de foudre*. He went into the shop and purchased the gift with a smile on his face. It cost very little, but the important thing was the thought behind it. He put the package into his overcoat pocket and continued on his way, threading his way through the crowds and chaos.

He walked into the main entrance of headquarters, said a quick hello to Mugnai, crossed the courtyard, and went up the stairs, wondering what kind of present he would have given Eleonora if they were still together. Perhaps a good book, or maybe a record by that group that was driving all the young people wild . . . what were they called? The Beatles. He would have given it to her after a nice dinner, at a restaurant with soft lighting. He imagined the scene and shook his head. Senseless fantasies. She probably had three boyfriends by now – all of them young, fun and intelligent, and vying with one another to be the best looking. Perhaps she had a beau for weekdays, one for Saturdays, and one for Sundays. Why should she have any thoughts at all for an awkward old police inspector, if not to curse the day she met him? He couldn't blame her, really. It had been all his fault. He, the stupid inspector, with his recklessness . . . if only that night . . . but no sense in tormenting himself, the only thing he could do now was forget, let time pass, and forget . . .

He walked into his office with his morale low, hung up his overcoat as if it was his armour, and only then realised that someone had said hello to him in the hall. He peered out of his door, but no one was there. Closing the door with a sigh, he walked across the room and flopped down into his chair.

He couldn't stand this daydreaming any longer. He needed to bring things to their proper conclusion, as if his life was a romance novel. Only three more years and he'd be up for retirement – that was what he needed to focus on. Sixty years old, damn it all. According to Rosa's friend the fortune-teller, who had read his cards a year earlier, one of these days he would meet a pretty fifty-year-old woman, a widow with children, and thus he, too, would be able to have his own children . . . and everybody would live happily ever after. And yet it was true that the fortune-teller had guessed a lot of other things correctly, aside from helping find the little Giacomo's corpse. She had foretold his meeting with Eleonora and the tragic end of their love story. Was it possible that the future was written in the cards? He never would have believed it . . . and yet . . .

It was a quarter past seven. He was eager to go home, to sit at the table with the fire burning, and to exchange stories with Colonel Arcieri. But his day wasn't done yet. He was waiting for Piras to come and give him his daily report and a copy of the will. He also wanted to assign Piras a new task, to find the chicken-plucker, Averino Buzzi . . .

He decided to have one more go at finding the mystery woman, though he wasn't very hopeful. He picked up the phone and called the headquarters of *La Nazione* newspaper. He asked to speak with his friend Batini, an old journalist who knew just about everyone. After exchanging Christmas niceties, he asked a favour.

'Sure, fire away.'

'Well, I know for certain that Antonio Migliorini – you know, the one who was run through . . .'

'Of course.'

'Migliorini had a mistress, a married woman, young, elegant, very beautiful, probably aristocratic, or at least from a very rich family . . . I was wondering . . . you wouldn't happen to know someone in the Florentine panoply of gods who could tell you who that woman was? I absolutely need to talk to her.'

'I've met a few of those people through my work, but I don't know them well. But I wouldn't even try; it'd be pointless.'

'Are you sure?'

'They would never tell me anything, even if they did know who the woman was. They live in a closed world, and no cracks are allowed. Also, it's not about finding a woman, but someone's mistress, which is very different . . . Maybe you, as a police inspector, could manage.'

'But how would I go about it? Who would I start with? I would have to ask randomly . . . and risk stirring up a hornet's nest, and probably for nothing.'

'I know what you mean. I'm sorry. I really don't know how I can help you.'

'Well, I tried. Thanks all the same.'

''Bye, Franco, hope to see you some time.'

'I'll drop in on you one day . . .'

Bordelli hung up and a few seconds later the phone rang. It was Agostinelli. He sounded tired; it had been a long day. He read him the brief file on Antonio Migliorini, but there was nothing of interest.

'I'm heading home,' he said.

'Thanks all the same.'

'If you want to help me, find Colonel Arcieri.'

'I wish I could, but I have no idea where to even start looking.'

'Try just the same; it's for his own good.'

'Fine, but I can't promise you anything.'

'If you hear anything, call me immediately, even at night, at home.'

'Wow, you must really be in love,' Bordelli said jokingly, but the admiral was not in the mood.

'I have to say, Franco, I'm tired of this job. For some time now, I've felt as though I've been living in an alternative world, a place where we breathe mysteries and falsehoods instead of air.'

'Come and work with us,' Bordelli said, repeating a phrase that his friend had said to him several times over the years.

'After years and years of working with passion, I find I'm simply looking forward to retirement. I count down the days like a prisoner.'

'Do you cross off the days on the wall?'

'Practically.'

'When you're retired, you must come and see me. I'll take you on long walks in the woods.'

'We're old, Franco.'

'There's a very large oak tree I'd like to show you.'

Dinner time was approaching, the traffic thinning out at last, and he reached Poggio Imperiale in a reasonable amount of time. Taking the Imprunetana di Pozzolatico, he drove along slowly, thinking of the long day just gone by. He was trying to put his thoughts in some kind of order, but without much conviction. But he truly did hope that Arcieri hadn't eaten yet. He was growing accustomed to the old carabiniere's pleasant company and their melancholy incursions into the past by the fire, with a glass of good wine in hand. He already knew he would miss them when they were over. By this point he considered the colonel a friend, and yet they still spoke to each other in the polite form and might keep on doing so forever.

He felt tired, but it was more a mental sluggishness than a physical one. This murder was proving a tough nut to crack. He really needed to make some kind of progress, but in which direction? Perhaps the most important thing was to relax and free his mind, but it wasn't easy. Piras had brought him the results of his research, but there wasn't much of interest, as he'd expected. Migliorini's sons, his sister Laura, his friend Giordanelli, Signora Amalia, all had alibis confirmed by other family members, friends or servants. Unless the murder had been a conspiracy, none of them had anything to hide. Additionally, none of them had shown the slightest uneasiness, just surprise, at being asked a question normally asked of a suspect. Piras, however, had rather skillfully explained to them that it was just a formality, more or less, and everything had gone rather smoothly thereafter.

Piras also had with him a copy of the will, several pages handwritten by the lawyer. Migliorini had left no personal document, just a list of the inheritors and the bequests intended for each, as well as a few minimal comments, as needed . . .

I, the undersigned, Antonio Migliorini, in full possession of my faculties, hereby declare that I am acting with the best of intentions in determining what follows, and I ask that all the heirs named herein accept my final earthly wishes in full serenity of conscience . . .

In reading 'what follows', one had confirmation of Migliorini's great generosity. The bulk of the inheritance went to his sons and grandchildren, including, of course, the two factories; then came his sister Laura and Claretta, who were bequeathed properties, government bonds and stocks. But a great many possessions, as Busotti Santi had already indicated, were left to people outside the family. Oberto and his mother received several apartments, some Treasury bonds and a considerable sum of money. Signora Amalia was given a *palazzina* in Vicchio di Mugello and a gold bracelet, which, however, must have been in the stolen case. Antonio's friend Butelli got all his cars, an old inlaid rifle, and a large garage in the centre of town. Juliette was to receive an entire palazzo in Fiesole and some jewellery that would no doubt have looked splendid on her person had it not been purloined by the killer. The remainder of the jewels were left to Claretta, including the ring that had been found on the carpet, which was already in her possession. Migliorini's friends Marinari and Giordanelli, who clearly had no need for luck to smile on them, were bequeathed only a few antique paintings of moderate value, as mementoes. At any rate, seeing these bequests, it was not difficult to understand why everyone spoke of Migliorini as a special, profoundly fair man guided by the noblest of sentiments . . .

Who would want to kill a man like that? It was almost certainly Migliorini himself who opened the door for the killer, and he must have known him well, since he was wearing his dressing gown. But who could it have been? An envious lout? A cuckolded husband? A rejected mistress?

This was getting nowhere. Bloody hell. Always the same questions, over and over . . .

And what if, on the other hand . . . He tried taking things a little farther, just to avoid being entrapped in a single view of things and to free himself of all the useless hypotheses he'd been formulating up until that moment . . . What if, indeed, Migliorini had led a double life? Perhaps he wasn't at all the way he seemed and harboured a secret, a perfidious side of his character that nobody in his immediate circle even suspected. Perhaps there was a Mr Hyde inside him that manifested itself in a world other than his normal one. Maybe he was a real son of a bitch who had sown the wind and reaped a whirlwind . . . Some kind of vendetta, in short, that had been conceived and ripened in rancour. It was certainly possible. Letting his thoughts go in this fashion, Bordelli could imagine just about anything, even that it was Martians who killed him or, better yet, Santa Claus . . .

Rolling down the dirt road leading to his beloved abode he decided not to think about anything. He felt like a fly trapped in a jar, and no matter where he hurled himself he ran only into glass. For the rest of the evening he wanted only to devote himself to the pleasures of the table and his discussions with the colonel . . . Speaking of whom, should he tell him what Agostinelli had said, or was it better not to upset him? He would decide later, depending on the situation.

He opened the door and, before crossing the threshold into the kitchen, smelled a wonderful aroma of food on the stove. Arcieri was indeed at the cooker, duly engrossed, and quite pleased to announce the evening's menu: chickpea soup with broken-up spaghetti, veal scaloppine with white wine sauce and, as a side dish, a new attempt at 'potatoes and onions' according to his mother's recipe.

'You can sit right down at the table if you like, it's almost ready.'

'I couldn't have asked for more.'

'I put the pasta in the soup as soon as I heard your car at the top of the road.'

'I guess working for the Special Services can be useful after all,' said Bordelli, thanking the heavens for having fulfilled his wishes in the best manner possible. He ducked into the bathroom to wash his hands well, like a good boy, then returned to the kitchen, humming to himself. Having restoked the fire, he put a couple of large logs in the hearth, uncorked a bottle of Balzini, and sat down at the table, awaiting the chickpea soup with his mouth watering. At last Arcieri turned off the flame under the pot.

'I added a bit of rosemary. It should taste pretty good,' he declared with satisfaction, approaching the table amidst a cloud of steam worthy of Totò.

'It smells promising,' said the inspector, pouring wine into their glasses. The colonel filled their soup bowls and then sat down across from him.

'And now a drop of olive oil and a generous dusting of Parmesan,' he said in the tone of a serious chef. He seemed at peace, almost cheerful; or at least the usual gloom was gone from his eyes.

'I love soup,' said Bordelli, passing him the cheese.

'I've never much liked to cook, but lately I seem to have developed a passion for it . . . Could it be old age?' Arcieri wondered aloud.

'We can discuss that later, in detail, but for now let me enjoy this wonder of cookery,' the inspector mumbled between spoonfuls. So far it was a placid evening, and it would have been a shame to ruin it by mentioning his phone conversation with Agostinelli.

'You have no idea how happy your appreciation makes me. I guess I now have proper confirmation that I am indeed old,' Arcieri continued, brow furrowed.

'So what am I supposed to say? At this moment, not even a beautiful woman could make me happier than this *pasta e ceci* . . . If that's not old age, I don't know what is . . .'

'Shall we have a contest to see who's older? I have an idea.'

'Let's hear it.'

'I would like to do the cooking for Friday's dinner myself. Without anyone's help.'

'That's a challenge for the very young.'

'So, what do you say? Will you grant me the honour?' the colonel asked.

'It's perfectly fine with me, but I'll have to hear what Ennio says. He was supposed to do the cooking. I don't know how he'll take it.'

'Just explain to your friend that it's a very special occasion for me,' Arcieri said in a serious tone.

'I'll see if I can reach him tomorrow.'

'You realise, of course, that I could be forced to flee from one moment to the next.'

'Let's not think about that for now,' said Bordelli, trying to smile.

'This may even turn out to be my last Christmas dinner,' Arcieri muttered sadly. The inspector refilled their glasses, and gestured a toast.

'Let's talk about serious matters . . . Are you sure you want to embark on such an endeavour? It won't be like cooking for two people, you know.'

'I love a good challenge,' said the colonel, imperceptibly raising his glass.

'I admire your courage.'

'I forget how many of us there will be at the dinner.'

'There were supposed to be seven of us, but the psychoanalyst will be out of town for the holidays . . . I think it's for love . . .'

'Then he's forgiven.'

'Have you already got a menu planned?'

'More or less,' Arcieri said mysteriously.

'Let's wait for Ennio's verdict, and if there are no problems you must tell me what to buy,' said the inspector, pleased to have brought the conversation back to lighter subjects.

'The scaloppine need another five minutes.'

'I'll try to control my temper.'

'No . . . I didn't mean . . . At any rate, as soon as you've finished your soup you can try to get in touch with your friend Ennio and settle the question straight away. The elderly can't tolerate uncertainty for very long. And anyway, it's only two days till Friday . . .'

'Maybe I should tell Ennio you need a sous-chef.'

'There's no need, thanks.'

'Not even me?'

'I'd rather do everything myself, if you don't mind.'

'As you wish.'

'Consider it my Christmas present to you.'

'I couldn't imagine a better one.'

'And you've given me a fine one too,' said Arcieri.

He patiently waited for the inspector to finish his soup, then took the empty bowls and headed over to the cooker to attend to the scaloppine. Bordelli went upstairs to phone Ennio, bringing his glass with him. He started dialling the number for Fosco's bar, then remembered that Ennio now had a phone at home and hung up. As he was turning the dial anew, he got the idea to play a joke on his friend, and put his hand over the receiver to disguise his voice.

'Hello?' said Ennio.

'Am I speaking with Signor Bottarini?'

'Yes, who is this?'

'Good evening, I'm the warden of Gorgona prison.'

'Why, what is this?' said Ennio, alarmed.

'The next time you're arrested, I would like to recommend that you stay in our luxurious penitentiary. We have splendid cells outfitted with all the latest conveniences, and magnificent views of the sea . . .'

'Good God, Inspector . . . I can't believe . . .'

'You already recognise me?'

'This is schoolboy stuff, Inspector.'

'How are you, Ennio?'

'I'm in a bit of a hurry. I was just on my way out.'

'A woman?'

'She's not a woman, she's a goddess.'

'Then you really must thank your Alfa Romeo,' Bordelli ribbed him.

'Actually, I was on my bicycle when I met her.'

'Then she really needs to see an eye doctor.'

'I'm running late, Inspector. Did you have anything pressing to tell me?'

'Absolutely . . . Well, it's just . . . There's been a slight change in plans regarding Friday's dinner. A friend of mine has offered to do the cooking, but only if it's all right with you.'

'And who's this friend?' asked Botta, a little surprised. Suddenly he wasn't in such a hurry.

'He's a retired general I met during the war, a superior of mine. I hadn't seen him for at least twenty years, when I ran into him in the streets of Florence, where he was passing through. He's staying at my house for a few days. He's a good cook, I assure you,' Bordelli exaggerated, almost blindly staking his bet on the colonel's abilities.

'Well, if you think it's all right, then it's all right with me too.'

'The fact that you give in so easily must mean you're in love.'

'You may be right.'

'I'm happy for you.'

'I gotta go, Inspector.'

'Break a leg.'

'Her name is Anita,' said Botta, hanging up. The inspector descended the stairs imagining Ennio in jacket and tie, hair slicked back with pomade, driving his red Alfa along the boulevards in the company of a beautiful woman, in love. He wondered whether Ennio had told her about his pilgrimages to half the prisons around the world.

'It's all settled: Friday's dinner is now officially in your hands,' he said to the colonel.

'I'll try to be equal to my crucial mission,' joked Arcieri, visibly pleased.

'When do you need me to go shopping?'

'Friday morning would be best. I'll make you a detailed list.'

'Yes, sir . . .'

They sat back down at table, to do justice to the scaloppine. They were truly excellent. As were the potatoes and onions, though Arcieri was still not satisfied.

Every so often Bordelli would remember his phone conversations with Agostinelli and wonder whether it might not be better to mention them. But then he would look over and see Arcieri's finally untroubled face, and in the end he decided to let it go.

To conclude the meal, they shared an apple, like two young brothers. As the inspector was clearing the table, Arcieri went into the sitting room and put a Mozart mass on the turntable.

After uncorking another bottle, they went and sat in the easy chairs by the fire and each lit up a cigarette. They sat there in silence, listening to the music. Throwing his head back, Bordelli closed his eyes. He was just drifting off to sleep when he heard the colonel's voice.

'Have you made any progress?'

'Eh? What was that?'

'On your investigation . . . The man run through with a foil . . .'

'Ah, yes . . . I mean, no . . . I'm still bogged down.'

'Not even some unlikely suspect?'

'Nothing whatsoever, I'm just feeling my way along,' said Bordelli, throwing up his hands.

'I'm sure something'll turn up sooner or later . . .'

'All I've got is a confirmation that Migliorini fell in love with a beautiful married woman much younger than him – tall, refined, and almost certainly from a prominent family, possibly even aristocratic. That's all I know.'

'It's already something, don't you think?'

'The problem is that nobody can tell me who this mysterious woman is. And I have no idea where to look for her. She's certainly not going to come forward of her own accord.' Sharing his sense of futility with another had a soothing effect on him.

'And why are you so interested in meeting this woman?'

'I don't really even know, but at the moment I've got nothing else to go on . . . Though, actually, there's also that old story of the chicken-plucker . . .'

'And what's that about?' the colonel asked, curious.

Tossing his butt into the fire, Bordelli refilled the glasses anew and started retelling the story of Averino Buzzi he'd heard from Butelli. When it was his turn, the colonel told him about some so-called partisan fighters who had holed up in an old mine during the German occupation and then come back out when it was all over with red bandanas round their necks . . .

Jumping from subject to subject, they found themselves again sailing through the past, letting themselves melt away ever so pleasantly into melancholy. They called forth memories more and more remote in time, when not downright buried. And they ventured far and wide, into the dreams and fears they had in childhood and the magic of certain imaginings, finding in their recollections the small events that had left indelible marks on their lives . . . *One evening, Mamma, when tucking me up, said to me . . . My father looked me in the eye, and I could see he was crying . . . That morning we woke up to snow, and I suddenly realised that* . . . They had fun telling stories, digging deep into their memories, as often happens when one finds oneself with an attentive listener. They didn't notice the time passing, even though the Sandman every so often made an appearance.

When they finally looked at the clock it was past two. Arcieri shook his head, as if he felt guilty.

'I made you stay up late again.'

'Apparently I like it,' said Bordelli. They stood up together and headed for the stairs, towards the realm of Morpheus. They were both in a bit of a daze, but only because they were tired and had drunk too much wine. Back from their long journey into the past, they were still surrounded by a host of ghosts.

'Another day gone by,' Arcieri said under his breath.

'Happens basically every day,' said the inspector, smiling.

They conquered the first floor, and Bordelli let his guest use the bathroom first, gesturing goodnight. While awaiting his turn he filled the stove with wood, then went into his room to tidy up the bed. He couldn't wait to lie down and sleep, so he could stop thinking about the mystery woman.

Hearing the colonel come out of the bathroom and head down the corridor, he went and brushed his teeth. Three minutes later he was under the covers, in the dark, curled up like a child seeking warmth. All of a sudden, as in a dream, he saw the eyes of a girl he had saved in the Abruzzi in June of '43, shooting at a drunken SS soldier who was about to throw her out the window. Now the beautiful child must be about thirty years old . . . Who knew where she was . . . Was she happy? What was her name? She had a rather unusual, sweet-sounding name . . . Damina . . . Delfina . . . No, actually, it was . . . Dorina . . . Yes . . . Dorina . . . Dorina Fante . . . More than twenty years had gone by, and he still remembered her name . . .

Before sinking into sleep he recited under his breath a few of his mother's lines of verse, which by now he knew by heart . . . *Summer will follow spring, winter fall, and so on till the sun shines hot above* . . . Then there was that sort of limerick . . . *I saw her on the metro with eyes just like black pearls,/a girl of gentle character, /a very pretty girl* . . . But when had his mother ever taken the metro? And what was she talking about in that sad poem that ended with those unforgettable lines . . .? *For my love to die like that,/on a night of frost,/was not my wish* . . . What was she referring to? When did she write it? He would never know . . .

At a quarter past eight he opened the door to his office. He had slept for only five hours or so, but was not overly tired, owing perhaps to the cold.

He sat down, reached for the telephone and set it squarely in front of him. He couldn't give up, he had to try again. Who was that beautiful creature with whom Antonio Migliorini had fallen in love? How on earth was it possible that no one knew anything about her? He laid out the list of the usual suspects and started ringing them up, one after the other. The children, the sister, the daughter-in-law, friends . . . Miraculously he managed to speak to them all, although in some instances it took more than one try. But nothing came of it. He had wasted two hours. No one had ever seen the woman. Relatives didn't even know she existed; they were thunderstruck by the news. Some of them even asked him for information, which was absurd.

He didn't call Juliette; he was certain she didn't know any more than she had already told him. He stopped to think about her for a minute and felt his heart race. Who knew whether they would ever see each other again. If he did ever see her again, it certainly wouldn't be as a client, but sometimes life was strange . . .

He also rang Oberto, but not to ask him about the mystery woman – after all, he was the only one who had been able to give a description of her, however vague. He was calling him on a whim, for no specific reason, merely in the hope that something else might have popped into his mind. But he wasn't at home. Oberto rarely was. And now he was even rich . . . The inspector wondered whether he would be a flashy spender or parsimonious. And what about Juliette? Would she stop practicing the world's oldest profession? Or was it more than a profession for her? At this point she could allow herself to choose and this definitely made things easier for her. Ah, there he was thinking about her again.

Someone knocked on his door. It was Piras. He didn't come all the way in, but just stood in the doorway, hand on the knob. He had been called out with Rinaldi and Tapinassi to a student protest. But he had news about Averino Buzzi, the chicken-plucker.

'He's been locked up in Pistoia prison for almost a year and has two more years to go. He stabbed two people in a fight, and he's a repeat offender.'

'So basically, another dead end.'

'I have to go now.'

'Thank you, Piras.'

'You're welcome, sir.' The Sardinian closed the door behind him and silence fell over the room again. But it wasn't the usual silence. It didn't have anything to do with the absence of sound. Rather, it was a kind of emptiness cloaking Antonio Migliorini's murder. He was like a corpse in the middle of a desert, surrounded by vast stretches of sand, the wind eroding any kind of trace. In the distance Bordelli could see a trembling, mysterious mirage of a woman without a face.

But he certainly wasn't going to let it get him down, damn it all. He needed some kind of distraction, to forget about work for a few hours. The sun shone through the dirty windows of his office, and above the rooftops he could see a sliver of clear sky.

He couldn't resist. He put on his overcoat and walked out, leaving his cigarettes behind. It was only eleven o'clock but the centre of town was already teeming with people. It was hard to make his way down the pavements. Cars and motorbikes crawled forward slowly, bicycle bells rang out in the air. The Christmas period was an ideal time for pickpockets.

He noticed that the majority of people around him were women, and they all looked beautiful. He devoured them with his eyes, enjoying even the minor details. He was constantly surprised by the infinite kinds of beauty that existed, and how attracted he was to women who were completely different one from the other. He looked around and felt the appeal of all types: an elegant lady, a wholesome girl, a breathtaking blend of chic and vulgar in a single woman, an angelic face, a hot tempter, a tired beauty, one shy, another bold . . . What common element did they all have that made his heart skip a beat? It was hard to say; maybe there was no common element. His was an impulse that went beyond reason and straight to the blood, almost animal. And it all stemmed from a single glance, after which everything else came into play, and very often the initial attraction would vanish down the drain, like toothpaste after brushing one's teeth. . .

Suddenly, as happened all too frequently these days, he imagined coming face to face with Eleonora, and he felt himself blush. He couldn't do anything about it, he felt terribly ashamed about what had happened. It had been his fault; he could never forget it. He'd been a fool, and letting himself be guided by idiocy was worse than committing a mistake. Faced with the impossibility of catching Giacomo's killers, he had forged on just the same, rather like David against Goliath. But in actual fact he had behaved like a real fool. He wondered how many other things he could have done instead. It occurred to him again that it was this very sense of guilt that linked him to Eleonora. He wanted her to forgive him, he wanted to feel that it was water under the bridge, that that wretched night had been forgotten and had not left any trace. He wanted to see her smile the way she used to, he wanted to know that she could still make love with the same joy as before . . . Was that really all it was? Was this the only reason he couldn't get her out of his mind? Or was he still in love with her? One thing was certain, the burden of the violence and humiliation that she had been subjected to would accompany him to the grave. Not even Eleonora's blessing could free him of that millstone. He had been bogged down with thoughts like these for a long time, and felt powerless to change the situation.

Taking smaller, less crowded streets, he reached Piazza Goldoni and started across the Ponte alla Carraia.

Dear Eleonora, this is the most difficult letter I have ever written . . . He tore up the fantasy letter in his mind and threw it into the Arno, imagining the scraps of paper floating lightly on the murky water. Past the bridge, he turned up Borgo San Frediano. The streets were crowded here, too, but there was less confusion, and it wasn't as hard to make his way along the pavements. Despite his glum train of thoughts he continued to eye women. It helped boost his morale. Actually, he not only looked at them, he scrutinised them, studied their details as an art historian would a painting.

Women let him believe that life had a meaning, even if he didn't know what that meaning was. Perhaps the admiration he felt for them was exaggerated, but he couldn't do anything about it. His literature teacher at grammar school had always said that man couldn't live without creating his own mythology, without an example to follow.

He felt at home in these streets. Every so often he needed to come back to them. He wondered whether anyone knew of an apartment for sale. He looked into a few different workshops to say hello, to chat with the artisans, and asked around.

'Go ask Pialla, I think I heard that he's selling a small flat on Via del Leone.'

'Thanks, I'll go now. If we don't see each other, happy Christmas.'

He continued on down the street. After about a hundred metres he pushed open the door to the workshop belonging to old Dario, also known as Pialla, for the tool, a plane, that he had been using practically since his birth in 1885. The workshop was full of furniture that Dario had collected from people's attics and cellars, which he would renovate and then sell. He was a tenacious old chap. It hadn't taken him long to get back on his feet after the flood.

'Hello, Inspector, how are things?'

'Not bad, and yourself?'

'Me? What can I do? I'm in the queue for the hereafter.'

'Just like everybody else, Dario.'

'I'm right at the front of the queue . . . already on my way out . . . and *there stands Minos, terrible and growling* . . .' Pialla said, quoting Dante's *Inferno* with a smile.

'Are you joking? They'll take you straight to heaven and ask you to restore St Peter's throne.'

'More likely they'll ask me to restore the gates to hell. Anyway, I want to be buried with my plane, I've said so in my will.'

'Don't think about it too much, Dario. All in due time.'

'At least I'll see my wife again. It's been twelve years since she left, and it feels like yesterday.'

'She was a fine woman, Maria was . . . And how is your son?'

'He's working at a garage in Campo di Marte. He couldn't care less about his father's workshop.'

'Things aren't the way they used to be, Dario. But people are freer; think of it as a good thing.'

'I'll try, but the thought that, when I'm gone, everything will be cleaned out doesn't make me too happy.'

'They'll put a plaque on the wall . . . *Here Lived Pialla* . . .'

'Pulling my leg, are you? Ah, before I forget, here's the number of someone who is selling a small flat on Via del Leone, third floor. A little past where you used to live, practically in Piazza Tasso. Do you have a pencil? Wait; let's call from here. It's easier.'

'Thank you.'

'I put the number somewhere over here . . . ah, here it is . . .' Dario dialled the number, talked to the fellow, and passed the phone to Bordelli. The owner lived in the hills around Careggi. They made an appointment to meet at five in front of the main entrance to the building.

'Thank you, Dario.'

'For what?'

'Have a pleasant Christmas.'

'You too, Inspector. Let's hope that next year is better than this one.'

''Bye, Dario, see you soon.'

The inspector turned down Via del Leone. Passing the building where he had lived for many years, he turned and looked up at his former windows on the third floor and thought again about Eleonora, and that wretched night when he'd driven her to her parents' house. It was quite possibly the saddest memory of his life after the death of his mother. Women had left him many times in his life, but losing her was completely different. He had seen her only once since then, in early March, in the centre of town. She had been on the other side of the street, walking arm in arm with her friend. She looked happy. But he hadn't had the courage to say anything.

He walked past the intersection with Piazza Piatellina and on towards Piazza Tasso, stopping for a moment in front of the building where they were selling the apartment to look at the façade. It was tall and narrow, a little run down, but all in all, not bad. Anyway, at five he would see the place and then decide.

It was past one o'clock and he was ravenous. To head back to the station along a different route, he reached Piazza Tasso and then turned up Via della Chiesa, then down Via dei Serragli towards the Arno. He crossed Ponte Santa Trinita, glancing at the new parapet they had rebuilt on Lungarno Acciaioli, after the flood.

He clearly remembered the dawn of 5 November. He had been forced to stay inside his house on Via del Leone and had spent the day looking at the river of mud coursing down his street, pulling everything along with it. As soon as the water level had gone down he ventured out onto the devastated streets, walking between debris and dead animals, seeing ruined automobiles and desperate people. Everywhere the air smelled of sewage and diesel. There had been dozens of victims, some of whom had died in the strangest of ways. Works of art had been destroyed, ancient books lost: the restoration would take decades. But Florence never lost its arrogance, nor its taste for joking. Even in the days directly after the catastrophe, people were telling jokes about the flood, some funny, others vulgar, some even cruel.

Opposing aspects came from the same Florentine 'soul': there was the fine Florentine wit, which could sweeten life with irony; there was also a vulgar, stupid and violent sarcasm, which smacked of cowardice. Florentines were capable of defending themselves verbally from a ferocious attack, but they could also strike a man when he was down. In other words, Florence was like fire: it could warm you but also burn you to a crisp. Bordelli had often thought about these things, each time in a new way . . .

He reached Piazza Santa Trinita, and to avoid the luxury shops on Via Tornabuoni, he walked down Borgo SS Apostoli. It was already lunchtime, the shutters on the shops had been pulled down, and there was far less chaos in the streets . . . *And hunger overcame Christmas*, he thought, altering Dante's words to fit the season.

That day he was a bit late in arriving at Cesare's trattoria, and when he came back out it was already time to head for San Frediano to have a look at the flat. It was best to go on foot; that would be much quicker.

Crossing the street crammed with nervous motorists, he felt light on his feet and was pleased about this. He'd eaten rather little and drunk less than half a glass of red. Totò had failed to undermine his resolve, not even by dint of *pappardelle sul cinghiale*. But it was no victory for virtue: he'd simply wanted to eat light because of the dinner planned for the following day.

He was a little worried about Arcieri, however. He'd tried ringing him at home from the restaurant's telephone, to ask him if he had the shopping list, since he himself was going to San Frediano and could buy some things in shops he knew well. As agreed, he'd let the phone ring just once, hung up, then called right back. But the colonel hadn't picked up. No doubt he'd gone out for a walk or fallen asleep.

Still, he didn't feel entirely at ease. People were after Arcieri, after all, and had even tried to kill him . . . But all this drama was starting to seem silly. Who on earth was ever going to find him in an old farmhouse on a hilltop? He would simply call back later, and Arcieri would most certainly answer.

Reassured by these thoughts, he dived into the madness of the streets, humming a melody that had stuck in his head, a song played often on the radio and sung by one of those British longhairs who made all the girls scream. He couldn't deny that some of those tunes were amusing, even engaging, though he couldn't understand a word of them.

The shop windows were ever more stuffed with sparkling displays of fake snow and flashing coloured lights, the streets festooned with strings of lights which during the day didn't make such a great impression. Whenever he saw a dog he thought of Blisk the Second and wondered whether the big white bear would ever come back to see him. Was he even still alive?

Someone was playing a bagpipe in the distance, and it sounded sad, even desperate, to him, bringing back a childhood memory. He was walking the streets of the centre of town with his father, looking for presents for his mother and grandparents. It was a very long time ago, a kind of mythic age, when the Christmas season was enveloped in a kind of agonising magical aura that dispersed over time until it vanished. He would have given up ten years of his life to go back to that time . . .

Coming out from the Piazza dell'Olio he saw across the street the sign for Alberti's, the famous music store, and thought that on his way back he could look there for a jazz disc for the colonel.

He suddenly thought of something he could do. Yes, it was worth trying. It might amount to nothing, and he certainly didn't want to delude himself. But then, thinking that even the tallest trees originate from the smallest of seeds, he decided to delude himself.

He turned onto Via de' Pecori and kept walking. When he came out in Piazza Antinori he ventured bravely down Via Tornabuoni and ducked into the Libreria Seeber, which was unusually crowded. Looking around for the young salesman who always recommended good novels to him, he found him upstairs, surrounded by a bevy of ladies barraging him with questions . . . They were asking him, for example, what to give a son who had just obtained a medical degree and wanted to become a dentist, or what to get for a lawyer brother-in-law who had a sailing boat at Viareggio, or for a nephew who was in his fourth year of Liceo Scientifico and loved movies, or for a husband who was an accountant but loved to go hunting, or for a dear retired lady friend who loved to read, or a very nice neighbour who collected antique irons . . . The salesman pretended to have the answer for every one of them, and was able to free himself promptly.

He then came over to Bordelli and greeted him with a slight bow. He immediately had two novels to recommend to him; one was a classic, the other just published, but Bordelli said that unfortunately, at the moment, he had little time to read and still had to finish the novels he'd bought a few months earlier. All the same, he was looking for a book to give someone as a present, and so he wanted some advice.

'Whatever I can do . . .'

'He's a lad of just sixteen and has probably never read a novel in his life. His parents are just poor devils who've been forced to stretch the law a little to get by, and he risks going down the wrong road. But he seems like a smart, sensitive kid, and so I'm deluding myself that I might be able to help him. But I need the right book, some kind of story to draw him in, something that talks in a sense about him.'

'I think I might know something that would work. Please follow me.'

They went down to the ground floor, wending their way through the crowd until they reached a shelf at the far end of the shop.

'This might work,' the salesman said, handing him a fine edition of *Oliver Twist*.

'Nice idea,' said Bordelli. 'Dickens might just be the one to work a miracle.'

'Shall I gift-wrap it for you?'

'Yes, thank you.'

While waiting to pay, he thought he might just be wasting his time, or that the whole thing might lead to a misunderstanding . . . *What's this guy want, anyway? To make us feel ignorant?* Moments later he was coming out the shop with the book in his pocket, and he headed for San Frediano.

It was almost five o'clock, and the sun was already setting. The streets were more and more crowded, and it wasn't easy to advance without bumping shoulders with someone. He often had to dodge and weave or even come to a complete halt, and the cumulative buzz of voices sounded like what you hear at intermission at the theatre. The lights in the display windows and the flashing decorations strung between the buildings hypnotised little children being dragged along by harried parents loaded down with parcels and irritated by all the confusion and too much walking. Little groups of young girls called to one another, laughing, often followed by lads in search of romance, and every so often amidst all the fine clothes and fur coats there appeared a beggar with hand extended, or a little woman selling chestnuts amidst a cloud of smoke. There was also the inevitable dotard with a cane trying to make his way through the throng, or a wizened old lady all alone, looking around with fear as if she had descended from another century . . .

Instead of hunting down killers, Bordelli was strolling through the centre of town looking at girls and buying Christmas presents. It made no sense, but what else, really, could he do? What was the point of sitting in his office juggling hypotheses and diddling around making useless phone calls? He had nothing whatsoever to go on, not the slightest lead to follow. Only some new development could pull him out of this quicksand. It was a terrible feeling. He'd had trouble with a case before, but never this bad . . .

At one point, amidst the stream of people he thought he saw a face he knew, a lad of about twenty with shadowy eyes like Oberto's . . . Who was it? He reminded him of something important, but what? Wending his way through the overcoats, he followed the young man, and when he finally reached him he pulled up beside him to have a look. The lad realised this, turned towards him, gasped in surprise, and came to complete halt. For a moment he seemed to want to run away, but then he calmed down and even gave a hint of a smile. At that point Bordelli recognised him.

'Ciao, Odoardo, how nice to see you,' he said, as the passers-by mumbled in protest.

'Hello, Inspector.'

They shook hands and went over to a nearby wall to avoid blocking the buffalo stampede.

'How are you? Still working with that architect?'

'Yes, I'm still working there.'

'Still a student?'

'No, I graduated a few months ago.'

'With the highest marks, I imagine.'

'Well, yes.' He seemed a little embarrassed, as if unable to find the words for what he was thinking.

'Do you still live in that big country house?' asked Bordelli.

'Yes . . .'

'All by yourself?'

'For now, yes.'

'Girlfriends?'

'Yes, I've got one.'

'Are you looking for a present to buy her?'

'I'm trying.'

'Well then, I'd better stop pestering you with questions, or it's liable to turn into an interrogation. But I'm glad to know you're well, and I wish you the best of luck in everything.'

He held out his hand again, and the young man squeezed it hard.

'Inspector . . . I . . .' Odoardo stopped, eyes veiled with tears.

'What's wrong? Is there some problem?'

'No . . . it's just that . . . well . . . I wanted to thank you for . . . I'll never forget what . . .'

'Forget about it, Odoardo, don't even think about it. I just did what seemed right at the time. You don't owe me anything. I wish you a very happy Christmas.'

By way of goodbye, he squeezed the lad's shoulder, and before Odoardo could say anything else, he dived back into the sea of people, thinking of how many hundreds of men and women he had met during his investigations over twenty years of police work. But he didn't remember all of them; that would have been impossible. On a few occasions he'd even made friends . . .. He'd met Rosa during a dragnet right after the war. Dante, for his part, was the brother of an elderly lady who'd been murdered a few years earlier by her nephews. Odoardo, on the other hand, had not become his friend; the difference in age was too great. But he would never forget him. The lad could easily be rotting in some penitentiary with no hope of making a life for himself; instead he was free, working at the profession of his choice, living in a beautiful house, and strolling through the centre of town in search of a Christmas present for his girlfriend . . .[24]

Crossing the Arno, the inspector looked at his watch. He was a little late, and so he quickened his pace. Good God, were there a lot of woman out and about! As though fallen from the heavens, *a miracol mostrare . . .*[25]

'Ciao, Fosco . . .'

'Well, hello, Inspector . . . Coffee?'

'Just a glass of water.'

'Water? Do you feel all right?' Fosco asked, with a smile. The inspector nodded in greeting to the group of four men playing cards at the back of the bar. Petty crooks, but with good hearts: they would never hurt a fly. As always a cloud of foul-smelling smoke hung in the air; ever since he had started cutting down, his nose had become quite sensitive.

'Do you have a token for the phone?' Bordelli asked.

'Go ahead and use my phone,' Fosco replied, placing the bar telephone on the counter.

'Thank you.' He dialled his home number, let it ring once, hung up and called back immediately. He let it ring for a long time, but Arcieri didn't reply. The door to the billiards room must have been left open because every so often he could hear the sound of someone shooting pool and the comments from the neighbourhood layabouts. He tried calling back after drinking his water. He let it ring once, as they had agreed, and then called back. Nothing. The colonel wasn't answering. Should he be worried? Had he been discovered? Had he fallen ill?

'You calling a married woman?' Fosco asked.

'What?'

'I see you're using a code.'

'You don't miss a thing.'

'Ha, that's nothing. I can recognise undercover cops at a glance. Even naked.'

'Well, that's lucky,' Bordelli said, knowing full well that Fosco dealt in contraband cigarettes. He knew it because every so often he had bought them too. He was a good guy, Fosco, much more sincere than some of their so-called politicians.

'Did you like the flat, Inspector?'

'How do you know about that?'

'A little bird told me.'

'This neighbourhood is worse than Murate,' Bordelli said, knowing that news travels mysteriously fast in prison.

'The only thing worse than Murate is the cemetery, Inspector,' mumbled Fosco, washing the cups.

'The flat wasn't bad, but I realised it wasn't for me. What would I do with two homes?'

'Too bad . . .' Fosco said, sincerely.

'I have to go, how much do I owe you?'

'Are you joking?'

'Thank you.'

'Not to worry, Inspector. Would you like some cigarettes?'

'I've practically quit.'

'Good for you.'

'Happy Christmas, Fosco. Try not to get into trouble.'

'If you see Father Christmas, tell him to pay some of my IOUs.

'Just behave, all right? Otherwise the Befana will bring you charcoal,'[26] Bordelli said. As he walked out of the bar, he waved briefly to the card players, who replied in kind. Stepping outside, he realised how smoky the bar had been.

He walked down Via del Leone, pulling his overcoat tightly around him, and when he got to the crossroads, turned right towards Piazza del Carmine. He was still worried . . . Why hadn't the colonel answered the phone? Was he just being careful? Or had something happened? If he thought too much about it, he risked making a mountain out of a molehill. Maybe Arcieri had been reading by the fire and had fallen asleep, or else the phone lines were down. It wouldn't be the first time. The poles carrying the phone lines to his house were rotten. In other words, there was no real reason to be worried. Still, he was eager to get home as fast as possible, so he could stop wasting his time with unpleasant thoughts. But first he had something else to do. It would only take a few minutes.

Walking past the church, he looked up at the large block of flats on the corner where the loan shark Totuccio Badalamenti had lived a few years back, before he was killed with a pair of scissors to the back of the neck, like a bull in the arena.[27] Bordelli was pleased to realise that he couldn't remember which windows were his. That time, too, he had broken a few rules, but he had never had any misgivings about them. He wondered whether Odoardo avoided passing in front of that building, or whether it didn't bother him anymore. He wondered who lived there now. That large apartment had been home to greed and humiliation for years. Did whoever lived there now know about Badalamenti or were they blissfully unaware that they were living in a flat where a murder had been committed? All ancient homes, and even simply old ones, had their stories – good things and bad, sometimes horrible things. It was better not to know. Sometimes it was ghosts telling their own stories, in their own way. Even the walls of his old country house had surely seen many things happen, and one day even they might come to the surface.

He stepped up his pace and, after crossing the piazza, turned right down Via Ardiglione, a long, dark, narrow street. Here, the stench of sewage and heating oil from the flood still hung in the air, even though the Arno hadn't reached more than a metre in height in that area.

He neared the end of the street and stopped under the low archway. He was just a few metres from where Filippo Lippi was born. Just above his head, under the arch, in complete darkness, he knew there was an ancient tabernacle that he had always liked. To see it, he had to light and hold up a match. It was possibly one of the most beautiful tabernacles in the city. If he reached up, he could even touch it. It was made of stone and sculpted in the manner of traditional altars. It had an oval opening, in which an elegant Madonna figure made of white gypsum stood protected in a deep niche painted lapis blue. Standing before the simplicity of that image, he felt the magic of childhood, the painful magic of nameless emotions, and he smiled, sadly recalling a past era that could never come back, but also could never be effaced . . .

When he felt that the match had burnt almost to the end, he tossed it aside and continued on down the road. He stopped just before a bend and knocked on a dilapidated door. After a minute he heard a woman's voice.

'Who's there?'

'It's Bordelli.'

'Who?'

'Bordelli . . .' After a few moments of silence the door opened and there stood Iolanda, hair unkempt, in slippers, a small child holding on to her skirt.

'Has something happened to Foresto?' she asked in fear. As a young woman, Iolanda had been gorgeous, the kind of beauty that caused heads to turn and made people bump into poles. Four children and a life none too easy had aged her quickly but her face still afforded a glimpse of her past beauty.

'No, not to worry. I was passing by and thought I would drop in. Is Matteo home?'

'What's he done?'

'When is Papa coming home?' the toddler whined.

'He hasn't done anything. I just wanted to say hello.'

'He told me you kept his arse out of prison. God bless you.' Two children were playing audibly at the end of a long hallway.

'Can I talk to Matteo?'

'When is Papa coming home?'

'That's enough whining, Mimma, Papa will be home soon . . . Come in, Franco. Matteo is in his room. Follow me. He has a slight fever, otherwise he'd be outside.'

'And school?' Bordelli asked, following her down the narrow, mouldy-smelling hallway.

'What about school?'

They walked into a small room with a bed and an old chest of drawers, the paint of which was peeling. Matteo was lying on the mattress; he was dressed and had his shoes on, but as soon as he saw Bordelli he sat up. His mother looked with disgust at a large poster nailed to the wall.

'I've got some potatoes on the stove,' she said, and walked away, the child still clinging to her skirt. The poster showed five long-haired young men with sneering faces. Underneath it said *The Rolling Stones*.

'You like them?' the inspector asked.

'They're cool . . .' Matteo said with a shrug. He didn't even have a record player. Bordelli was in a bit of a hurry to get home for the colonel's sake, and he promptly took the book out of his coat pocket.

'I brought you this,' he said. Matteo took the package suspiciously, unwrapped it, and saw it was a book. He didn't look too happy about it, but thanked the inspector anyway with a few mumbled words. Bordelli tried not to feel discouraged.

'He who reads doesn't get tricked by the Cat and the Fox,' he said.

'Huh?'

'Don't you know Pinocchio?'

'Sure . . .'

'Try reading this, you might like it.'

He looked at the shy, thin boy. His eyes were wide with curiosity; he was so different from his father. Everyone in San Frediano remembered the big fight that took place fifteen years ago, when Foresto had battled it out with that beast, Lordo, who was a real son of a bitch and had stolen the bicycle of Marietto, a poor kid from the neighbourhood who was hanging on by the skin of his teeth. Legend had it that they had started punching each other after lunch and finished at dinner time, their faces purple from the blows. Then they all went to eat at I Raddi, even Marietto. Clearly Matteo would never make his way with his fists; he just wasn't that type of person.

'Try not to end up in prison. I assure you that it isn't fun at all.'

'I know . . .' the boy said, pouting. Bordelli didn't want to bore him with more lectures. He had planted the seed, what else could he do? He could only hope for a miracle – that the seed would sprout.

''Bye, Matteo.' He held out his hand and they shook, and then he left. He peeped into the kitchen, which was as spare as the rest of the house.

'I'm leaving. Don't mind me, I'll let myself out. Happy Christmas.'

'You too, Franco. Do you want some cigarettes?'

'I'm quitting, thank you. Say hello to Foresto . . . 'Bye, Mimma.'

'Say goodbye to Franco, Mimma.'

'No matter . . . 'Bye, sweetie, be good.' He waved to the little girl and made his way down the dark hallway. To open the door he had to throw two or three bolts. He went out and walked back down the deserted alley, careful not to trip on the uneven flagstones. Passing back under the Madonnina, he glanced up but didn't stop. He was in a hurry to get home but had to go back to the office to get the car; he would try to call the colonel one more time from the office. As he passed under a street lamp he peered at his watch. Quarter past six. He picked up his pace, anxious to get home. There was no one around: it seemed almost impossible that just a few blocks away the streets and piazzas were thronging with people.

Mimma was truly adorable. He started thinking about how difficult and fun it was to raise kids. And how sad it was to grow old alone, to die without having a son to hold your hand. His mother had left this world peacefully, with him reciting D'Annunzio's most famous poem to her. At such an important time as death, he too would have been content with the same things: a child and a poem. Maybe even a poem by his mother, to bring things full circle . . . He tried to put these thoughts out of his mind, to escape the clutches of sadness.

He crossed over the Arno and, in the hope of avoiding the busiest streets, took Via del Moro, where one could walk without being jostled by pedestrians. He was about to head straight to San Lorenzo, but then remembered the present for Arcieri and turned down Via del Trebbio. The idea of stopping at Alberti's to buy a jazz record calmed him down, as if that gesture signified that everything was all right, that the colonel was fine, and that the only thing he had to worry about was the menu for the big dinner the following day.

He even thought about ringing Juliette and inviting her to dinner, just on the spur of the moment. My God, how fascinating she was. She looked like a sixteenth-century Madonna, painted by a painter who had fallen in love with his model. Her gaze was a touch languid, just enough to be sensual, her manner refined yet insolent, and expressed mostly through her smile. Her lips looked as if they had been created especially for amorous skirmishes . . . would it be dangerous to kiss her again?

Outside Impruneta he stepped on the accelerator, feeling agitated. It was past eight. To avoid the delirium of the centre of town, he'd taken the avenues, but they had been almost worse. It had taken him nearly an hour to get from headquarters to Poggio Imperiale, and he was trying to make up the time lost. What the hell had happened? Why didn't the colonel answer the phone?

He'd tried calling him again just after seven, as soon he'd got back to the office. After the first warning ring, he'd called back and let the phone ring for a long time, hoping to hear someone pick up.

He kept imagining how he would tell the story: I'd just bought a jazz record at Alberti's for the colonel for Christmas, and then, when I got home . . . And he pictured the most horrid scenes of death . . . An iron wire round his neck, face livid, eyes popping out of his head, tongue extended and black like meat gone bad . . . Or else with his throat slit and blood everywhere, even on the ceiling . . . Or hanging from a beam . . . Or bludgeoned to death and unrecognisable . . .

Perhaps he'd been wrong not to leave him in the city, disguised as a hobo. Bringing him to his home in the country had amounted to a death sentence. Another mistake, another regret to carry around for the rest of one's life. He was ageing poorly. Maybe he should take early retirement.

Biting his lip, he swore that if the colonel had been murdered, he would find his killer . . . Well, actually, so far he hadn't even been able to find the 'mystery woman', so one could imagine how far he would get with professional killers, probably from the intelligence services . . .

He came up behind a lorry climbing slowly and spitting black smoke. Flashing his high beam, he passed it right before a bend in the road. Just as he was getting back into his lane, the headlights of a Fiat 600 coming on at full speed appeared, its horn blaring like Gassman's Lancia in *Il Sorpasso*. He had to calm down. Whatever had happened, it was already too late. He managed to slow down, but only for a brief stretch.

Crossing the central square in Impruneta, which was dark and deserted, he headed on for home with his heart racing. When he turned onto the dirt road his mouth was completely dry. He was breathing with his mouth open, and despite the cold his forehead was bathed in sweat. From about a hundred yards away he saw the threshing floor at the bottom of the hill, dimly lit by the small lamp over the front door, and tried to see whether he could spot anything unusual. The kitchen window was illuminated, the front door was closed, and everything seemed calm.

At least twice during the war he had let himself be deceived by appearances and ended up in an inferno. Now he regretted not having his regulation handgun, which he always left in his office, in the bottom drawer of his desk. Then he remembered he had another one in the glove compartment, wrapped in chamois, an old Guernica 7.65 from his San Marco days. He grabbed it, lifted the safety, and slipped it into the pocket of his overcoat. He continued driving at a walking pace.

Pulling the car up outside the front door, he turned off the headlights and got out, pistol in hand, looking around and listening to the silence. There was a half-moon in the sky, but in the ambient darkness it was almost as good as a street lamp. All quiet. The usual dogs barking in the distance, the sound of the wind, the creaking of a cypress tree. He went over to the kitchen window to have a look, holding his breath, and saw, behind the curtain . . . the colonel busy at the cooker, the table set, the fire lit. He could feel his muscles relax, and he began to breathe again. He even started laughing. He would never tell the colonel what he'd thought and lived through during the last half-hour.

He put the gun back in his pocket, thinking it was probably best to keep it within reach for the time being. He went back to the car to fetch his present for Arcieri, and as soon as he entered the house he hid the record in the broom closet. He would give it to him later, calmly, after dinner, as a real surprise, hoping he had correctly guessed the colonel's tastes. He entered the kitchen, trying to banish from his memory all the macabre scenes he'd imagined. They greeted each other like two friends living under the same roof.

'You're home early tonight,' said Arcieri.

'I tried calling several times this afternoon with no answer, and I got a little worried.'

'After lunch I went out for a short walk nearby, and then fell asleep until just a little while ago.'

'How nice to come home and find dinner ready and waiting,' said Bordelli, not letting him know how worried he'd been.

'It would be even nicer if I was a beautiful woman.'

'If you were a beautiful woman you'd be with a hot-blooded youth.'

'My potatoes and onions came out a lot better this evening.'

'God be praised . . .' said Bordelli, who was very hungry.

'I'll put the pasta in the water.'

'For the moment, I think I'll put this up here,' the inspector said casually, setting the pistol down on top of the hutch, next to Jeremiah.

'Has something happened?'

'No, I'd just forgotten I had it in the car. It's better to have it in the house. You can take it with you whenever you want.'

'That's very good of you.'

'Let me go and wash my hands, and I'll be right with you.'

He was dead tired and couldn't wait to sit down at the table.

Ten minutes later they had two plates of steaming spaghetti and tomato sauce in front of them.

'I've also made a frittata with cauliflower.'

'Excellent,' the inspector mumbled between two bites.

'Any news on the mystery woman?' Arcieri asked almost cheerfully.

'Mind if we talk about something else?' said the inspector, looking defeated.

'All right, I won't mention it again . . . Listen, do you think I could use your Olivetti tomorrow?'

'Absolutely. No need to ask.'

'Thank you.'

'Want to write your memoirs?'

'That's the last thing I need . . . Better they were buried along with me.'

'An epic poem? A sonnet?' the inspector ribbed him.

'No, I just want to write a letter, but don't ask to whom,' said the colonel, giving a faint smile.

'If it's for a woman, I think I've got a fine fountain pen lying around somewhere.'

'That would be more elegant, I know. But I have clumsy handwriting, and it costs me great effort to make it legible.'

'Well, if it makes you feel any better, my schoolmistress used to call me *chicken-scratch*,' said Bordelli, remembering how embarrassed he used to feel about it.

'Hitting those keys isn't so easy for me, but at least people can read it afterwards.'

'I hope the Olivetti still works.'

'The Lettera 22 model is a tank, a bit like your Volkswagen.'

'And do you type with your two forefingers, like all carabinieri?'

'Why? Is there any other way to do it?' Arcieri said, smiling.

The inspector was truly happy to see his new friend so calm. Sooner or later, however, he would probably have to tell him about Agostinelli, though he knew it would not be a pleasant conversation.

'Is your shopping list ready?'

'It's still all in my head. I'll compile the dossier after dinner.'

'With the Olivetti, I hope.'

'No need to worry. I'm pretty good with block capitals as well.'

Bordelli had always trusted his admiral friend in the Special Services, ever since they'd served on the same vessel at the start of the war. But there might also be some underhanded individuals around Agostinelli with other intentions, who used the SID for different purposes, perhaps even for some hidden power. As Arcieri had said about the Freemasons, one could find bad apples in every bushel.

'These potatoes are a masterpiece.'

'Not quite yet.'

'The great masters are never content.'

In the end Bordelli decided not to tell the colonel anything for another few days, so as not to get him upset again. He would rather do it after Christmas.

They kept on chatting serenely, joking, eating heartily and drinking wine. They hardly seemed like a colonel being hunted by killers and a police inspector who'd taken justice into his own hands.

After dinner Arcieri busied himself washing up, insisting that he do everything himself. He cleared the table, put the leftovers in the fridge, and started washing the dishes, humming a Duke Ellington melody. Just a week earlier he would never have imagined he would so quickly find anything remotely resembling such serenity. It seemed like a miracle to him. But it was only the first step in the long march that awaited him, and he dreamed of soon regaining his normal freedom of movement. His dream was to be able to sleep in his own house again and to travel freely . . . Would he manage? Or would his mysterious enemies succeed in burying him? By now he was accustomed to such questions; they no longer weighed so heavily on his mind. Now he could blithely wash the dishes, hum Duke Ellington, and wonder whether he might just manage to live through it all.

The inspector put a nice big log on the fire and, after uncorking another bottle of wine, sat down in an armchair, waiting for the colonel to finish before smoking his first cigarette of the day in his company. He felt dead tired and very nearly forgot the jazz record he'd hidden in the closet. It was anybody's guess whether he'd picked the right music. The salesman at Alberti's had assured him that any jazz aficionado would consider the disc a masterpiece.

With an unlit cigarette between his lips, he tenderly recalled when his dad would do things to make him believe that it was the Baby Jesus who brought him his Christmas presents. On Christmas Eve Papa would set the alarm for 3 a.m., and secretly get up on tiptoe. By the light of an oil lamp, he would then construct a large Nativity scene, cover the tree with coloured ornaments and tinsel and arrange his presents under the tree. It would take him several hours, all the while taking care not to make the slightest noise. The following morning he would go and wake up little Franco and his mother, and, holding their breath, all three would enter the living room, where they were greeted by a big surprise: the Baby Jesus had come in person during the night and brought gifts! He, little Franco, believed it all. He would feel his heart race and in his excitement didn't notice the dark circles under his father's eyes and his continuous yawning. He would just look around, mouth agape . . . the coloured ornaments . . . the crèche . . . the ox and the donkey . . . the presents . . . It was like waking up in a dream . . .

'Feel like going to bed?' the colonel asked him softly, sitting down in the armchair opposite him. Bordelli opened his eyes and realised he'd nearly fallen asleep. His unlit cigarette had fallen between his legs.

'Not yet, but I don't know how much longer I can hold out.'

'I'm pretty tired myself, and tomorrow's going to be a busy day for me.'

'How about a cigarette and a glass of wine before beddy-bye?' asked Bordelli, holding out the packet for him.

'Sounds reasonable to me,' said the colonel, taking a cigarette and lighting it while the inspector lit his own.

'And the shopping list?'

'I left it on the table.'

'All right if I bring everything to you at lunchtime?'

'If it's not too much trouble for you, I'd rather have everything in the morning,' said Arcieri, feeling a little embarrassed.

'You're the cook. I'll get up early tomorrow and go into town.'

Bordelli refilled their glasses and they gestured a toast in the air. As if by tacit agreement, neither of the two spoke of mystery women or killers. Only three days remained till Christmas, and the dinner they were planning for the following day was supposed to make them briefly forget their troubles.

Bordelli tossed his cigarette, only half smoked, into the fire, and got up.

'Before I go to bed, there's something I wanted to give you,' he said, and he left the room. He returned with a flat, square object in his hand, wrapped in fine blue paper and tied with a golden ribbon. He handed it to the colonel, who looked at him in surprise.

'For me?'

'I hope I guessed right.'

'You really shouldn't have done . . .'

'Just a little Christmas present,' said Bordelli, sitting back down.

Arcieri untied the ribbon, and when he removed the wrapping

he couldn't refrain from smiling. It was an album by John Coltrane: *A Love Supreme*.

'I thank you with all my heart. I'll listen to it tomorrow while preparing the dinner.'

'Do you know it?'

'Yes, but not very well. It's modern jazz . . . I'm very curious about it.'

'Another little splash of wine?' Bordelli refilled their goblets, as the colonel kept studying the album cover with excitement.

It seemed like forever since Arcieri had listened to some good jazz, and he began to feel nostalgic for his collection of classics. Would he sooner or later manage to get his hands on those magnificent records again? Duke Ellington, Count Basie, Glenn Miller, Charlie Parker, Art Tatum, Billie Holiday . . . He nearly felt like crying.

'Music . . .' he whispered, not knowing what else to add. Bordelli smiled, downed his glass in a single gulp, and got up again.

'I think I need to lie down.'

'Goodnight. And thanks again . . .' said the colonel, remaining seated.

Bordelli climbed the stairs, put a bit of wood in the stove, and quickly brushed his teeth. Five minutes later he was under the covers with the light off. It was barely eleven o'clock, and he never went to bed so early. But over the past few days he'd been feeling more and more tired and now needed to recover his strength. A soft wind was blowing outside, and every so often he heard a creaking sound . . .

Some thunder very far away, and already his memory was off and running . . . A summer evening, an open window, rain falling hard, the scent of wet earth . . . Mamma had gone to shut the windows and then sat down on the edge of the bed . . . *Sweet is the company of one no longer hurried* . . . His mother's poems, rediscovered by chance among the old family photos . . .

He turned onto his other side and suddenly thought he smelled Eleonora's scent on the pillow – her hair, her breath, which reminded one a little of warm bread just out of the oven . . . But it wasn't possible. Eleonora had never been in that room, in that bed . . . He drifted slowly into a somnolent state peopled with ghosts, and as he was falling asleep a painful episode from twenty-five years earlier came back to him . . .

It was June of '42, and Italy was still fighting alongside the Germans in the mad hope of winning the war. Young Lieutenant Franco Bordelli was assigned to board a heavy cruiser sailing to Malta with the task of intercepting and sinking an Allied reinforcement's convoy. But that was not how things went. A British submarine travelling alone had fired a torpedo right on target and fled immediately after the strike to avoid depth charges. A serious breach in the hull had the cruiser listing and shipping water, even though all the watertight bulkheads had been promptly shut to stem further flooding. In the meantime the danger of new attacks was warded off by the arrival of four Italian submarines, which immediately began sounding the area. Everyone was waiting for the rescue vessels, but they wouldn't get there for another two or three hours. Following the initial moments of agitation, it was discovered that four sailors were trapped in an engine room. They communicated with the bridge through the speaking tube, saying that water was coming in through a crack in the hull at a speed of about four centimetres per minute. After a swift and careful investigation it was established that there was no way to extract the engineers. The hatches had all been jammed by the blast, and the spaces between the engine room and the upper levels were flooded. There was no way to save the four sailors, and the ship's captain made the painful decision to tell them this. The sailors climbed up as high as they could in order to breathe, but soon the water was up to their shoulders. They had only a few minutes left, and they used them to dictate, through the metal tube, a brief letter of goodbye to their families, which the officers transcribed with tears in their eyes. The four sailors' last moments of life were accompanied by broken phrases and the pitiless gurgling of the water as it came up to the ceiling, as the captain and other officers listened with their caps in their hands. Nobody knew yet that just a few hours later the whole ship would go down in a few minutes, under a barrage of bombs rained down on them by a British squadron, even as the cruiser was being towed by an Italian destroyer that had come to the rescue. Hundreds of crewmen died in the explosions or drowned in the sea, including the captain, who was determined to be the last to abandon ship, not only to honour the Navigational Code approved by royal decree less than three months before, but above all because he had always shown outstanding bravery. Of the entire crew, only a few dozen men survived, and Bordelli was one. He'd come out alive as if by miracle, as was to happen so many other times during that bloody war . . .

'I'll take three kilos of potatoes as well.'

He had woken up early, even before the alarm rang. A long, hot bath, a cup of coffee with Arcieri, and by eight o'clock he was in Impruneta doing the food shopping. Greengrocer, butcher, baker . . . it was fun, he was relaxing. A nice dinner with his friends would do him good.

While he was at the butcher's he remembered the Countess Gori Roversi, the owner of the castle on the hill across from his house, and he asked the butcher whether he had news of her.

'You mean the nutcase? Haven't seen her in ages. Can I get you anything else?'

'No, thank you.'

He had to stop at the 'bazaar' to buy two mixing spoons, a potato peeler and a terracotta baking dish – under strict orders from the colonel-chef. The shop was full of ladies chattering on in an almost incomprehensible language. He took his place calmly in the queue, enjoying the slow rhythms of country life.

He left the shop half an hour later, knowing everything about Cesare's new cow, the priest's sciatica, and poor Ginetta, who twisted an ankle when she slipped and fell in the vegetable garden.

He loaded everything into the car, and then on his way home stopped at a farm to buy some *olio novo*. The olive grove stretched downhill from the farmhouse; he could see the whole valley below. Chickens roamed about, and a skinny dog on a chain barked unconvincingly. He knocked on the door, but there was no answer so he called out. Moments later, a window on the first floor opened. A wizened old woman peered out, head wrapped in a kerchief.

'Who are you looking for?' She sounded like the witch in 'Snow White'.

'Good morning, I was wondering if I could buy some oil?'

'Let me call him . . . Vasco! Vascooooo! Someone here for oil!' she yelled down towards the valley. She closed the window forcefully, and all fell silent once again. Five minutes passed, and an old man finally came walking out of the grove. He had a cap on his head, and a hunched back. He was small and thin, had few teeth and a ruddy face, but his eyes had the glint of intelligence.

'How much do you need?'

'Would ten litres be possible?'

'You tell me . . . ten litres comes to five thousand lire.'

'Fine.'

'Did you bring a container?'

'I forgot. You don't have any bottles?'

'How about two five-litre jugs?'

'Perfect.'

'The jugs cost two hundred lire each,' the farmer said, walking towards the house. He pushed open the front door. It was unlocked. They walked through a darkened kitchen, which was poor but welcoming. Embers glowed in the large fireplace. They went through a doorway with a heavy door, and down a narrow passageway that descended gradually. At the bottom was another large room with several other doors. The old man pulled out a big iron key and turned it an infinite number of times, the clunking sound breaking the silence. They went down four or five more steps, and then the old man rotated the light switch. A light bulb covered with cobwebs barely illuminated the small cellar, but Bordelli could see that the ceiling was made of bricks and the floor of stone. Lining one side of the room were wine casks and in front of them were two *orci*, giant terracotta jugs. The farmer lifted the cover on one of the jugs and invited Bordelli to smell. Bordelli leaned over and the fine aroma made him smile with pleasure. Slowly, the old man took a ladle and funnel down from a hook, then placed two straw-covered jugs on a makeshift table and started to fill them. The oil was an intense green, the colour of Juliette's eyes. It cost five hundred lire a litre but was well worth it.

'It's hard work, by God, but not for nothing,' the old man said solemnly.

He finished filling the jugs, plugged them with big corks and gave one to Bordelli to carry. They went back upstairs and outside.

As they were standing next to the Beetle, 5,400 lire exchanged hands.

'Remember that oil fears only three things: heat, cold and light,' the old man said.

'I won't forget.'

'We slaughter a pig in January and this year's wine is ready in March.'

'All right, thank you. Goodbye.'

Bordelli got into his car, but before he could close the door the old man stepped forward.

'Are you the one who bought La Poderina, the house that belonged to Marchese Bellincioni?'

'Yes, that's me.'

'You're the one who works for the police?'

'That's right.'

'I thought you might be.'

'Thank you again. Goodbye.'

'La Poderina is a nice farm, but a lot of bad things have happened there.'

'Bad things? Like what?'

'I don't need to tell you. Just bad: you know what "bad" means, don't you? Seems there's ghosts in there, too.'

'Ghosts? I haven't seen any.'

'Some people swear to it. That's what they say . . . Anyway, a lot of bad things have happened there, I can tell you that . . . But I guess I'll be heading back to the fields now; it looks like it's going to rain again after lunch. Take care of yourself.'

The old man waved and started walking back to his clods.

Bordelli started the engine, manoeuvred around the chickens scratching the ground, and headed down the dirt road. He was curious to know more about these 'bad things' . . . One day he would have to ask around. He didn't even know that the farm was called La Poderina. Ghosts, no less. Well, he wouldn't mind running into a ghost; he would gladly have a chat with one.

He reached the house and unloaded the shopping with the colonel's help. He warmed up a little coffee and drank it sitting at the kitchen table, while Arcieri poked through the bags, checking to make sure that everything was there.

'Did you remember the pancetta?'

'I got everything, don't worry,' the inspector reassured him. Before leaving for Florence he wanted to prepare four bottles of *olio novo* to give to his guests that night. He filled them up and left them in the kitchen cabinet. The colonel had already started to prepare the dinner with the concentration of a chess player.

It was half past ten. The inspector put on his overcoat with a sigh. He didn't like the idea of going into the office without anything to do.

'See you this evening, Colonel.'

'If you don't mind, I'd rather not see you until at least half past eight.'

'As you wish, General . . . By the way, what will your name be tonight?'

'Let me think . . . what do you say to Bruno Fucilieri?'

'Allow me to introduce to you General Fucilieri . . . sounds good,' the inspector said, satisfied.

'What time will the others arrive?'

'Around nine.'

'Perfect. Can I take some cabbage from the vegetable garden?'

'You can do anything you want.'

'Don't eat too much for lunch.'

'I'll just have a sandwich,' Bordelli said, giving his friend a military salute. He walked out of the house and left his cigarettes behind. It had now become a habit for him to go the whole day without smoking. Driving down to Impruneta, he hoped the day would pass quickly.

When he turned down Viale dei Colli he suddenly found himself in a long queue of automobiles moving at a snail's pace. He turned on the radio. As he listened to song after song, he reviewed everything he had learned about Antonio Migliorini, but the conclusion was always the same: absolutely nothing. He simply had to talk to the mystery woman.

The morning was more or less over by now, and after a panino at the grocer's in San Gallo, he went back to the office. He'd avoided Totò's kitchen for fear he would eat too much and ruin his appetite for the evening's dinner. The afternoon promised to be long and boring. It had even rained, as the peasant had predicted, but had stopped over an hour before.

A few hours earlier, round about midday, Piras had ducked in to tell him he'd received a call from a small police station near Grosseto. A pimp had been found dead along a dirt road in the country, inside a Ford Mustang, strangled with a woman's stocking, and for a few moments Bordelli had been undecided as to whether he should go in person, in hope of escaping that feeling of immobility. But in the end he'd sent Junior Detective Silvis along with Rinaldi and Tapinassi, among other reasons because the death of someone who lived by exploiting women didn't really interest him all that much.

What he really couldn't swallow, on the other hand, was that Antonio Migliorini's killer would spend Christmas free as a lark, possibly even with his family, surrounded by love and affection . . . But what could really be done about it? He'd tried everything, mapped out every hypothesis, delved into every little detail, looked for the needle in the haystack and hadn't found it . . . Bloody goddam hell . . . All he could hope for at this point was that the killer would fall out of the sky, preferably straight into his arms.

He stood up in a huff and started pacing back and forth in front of the window, trying to calm down. Never had he paced so much in his office. Who needed trails through the woods?

He didn't want to ruin his dinner; that would have been pointless. Better to wait for Christmas to be over, and then start over again afterwards, beginning with the photos of the corpse. He would dive headlong into the forest of declarations dancing around in his head, and maybe sooner or later a little spark would kindle a flame . . . Even though, truth be told, he didn't have much hope of this. If only he could talk to Migliorini's mistress . . . Had they really been so much in love? If so, then why hadn't she come forward? Was she so convinced she didn't have anything important to tell anyone? Nothing that might help unmask the killer? Or was she merely afraid of making her secret relationship public? Or was she wallowing in grief and would sooner or later show up at the police station?

He kept asking himself a thousand questions, each more useless than the last, a bit the way he did when tormenting himself over Eleonora . . . *And what if it really is so? And what if it really is* not *so?* It was the silliest way to avoid getting anything done. He used to do the same thing as a child. He would fixate on one thing and then be unable to think about anything else . . .

The ringing of the telephone pulled him out of the mire. It was Commissioner Inzipone. He was leaving for Umbria later that afternoon, dragged away by his wife, and would be back after Epiphany. He'd left the hotel's telephone number with the radio switchboard, just in case. They exchanged holiday wishes, with no mention of murders or investigations. The shortest of phone calls. Aside from work, they never had much to say to each other.

The inspector resumed pacing back and forth, hands in his pockets. It made no sense to keep turning things over in his mind; it was clear by this point that he was incapable of moving forward so much as one step. To avoid getting further bogged down, he tried to ask himself some questions of another nature . . . Such as: What was the colonel going to make for antipasto? What did he need the pancetta for? Would the potatoes and onions finally come out the way his mother used to make them?

Still, he continued to think bitterly that the killer might just get away with his crime, unless something unexpected were to turn up. Beyond all reason, he imagined a surprise phone call, a precious revelation that would shed light on the motive for the murder, or even the name of the person who had thrust the foil into him . . . Why had Antonio let his killer into his house? Was he a friend? Or was he a blackmailer? What had happened to the jewels? Why did Antonio open the safe? Had he been threatened, or did he trust the person in front of him? How had his wife's engagement ring ended up on the carpet? And why hadn't the killer taken it?

Without realising it, he was already facing a new army of questions without answers – always the same ones, actually – and all he could do was beat a hasty retreat. He would have to try again after Christmas . . . He swore to Antonio he would give it his all . . . But for now it was best to let it slide. He felt confused, powerless, as though in the face of an impossible task – like cutting down the great oak at Monte Scalari with a bread knife.

He stopped in front of the window and contemplated the cloudy sky, realising that he was now calling Migliorini by his first name, *Antonio*, as if they were friends. After hearing all that everyone had told him about the man, he almost felt as if he remembered the sound of his voice, the way he moved, and even his smile. It was as though he could talk to him and hear him answer . . .

'Ciao, Antonio, just give me a little time and, you'll see, I'll find your killer.'

'*My dear Franco, don't be upset. I know perfectly well who ran me through like a goose on a spit. I'm just sorry I can't tell you, but such is the law of the dead: they know everything and can't tell you anything.*'

'I want the killer to pay for what he did.'

'*It matters not at all to me, but if it keeps you from sleeping at night . . .*'

'Listen, is it really true you were so generous? Sorry to ask, but sometimes people who seem too good turn out to be monsters.'

'*My actions were guided only by my feelings, and I was fortunate to be able to afford to do many things. If I'd been poor, nobody would be saying how generous I was.*'

'I'm told you felt guilty over the death of your wife, and Oberto's father . . .'

'*What choice did I have? Regret is something we can't control, just as we can't control our hearts. But now I must go . . .*'

'Wait . . . What can you tell me about Juliette?'

'*Juliette . . . Juliette . . . What a marvellous woman . . . I know you kissed her, and I'm a little jealous . . .*'

'It happened only once.'

'I really must go now. If you don't manage to find the killer, don't make a big deal out of it. It's of no importance to me.'

'Thanks for the encouragement.'

'Farewell, Franco. I wish you a pleasant evening.'

'Farewell, Antonio,' he whispered with a smile, even waving his hand imperceptibly. He felt mildly relieved. He would get the investigation moving again after Christmas and would not give up – but for now it was better not to think about it. He needed to clear his head, to spend a quiet evening eating and drinking in the company of friends, in front of the fire.

It wouldn't be long now. All he had to do was make the slow, empty afternoon go by as quickly as possible. In the meantime he might as well ring up his cousin Rodrigo and wish him a happy Christmas. The conversation was certain to be amusing, which would help the time pass. His cousin taught grammar-school chemistry, was a devotee of rationalism and seemed to consider irony a degenerate form of human thought. It mattered not a whit to him that the cream of modern Western philosophy had often used irony to expound their ideas to the world – men like Voltaire, Schopenhauer, Nietzsche . . . Things, to Rodrigo, must be expressed clearly and with no turns of phrase designed to trigger giggles from simpletons. To him, *Candide* was a useless book, a little story with nothing noble in it whatsoever. Even falling in love was something he lived out as high drama, perhaps because it involved a sort of chemistry that eluded programmes and formulas. Rodrigo had moved to the country a year before he did, and had been living now for a number of years with a woman he had tried to resist to the point of silliness. He was, in short, the person most different from him that Bordelli had ever known, and the level of incomprehension between them often reached extraordinary levels.

The inspector dialled the number, hoping to find him at home, and, just to strike the right pose, he put his feet up on the desk.

'Hello?' said a warm female voice. Bordelli had never met Rodrigo's girlfriend, but her voice suggested a very charming woman.

'Hello, I would like please to speak with the esteemed Professor Callegari.'

'Who's calling?'

'I'm the Italian representative of the Nobel Committee,' the inspector said in a serious tone. There were a few seconds of silence.

'Rodrì, I think it's your cousin,' said the woman, putting down the phone.

Bloody hell, she'd unmasked him straight away. Apparently Rodrigo had told her about him and described him as some kind of good-time Charlie who was always kidding around. The esteemed Professor Callegari took a good while to come to the phone.

'Hello?' he said, already irritated.

'Ciao, Rodrigo, it's your cousin.'

'I know, I was just told that.'

'What did you tell her about me, anyway? That I'm some kind of joker? Or would you say I'm more of a cut-up?'

'Please get to the point.'

'When are you going to introduce your girlfriend to me?'

'Why do—'

'Well, we're cousins, after all.'

'So what? Cain and Abel were brothers.'

'Are you worried she might fall in love with me?'

'Listen, I haven't got much time . . .'

'How's Zia Camilla doing?'

'Fine.'

'Please give her my best wishes for the holidays.'

'I shall.'

'And a happy Christmas to you and your mysterious girlfriend as well.'

'She's not my girlfriend, she's my wife.'

'You got married?'

'That's what I just said.'

'Of course, I just meant . . .'

'You meant what?'

'Well, just that I didn't know you'd got married.'

'Then why don't you say, "I didn't know you'd got married," instead of asking stupid questions?'

'Well, it was a rhetorical question . . .'

'I'm well aware of that, and I hate rhetorical questions.'

'And when did you get married?'

'I have to go . . .'

'That was not a rhetorical question.'

'You can't possibly care when we got married.'

'Why not?'

'You really have to excuse me, but I've got things to do.'

'I bet you're correcting homework papers with your ruthless red pen . . . It must be thrilling to go hunting for mistakes like that . . .'

'I don't like your tone.'

'I meant that in all earnest.'

'You are *never* in earnest.'

'Come on, don't you think you're exaggerating a little?'

'If I thought I was exaggerating, I wouldn't have said what I said. I'm not like you.'

'Oh, come off it, Rodrì . . .'

'And don't call me Rodrì.'

'Your girlfr— I'm sorry, your wife called you that.'

'I don't see the connection.'

'I was just kidding.'

'I assure you that at this moment I am really in no mood for kidding. And, besides, there was nothing amusing about it.'

'Well, I hope you are able at least to kid around with your wife. Women love to laugh.'

'My wife is not *women*, she's an individual with her own specific traits.'

'Yes, and I bet you even know her exact chemical make-up. Thing is, for me, that's not enough to guarantee a good relationship.'

'Generalisation is one of the worst scourges the world has ever known,' Rodrigo continued. He seemed to be warming up.

'I'll agree with you on that . . . Happy?'

'Delusion arises from the human need to simplify reality to avoid losing oneself in complexity.'

'Good God, man. You weren't such a nitpicker as a boy.'

'I'm not a nitpicker and I have no desire to continue this pointless conversation, and so I have no choice but to say goodbye.'

'Wait just a second . . . Did you know I've been living out in the country for almost a year?'

'Of course I know; my mother told me.'

'Why don't we get together on Boxing Day? That way I can meet your wife.'

'I don't think that's such a good idea.'

'Why not? You two could come here round about noon, we'll go for a walk in the woods nearby, and then we'll have lunch together . . .' said Bordelli, knowing it was like asking a cat to dive into the sea. Rodrigo heaved a big sigh by way of conclusion.

'I really see no need for that. Have a good Christmas,' he said, and hung up.

Bordelli smiled, thinking that sooner or later he would pay him a call at home, unannounced. He was quite curious to see with his own eyes what kind of woman would have the courage to marry a man like him. On the other hand, who could say . . . Perhaps with his wife Rodrigo was a completely different man, sweet and affectionate, maybe even witty. After all, people really were like chemical elements, which behave differently depending on the molecules they combine with . . . He had to remember to bring up this important consideration on the human soul the next time he spoke with Rodrigo, who was sure to appreciate it.

It was barely half past three. There was still an eternity to go before dinner time, and all he wanted was for the time to pass. Normally he didn't feel this way when confronted with a murder case, but by this point he had realised that dogged determination would be pointless. If you haven't got a seed to plant in the ground, you cannot hope that a plant will sprout. He would deal with it all after Christmas. And maybe he would get lucky.

So what could he come up with next to make the minutes pass? Start writing his war memoirs, as Piras has suggested? Hole up in the guard booth with Mugnai and do crossword puzzles? At last he had an idea. He put on his coat and went out to the courtyard, got Rosa's present out of the Beetle, then went to the station's depository and requested a bicycle. A fine black model, with duck brakes. It had been years since he'd last ridden a bicycle, and as soon as he climbed onto it he felt like a bear at the circus. He rode it round the courtyard a few times, to gain some confidence, then rode it straight out of police headquarters, diving into the sea of cars and human beings thronging the downtown streets, continuously ringing the bell. Piazza del Duomo looked like the exit of a football stadium, except that there were a lot more women about. He couldn't ogle them for very long, however, because he risked running someone over. Maybe even Eleonora was somewhere in that crowd . . .

'Come on . . . give it to me!' Rosa squealed in excitement, following him into the living room. In one corner was a small Christmas tree laden with trimmings, and on a round side table there was a minuscule crèche with three shepherds and two sheep.

'But you mustn't open it until Christmas,' Bordelli said.

'Ohhhh!' she complained, trotting behind him on her high heels. Her blond hair was in curlers but before opening the door she had found the time to put on some bright red lipstick. Bordelli let himself flop down on the sofa, somewhat exhausted. He had carried the bicycle all the way up the stairs to the top floor and left it in the hall of Rosa's flat.

'People open presents on Christmas night.'

'I won't open it, I promise . . .' She continued to tell herself this, as her cats chased each other through the flat.

'Swear on it.'

'I swear on the blue Madonna!'

'And who might that be?'

'No one, never mind . . . please, give it to me, I won't open it . . . Briciola! Get down from there right away!' The kitten leapt off the Christmas tree branch, causing a decorative ball to fall to the ground and roll out of sight under a piece of furniture. Gideon promptly ran after it.

'Will you really be able to wait?' Bordelli asked, taking the package out of his pocket.

'What a bore you are!'

'Put it under the tree like a good girl.'

'Yes, Daddy . . .' Rosa said, grabbing it out of his hand. She ran and sat on the armchair and put the present on her knee.

'Be careful, it's fragile,' Bordelli warned.

'Let's see if I can guess . . . is it a cup?'

'I'm not going to say anything.'

'A vase for flowers?'

'You'll find out at Christmas.'

'Oh, please . . .' she said, pulling on the ribbon to undo the bow.

'You swore, Rosa.'

'What's that? I can't hear you . . .' She undid the package ever so slowly, biting her lip, and as soon as she saw the present she broke into laughter.

'You just don't know how to wait,' said Bordelli resignedly.

'I get it! You're telling me that I'm a little piggy,' she said, laughing.

'Or maybe you're thrifty.'

'How funny! I already have a name for it . . . Trogolino!' She picked up the little pig and kissed its snout.

'Don't you have a present for me?'

'I changed my mind. I'll give it to you on Christmas night, otherwise you'll unwrap it early.'

'I swear I won't.'

'Who believes you? I swore it, too, and look what happened . . . No, no, no, I'll give it to you on the afternoon of Christmas Eve.'

'What difference does it make?'

'You said it yourself, no? Presents are opened on Christmas night.'

'And if I can't come on Christmas Eve?'

'That's your problem . . . Then it means that I'll give it to you after Christmas, unless I've already given it to someone else,' Rosa said with a giggle, cuddling her little pig.

'You wouldn't have the courage to do that.'

'Listen here, you big lout . . . Are you coming to see me on New Year's Eve?'

'Where?'

'What do you mean, where? At the Casa del Popolo in Osteria Nuova! Me and my girlfriends are putting on a song-and-dance show.'

'Are you sure you know how to sing?' Bordelli asked, remembering how tone deaf she was.

'Who cares? You think the people in the government know what they're doing?'

'Well, if you put it like that . . .'

'So, will you come?'

'I'll try,' Bordelli said, knowing already that he wouldn't go.

'*Non ho l'etàààà, non ho l'età per amaaaaartiiiii . . .*'[28] Rosa sang. 'Don't make any stupid jokes now!'

'I didn't say a thing.'

'Be careful what you say, Monkey.'

'I could really use a back massage,' Bordelli said, taking off his shoes and lying face down on the sofa, hoping that Mamma Rosa wouldn't say no. She laughed and put Trogolino up on a shelf, but still in view. Then she went and put a record on the turntable at low volume, and the nasal voice of Fred Bongusto filled the room. She turned off all the big lights and lit a small lamp.

'Now, let's see what I can do for you,' she said, climbing on top of him. She raised his shirt and started to work him with her hands, as if she was kneading dough.

'Oh God, that feels good . . .' Bordelli mumbled, his eyes closed.

'*Una rotonda sul mareeeee*,' Rosa sang with Bongusto.

'What are you doing for Christmas?'

'I'm having a dinner here with my girlfriends on Christmas Eve . . . and not just hookers.'

'Ex-hookers too, you mean?'

'Silly . . . Watch out, you're in my hands now.'

'Ouch! You're hurting me.'

'That'll teach you . . . by the way, did you manage to see that Juliette woman?'

'Who? Ah yes . . . I talked to her . . .'

'What's she like?'

'Not bad at all,' Bordelli said, blushing.

'They told me she's beautiful.'

'She's not my type,' Bordelli lied.

'And you call me a liar!' Rosa said, continuing to pound her Monkey's tight muscles. Rosa had the hands of a fairy, and gradually Bordelli managed to unwind and loosen up. After a bit Briciola jumped up on the sofa and snuggled next to his head, licking her paws and purring . . .

Rosa's warm hands, Bongusto's voice, Briciola's purring . . . Bordelli was swimming in a sea of serenity he would gladly have drowned in. It had been too long since he had felt so good, without a care, nothing weighing on his conscience, no women to wait for . . . Suddenly Briciola got up and came and whispered in his ear: *I know who killed Antonio . . . I know who killed Antonio . . .*

'What?' Bordelli said, waking up. The music was over, Briciola was gone, Rosa was sitting in the armchair knitting, and instead of curlers she had beautiful blond curls.

'Welcome back, Monkey.'

'Oh God . . .'

'It's such a pleasure to talk to you.'

'I'm sorry . . . I'm just so tired . . .'

'It's been more than three hours, and you've been snoring like a train.'

'What? What time is it?'

'Almost eight o'clock.'

'Oh my goodness . . . I have to go.' He pulled himself up, confused.

'A lady?'

'Not just one . . . I have to take five beautiful women to dinner, and all of them are in love with me.'

'Ah, a science fiction kind of evening,' Rosa said, breaking out in laughter. Briciola and Gideon were sleeping on the armchair next to her, and they barely wiggled their ears.

'Go ahead and laugh, but when I was young, I wrote so many letters to girls I had to use carbon paper.'

'You mean at the time of Garibaldi?' And she broke into laughter again. Bordelli shook his head and continued to tie his shoes, yawning incessantly. He got up with difficulty, and went to kiss Rosa's hair.

'You're such a sweetheart.'

'That's what most men say when they leave,' she twittered, resting her knitting on the table. She accompanied him to the door and planted a kiss on his mouth. Bordelli put on his coat, buttoned it up, and pushed the bicycle out onto the landing.

'I'm not that old,' he said, and went down the stairs with Rosa blowing kisses after him.

Once outside the building, he got on the bike and started pedalling. A few hours earlier he hadn't known what to do with himself and now he risked being late. The cold woke him up. The main streets were so packed that it was hard to get by even on bike. To speed up his journey he took side roads and one-way streets, rode on the pavement and pedalled fast, almost always standing up, proving to himself, yet again, that he had better stamina since he'd stopped smoking. Indeed, you could almost say he'd been rejuvenated . . . and was therefore more worthy of a girl like Eleonora.

When he turned onto the dirt road leading to his house it was already half past nine. Once back at the station, he'd left his bicycle with Mugnai and hopped into the Beetle, knowing he was already late for the party. Never so much as now did he wish he had the mythic Sergeant Spatafora's Ferrari under his bum, with its flashing cherry on top.

He'd handled the avenues with great patience, crushed in traffic such as he'd never seen before in his life. Peering into the cars around him, he'd glimpsed scenes of every imaginable variety, parents slapping teary children, young lassies in love covering their swains in kisses, couples quarrelling, men reading newspapers behind the wheel, young men trying to woo girls on the pavements . . .

He'd even had time to think back on 'Armandino' Spatafora's most famous exploit, a feat that was duly recounted to every novice policeman to land in the commissariats and station houses of Italy. Some years before, Sergeant Armandino had chased an elusive armed robber halfway across Rome in his Ferrari, finally careering down the Spanish Steps. The robber was said to have commented, as they were putting the cuffs on him, 'Bloody hell, Sergeant, you drive too fast!'

The Christmas traffic hadn't begun to let up until after Poggio Imperiale, where the Beetle was at last able to shift out of first gear. A proper nightmare, in short. He couldn't even bear to imagine the chaos of the following day. And after that, Christmas Eve, which would fall on a Sunday, with the shops staying open all day. In brief, it was best to stay at home and hoe the garden until after Christmas.

He pulled up on the threshing floor alongside the guests' vehicles: Diotivede's Fiat 1100, Botta's Alfa Romeo, Piras's Fiat 600 and, just past them, Dante's Moto Guzzi Falcone. Upon entering the house his senses were greeted with a pleasant scent of cooking against a gentle background of jazz music dominated by the free, sinuous ramblings of a saxophone.

The situation in the kitchen was calm. A lovely fire was burning in the hearth, and two lamps in opposite corners of the room emitted a soft, restful light. Arcieri was sitting in an armchair wearing his new clothes and chatting amicably with the guests, while the skull atop the hutch observed the scene with its customary irony. The table was laid out with as much elegance as Bordelli's house had to offer. There were linen-covered trays on the shelves of the hutch, and Balzini wine was already swirling in the guests' tulip glasses. Dante was the first to notice the inspector.

'We were worried we might have to dine without you, Inspector,' he said through a cloud of cigar smoke.

'Sorry I'm late, the traffic was awful,' Bordelli said by way of justification, quickly washing his hands in the kitchen sink.

'General Fucilieri was just telling us about when you two first met, at Monte Cassino.'

'There'll be time for stories later. What do you say we all sit down at the table now?' said Bordelli, who'd eaten only a panino all day.

'*Now they laid hands upon the ready feast . . .*'[29] Dante quoted with his Homeric voice, then took a last puff on his cigar before throwing it into the fire.

Botta was the first to sit down, visibly curious to discover whether the general had been a worthy replacement for him at the cooker. Diotivede uncorked another bottle and, exchanging a meaningful glance with the skull, sat down at the head of the table. The glance did not escape Bordelli's notice, and he took advantage of it to inform everyone that the death's-head had been named Jeremiah.

'I just knew you two would become fast friends,' said the forensic pathologist, tucking one end of his napkin into his collar. Piras offered to help the general, but Arcieri wouldn't hear of it and ordered him to sit down. Then he went back to the cooker to turn up the flame under the pot with the pasta water.

Clapping his hands, he called everyone to attention.

'May I bring in the starters?' he asked the crew, as Bordelli filled their glasses.

'We're ready to make the sacrifice,' said Dante.

'It's started drizzling outside,' said Botta.

In the meanwhile the music had stopped, and for a few seconds everyone perked up their ears to listen to the murmur of the rain on the fields, broken up every few seconds by great gusts of wind.

'Sounds like a squall out there,' said Diotivede, seeming pleased.

The colonel set two trays down on the table, one full of still-warm toasted bread waiting to be doused with olive oil, the other covered with multicoloured *crostini*. It was the start of an unforgettable dinner . . .

General Fucilieri saw personally to serving the guests, who became more and more impressed with the excellence of each new course, and their glasses were continually filled. The soft light lent itself to conversation and confidentiality. The atmosphere was reminiscent of old country inns, where the fire and the wine were a much-deserved recompense after a long day of toil. Eating and drinking, they talked in relaxed fashion about everything from politics and recurrent dreams to the Great Flood, walks in the woods, Sardinia and women's legs . . . They took turns uncorking bottles, which then were emptied promptly, and Piras got up twice to add a log to the fire.

When Arcieri brought the skillet with the potatoes and onions to the table, he nodded meaningfully to Bordelli, as if to say that they had at last come out the way he wanted – that is, the way his mother used to make them. When Bordelli tasted them, he knew exactly what he meant.

Outside it began to rain harder, and every so often the wind howled down the chimney, as in certain stories of Chekhov. Arcieri had drunk a fair amount and now looked around with a blissful expression. The inspector was happy to see him so placid; it didn't matter that it was also thanks to the alcohol.

When the last bite of meat and the last spoonful of potatoes and onions disappeared from their plates, there was a long round of applause for the chef, topped off by warm compliments. Arcieri was touched, and he stood up and took a bow, like an actor. He'd acquitted himself quite well as a cook, and the results were plain to see.

Glasses were raised for a toast, then they all cleared the table to make way for the dessert dishes. The pudding was to be an apple tart made with the general's own two gifted hands. Ennio got busy cutting up the pie, which was dispatched in no time amidst comments of approval and moans of delight. There was another round of applause, and the inspector looked over at Botta.

'What do you say, Ennio? Did the general pass the test?'

'I don't know, I'll have to think about it . . .' said Botta, putting on a pompous air, then chuckling as he reached over to clink his glass with Arcieri's.

'The demon makes its way into the soul by way of the mouth, as the monks of the Middle Ages warned us,' said Dante, putting an unlit cigar between his lips.

'*Never trust anyone who knows not how to eat*, a present-day crime pathologist warned,' said Diotivede, grinning like an obnoxious little boy.

'It's easy to be nice when your belly's full,' Botta said, continuing the debate.

Piras allowed himself a smile, but didn't take part in the game. Bordelli stood up to poke the fire and, before sitting back down, opened a door in the hutch, took out the four bottles of olive oil he'd prepared, and lined them up on the table.

'These are for you . . . *Olio novo*, as they say in these parts.' And, ignoring the buzz of thanks muttered by all present, he went and took his present for Diotivede out of his jacket pocket.

'And this is for Pepion, from Santa Claus himself.' He set a beribboned little packet down on the table.

'I'm jealous,' said Botta.

'Of course you are,' said the inspector, sitting back down.

Diotivede picked up the packet. All eyes were on him, awaiting the great event. Arcieri swirled his wine in his glass, looking amused. The doctor removed the ribbon, opened the packet and took out his present.

'A masterpiece,' he whispered, quite serious.

'I knew you would appreciate it,' said Bordelli. They were all terribly curious to see that work of human genius from up close and respectfully passed it to one another, impressed by such imagination, finally returning it to its rightful owner, who set it down delicately beside his wine glass. It was a most tasteful little skeleton sitting on a toilet, with a tiny top hat on his head and two shiny red stones for eyes. Not only was it of immense artistic and educational value, but it was also quite useful, in that it served as a key chain.

'Please thank Santa for me; it's the most wonderful present I've ever received,' said the doctor, to the laughter of all except Piras, who only smiled in silence.

'I've also got something for you,' said Diotivede to Bordelli, getting up from the table.

'And while we're at it, I've brought a present as well,' said Dante, following the doctor to the coat rack.

'And here's mine,' said Botta, taking a small packet out of his pocket.

Piras said nothing, but followed the others to the coat rack and took something out of his coat pocket. The four beribboned packets were lined up on the table, and the inspector stood up and opened his arms.

'I thank you all, but you really shouldn't have gone to the trouble. I'm as curious as a village housewife, but I'm going to resist the temptation to open them now. I will put them under the tree and wait until Christmas morning, the way I used to do as a boy.'

'What tree?' asked Diotivede, looking around.

'Well, I haven't bought one yet . . .' said the inspector, and he scooped up the packets and went and set them on top of the hutch. After putting two logs on the fire, he sat back down and refilled everyone's empty glasses. They all knew that the moment had come to tell their stories, and they started exchanging glances to see who would go first.

Dante lit his cigar and took a few puffs, emitting a cloud of smoke that made Piras wrinkle his nose, and the inspector took advantage of the situation to offer cigarettes to anyone who wanted one. They all lit up except for the Sardinian, who, to escape the smelly smoke, went and sat down by the fire, bringing his wine glass with him. Diotivede stood up with a sigh, went over to the hutch, grabbed the death's-head and set it down in the middle of the table.

'I didn't want him to die of boredom all alone up there.'

'You're quite right,' said Arcieri, smiling. Botta emptied the seventh bottle of wine of the evening, pouring a little into everyone's glass.

'Shall we have one more round of red before we move on to the *vin santo*?' asked Bordelli.

They all agreed that it was best to stay with the same wine for the time being, since it was so delightful, and Botta volunteered to get up and open another bottle, which he uncorked and set down in the middle of the table as Dante began to tell his story . . .

'This story took place in 1959, but we could say that it dates back to the end of the last century, and specifically to far-off 1892, which, if I am not mistaken, was the same year that D'Annunzio published *L'innocente* – though that really has nothing to do with the story . . . My memory skips around, you see . . . forgive me for digressing, let me get back to the story . . .' Dante took a sip of wine, and after a long pause he picked up where he had left off.

'A dear friend of mine, a professor of philosophy, woke up one morning with a nagging pain in his lower back, near his spine. At first he ignored it. He was almost seventy and figured that such pain was normal for a man his age. But the pain didn't go away, so he took an aspirin before going to bed. He tossed and turned for most of the night, trying to find a comfortable position, but eventually managed to fall asleep. The next morning, the pain was still there. It stayed with him throughout the day. It felt as if someone was pinching one of his muscles, near his backbone. Things continued in this manner, with him taking aspirin, hoping and waiting for the pain to go away. But it didn't. It was always there. It didn't get worse and it didn't get better, so one day the professor decided to get it examined. The doctor could make nothing of it and suggested he go to Santa Maria Nuova hospital for X-rays. The professor chose to wait a few more days, hoping that that the nagging pain would go away on its own. The idea of subjecting himself to this mysterious thing called X-rays didn't thrill him. After all, it might just be stiffness from the cold or an enflamed nerve. But when he realised things weren't getting better, he gave up. He went to the hospital and undressed like a good boy, and put his trust in the power of X-rays. The radiologist developed them, looked them over, and stood there scratching his head. There was something there – he could see it. Something rather like a foreign body with a strange shape, very different from anything he had seen before, but he couldn't say any more than that. He suggested that the professor find a good surgeon. For his part, the professor couldn't take the pain any longer, and a week later he was on the operating table. A well-known doctor from Careggi cut into him. After removing the foreign body he looked at it carefully. When he realised what it was, he exclaimed out loud. He had never, in his long career, seen anything like it . . . Do you know what this foreign body was? I'll let you think about it and guess,' Dante said, topping up his glass. No one said a word. Diotivede was perplexed. Dante lit his cigar, and stared as the wide ribbons of smoke climbed slowly towards the ceiling. After a few minutes of silence he revealed the mystery.

'It was the atrophied fetus of the professor's twin, which he had been carrying inside his body ever since he was born.'

Again there was silence, this time due to amazement. They tried to put themselves in the professor's shoes and understand what he must have felt. But Dante had more to add.

'The professor had spent his whole life regretting the fact that he didn't have a brother or sister, without ever imagining the truth. It made him cry to think about it. He felt guilty, as if he had killed his brother. Philosophy was of no help.'

Having finished his story, he went back to nursing his cigar. His white mane looked even wilder than before.

'And what about the twin?' Diotivede asked.

'The atrophied fetus? The professor took it home with him in a jar of formaldehyde and kept it on his dresser in his bedroom. At night, before turning off the light, he would wish him goodnight. He had even given him a name, but I don't remember what it was,' Dante said with a grin. Bordelli looked at the skull, sitting there in the middle of the table, and imagining the fetus next to it, he remembered a line from D'Annunzio . . . *Suspended between the cradle and the grave . . .*

'Whose turn is it now?' Dante asked, blowing smoke through his nose.

'How about you, Ennio?' the inspector asked. Botta pushed his empty glass towards the bottle and it was immediately refilled. You could tell he wanted to tell a story; he was only looking for the right words to start. Amid the silence they could hear the logs burning, the rain falling on the fields, the wine being poured. After a very long minute, he began . . .

'Every time I think about it, I get emotional. It must have been 1932 or '33, several years before the start of the war. I was about ten years old, kicking a ball around with my mates in a courtyard on Via Camaldoli, a few blocks from my home. Growing up in San Frediano, we kids were always free to roam. My mother never knew how I spent my afternoons. There were eight of us, two goalies and six of us scrambling for the ball. We were all trying to show off, launching shots from great distances, in the hope of scoring a goal. The other team was winning. I would have given my life to help my team win! When I got the ball I kicked it as hard as I could, but not very well . . . I saw it fly up high, too high, and crash straight through a window. The glass shattered, and we just stood there, looking. Then an old lady with curlers in her hair came to the window. She looked down into the courtyard and asked who had done it. My mates all looked over at me, while I pretended nothing had happened. It was obvious I had done it. She called out to me and told me to come up to her house.

'"Me?"

'"Yes, you. Come upstairs . . ."

'I stood there awkwardly, then went towards my destiny with head bowed. I was afraid the old lady would tell my father. I had already made up my mind to get down on my knees and beg her not to tell him. My dad would pay for the glass, but I would pay with a proper thrashing. Not to mention the cloud that would hang over our house . . . We were poor, and every penny wasted was a tragedy.

'I got up to the first floor, my heart beating fast. The old lady ushered me into her living room and sat me down in an armchair that smelled of cats. Not far away were the shards of glass. I tried not to look at them.

'"I know who you are. You're Nando Bottarini's son."

'"Yes . . ."

'"What do we do now?" asked the old lady, turning slightly to look at the broken glass.

"'I'll pay you back, a little bit at a time . . . I promise . . ."

"'And how will you manage that? It's expensive, you know." She didn't seem angry. Actually she was very calm, and this scared me even more.

"'You're not going to tell my father, are you?"

"'We'll see."

"'I'll pay you back . . . I'll work . . ."

"'Listen, have you ever read a book?"

"'Huh?"

"'I see . . . Here's what we're going to do. I won't tell your father a thing, but you must come here every afternoon, to my house, for an hour, and read a book out loud . . ."

"'A book?" The very idea bored me to death.

"'If you accept, no one will know a thing about it, and I will replace the windowpane at my own expense. What do you say? Will you do it?"

"'I don't care much for books," I mumbled.

"'Ah, I see. And tell me . . . how many have you read?"

"'Um, not sure, at school . . ."

"'You've never read a book in your life, and you know it."

"'They're boring. That much I know."

"'Do you like potato ice cream?"

"'Potato?"

"'Yes, potato ice cream . . . Do you like it?"

"'I don't know . . ."

"'What do you mean you don't know?"

"'I've never had any."

"'You see? So how can you say that books are boring, if you've never read one?"

"'Well . . . I . . ."

"'You have three seconds to answer me. Accept my proposal or I will tell your father. One . . . Two . . . Thr . . ."

"'Fine!" I said, practically shouting. I hated that old witch. Why did she want to force me to read a boring book? What did she care? The old hag. She accompanied me to the door, saying that she would see me the next day at four. I went back out to the courtyard with my hands in my pockets. My mates surrounded me to ask what happened.

'"I've taken care of everything," I said, trying to sound tough. The old lady came to the window and waved. I dragged my mates away from there and we went to play in another courtyard.

'The next day I thought of a lie to tell my friends so I could get out of playing, and I headed off to my appointment with boredom. At four o'clock I knocked on the old lady's door, ready for the torment. We went into the living room. The pane had been replaced. I hated that window. The old hag had me sit down in the same armchair as the day before and she put a book on my lap. I read the cover . . . Jack London, *White Fang* . . . What a weird title. Luckily it wasn't too long, I thought to myself. I pretended to be interested.

'"You can open it, it's not dangerous," the old lady said, with a smile. She was sitting on the sofa, looking at me. I opened the book, and after a bunch of white pages, I read the title again, *White Fang*. I turned the page and found myself in front of a wall of words . . . That was exactly how I saw them, a high wall that I had to climb over. I read the first words to myself, more than once. I remember them to this day: *Dark spruce forest frowned on either side of the frozen waterway* . . . But I couldn't bring myself to read out loud . . .

'"Cat get your tongue?" the old lady asked.

'"Yes . . . No . . . I'll start now . . ." I imagined my friends hiding behind the furniture, waiting for me to start reading so they could burst out laughing. If they found out, they would rib me about it for the rest of my life.

'"Stalling will get you nowhere. We'll start counting an hour when you start reading."

'"I'm going to start now . . ." Old hag, I thought to myself.

'"It's easier than you think," she said. I hated her with all my heart, and after taking a deep breath I started to read, my face as red as a bell pepper. I got to the end of the page, but I was too upset and didn't understand anything.

'"Start over from the beginning . . ." said the old woman.

'"*Dark spruce forest frowned on either side of the frozen waterway* . . ." Now I was a little calmer. I read to the bottom and turned the page and kept going. It wasn't really that bad, I said to myself. Not as boring as I thought. Actually it was pretty good. But I didn't want to admit it, that would been like conceding victory, and I preferred to keep thinking that books were boring. Mostly I didn't want the old lady to be right. But each time I got to the end of a page, I wanted to keep going and I felt I could see the scenes that I was reading. Gradually I forgot to feel embarrassed. I even forgot the old lady, who was sitting there listening to me. I read slowly, trying not to stumble over the words. When I got to the end of a chapter, I started to turn the page, but the old lady stopped me.

'"That's enough for today," she said, standing up. I looked at the clock on the wall. A whole hour had passed and I hadn't even noticed. I closed the book, a little dazed . . . I felt like I was still in the snow, next to White Fang.

'"You read very well," the old lady said, adding that she would be expecting me the next day at the same time. She saw me to the door and I left, my head spinning. As soon as I got outside, I forced myself to think again that books were boring, that books were for nerds, and I went to look for my friends and play football.

'But that night, in bed, I thought about the story of White Fang, and I wanted to know how it continued. The next day I arrived at the old lady's house a little before four, eager to read. Another hour flew by. It felt like I was living inside those pages.

'I went back every afternoon and sat in that armchair and read out loud. In a few weeks I finished the book. When I closed the book I had a knot in my throat.

'"So what do you say now? Was it boring?"

'"I liked it," I mumbled.

'"If you'd like I can lend you another book . . . actually, I'll give you one as a gift." She went to her bookshelves and took down a book by the same writer, *The Call of the Wild.* I opened it immediately and read the first sentence. *Buck did not read the newspapers, or he would have known that trouble was brewing* . . . The old lady closed it and accompanied me to the door. She patted me gently on the head.

'"Now you're free . . ." she said solemnly. Only many years later did I understand that she was not referring to our pact, but to a far greater kind of freedom.

'I went downstairs. Before going out, I hid the book under my shirt. I took it home straight away and hid it under my mattress.

At night I would pull the cover up over my head and read late into the night with the help of a tiny flashlight, so no one would find out. It was a beautiful book, and when I finished it, I reread it twice. I had stolen the flashlight from a stand at the flea market – without it I would have read much less because my mother always turned out my light at nine o'clock.

'I went back to the lady's house and she gave me other books, saying she was very happy she'd saved me. Sometimes I went and got books from a bookshop, without actually paying for them. But how can you call a penniless kid who steals a book to read a thief? Sure, after I read them I'd often try and sell them back to one of the stands at the market, but that was only because there was no place in my tiny bedroom for them. Basically the more I read the more I liked reading. I travelled to other worlds, I cried and laughed along with the characters, I felt all sorts of emotions . . . I still spent my afternoons playing football with my friends, but soon they seemed like snot-nosed babies to me. When I went to see the old lady she talked to me about poets, writers, and even important characters in history. She told me she had taught school for thirty-five years and now that she was retired she felt very empty.

'One thing is certain: if I hadn't broken that glass, I would have stopped going to school not long after. But instead, I graduated from secondary school and even went to university for one year, without ever sitting for any exams, though. I'd enrolled in Law, but in order to help out at home, I had to do other things . . .'

'How can you call a young person who has no money who steals to study Law a thief?' Bordelli asked with a smile.

'You took the words right out of my mouth, Inspector.' Botta's eyes were glistening, and he had a seraphic smile on his face.

'Do you still read novels?'

'Of course . . . not as many as when I was a kid, but at least five a year.'

'And do you pay for them?'

'It would be sad to abandon the good habits I had as a child, don't you think? Long live books and women,' Botta said, raising his glass. They all toasted books and women. A flash of sadness crossed Arcieri's face. He was surely thinking of his chimera, the beautiful Elena. Bordelli waited for Arcieri to put down his glass so that he could refill it. He looked at the colonel tenderly: he was sitting as straight as a pole, but it was apparent that he was suffering inside, thinking about a ghost from the past . . . just like Bordelli himself . . .

Piras was sitting in an armchair, away from the smoke, but his silence was full of life. A strong gust blew outside the house, shaking the trees. At the same time, a dog barked in the distance. Diotivede's eyes shuttled lazily between the fire and Jeremiah, his usual childish frown on his face. The inspector had no trouble imagining him as a child with thick glasses, trying to explain the workings of the human body to his friends.

'You could go next . . .' Bordelli said. The doctor gave a hint of a smile, pulling himself up in his chair and resting his elbows on the table. He stared at the skull, then reached out and patted it.

'To be or not to be . . .' he said. The inspector looked over at Botta to see whether he had understood the reference, but Ennio had not blinked . . . That broken window had really worked miracles . . .

'This story has a sad ending, but it's a sweet story,' Diotivede continued. He asked for a cigarette, though he didn't usually smoke, and then leaned back in his chair. It was raining hard, and the sound of the rain falling on the fields blended with the crackling in the fireplace . . .

'Nicola Obinu was a dear friend, a man of great integrity, with a will that I always admired . . .

He was born in 1890, in Nuramini, a small town in the province of Cagliari, into a family of modest means. His father was a baker and had to work like a mule in order to send his son to school. Nicola was short but his pride made up for his stature, to the degree that sometimes he seemed almost imposing. Ever since he was a child, he had had the courage of a lion. Once, at the age of ten, he got bitten by a dog and, to disinfect it, he burned himself with a red-hot piece of iron.

After completing secondary school at the age of eighteen, he decided to go to the mainland to study Engineering. No one could stop him. He arrived in Pisa with a shabby suitcase and a small amount of money in his pocket. He lived in a dilapidated boarding house, which he shared with the cockroaches, and paid for his studies with endless sacrifices. At night he copied out lecture notes and handouts by candlelight, later selling them to other students. But he still didn't have enough money. So, on the weekends he would go out to the countryside to catch butterflies. He would pin them to a piece of cardboard, identify them, and sell them to collectors. This was how he managed to survive and pay for his studies.

During his third year of university he moved to Padua, where he took classes in mechanical and industrial engineering. He was an exceptional student and soon the teachers invited him to conduct classes and assist with exams. He graduated with honours and his thesis was published for the benefit of future students. His professors were convinced that he would have an academic career, but he had other plans, and he chose to go to Milan to look for work.

The first few months were not easy but eventually he found work as a designer in a small factory; with his salary he could afford to rent a proper apartment. Two years later, young Gavrilo shot Franz Ferdinand and his wife Sophie and the war broke out. During the conflict, Obinu's expertise earned him an appointment as a military radio officer, as well as a couple of medals for his efforts. At the end of the war he went back to working at the same factory, but he now felt that it was beneath his skills. In 1921 he arranged a meeting with someone in the new Italian Underwater Cables Company, and after a brief interview, was hired. His talents gradually carried him to increasingly important positions. He earned good money and eventually bought himself a small apartment not far from the Duomo.

In 1928, at almost forty years of age, he got married to a beautiful girl much younger than he, whom he had met in Versilia, on the Tuscan coast. She was from the petite bourgeoisie of Lucca. From the start theirs was a turbulent marriage, with quarrels and jealous scenes where both were too proud to give in. Despite this, over a ten-year span they had three children: two daughters and a son.

Obinu was very well respected and in 1933 was selected to

be one of the technicians who followed, by radio, Italo Balbo's famous Atlantic crossing with a squadron of twenty-five seaplanes.

In late 1936, he left the company to accept an important post at FIVRE, a modern Milanese factory that produced valves, which was founded by Magneti Marelli, and he soon became a manager. When war broke out he stayed at his job, where he'd become indispensable to the war effort. This didn't change after September the 8th.[30] *One morning during the German Republic of Salò, he was approached by a supposed partisan who offered him a suitcase full of money in exchange for some electronic material. Nicola refused firmly, but not because he was sympathetic to the Republic. It was, for him, an ethical question. He had been asked to steal, and this was inconceivable for him. Some years later he found out that on that occasion his life had been at risk. The man with the suitcase of money was not a partisan but a spy for the regime sent by the Germans to evaluate his behaviour. He'd had a pistol in his pocket, and had he accepted the deal, he would have been killed on the spot.*

Not long after, Obinu found himself in another life-threatening situation, but this time of his own doing. During the Nazi retreat he led a risky operation to save the expensive machinery that belonged to the company, which would otherwise have been taken to Germany. He and a group of collaborators dismantled the machines during the night, took the parts out to the countryside, and hid them in the haystacks of abandoned farmhouses. Despite this act of courage, after the liberation he was arrested for collaborating and sat before a People's Tribunal. It was a serious accusation: those who had shown allegiance to the Fascists risked summary execution. During the trial a man came running in – a craftsman, a hulk of a man who knew Engineer Obinu very well. Holding a chair high over his head, he shouted, 'The first person to touch the engineer will have this broken over his head!' No one had the courage to contest him; the trial continued under the giant's watchful eye. By the end the truth came out, thanks to several witnesses who told the story of how they had hidden the precious machinery. The engineer had risked his life for his country without any personal interest. Not only was he acquitted and even applauded, but his acts did not go unnoticed by the directors of Magneti Marelli, who rewarded him by naming him co-director general of FIVRE.

He was given a very high salary, commensurate with his new role, which covered a wide range of responsibilities, from creating new designs and issuing contracts to developing strategies to conquer new international markets.

Two years later he moved his family to a new apartment in Via del Corso that he had purchased easily. Milan was in full rebuilding phase, and business was better than ever. But the quarrels with his wife persisted, and in fact grew more frequent. By then they fought about every little thing, for no reason at all, just out of habit. Every occasion was good for pulling long past episodes out of the drawer, to be used as weapons. She knew where to find his weak spots and went after them pitilessly, while Nicola also knew how to be cruel, both with words and with silence. What kept him going was his work. He didn't hold back, probably so that he would be away from home as much as possible. At the office he was respected and appreciated, people listened to him and obeyed him, and he tried to regain his bearings during those hours in order to face new challenges at home.

His tenacity was unshakeable, and his desire for adventure had not yet been quelled. In 1956 he resigned from Magneti Marelli with a moving and elegant letter, with the serious intention of throwing himself into business. He sensed a ferment in the air that he didn't want to let get away, and at the age of sixty-seven, together with a friend, he founded Elettritalia, a company that initially sold washing machines, both Italian and German. Then it was televisions, and then replacement valves, which he bought from FIVRE. Within a few years forty Elettritalia shops had opened all across Italy, accompanied by a tight network of representatives who travelled all the way to small villages in the countryside or at the tops of mountains.

Rivers of money poured into the company coffers, and Nicola bought real estate, land, hotels. He had a large villa built for his daughter, who had married an engineer, in an exclusive part of Florence. At that time he also acquired a beautiful three-storey villa with a large garden, not far from the other, and 'suggested' to his wife that she go and live there. He accompanied his suggestion with a few practical details: he would pay for a driver and a waiter, and every month he would give her the considerable sum of five hundred thousand lire. She would live near her daughter, in a beautiful city of art, and once a week he would go and see her. It didn't take his wife long to decide, and she accepted the proposal, mainly because she couldn't stand Milan.

But Nicola had a secret. He was in love with Elisa – a young, petite, delicate woman who shared his affections. He had considered the situation for a long time before compromising himself, but in the end he decided that it wasn't right to renounce one's most heartfelt sentiments. He hired his lover as his secretary in order to be closer to her. They saw each other secretly after work, and were exceedingly careful. No one must know about his real bond with Elisa, neither at work nor in the family. Of course, Roman, his driver, understood straight from the start, but he pretended not to notice, and would never have told anyone. Roman was from Friuli, as solid as a rock, and would have walked through fire before betraying Nicola's trust.

Nicola went to Florence every week to see his wife, as promised, and they would inevitably quarrel. This routine went on for several years. The children had, over time, come to see the situation for what it was, and his wife too, and he knew well that they understood, but no one ever dreamed of talking about it. Until one day the son felt the need to talk to his father. The young man told him that he needn't worry, that it was understandable, and that if he was happy with Signorina Elisa he had no problem with it. But Nicola vehemently denied the evidence and acted as though he were offended.

Time passed with no major changes, except a steady increase in the salary of the man who had made his way in the world all by himself, through great sacrifice. His wife was in Florence, his true love in Milan.

At seventy-five, Nicola decided to retire, or almost. He bought a small office in the centre of town, where he went for a few hours each day to oversee his investments. The office had two rooms, one for him and one for his 'secretary'. At work, even when they were alone, they continued to use the formal address with each other. On the street they kept a distance of a few steps, with Elisa ahead and he behind. On Sunday mornings, when they went to get a coffee in the Galleria, they would sit at two separate tables, and merely glance at each other with feigned indifference. Only in the intimacy of the home could they really get close and drop the formalities. Obviously they never lived together and never woke in the same bed. Roman would come to get Signorina Elisa at midnight and take her home to her apartment.

One terrible day, Nicola fell ill, and after a long period in hospital he was sent home in a wheelchair. He looked as if he had aged ten years: he struggled to speak and his hands shook. He could no longer live on his own, and for the first few days two full-time nurses were hired. The daughter who lived in Florence, in agreement with her husband, decided that the best thing was to bring her father into her own home. They asked Roman to come and stay with Nicola and look after him, and Roman accepted without thinking twice. Roman would shave him, wash him, feed him, and often scolded him. He couldn't stand seeing his employer so defenceless, and he would swear at him in dialect, prodding him to pull himself together.

A week later, Nicola's daughter and husband went to Milan to take care of some pressing business, and they invited Elisa to lunch. It was a very desolate hour. Elisa's eyes were vacant, she didn't touch her food, and she drank only a sip of water. She spoke very little and only to say that her life no longer had any meaning. She would never see Nicola again, she said, and so she would rather go away – that is, she would rather die. The daughter's husband tried to make light of it and jokingly said that if she chose gas she should remember to turn off the mains otherwise the whole building might explode.

Some people talk about it and never do it . . . But two days later Elisa really killed herself. She chose gas and she hadn't forgotten to switch off the mains. They found her on the kitchen table with a pen in her hand. Under her head was a letter

> *addressed to Nicola Obinu's eldest child, in which she openly confessed her feelings for the only man she had ever loved. Towards the bottom of the page the writing became a little sloppy, and the last lined ended in mid-sentence with a kind of smudge . . .*

'At first they told Nicola that his secretary had fallen ill, then that there had been complications, and only after several days did they say that she hadn't made it. He cried, chin quivering, but said nothing. A few weeks later, Nicola's condition grew worse, and it was clear that he didn't have much time left. His entire family gathered at his bedside, even the youngest grandchild. His wife stood at the front of the group, not breathing a word. Roman remained in a corner, wringing his hands, eyes red, every so often mumbling something in dialect. Nicola looked at each of them carefully, letting his gaze rest on each for a long time. He looked serene, almost as if he was smiling. Heaving a long sigh, he gave up the ghost, after murmuring the name of his secretary and lover . . . *Elisa*.'

Diotivede had reached the end of his story and, thinking it over, turned and gazed at the fire . . . *Elisa*. The name continued to hang in the warm air, as light as a feather. No one said a thing. Even Jeremiah seemed touched.

It took them all a few minutes to realise it was raining hard, and they glanced at each other in silence. They could feel the darkness surrounding the farmhouse . . . *Elisa* . . . It had a delicate sound, which Bordelli transformed into the name that was closest to his heart, *Eleonora* . . . The colonel had surely done the same, as had the others . . . *Elisa* . . . None could say whether he, too, would have the strength and lucidity before dying to murmur the name of a woman . . .

Piras was visibly moved; Obinu was his compatriot. He had surely recognised in him the tenacity of the Sardinians, who could face any hardship with strength and patience. He got to his feet and put another log on the fire, had his glass refilled, and went back to his place, away from the cigars and cigarettes. He knew it was his turn now, but he enjoyed taking his time. There was no hurry. Their silence seemed timeless, an invitation to let one's thoughts wander. The rain continued to pour down hard, reminding them all of the flood. Who knew for how many years, at every drop of rain, the Florentines would still think of that 4th of November.

The inspector gestured to Botta to open another bottle, but of *vin santo* this time. Ennio opened it with pleasure, filled the glasses, and sat back down beside the fire, facing Piras. Amidst a clutter of dirty dishes and fruit on the table, Jeremiah reminded the guests of their final destiny . . . *Chi vuol esser lieto sia*, Bordelli thought to himself, recalling Lorenzo de' Medici's 'Canzona di Bacco.'

Piras shifted position in his armchair and, after taking a sip of *vin santo*, raised his glass with the hint of a smile. '*Custu sì chi recrea', ccustu sì chi l'iffrisca 'ssu gagaiu! Si assa-zo prus abba in bida mea mi falet unu raju!*' he said.

'Care to say that in Italian?' the inspector asked.

'"This is restorative! This soothes my throat! If I ever touch water again may I be struck down by lightning." It's a little rhyme that my grandfather always said when he drank *filu' e ferru*, the Sardinian grappa.'

'I've had the stuff: it's pure fire,' Dante commented.

'A wise man, your grandfather,' Botta said.

'He didn't invent it. I think it was part of a poem written in the late 1800s by a priest.'

Ennio laughed. 'I can imagine his sermons.'

'If I ever visit your father, I'll need an interpreter,' Bordelli added.

'That's not the language they speak in Bonarcardo; my maternal grandfather was from Mamoiada,' Piras explained. Diotivede's interest was aroused.

'*Filu' e ferro* . . . why do they call it "iron wire"?' he asked. Piras was about to answer, but Botta sat up straight and raised a hand, as if he was at school.

'I know this one, I learned it when . . . on holiday on Asinara.'

'A real man of the world,' the inspector said ironically, hinting at the fact that Botta had done jail time on Asinara, but Ennio ignored him in order to explain.

'The name *filu' e ferru* came into being a few centuries ago, during a period of prohibition: It comes from the iron wire that people stuck into the ground to mark where the grappa had been buried, together with the equipment necessary for making it.'

'Exactly,' the Sardinian said, and Botta crossed his legs with a satisfied air.

'Did you also learn how to cook on Asinara?' Bordelli asked.

'Don't ask pointless questions, Inspector. I know how to cook in all languages.'

'So, next time we'll have a good Sardinian dinner.'

'Whenever you like,' Ennio said, looking over at Piras.

'You and Pietrino can go head to head, he's a good cook too,' Bordelli said, trying to provoke Piras.

'That's fine with me. We can even play cops and robbers,' Botta said with a laugh. Piras smiled at the reference to both their professions, but didn't take him up on the challenge. Slowly taking another sip of *vin santo*, he looked around to see whether the others were ready to listen. General Fucilieri was silent but his gaze was serene. There was another round of *vin santo*, and Dante relit his cigar. Piras waited for complete silence, and then began to tell his story . . .

'This story is about what happened to my paternal grandfather's brother in the late 1800s. His name was Salvatore, he was the youngest of five children, and he was seven years old at the time. In the woods above Santi Lussurgiu, not far from where he lived, there was an old lady who lived all alone in a run-down stone cottage. No one knew what her name was, they just called her *sa bezza*, "the old lady" . . .

They said she was a witch, and mothers instructed their children not to bother her. She was no joke, that witch . . . Be careful, she kills children and roasts them on the spit like suckling pigs. But when you're young, the desire for adventure is irresistible. One afternoon, Salvatore and the other kids decided to go and spy on the old woman, and so they climbed the hill. They were careful where they walked and kept their voices low. They didn't want to end up on a skewer and be cooked over a fire, but it was this very danger that drove them forward. Salvatore was the youngest in the group and ran hard so as not to be left behind. The other kids had fun scaring him, but they were scared, too. They walked for a long time in the woods looking for the stone house and finally found it. It was in the middle of a small clearing.

Smoke was coming out of a stovepipe that poked through the roof. She's cooking a child, one of them whispered. Let's go and see, said another. They made their way forward, practically slithering on the ground, to the edge of the clearing, hearts pounding. There were no windows on the side they approached, and the old woman couldn't see them. 'Wait for me here,' Walter, the oldest one, said. 'Let's go home,' said Salvatore, trembling with fear. Walter stood up and ran to the cottage, pressing himself up against the wall. Two others followed him, and gradually everybody else, including Salvatore, who would have done anything not to be left on his own. 'Please let's go home, let's go,' he begged. 'Hush,' said the others. Walter went round the corner and made his way along the wall until he got to a window; the rest of the kids followed suit . . . and just then sa bezza *came out, her hair standing straight up on her head, and her big wrinkly mouth twitching. She shouted and ran after them, waving her stick. The kids ran off as fast as they could, followed by the old witch, who was shouting and laughing at them. 'She's going to get us!' they said, dashing between the trees. The old woman was as fast as a hare, and just kept getting faster. Salvatore had been left behind, and he thought his heart would burst. He thought she'd grab his hair any minute. He didn't have the courage to turn round, but was convinced the situation was hopeless. He saw himself skewered and roasting like a* porcheddu. *His mates had disappeared; no one could help him . . . Now she's going to get me, now she's going to get me, he thought . . . Instead, he managed to reach the town, but didn't stop running until he got to his front door. He rushed inside and huddled down by the fire. He couldn't believe that he was safe. He was shaking like a leaf and his heart was beating fast. His mother asked what had happened. 'Nothing,' he said, 'I'm just a little cold.' 'We'll be eating soon,' his mother said. Her husband came home, tired after a long day out with the flock, and sat down at the table. He wanted to take off his boots but his back ached, so he beckoned to Salvatore to come and help. The child looked at him vacantly, but didn't move. 'Come here,' his father said. But Salvatore stayed where he was. His mother said to leave him alone, that the little chap was cold. But his father didn't agree with this approach and, mumbling and swearing, he got up to teach his son to obey. He raised his hand in the air to slap him. But Salvatore didn't cover his head as he had done other times. It was very odd. His father lowered his hand and waved it in front of Salvatore's eyes, but the child seemed not to see it. His mother came over, worried, and also tried to get his attention by waving a hand a few centimetres from his face . . .*

'It didn't take them long to realise that their child had gone blind. His fear had blinded him,' Piras concluded.

'*Mamma mia*,' mumbled Botta.

'He died when I was a child, but I remember him well. He was always in a good mood and nice to everyone. Sometimes I would read to him in front of the fire and he would doze off. The incident had made his other senses more acute. He recognised people by their smell, and he could even distinguish the colour of fabrics simply by touching them. I saw him do it with my own eyes. But above all, he was very generous. Despite his condition, he did everything he could to not be a burden to the family; he always made himself available to others. He was a great man, and he taught me a lot,' the Sardinian concluded, holding out his glass for more wine.

Dante nodded, with a solemn air. 'Man is a marvellous creature,' he declared, surrounded by a cloud of smoke.

'Not always . . .' Diotivede mumbled with a cynical smile.

'As Pascal said – more or less – man's beauty lies in his contradictions,' replied Dante, exhaling smoke through his nose.

'And what about women's beauty?' Botta asked.

'I propose another toast to women,' Diotivede proposed, with a rascally smile. They raised their glasses in an almost religious silence. Bordelli felt a pleasurable melancholy in the air, a regret for things that they had never experienced and that were impossible to express in words.

He exchanged glances with the colonel. They were the only ones left to tell their stories. Arcieri understood that the inspector wanted to be the last and was glad to grant him the honour. He took another sip of wine and listened to the rain. Over the course of the evening, during the moments of silence, he had revisited the ghosts in his memory. He had finally decided which story to tell . . .

'In July 1944 I was advancing towards the Southern Sector of Florence behind a British division, as a liaison officer between the English and Italian Secret Services, under Badoglio. We walked through the towns of the Val d'Elsa, Castelfiorentino and Certaldo. I had a couple of secret missions to carry out. One of them was for SIM, a nasty affair I can't even tell you about today . . . you have no idea how it feels, at my age, to have spent one's life surrounded by intrigue . . .' he said bitterly, halting to take a sip of wine.

Bordelli was amazed to hear Arcieri opening up to people he didn't know at such a delicate time in his life, but the colonel gave him a reassuring glance. The others looked at the colonel in silence, trying to imagine some of the adventures he might have been through. The colonel smiled a little and continued.

'The other mission was for something private, for a publisher from Florence, a friend of an enemy. It had to do with an ex-minister who was involved in press and propaganda . . . But forgive me, I'm wandering again . . . it happens a lot to elderly people, especially when they drink too much . . . what was I saying? Ah, yes, of course . . . On our way to Florence, the British division stopped in a rather large town along the main road. People welcomed us somewhat unenthusiastically. The poverty, the fear, the deaths . . . It certainly was not easy to celebrate. But the arrival of the Allied soldiers represented life over death, and their relief was palpable.' Arcieri took another sip, perhaps to catch his breath.

'This *vin santo* goes down so smoothly and pleasantly, but I have to go slowly . . . Anyway, the officers were assigned rooms in confiscated hotels and homes, those that were still standing, of course. They gave me some keys and an address. I was given the house of the town chemist. It was on the main road, in an area that had not been bombed. Not far away, entire neighbourhoods had been reduced to ruins, especially near the railway lines.

'The house was a three-storey building, with a small balcony. And I had it all to myself. The chemist had been sent off to the country with his family. The heat was exhausting and I couldn't wait to take off my uniform. The English had given Italian officers uniforms from their dead soldiers. Some still had bullet holes and bloodstains on them. Luckily I still had my Italian uniform, onto which I had sewn the British patches. But I didn't have a change of uniform and could no longer stand the smell of sweat and dust.

'When I opened the door of the house, I felt as if I was walking into a grotto. The air in the dark foyer was cool and dry, and a great relief. The thought of lying down on a mattress made me very sleepy. I could barely stand up. I had not slept in a real bed for months, and never for more than three hours at a time. With great effort I climbed the stairs to the first floor, propelled by curiosity. I found myself in a large living room, sober but elegant, with a balcony that looked out onto the street and a door that led to the chemist's study. The wide stone staircase continued up towards the second floor, where the bedrooms probably were, but I didn't have the strength to go on. I got completely undressed and left my clothes where they fell. The air was stuffy, so I opened the French door that gave onto the balcony. I lay down on the sofa, which felt as soft as a cloud, and fell asleep instantly. You could almost say I passed out. A few hours later I was awakened by some noise. I opened my eyes and realised that the sound was coming from the street. Men and women were shouting: "Fascist," "Beast," "Murderer . . ." I put on my trousers so I could have a look from the balcony. A crowd of restless people filled the road and in their midst was a man in a torn and bloodied white shirt. He covered his head with his hands to protect himself from the slaps and punches. This was the period when people were hunting down Fascists, a time of summary killings and personal vendettas. I had seen several such scenes over the previous months.

'The situation was deteriorating. The man kept charging in every direction, trying to escape the lynching, but he couldn't get away. They would have torn him to shreds, and even though he may have been a Fascist I couldn't stand this kind of thing. How long would it take for the military police to arrive? Suddenly the man raised his head as if to catch his breath and I saw he had dark hair with a white streak . . . I felt a shiver go up my spine . . . I knew him . . .'

In October 1922 Bruno Arcieri was twenty years old. He was doing his mandatory military service in Lucca, in the infantry, and was housed in a barracks situated adjacent to the Renaissance walls of the city. He had obtained his secondary school diploma after wasting a few years and was uncertain what to do with his life. He felt an urgency inside that he didn't know how to direct or dominate. He was confused, in short. He would wake up earlier than the others, when it was still pitch dark. During the day he felt overwhelmed by a terrible anxiety he was unable to quell, not even after the strain of long marches. He couldn't stand the life of the conscript, finding the violent manners of the NCOs and petty officers intolerable. Those early mornings, however, offered him an escape, the almost angry pleasure of a few hours of solitude and silence. At the end of one of the corridors of the barracks there was a small window with no bars on it that looked out onto a tiny courtyard surrounded by high brick walls. At four in the morning Bruno would lower himself down the wall and out into the fresh air. Then he would climb up the rampart's earthen embankment until he reached the causeway. Shivering with cold, he would run the length of the walls around the city to keep warm. The view was magnificent. On the clearest mornings he would watch the sun rise over the frosted landscape, the pink light colouring the foliage of the trees and flooding the rooftops of the sleeping city. His jog along the parapet helped loosen the vice that he felt around his chest; these excursions helped him survive. He returned to the barracks just before reveille, and no one was any the wiser. But he was undisciplined: sometimes he answered badly or didn't show up for evening roll call. Often he was sent to the barracks' prison for punishment. Shut up in a small, dark, smelly cell with only bread and water, his anguish only intensified. The forced immobility drove him crazy. He concocted wild plans to escape from his cell, or even from the barracks. Despite all of this, he decided that – at the first opportunity – he would sit for the examination to become an officer in the Carabinieri. The idea had come to him during one of his punishments, perhaps as a kind of revenge.

'But I still haven't told you who the man was that the crowd was lynching . . .' Colonel Arcieri, alias General Fucilieri, continued.

On 28 October 1922, all the barracks in the kingdom of Italy were put on full alert. Mussolini was marching on Rome, and all conscripts had to be in their rooms, on their cots. Truth be told, no one really knew what was happening. There were confusing rumours, often contradictory in nature. Arcieri had been thrown directly into a cell. His superiors didn't want to take any risks; a hothead like him might make trouble or escape. No one wanted any problems, at least for the next forty-eight hours. Bruno was like a beast in a cage, ranting and raving in the dark cell, feeling lonelier than ever. After a few hours the cell door opened, and another soldier was thrown in with him, a young man from Certaldo with dark hair with a white streak in it. They started talking. The lad was very agitated. He too had been thrown in for security reasons. He belonged to one of the 'glorious' Fascist squads, and had been singled out by the Political Police. Bruno had never appreciated Mussolini's bravado, and he said so openly, airing his opinions. And so the two prisoners started scuffling. It was simply because of their ideas: their respective visions of the world and of life were incompatible. But they didn't quarrel for long. They were just two kids bitter to find themselves both in the same situation. In the end they forgot their differences and spent the night talking, though avoiding certain topics. Bruno expressed his apprehensions to his cellmate, and even told him about his secret excursions along the ancient walls of the city. When they got out of there, Bruno thought they might even become friends. And then the news came that the March on Rome, combined with pressure from notable Romans, landowners and industrialists, had convinced the king to hand the government of the country over to Mussolini. For Bruno this political disappointment represented one of the deepest wounds of his life, and it only added to his personal anguish. He continued to console himself with his early morning excursions along the walls of the city, always with the utmost caution. One day in January 1923, upon returning from a brief leave, he received a telegram from Milan: his father had had a heart attack and was dying. Bruno wanted to go home immediately and asked to speak to his commanding officer to obtain special leave. But his conduct and the days he'd spent in confinement weighed against him, and his request was rejected. So he asked to speak to the commanding colonel, who had the reputation of being a man of good sense. The colonel was quite stern. He told him that he would reconsider the situation but warned Bruno that he should obey orders and fall in with the discipline. Bruno could find no peace. That night, lying on his cot, he couldn't sleep. He thought of the long walks in the country he used to take with his father, or the day they had laughed and laughed, or the one night they had confided in each other . . . He thought of all the things that he would never be able to tell him, from his fears to his unspoken dreams. He had to go home and say goodbye to his father before he died. He got out of bed and dressed in a hurry, without washing. It was very cold. The windows in the latrine were open and the water in the pails was covered with ice. He walked over to the window without bars and lowered himself down into the courtyard. The light of an enormous moon made the frost shine, and he could see perfectly. It was a magnificent night, but he had other things on his mind. He had only a few lire in his pocket, just enough for the train ticket. They would try him for desertion, but he didn't care. He only wanted to embrace his father one more time. With his hands frozen inside his gloves he started to climb up towards the top of the rampart; he knew exactly which stairs he had to take to get to the station. But when he reached the walkway he was met with an unpleasant surprise. Two guards were there, waiting for him, under orders of the commanding officer who had denied his leave. As they brought him back to the barracks he realised who had squealed on him. No one knew about his escape route except his cell companion, the Fascist with the white streak in his hair, to whom he had stupidly confided during that long, anguished night. He spent fifteen days in confinement in total despair. He never saw his father alive again and couldn't even go to his funeral. After two months they granted him leave to visit the cemetery. At his father's grave, Bruno wept in anger, swearing at the young Fascist who had betrayed him.

'I hadn't seen him since that night in the cell, and suddenly there he was before my eyes. I watched that ferocious scene from the balcony, remembering how, because of him, I hadn't been able to say goodbye to my father. The white streak of hair bobbed about with every punch he took. I felt no pity for him, but that violence, that blood, disgusted me. After the horrors of three years of war, the brutality and suffering were intolerable. Twenty years earlier I might have been able to kill that man with my bare hands, but now I couldn't let the crowd tear him to bits in front of my eyes. I put on my uniform jacket and stepped out onto the balcony.

'"Stop! That's enough!" I shouted. The crowd's fury diminished and then abated, and in the sudden silence everyone looked up at me. Their eyes were full of hate and their mouths twitched nervously. Even the Fascist looked at me in astonishment. I couldn't tell whether or not he recognised me. His face was covered with blood, his eyebrows were split, his eyes puffy and half closed. He had no shirt on, and his strong build contrasted noticeably with the gaunt bodies surrounding him. War and poverty, that's what his glorious Duce's promises had brought. And, as if that wasn't enough, the Germans had invaded Italy.

'"What's going on? What has this man done?" I asked in a peremptory tone.

'A young man waved his fist in the air and started to shout. "He's a Fascist rat! People like him have done terrible things!" There were mumbles of approval, and someone repeated his words more or less. I saw the crowd surge, ready to start pummelling him again.

'"And what were you doing, while I was fighting the Germans?" I asked, to buy time, looking them in the eye. The young man lowered his gaze, perhaps frightened by my uniform. The Fascist looked around, as though feeling lost. A woman made her way forward and stopped under my balcony.

'"So you feel sorry for a Fascist pig?" she asked with anger. Other voices around her mumbled similar phrases: "Why are you defending a good-for-nothing?" "Who are you?" "What do you want?"

'"I'm an Italian like you . . . and an anti-Fascist."

'"So don't stick your nose in our business . . .we'll take care of this bastard," a man shouted. I had very little time to find the right words if I wanted to stop the lynching. The crowd was like a shapeless, brainless beast and I could sense its desire for blood. I rested my hands on the terrace railing and thought of the Duce on the balcony of Palazzo Venezia. I had often watched him in the newsreels at the cinema, and each time I was impressed by how much power he exerted over the human ocean gathered in the piazza. Now here I was, in a similar situation, even though the crowd below me was hardly an "ocean". Speaking from the balcony of my own Palazzo Venezia, I thought of how many people had cheered Mussolini on. I don't know how, but I started to imitate the Duce's intonations, and even that ridiculous manner of his of bouncing back on his heels.

"'Listen to me very carefully, all of you . . . So this man is a Fascist? A dirty bastard who has committed terrible crimes? Let's assume for a moment that this is true . . . And what are you doing, if you lower yourself to the same level as the Fascists? If you become like them, it will be the worst kind of defeat; it will mean they have succeeded in changing you . . . So, how are you any different from the Fascists? If you kill as a group, you will each think that you didn't do it, whereas you will all be killers . . ." I went on like this for a bit, sweating in the heat. The sentences came to me by themselves, and I didn't care if I started repeating myself. One by one I saw them lower their heads, and I realised that the lynching was over. I dashed down the stairs and into the street. They stood aside for me, letting me through, staring at me in silence. I went into the middle of the crowd, took the Fascist by the arm and dragged him into the house. I locked the doors behind us and took him up to the first floor. I peered out from behind the curtains, waiting for the last person to be gone. Then I went up to the Fascist. His face was as swollen as a football, and he was dripping blood.

"'Do you remember me?" I asked him. He didn't answer. I thought of my father and punched him in the stomach, causing him to fall to the floor and writhe in pain.

"'Now do you remember me?" I asked, biting my lip. He got up slowly, trembling in fear, leaning on the wall for support.

"'Yes, I remember," he said without looking at me.

"'Back in Lucca, in '23, you ratted on me . . ."

'"Yes . . ." he said, breathing heavily, knowing he couldn't deny it.

'"Tell me why."

'"I don't know . . ."

'"They locked me up . . . I couldn't go and say goodbye to my father on his deathbed . . ."

'"I'm sorry." He seemed sincere, but maybe he was just terrified.

'"I was tempted to leave you out there just now."

'"Why didn't you?"

'"I don't know . . ."

'There was nothing else to say. I waited for a few more minutes, then gave him an old shirt that I found in a drawer. I accompanied him to a back door and opened it.

'"Get out. The next time I'll let them tear you to bits."

'"Thank you . . ." he whispered, incredulously. After a moment's hesitation, he ran off. I was left alone with the memory of my father's grave, and I managed not to cry.'

Arcieri rubbed his eyes and asked whether someone would fill his glass. After taking a sip he looked deeply into the fire. The rain was falling lightly now, with a gentle sound.

'Did you ever see him again?' Botta asked darkly.

'Never . . .' the colonel said. They sat there silently, as always happens after a sad story. Piras was as still as a stone. His dark eyes reflected the flames.

More wine was poured, and another log was put on the fire. Bordelli put a cigarette in his mouth but wasn't ready to light it. It was his turn now. As he searched through his memory, troops of figures came marching forward, some mere sketches, others more sharply defined. He had to choose one. A story he'd been told just after the war, by a friend of his father, came to him:

The German occupation, the Tuscan countryside . . . A girl, her mother and her aunt had to cross some fields to find something to eat in the nearby town. They were supposed to bring their documents, but the girl's were stuck inside a dresser that was warped shut. 'Come on, what do you think's going to happen? That today will be the one day they stop us?' But stop them they did, and they checked their documents. The two women's papers were in order but the girl was taken away, never to return home again . . . No, he didn't want to tell that story, it was too sad a way to end the evening. Finally he remembered a story that had been buried in his memory for years. He might never have recalled had it not been for that occasion. The others looked at him, waiting patiently for him to begin . . .

'Not much time had passed since the hellish months at Monte Cassino. The Germans, in angry retreat towards the Gothic Line, left a river of blood behind them. At this point it was more a matter of revenge than of war to them. Their Italian friend had betrayed them, and he would pay dearly.

'During the advance to the north, my battalion had the job of patrolling the dangerous areas. We had to find, and in some cases confront, the German positions. Quite frequently we had to shoot. Other times we entered towns just after the German columns had fled. We never knew what to expect.

'One afternoon in June, in the southern part of the Marches, I went out on patrol with three of my men. After an hour's march, we reached the edge of a village. We approached with the usual caution. We got to the first houses but didn't see anyone. The silence didn't necessarily mean that the Germans were still there; by then, we were used to not being welcomed with the sound of bells. We approached the main piazza with our machine guns in hand. The whole town was gathered in front of the church. They looked like ghosts. They were speaking softly and several people were crying. They didn't come towards us or embrace us the way people usually do with liberators.

'When we got closer, they told us that the Krauts had arrived suddenly and had left barely an hour before. They didn't stay long but had had enough time to sack the town, rape a few girls and kill seven people, including the parish priest. Luckily, many people had escaped. We were surrounded by spectres. You could feel the terror the town had experienced. They had put the corpses in the church, and we went to see them. Four men, a boy, one woman, and the priest. They would be buried the next day in the cemetery, without coffins.

'As we were about to go back to our camp, a woman asked if we were hungry. She could only offer us some stale bread, a plate of beans, and a slice of salami. We accepted the invitation without thinking twice. Anything was better than the Allied tinned food, which we disliked almost as much as we did the Nazis. We made our way into a humble kitchen and sat down at the table. Two adolescent girls huddled on a bench, watching us from a distance. The woman filled our plates and offered us each half a glass of wine. We ate in silence, enjoying flavours we had all but forgotten. After a bit, a man came out, his face full of bruises and dried blood. It was the husband – his name was Tommaso. The wife was called Maria. In addition to the two teenage girls, they also had a two-year-old daughter, who was sleeping. They were lucky to be alive, they said. It had been a miracle. And with tears in their eyes they told us what had happened . . . The Germans had arrived suddenly, and started breaking down people's doors . . .

They hadn't been able to get away. Hearing footsteps on the stairs, Tommaso pushed his wife and two daughters into the room next door in the absurd hope that they would be saved. When, a few seconds later, someone broke down their door, he was certain he would be killed. He prayed that at least Mary and the baby would survive. There were four Germans, each one bigger than the next. They threw him to the ground and started kicking him. They shouted something at him that he didn't understand and then broke out in laughter. Tommaso heard the sound of their officer's footsteps coming calmly down the hallway. And then there he was, in shiny boots and an impeccable uniform. He was smoking a cigarette in a long, ivory cigarette holder. He looked around with a disgusted air, bothered by the bad smell, as if he had walked into a chicken coop. With a gesture he ordered the giants to drag the Italian bastard close to the window so he could see him better. He smiled wanly and pulled his Luger out of his holster with a bored look. He pointed it at Tommaso's head. At that very instant the two-year-old daughter ambled across the room towards her father. Tommaso managed to pick her up, hugged her and kissed her head desperately, without looking at the barrel of the gun that was pointed at him. The soldiers laughed and pushed him around. Drily, the officer ordered the four beasts to leave. A second later, they were gone. Tommaso put the child down on the ground, trying to convince her to leave, to go back to her mother, but she wanted to be held. Maria watched the whole scene through the keyhole, terrified, not knowing whether she should go out and try to save the baby or if it was better to stay hidden to protect the two older daughters, who were so pretty that heads turned when they walked down the street. Maria prayed to the Madonna, and rubbed the medallion that she wore around her neck. The SS officer took a step forward and gave the father and daughter an awkward smile. The little girl looked around playfully, as if the two adults were involved in a game. The German raised his gun and pressed it to her little head. Tommaso saw the madness in his gaze and trembled with fear, but also with anger; a two-year-old should not die like that. Waiting to die together with his daughter, he closed his eyes, humiliated by the fact that he couldn't do anything. The shot from the Luger echoed through the room and the glass in the windows shattered. Tommaso opened his eyes, amazed to be alive, and saw the officer biting his lip, as though moved. He didn't understand what was happening until he heard the German say in an awkward Italian, 'I, too, have small child in Germany.' The Nazi put his Luger back into the holster and after a long sigh walked quickly out of the room, drying his eyes. Tommaso collapsed to the floor and started to laugh, cry, and kiss the little girl's hair. The mother and the two girls ran out and hugged him too . . .

'When we got up to leave, they embraced and kissed us. That night I dreamed of the whole scene, just as they had described it to me, and I woke up looking for my machine gun next to my cot,' Bordelli concluded, putting his cigarette out in the ashtray. The child was probably twenty-five or so now . . . He wondered whether she remembered those moments.

'It's almost a fable,' Dante said in a deep voice.

'What a horrific story,' Diotivede commented.

'Precisely . . .' Dante replied.

'But they were saved . . .' Botta said, with tears in his eyes.

'We should marvel at the power one man can have over the life of another, not at the gesture of a Nazi in a moment of lucidity,' said the forensic pathologist, pouring himself some more wine. The colonel was deep in thought, and Piras stared silently into the fire.

'All the same, it is a moving story,' murmured Dante, with a smile. Botta wanted to have the last word.

'However you put it, it was a female who saved the family . . . so I'd say it's time for another toast to women . . .'

They continued to sip their *vin santo* and chat about this and that. They drank with great gusto, and though they'd already downed a great many glasses, they didn't feel too drunk. Perhaps just a bit melancholy . . .

After they'd emptied their umpteenth bottle, the sad moment for goodbyes finally arrived. Time had flown, and it was very late. They could have gone on forever, telling stories and listening . . .

Handshakes, overcoats, bottles of olive oil, umbrellas, car engines starting up . . . Minutes later there was only the sound of the rain. Jeremiah was surrounded by dirty dishes and empty glasses, but looked more serene than usual.

'Your friends are very nice,' said Arcieri, sitting back down. Bordelli answered with a smile and then put the death's-head back on top of the hutch.

'Think you'll feel like going for another walk in the woods tomorrow?'

'Are you asking me or Jeremiah?' asked the colonel, smiling. Bordelli turned and looked at the skull.

'I don't think I could live without him at this point.'

'Yes, but he never lends a hand with the housework . . . Though the dishes are mine to do. I mean it.'

'Reveille at eight?' asked Bordelli, yawning. Arcieri dug into his pocket.

'I have a present for you.'

'Another?'

'Don't expect a winged horse,' said the colonel, getting to his feet. He had a sealed letter in his hand, which he set down on a corner of the table.

'What is it?' asked a curious Bordelli.

'Goodnight, Commander.'

Arcieri bowed slightly and headed up the stairs. The inspector imposed some order on the kitchen, waiting for the bathroom to be vacated. He would open the envelope in bed. For the life of him, he couldn't imagine what it could be.

His head was spinning slightly, but one couldn't really say he was drunk. He felt vaguely euphoric, but also a little sad, and there was something pleasurable about this mix of emotions. He placed the dirty dishes and glasses on the counter beside the sink, lining up the empty bottles on the hutch without bothering to count them. He removed the stain-covered tablecloth and tossed it into the laundry hamper, which he kept in the broom closet next to the entrance. Once a week he would take the hamper to a laundress in the village, who had four washing machines in her house. A few days later he would go and pick up his laundry, all nice and ironed. Eventually he would have to decide whether to buy his own washing machine, preferably a German brand.

He had a look at the fire to make sure everything was in order, put Arcieri's 'present' in his pocket, and went upstairs. The bathroom was free. As he was brushing his teeth he recalled bits of the stories he had heard that night and let himself be carried away by the images . . . The stink of formaldeyde, the shock of white hair, the witch chasing after the children . . . It was as if he'd read a novel.

After loading the pot-bellied stove for the night, he went into his bedroom, leaving the door ajar to let a bit of heat in. He lit the lamp on the bedside table and quickly got undressed. Once under the covers, he opened the colonel's envelope. Inside was a sheet of paper folded in four, as well as a smaller, sealed envelope. He unfolded the sheet and found a typewritten letter . . .

Dear Inspector,

You already know that when I feel strong enough to leave this magnificent castle, I will try in every way to find out what lurks behind the fake suicide of that Florentine youth. I feel it is my duty, and I shall stop at nothing. But if one day you learn that I have died, especially in an accident, or even by natural causes, please do not be deceived by appearances. And then, if you can, please try to find out, for my sake, what happened to that lad.

Now comes the hardest part. It's one of those things that one cannot express out loud.

We'd met a few times in the past, before this most recent occasion. I liked you at once, despite our profound differences, or perhaps because of them. You seem to me a sincere person, and for my part I have always detested deception . . . Fancy that, given the job I had for so many years.

You took me in at a very difficult time in my life, and I was able to get to know you better. But I have also got to know myself better. In this house I have succeeded in reducing, a little, the tension that has had me in its grips for so long. Perhaps it's also thanks to your wine. I have told you things I had never told anyone before, and even when alone I've been able to free myself of my own ghosts. You see, Bordelli, I've never had any friends. I mean real friends. The kind in whom you can confide your innermost secrets without fear. I have spoken to you about Elena, the most important person in my life. I'd never have imagined myself capable of it.

One last thing: as you may imagine, the present I was referring to is not this letter. You'll find it in the other envelope. And there you have it. I've said what I wanted to say. When we see each other again over coffee tomorrow morning, please pretend you never read these lines.

Goodnight.

Bruno

His name was written by hand. Bordelli smiled, realising, with some amazement, that the colonel was right . . . There were certain things one could not express aloud. Feeling terribly curious, he opened the second envelope and found another typewritten sheet of paper. An unexpected surprise, one that took his breath away . . .

I have succeeded in finding the 'mystery woman' you've been looking for. I cannot tell you her name, because I swore not to do so. The lady has agreed to meet with you, however reluctantly, on the condition that she be allowed to conceal her identity. When you meet, she will dress up in such a way as to be unrecognisable.

She is married and terribly afraid her husband might get wind of something. Her fear is that her relationship with the murdered man (whose name, I'm sorry to say, I cannot remember at present) might come to be known, and she wants at all costs to avoid a scandal. The appointment is for Sunday, the twenty-fourth, at half past five in the evening. You must wait for her in Via del Corso, at the corner of Via de' Cerchi, directly under the Red Cross shrine, with an unlit cigarette in your mouth. She will make herself known to you. You must follow her at a safe distance and go into a place of the lady's choosing. You'll have half an hour, at the most, to talk, perhaps less. The lady also advises you to arrive on time. She will walk past the shrine at half past five on the dot. If she finds nobody there, she will leave. Break a leg . . . or, as they say in the navy, up the whale's arse . . .

Bruno

Bordelli set the letter down on the bedside table and lay there staring at the ceiling. He was wondering how the hell the colonel had managed to . . . But what a fine gift indeed. One could only imagine how hellish the centre of Florence would be at half past five on Christmas Eve . . . Would talking to the woman really be of any use? He sincerely hoped so, otherwise he didn't know what he would do . . .

Before turning out the light, he read a poem by his mother, one chosen at random, and, like the first time, he was struck by the simplicity of her lines. As he was falling asleep he kept repeating them in his head, embracing the pillow . . . *In an autumn as sweet as back then . . .*

Colonel Arcieri never told Bordelli how he'd managed to find the mysterious woman. It was a gift, and one never leaves the price tag on a box of chocolates.

It hadn't been easy. But compared to what the inspector had done for him, it was nothing. After Bordelli had told him about the elegant woman and how he didn't know where to look for her, Arcieri had decided to try to lend him a hand. If she was a lady of the upper bourgeoisie or aristocracy, he had a good chance of finding her. He just had to be careful not to make waves and to use discretion. Above all, he had to avoid being seen by those who wanted him dead . . .

Bordelli left the house early in the morning, saying that he would be back in time for dinner. The colonel waited to hear the Beetle climb the dirt road and then rushed upstairs to get dressed. He didn't have any time to spare if he wanted to get things done and return to the house before the inspector.

He opened the closet where he had put the new clothes that Bordelli had bought him. But he changed his mind right away and put on his old clothes, which were too big for him. It was better if he looked like a beggar. He put on a woolly hat and wrapped a scarf around his neck and up to his nose. His overcoat reached his ankles. He remembered having seen a pair of sunglasses in the living room and decided to borrow them. No one would recognise him in such a guise. He opened his change purse and counted out his last three thousand lire. That was all he had left. He put the keys to the house in his pocket and pulled the door shut behind him. The sky was clear but it was very cold and he had to keep his hands in his pockets. He walked uphill without much effort. The walks in the woods had helped him regain his stamina.

Finding the mystery woman might not actually lead anywhere, but that was another matter. Right now, the main thing was to give the inspector a pleasant surprise. Arcieri seemed to recall that the village was about three kilometres away. He didn't want to risk tiring himself out, so he walked slowly, enjoying the view of the distant hills. It touched his soul: he felt like a boy skipping school . . . And up above loomed the castle, gloomy and black, with its underground rooms where disobedient children were banished . . .

He knew to whom he had to talk in order to chercher la femme. *Another woman, naturally. A woman his age who knew all the important families in Florence and often their private affairs as well. Her name was Serenella Giusti Cattani; Nelli, to her friends. It had been almost twenty years since he had last seen her, right after the war. She was very beautiful, even if her beauty was somewhat disturbing. She had always reminded him of an Etruscan sculpture he had seen in Rome, at Villa Giulia – the sarcophagus of the Bride and Groom.*

Nelli was very reserved and never got upset. She looked at the world with irony and detachment, but she was also capable of reading people's looks and perceiving what was hidden behind appearances. Somewhere she had a husband, a diplomat who was always travelling for work, but she seemed happy to be on her own. She had a hard time getting close to other people, and she had even kept her distance from Elena. She felt a sincere sympathy only for Arcieri, a captain in the Carabinieri, a world to which she didn't belong. They used to meet twice a week in the centre of town for a drink, just the two of them, and talk about a million things . . . Elena was even a little jealous . . .

He reached the village and walked to the church square, where he entered a bar to ask when the bus left for Florence. It would be another forty minutes before the next departure. He also inquired as to the return trips. The one most likely to get him back in time left Santa Maria Novella at 4.35 p.m.

'Do you have a telephone?'

'Over there,' the barman said, nodding towards a small door at the back of the room.

'A coffee, please . . . and three tokens for the telephone.'

He closed himself in the booth, which stank of cigarette smoke. The floor was covered with a filthy carpet riddled with cigarette burns. Flipping through the phone book, he found the number he needed, that of an exclusive club that Serenella had always frequented. Having had no news of her for so many years, he preferred not to call her at home. He put a token into the phone and dialled the number, being careful not to make a mistake. After a few rings the token dropped into the device with a clink, and he was greeted by a most polite young secretary with all the warmth of an ice cube.

'Good morning, I'd like to leave a message for Signora Cattani,' he said drily.

'Your name, please?' the girl asked, with the tone of someone who already has a pen in her hand.

'Please tell the signora that . . . Elena's fiancé called . . .' Arcieri said, feeling slightly ridiculous. But he was almost certain that Nelli would understand, or at least so he hoped.

'You can't tell me your name?' the secretary insisted somewhat aggressively.

'Here is the message, if you would be so kind: "I shall be at the Osteria del Ghetto today for an aperitif before lunch . . ." Please be sure to tell Signora Cattani that she must come alone . . . thank you.' He hung up the phone and exited the foul-smelling cabin with a sigh of relief. He hoped that the secretary would rush off to find Signora Cattani to give her the strange message. His coffee was waiting for him at the bar, no longer hot, but fine nonetheless.

Of course Serenella would understand the message; of course she would come to the meeting. 'Rendezvous at the Osteria del Ghetto for an aperitif.' In the late thirties, the Osteria del Ghetto was their name for Caffe Paskowski, in Piazza della Repubblica, because of the old Jewish ghetto that used to be located there.

He didn't want to be seen strolling around, so he waited in the church. The roof of the basilica was so high it almost gave him vertigo. He sat in a chilly pew, counting the minutes. Here and there a few old ladies with kerchiefs tied under their chins were praying. One of them rocked and nodded back and forth, back and forth . . . Arcieri almost fell asleep.

He finally boarded the bus for Florence, which at that hour of the day was almost empty. Sitting behind the driver were two well-dressed ladies chatting about holiday events and common friends. At the back of the bus was a young soldier with dark circles under his eyes. Arcieri hoped for his sake that the fatigue was due to pleasurable activities. He well remembered how it felt to be that age; it seemed like yesterday. It saddened him, but it also left him feeling bitter. The years had passed too quickly. Who knew what it would be like to see Serenella again at the Osteria del Ghetto . . .

But Arcieri didn't want to lose himself in nostalgia and so he focused on the countryside out of the window: the hills dotted with large villas and small churches, the vast olive groves, the abandoned vineyards, the well-kept vineyards . . . and he thought about the day ahead. Serenella knew everything about everyone, and what she didn't know she could easily find out. But she was no gossip either, and he would have to let her know just how serious the matter was.

The bus stopped periodically along the Imprunetana for passengers, reaching Florence in about an hour. Arcieri got off at Porta Romana and walked towards the centre of town, looking distractedly at the shop windows decorated for Christmas. Via Romana was crowded with cars and scooters. It was hard to breathe with all the exhaust fumes. The pavements were a-bustle there as well, and more than once he was forced to walk in the middle of the street. Every so often he saw himself reflected in one of the shop windows and barely recognised himself in his present dress. Before reaching Piazza Pitti, he turned up Via Maggio to avoid the crowds on the Ponte Vecchio. Just over a year ago he had walked up that very street, the muck coming up to his ankles, past wrecked cars and dead animals. The black water line on the façades of buildings looked like a wound to display to the world, for its amazement and compassion.

He found himself looking into the eyes of the passer-by, men as well as women, to see whether any of them represented a danger. Who knew whether it ever occurred to those looking for him that he was still in Florence. Living at the inspector's house gave him a sense of safety, but being in the city was risky . . .

What if someone was following him? A pistol with a silencer, a single shot, and before anyone knew anything the hit man would be lost in the crowd . . . He tried to stay calm by reminding himself that his face was covered with a scarf and that he was wearing sunglasses.

He crossed Ponte Santa Trinita and continued up Via Tornabuoni, where there were even more tourists. This was the elegant part of the centre of town, and the windows were dressed sumptuously. There were only a few days left until Christmas, and people walked in and out of shops with their arms full of packages. Seeing boys with long hair or girls dressed in strange ways no longer amazed him. There was something beautiful about those young people. Their eyes revealed the light-heartedness of people who had not been through war . . . Although, at times, he did notice some dark, impatient looks, like those of a caged animal.

He had more than thirty minutes to wait before his rendezvous with Serenella, but after all the morning's activity he was feeling rather hungry. He went to the Bottegone, at the corner of Piazza del Duomo, and it was as crowded as ever. He ate a small sandwich at the bar without taking off his dark glasses, ignoring the bartender's suspicious glances. It might have been imprudent to come down to Florence, but he deeply wanted to complete his mission and find the mystery woman.

While waiting for the rendezvous, he strolled down the busiest streets, letting himself be pushed along by the flow of people. A few of them looked at him suspiciously, but for the most part they ignored him. Everyone was absorbed in their Christmas shopping. Indeed, he too had come to town to look for a gift, and he sincerely hoped to find it.

He repeatedly walked up and down the same streets, checking the hour on the public clocks. It wasn't at all like walking in the woods, where memory could take wing.

At half past eleven he peered into the windows of Caffe Paskowski. He was shocked to see that everything was exactly the same as he had left it thirty years earlier. A few of the tables in the tearoom were occupied, and in the far corner he saw an elderly lady sitting alone. He recognised her instantly . . . it was

Serenella. She was probably almost seventy now, and she looked her age. Her hair was completely white.

Arcieri headed for the entrance of the café, heart filled with nostalgia. To look a little less shabby he took off his dark glasses and his odd woollen cap, and ran his hands through his hair. Upon entering he heard the wild notes of a current song; it sounded almost violent. Two customers at the bar turned to look at him, curious about this strange, poorly dressed man. Arcieri barely had time to look into the tearoom when a young waiter came up and asked him kindly to leave. Serenella watched the scene from a distance and clapped her hands gracefully to get the young waiter's attention.

'The gentleman is with me,' she said, glaring at him.

'Forgive me . . . I . . . I had no idea . . . Please, sir, please sit down . . .' He accompanied the colonel to the lady's table, helped him take off his overcoat, and disappeared. Arcieri sat down facing her, and gently took her hands.

'Rendezvous at the Osteria del Ghetto,' he whispered.

'Yes . . .'

'How are you, Nelli?'

'Bruno . . .' She was also visibly moved. She was smiling and had tears in her eyes.

'You're beautiful.'

'That's the only lie that I love to hear.' She truly was beautiful, and as elegant as ever. She wore a matching skirt and blazer, and a string of pearls; a black and white checked overcoat hung over the back of her chair.

'Let me look at you,' Arcieri said. She looked at him with her big green eyes, slightly alarmed.

'What's happened to you, Bruno?' she whispered.

'It's too long and complicated a story to tell you now.'

'But are you well? Do you need anything?' She gazed at his baggy clothes, his tired face. Arcieri looked around, and noticed that people at other tables were staring at them. And with good reason. It was unusual to see an elegant lady with a vagrant.

'Shall we take a little walk?'

'As you wish.'

They got up in silence. Arcieri helped her put on her coat, as he had done so many times in the past, then donned his own heavy overcoat. He also put on his sunglasses and his pom-pom cap, Serenella observing him with some surprise. The waiters respectfully said goodbye as they left the café and stepped, arm in arm, into the crowd flooding the streets. They walked towards Via Tornabuoni, paying little attention to the windows dressed with streamers and colourful ornaments.

'Are you embarrassed?' Arcieri asked her softly.

'Of what?'

'To be walking with a vagrant.'

'You're the most elegant man in the world,' Serenella said, with the sweetest of smiles. Arcieri asked after her family, and she said they were all well . . . except her husband, who had died ten years earlier, in Brussels, in a prostitute's bed. Arcieri told her briefly about his accident, his months in hospital, adding that he needed to stay in hiding for some time, but that he couldn't tell her any more than that. Mostly because he didn't know any more himself.

'You're making me worry,' Serenella said, squeezing his arm.

'And to think that I'm retired . . .' he muttered with a smile. They walked across the bridge, the sunshine almost warming them, and headed down the Lungarno. Turning onto a few narrow streets, they made their way to Piazza Santo Spirito, which was notably less crowded than the rest of town, and sat down on a bench. The beautiful, bare façade of the church was lit up with sunshine. Six or seven long-haired hippies were sprawled on the steps in front. One of them was playing a guitar.

'Can you at least take off your glasses?' Serenella asked gently. Arcieri took them off to please her. Then he took one of her hands and told her he needed to ask her a favour.

'I need to find a woman.'

'Oh my God, Bruno . . .' Serenella exclaimed with some delight. Arcieri smiled too, imagining his friend acting as a procuress.

'Not in that way, for goodness sake . . . I need your help in identifying someone, a woman from your social circles.'

'Can you tell me why?'

'First tell me this: did you know the entrepreneur who was killed, Antonio Migliorini?'

'So it's a serious matter,' Serenella said with a frown.

'I wouldn't bother you with anything frivolous.'

'I learnt of the murder just two days ago, when I got back from London.'

'Did you know him well?'

'Didn't you say you were retired?'

'It's not my case. I am trying to help the inspector in charge of it, even though leaving the house is very risky for me.'

'Memento audere semper . . .[31] *isn't that your motto?'*

The people passing by could never imagine what the strange elderly couple was talking about.

'Tell me about Migliorini . . .' said Arcieri.

'I can't say that I knew him very well. I met him a few times on social occasions.'

'When was the last time you saw him?' Arcieri asked. Serenella thought about it for a second, staring into space.

'Yes . . . I think it was in early November at a dinner at the Cacciaguidi home. Antonio was not much of a socialite. On the contrary, it was something of an event when he did make an appearance. But he was always cordial with everyone and quite chivalrous with all the women. Once in a while we talked, and I have to admit that I liked him. He was likable, gallant, and mostly I felt that he was sincere.'

'Do you know who his lover was?'

'So she's the woman you're looking for . . .'

'Yes. Do you know who she was?'

'No . . . no one knew anything about Antonio's private life. He was very reserved. But they said that he had a way with women, and this doesn't surprise me at all. He was very charming.'

'I'm starting to feel jealous.'

'I don't mind,' she murmured with a Mona Lisa smile. Had they been twenty years old, this would have been the ideal moment for their first kiss.

'Help me find that woman,' Arcieri said, thinking of what a wonderful Christmas present it would make for the inspector.

'I can try.'

'I know very little about her. She is definitely married. The only person who has ever seen her is the gardener, and just once. He described her as a beautiful woman, about thirty years old, tall and thin, very elegant. He couldn't give me any more information because she'd covered her head with a scarf and was wearing dark glasses.'

'The world is full of women like that,' Serenella said.

'The inspector has been unable find out anything else about her. Migliorini's friends and relatives have never even heard of her.'

'That doesn't surprise me.'

'You have to help me, Nelli.'

'Although, on second thoughts . . .'

'What?'

'It's just an impression, and I can't promise you there's anything to it.'

'Tell me all the same.'

'At that dinner at the Cacciaguidi house, I saw Antonio exchange short but intense glances with a beautiful woman. At a certain point I even thought to myself that they looked like a couple in love. And she could indeed be said to resemble the woman you've just described.'

'Who is she?' Arcieri encouraged her.

'Do you recall the Marquis Pierguidoni?'

'Of course, Pierangelo Pierguidoni . . . the fat bloke who used to go around boasting that he was friends with Pavolini and Mussolini . . . a fine fellow, that one, a perfect Fascist . . .' Arcieri said scornfully.

'That's quite enough, Bruno, it's all water under the bridge . . . and I assure you that Pierangelo is not the way you think. He may not be the bravest man in the world, but during those dark times he certainly didn't do anything too terrible.'

'All Italians who applauded Mussolini did something terrible, dear Nelli, even the most innocuous.'

'You're always so drastic . . .'

'Let's not talk about these things; let's talk about that woman,' Arcieri said impatiently. Serenella caressed his hand.

'Last year, the marquis's eldest son, Pieramedeo, married the

daughter of a Sicilian baron who has property in Tuscany . . . She is the woman I am thinking of.'

'Do you know her well?'

'As much as a woman my age can know a thirty-year-old, but our paths do cross quite often.'

'I want to talk to her . . .'

'And what if she isn't the one?'

'Do you have her telephone number? What is her name?'

'I'll whisper it to you, since it's such a secret.' Serenella leaned towards him and whispered the woman's name in his ear.

'I guess two surnames weren't enough – she had to have four,' mumbled Arcieri, shaking his head.

'And she deserves every one of them because she is truly beautiful,' Serenella said with sincere admiration.

'I beg you, please try and call her right away.'

'Oh my . . .'

'I can't do it personally. A phone call from an outsider would just scare her. She might even think I am trying to blackmail her. I need your help, please don't tell me you won't . . .'

'These are delicate matters, Bruno.'

'If she answers, try and ask her if she really was Migliorini's lover. You have just the delicate touch to do so successfully,' Arcieri continued, as if his friend had already accepted.

'It's embarrassing . . .' Serenella protested weakly, but for Arcieri it was already settled.

'And if she is indeed the one, tell her that I absolutely must talk to her. I will call her back whenever and wherever she wants, but it must be as soon as possible, even today, which would be best of all. But please don't give her my name for any reason whatsoever. You need only vouch for me. Reassure her that she can trust fully in my discretion . . .'

He anxiously waited for Serenella to give in.

'It will be most unpleasant,' she said, smiling sadly, and she began to rise from her chair. Arcieri stood up with her and kissed her hand.

'You're a dear,' he murmured. And he watched his agent Serenella set off on her important mission. Then he sat back down and saw her enter a bar nearby. He put his sunglasses

back on, hoping she wouldn't return at once with the news that she hadn't been able to talk to the Sicilian lady with four surnames.

After five or six minutes passed he started to feel calmer. Serenella must have reached her, and they were surely talking. Perhaps Migliorini's name had already been mentioned . . . Was she really the one?

Serenella came out of the bar fifteen minutes later. As she was walking towards him, Arcieri tried to judge from her expression whether the mission had been a success.

'How did it go?' he asked. Serenella sat down next to him.

'You're still wearing those glasses?'

'Don't leave me hanging, please,' Arcieri said, taking them off.

'She is indeed the one.'

'Good . . . Was it hard to get her to talk about it?'

'Let's say it wasn't easy. I had to approach the subject in a very roundabout fashion. She is terribly afraid of her husband.'

'Did you tell her I need to talk to her?'

'At first she refused, but I managed to persuade her. I gave her my word that she can trust you.'

'When can I call her?'

'Straight away, if you like.'

'What's her number?' Arcieri said, already standing. Serenella rustled through her purse and handed him a little address book.

'Now it's my turn,' Arcieri said, putting his glasses back on and striding off towards the bar. To pass the time, Serenella took a Maigret novel out of her purse and started to read. Becoming immediately engrossed in the story, she lost track of the time.

She didn't come out of it until Arcieri sat down beside her.

'You seem pleased.'

'Mission accomplished.'

Arcieri was smiling. He returned the address book to her and took off his dark glasses before Serenella could say anything.

'It took you more than half an hour,' she said, looking at her watch.

'Let's just say it wasn't a walk in the park.'

'What exactly was your mission?'

'I needed to persuade her to talk to the detective,' Arcieri said with satisfaction. Serenella folded her hands.

'She must have suffered a great deal from Antonio's death, poor dear.'

'Her voice is lovely.'

'Now it's my turn to be jealous,' Serenella said, putting her little book back into her purse. Arcieri took her hand in his.

'May I have the honour of lunching with you?'

'How could I possibly refuse?'

'But I need to ask you another favour.'

'I just hope it's not another phone call . . .'

'No, it's much worse than that . . . for several months now I haven't dared make any withdrawals from my bank account, in order to not leave any trace . . . and so . . .'

'How terribly scandalous,' she said, laughing.

'In theory I've invited you, don't forget.'

'But only on one condition,' Serenella said, rustling around in her purse again.

'What condition?'

'No one will ever see me pay for a man.' She furtively slipped a five-thousand-lire banknote into his pocket and invited him to get up.

'You know I'll make good on my debt.' He took her arm and they slowly walked off.

'Where are we going?'

They went to a trattoria in the neighbourhood and were seated at a table amidst local craftsmen who were already enjoying their coffee. The place smelled of rustic cooking. Serenella had never been in a place like that, and she seemed to enjoy it. Their presence aroused quite a bit of curiosity; the other diners looked at Serenella and Arcieri as if they had dropped out of the sky.

After years of not seeing each other, it was normal to start reminiscing about old times. They talked in a whisper, so as not to be heard. The craftsmen left their money on the table, said goodbye to the host, and went back to their workshops. The two of them were finally alone. Serenella caressed his cheek.

'Have you seen Elena?'

'Yes . . .'

'How is she? I haven't heard from her in years.'

'She's well. . .' Arcieri said curtly. He didn't want to talk about Elena. Serenella understood and didn't press him any further. They continued to talk about their old friends and about things that had happened in the past twenty years. They had so much to say, but it wasn't just the words that were important. Even their gazes evoked a world that no longer existed, a period of time for which they didn't know whether they should feel nostalgic or not.

The waiter started turning the chairs upside down on the tables, in order to mop up. It was time to leave. How quickly it had all gone. Arcieri paid the bill, with Serenella watching in amusement. As soon as they left the trattoria, he tried to give her the change, but she refused.

'I am sure you will honour your debt,' she said, feigning seriousness.

'If I don't, it's because I'm dead.' Arcieri put on his dark glasses again and she didn't dare protest. They walked off towards the Arno, enveloped in a veil of melancholia. They strolled arm in arm, ignoring the puzzled gazes of passers-by.

'And what will you do now?' Serenella asked.

'Don't worry about me. I ask only one thing of you: don't tell anyone that you saw me. Don't mention a word to anyone, please. It's more important than you think.'

'I won't say a thing, Bruno. You can count on that. But you can't stop me from worrying,' Serenella said, attempting to smile. As soon as they crossed to the other side of the river, Arcieri stopped.

'We'll say goodbye here. I would rather you didn't see which way I went.'

'So that I won't be able to say anything even if they torture me.'

'Precisely.'

'Will another twenty years pass before I see you again?'

'In twenty years it will be my ghost that will come to see you,' Arcieri said with a smile. He took off his glasses and they said a wordless goodbye with a long embrace. Serenella turned away

and headed down a crowded Lungarno. Arcieri stood watching her for a few minutes then put his glasses back on and continued on his way. He felt terribly sad, and tried to cheer himself up by reminding himself that he had found the mystery woman. And not only . . . He had inveigled her into meeting with him. He was certain that the lady with four surnames would keep her promise.

All at once he spotted Bordelli at the far end of Via Tornabuoni. He stopped in his tracks. The inspector was skirting the crowds on the opposite side of the street. When Arcieri saw him walk into the Seeber bookstore, he rushed off, like a kid worried about being caught doing something wrong. He imagined Bordelli thought he was at home, reading a book by the fire.

When Arcieri reached Santa Maria Novella, it was past four, and the bus left at 4.35. Outside the Carabinieri compound was a crowd of students with banners, some of whom were seated on the ground. A bearded, long-haired man shouted anti-Vietnam war slogans into a megaphone, and everyone repeated them in unison, as if it were a mass. Here and there he saw spray-painted graffiti on the walls of various buildings . . . They reminded him of the slogans he had seen more than twenty years ago, which were done with paint and brush and were as blunt and bitter as poverty and suffering themselves: NO FOREIGN OCCUPATION! LONG LIVE THE KING! IF YOU HONOUR THE REPUBLIC YOU DISHONOUR THE FAMILY. *Now instead they read:* USA KILLERS, OUT OF VIETNAM, NO MORE BOMBS. *There were other slogans that praised the hippies and flower children, and others still in English. Young people were fed up with the old world of their parents . . .*

Arcieri walked away from the crowds and confusion. Minister Taviani had a fine kettle of fish to deal with, he thought. While waiting for the bus he decided to walk around a bit. On the far side of the piazza he stopped to look at a marble building . . . Hitler and Mussolini had walked out of that door with their hit men one May morning almost thirty years earlier to an exultant crowd. He had been there and watched that scene, biting his lip.

Back then he'd been struggling with an unpleasant investigation involving the rape and murder of a number of girls, and he'd had to defend himself from a nameless party official who had tried to manipulate him like a puppet. That was when his career as an agent in the Special Services started . . . Damn his memory, it never behaved. And all because he was getting old.

To pass the time he decided to go inside the station and look at the timetable. Milan, Pisa, Salerno, Brussels, Paris . . . so many suitcases, legs, eyes on the move . . . not to mention shady-looking figures feigning indifference.

He couldn't risk being stopped by a policeman, so he left after a few minutes. Mixing in with the crowd on Via Nazionale, he elbowed his way forward. When he reached Piazza Indipendenza, he turned round and came back.

He arrived at the bus station just in time to board. The seats were almost all taken, and people were talking loudly. He found a place at the back of the bus next to a boy sleeping. A sudden jolt, and they were off. It was still light but night was descending upon the city. Arcieri continued journeying through his memory, talking to his ghosts, and by the time they reached Porta Romana, he was already asleep.

The driver woke him up with a gentle tap on the shoulder. The colonel apologised and hurried off the bus. It was dark. The piazza was empty. Suspended in the night sky from a very tall trellis was a large, illuminated red star, the symbol of hope for the oppressed.[32] *One of many hopes betrayed, he thought to himself. Man had an extraordinary talent for sullying everything he touched.*

Arcieri removed his glasses and set off towards home at a steady pace. The street lamps were no brighter than candles, and past the town they grew ever rarer. He could barely see where he was going, and was helped only by the moonlight. In the distance he saw the dark outlines of the hills speckled with lights. He shivered with cold, and could see his breath.

Before he knew it, he was heading down the dirt road that led to the house. Not even the shadow of a street lamp there . . . He heard dogs barking, and other dogs barking their distant replies. He couldn't wait to get into the house and close the door behind him. The last stretch of road was a descent full of rocks and potholes, and he very nearly fell twice.

He felt great relief when he walked into the house, and as he stoked the fire he realised how very tired he was. He warmed himself in front of the blaze without even getting undressed. As soon as he felt better he took off his scarf and hat and removed his overcoat. He went to put a record on the gramophone and then quickly washed all the dishes. He had become quite skilled at that noble job.

He relaxed in the armchair in front of the fire with a book in his hand. It was as if he had never gone out, but in fact he had travelled in time and returned with the mystery woman. He didn't want to tell Bordelli right away, preferring to wrap his offering up like a proper Christmas present.

He started to read a story by Melville that he knew rather well and after a few minutes he fell asleep, just as he had done on the bus.

He dreamt he heard the wail of an air-raid siren, as if the bombers were on their way, and when he pulled himself out of it he realised that the phone was ringing. It made him nervous, as if that connection with the outside world was dangerous. He couldn't be sure it was Bordelli; if he had sounded the signal, Arcieri hadn't heard it in his sleep. And so he decided not to answer. When the phone stopped ringing he felt a distinct sense of relief.

He tried to read some more, but no longer felt calm. That phone call had got him worrying again. He had to try to distract himself. It was past seven. He closed the book and started cooking slowly under Jeremiah's haughty gaze. A tomato sauce for pasta, four eggs for a frittata, and, once again, potatoes with onions.

He didn't feel like eating alone and hoped Bordelli would come home for dinner. Concentrating on the cooker, he managed to calm his nerves. He was thinking of the next day's menu and had only to write it down and turn it over to the secular arm . . .

When he heard the Beetle pull up outside, dinner was almost ready. The table was set. The only thing missing was the wine, but that was Bordelli's job. He heard the front door close and a moment later the inspector came into the kitchen. They greeted each other like two friends who have been living together under the same roof for a while.

'You're home early tonight,' said Arcieri.

'I tried calling several times this afternoon with no answer, and I got a little worried.'

'After lunch I took a short walk nearby, and then fell asleep until just a little while ago.'

'How nice to come home and find dinner ready and waiting,' said Bordelli.

'It would be even nicer if I was a beautiful woman.'

'If you were a beautiful woman you'd be with a hot-blooded youth.'

'My potatoes and onions came out a lot better this evening.'

'God be praised . . .'

'So you really don't want to tell me how you found that woman?'

'What woman?' said Arcieri, looking out over the valley. They were sitting on a flat boulder right in front of the large abandoned house at Pian d'Albero, in the hills above Figline Valdarno. It was a fine sunny day, though quite cold. One could see a few strips of snow here and there, now melting in the sun.

They'd left the Beetle down at La Panca mid-morning and walked for almost two hours straight along a trail that snaked through the woods, surrounded by the dark trunks of leafless chestnut trees. When they came within sight of the ruin, Bordelli had told the colonel about the battle that had taken place between partisans and Nazis at that house in June '44, ending with some forty dead, including children. Amid the silence they could still imagine the scene, still hear the Germans' guttural cries, which they both remembered well from the war.

'I was simply curious and would like to know how you did it.'

'Did what?' said the colonel, smiling.

'Okay, I won't insist.'

'The fact of the matter is that I can't tell you anything. I gave my word.'

'Then let's not discuss it any further. The most important thing is that you found her.'

'I truly hope it will be of some use.'

'Well, at least I won't be spending all my time staring into space.'

Bordelli was very grateful to the colonel for this lovely surprise and couldn't wait to speak with the mystery woman.

'Shall we head back home?' asked Arcieri, getting to his feet.

'It's true I'm starting to feel hungry.'

'We need to finish the leftovers.'

'Who could ask for more?' said Bordelli.

They headed back out on the trail of frozen mud, their breath visible in the air. The colonel no longer limped and didn't even seem to mind the effort of the walk.

'I have to confess something to you,' he said.

'Go ahead; consider me your parish priest.'

'Forgive me, Father, for I have sinned . . . A few days ago, in the evening, when you didn't come home for dinner . . . I was unable to read . . . I felt a bit restless, I needed to move . . . And so I took the liberty of visiting some of the forbidden places in your abode – those abandoned rooms on the ground floor where spiders reign from cobweb thrones. But I didn't touch anything.'

'*Ego te absolvo a peccatis tuis* . . .' the inspector mumbled, tracing a cross in the air with his hand.

'I just can't help myself. Ever since I was a boy, I have been fascinated by cellars and attics. They are the warehouses of memory and can trigger the imagination.'

'I also like to rummage through old stuff, but I still haven't found a suitable moment for sifting through those rooms.'

'So I wanted, in fact, to ask your permission to poke about in there.'

'Please feel free, *mon colonel.* But if you find a lost treasure, we split fifty-fifty.'

'I noticed two very interesting trunks.'

'Beware of scorpions.'

They continued chatting, dodging some large, half-frozen puddles, taking care not to slip and fall. For a long stretch the path practically turned into a torrent, and they had to step on the biggest rocks to keep going. Then they trudged uphill, and after turning a bend, Arcieri grabbed Bordelli's arm.

'There's someone there . . .' he whispered.

'Where?'

'Behind those shrubs there, by the boulder.'

'Yes, now I see him.'

There was a motionless figure, bent at the knees, head poking out above the shrubbery.

'What should we do?' asked Arcieri, never taking his eyes off the apparition.

'You wait here, I'll go and have a look.'

The inspector went on alone, seemingly unruffled. As he was about to reach the boulder, a rail-thin young man in oversized clothes and a crew-cut leapt out from behind the bush and planted himself in the middle of the footpath. Bordelli recognised him and breathed a sigh of relief. He'd seen him once a few years earlier, in that same area, and learnt his story from an old hunter he'd met in those woods. Everyone called the lad Giuggiolo, and it was obvious at a glance that he had a few screws missing.

'Ciao, don't you recognise me?' said the inspector.

'Don't tell anyone . . . Don't tell anyone . . .' the lad whispered with his head down. He was constantly moving, as though dancing on hot coals.

'What am I not supposed to tell anyone?'

'The devils . . .'

'The devils?'

'There's devils aplenty out here . . . They hide under the rocks . . .'

'And what are they doing there, under the rocks?' asked Bordelli, shrugging. It wasn't easy to talk to Giuggiolo.

'I heard them just now . . . They scream like pigs at the slaughter . . .'

'No, go on . . . I heard them myself. They were just joking.'

'This is all mine, out here . . . Wherever I step is all mine . . .'

'You like to walk in the woods, do you?'

'Wha'd Santa bring you for Christmas?'

'A mysterious woman . . .' Bordelli turned and gestured to the colonel to let him know that all was well.

'That man over there is Bachicche . . .' Giuggiolo mumbled, ready to run away.

'No he's not, he's a friend of mine.'

'He's Bachicche, I tell you . . . I know from the smell . . .'

'Well, he surely won't eat you.'

'Bachicche . . . Bachicche . . . Even if you kill 'im he always comes back, that one . . . I don't like him so near . . .' Then he spat into his hands and dashed down the hillside, babbling all the while and sliding through the trees as nimble as a hare.

By the time Arcieri came forward Giuggiolo was already at the bottom of the slope, before vanishing into the underbrush.

'Who was that?' Arcieri asked, curious.

They resumed walking, without hurry, and Bordelli told him the boy's sad story, as he'd heard it himself. During the war, Giuggiolo was just a little boy, and of course nobody called him Giuggiolo at the time. He'd witnessed the hanging of his whole family from the oak of the abbey by a drunken SS unit, and when his turn came he was saved by a miracle . . . But lost his mind in the process.

They started talking about human cruelty, asking themselves how anyone could hang an eight-year-old child with their own hands. Of course, the Italians themselves had done worse in Ethiopia, wiping out whole villages with mustard gas and other chemical weapons. And you could be sure the Black Brigades under the command of the ever so refined criminal Pavolini weren't wringing their hands over the age of the partisans they killed.

'Sometimes I wonder . . .' Bordelli began. Surely, he thought, some of those *fine lads* who had killed and tortured in wartime had gone home, raised families, gained weight, and now kissed their beloved children goodnight every evening and fell asleep in their slippers in front of the telly . . . Did they ever think back on what they had done? Did the Germans who had hanged Giuggiolo and his whole family ever stop and think back on those moments? And how about the soldiers at Sant'Anna, who'd murdered women and children? What did they feel? Were they able to justify themselves and go lightly into the world? Or did they have great boulders weighing on their consciences?

'Well, what man doesn't have some weight on his conscience?' Arcieri asked with a sigh.

The inspector was chewing his lip, thinking of what he'd done just a few months earlier, convinced he was in the right. The responsibility for those murders was his alone; he had to bear that weight unaided. Not that he wanted to lighten his load or try to justify himself. Still, in spite of everything he wished he could talk about it with the colonel at that moment, even though he knew he wouldn't. Perhaps it was the growing friendship he felt for Arcieri, or the simple, very human desire to get something off his chest . . . And so he let slip an allusive statement.

'Sometimes we can commit grave mistakes, even crimes, in the name of Justice, and that's when confusion begins to take hold in our conscience . . .'

Out of the corner of his eye he saw Arcieri turn and look at him with a troubled expression.

The old Special Services colonel had realised that Bordelli was talking about himself. He was quite used to reading between people's words, to look for hidden meanings. He didn't even do it deliberately; it just came to him naturally, since for so many years he'd been forced to devote himself to the art of 'deciphering'. Since childhood, however, he'd learnt that the meaning of a statement must be sought above all in the tone of voice with which it is uttered. Bordelli was clearly referring to some weight he was carrying on his shoulders, even though he had spoken more generally. And Arcieri knew what it meant to have secrets that one could never admit to. They were like blots or rents in the canvas of a magnificent painting that one tried at all costs to maintain in a state of perfection, in the vain hope of preserving an unattainable ideal of beauty. In short, prodding one's own remorse was never pleasant, but Bordelli's words had now reawakened old memories in him, which he might as well bring out into the light . . .

'You're right, Inspector. It is possible to commit some very grave injustices in the name of Justice – indeed, it's all too easy. It happened to me over thirty years ago, but when I think about it now I still have that weight on my conscience . . .'

'Do you feel like telling me about it?' asked Bordelli, almost pleased to have company in the misery of his remorse. The colonel nodded.

'Nobody really knows the whole story of this affair, aside from myself . . .'

Milan, 1935. Arcieri was a young officer in the Carabinieri, and the only espionage he was familiar with was in the novels he had read. At the time he was hunting down a dangerous madman as big as a bear, a maniac who had kidnapped a little girl and disappeared with her. They knew the man's name was Gino Brambani, and they knew who he was, but they had no idea where he might be hiding out. The days went by. Nobody hoped any longer to find the girl alive, and a sorrowful sense of defeat hung in the air at headquarters. Brambani was a psychopath, someone able to kill another human being without thinking twice, and yet he enjoyed a certain protection by the state, by virtue of his having been a 'Fascist of the first hour'. In 1921 he'd been one of the fiercest of the squadristi, *those bloodthirsty stormtroopers whom the bourgeois fascism of the 1930s had shunted into the background and kept under close surveillance, but also defended. In his efforts to try to discover the man's hideout, Arcieri had importuned a great many party bureaucracies, from the Gruppi Rionali to the Casa del Fascio, all the way up to the Federal Secretary. But he'd come up against a wall of secrecy and was even subjected to some veiled threats accompanied by less than reassuring smiles. He did not intend to give up, however, and at some point had spent an entire day interrogating a small fish in the Milanese underworld, which at the time was quite different from that of the post-war boom economy. There developed at times a certain familiarity, even friendship, between hoodlums and carabinieri, but if the delicate balance was broken at any time, all bets were off. And then the interrogations could get pretty harsh, with no hard and fast rules, and no lawyers to interfere. Slaps, punches, lighted cigarettes stubbed out on the backs of hands, and worse. Nobody made a big deal out of it, neither the cops nor the hoods. That was just the way things were, and it was perfectly possible that the following day the sergeant and the hotel thief might go out for a coffee together as though nothing had happened.*

With the kidnapped little girl very much on his mind, Arcieri had been rather rough with that street punk, but in the end he'd succeeded in obtaining what little information the guy knew, which helped provide him with a hint of a lead. It was possible that one of the people protecting Brambani was a seller of dried fish and legumes with a shop at Porta Romana. His name was Amerigo Cerutti. He apparently belonged to a group of men who liked to amuse themselves in special ways. Drugs, parties with very young prostitutes, gambling . . . There was something for every taste, but what they all shared was a passionate faith in the Duce. Wanting to get to the bottom of this affair at all costs,

Arcieri pulled out all the stops. He was acting in the name of Justice, and was therefore acting correctly. At least, this was what he kept repeating to himself. At the time anti-Fascism was the last thing on his mind. Like so many others, he simply went on with his life 'in spite of' the regime, by ignoring it. There was, in short, no ideological motivation for his actions. He simply wanted to find the girl.

He knew a chap, an old, forever frightened communist who lived on his gains from reselling stolen goods and from his modest professional activity as a photographer. Arcieri also knew about some publishing the man had done for an anti-Fascist organisation but had not passed this information on to the Political Squad. Thus he had, in short, the power to ruin the man, and he blackmailed him by asking him to track down, in short order, some zesty erotic photos of a homosexual flavour. The photographer blanched and nearly started crying, but Arcieri would not bend. It was the photos or jail, he said. And a few days later he got what he wanted. Now he could open the second act. He went and paid a call at Cerutti's shop when it was full of customers, and without being seen he slipped the photos under a large sack of lentils. The next day he organised an apparently routine check on the shop, as part of the effort to prevent fraud in the foodstuffs market, and the photos were quickly discovered. Cerutti was brought into the Carabinieri station for questioning and locked up in a cell. Arcieri let him stew in his juices for an hour or so, then went in alone to talk to him. He found before him a frightened man who wouldn't look him in the eye, broken inside, like a toy that no longer worked. Cerutti swore he had nothing to do with those lewd photos, and by way of reply Arcieri asked him what his wife might think if she saw them. The poor man burst out in tears, still swearing, in God's name, that he . . . He was terrified. He knew well that those photos would not please his Fascist comrades one bit. Suddenly Arcieri became nice again, and understanding, telling him that he could make those photos disappear as if by magic. No one would ever know anything about them, especially his wife . . . But in exchange, Arcieri wanted some specific information: Brambani's hideout! There were only a few seconds of silence, and then Cerutti spilled the beans. Arcieri didn't set him free at once, however. He wanted first to be certain he'd told the truth. And he promised him that he would burn the photos.

A few hours later Arcieri found himself at the hydroport of Milan on a cold January night with a pistol in his hand. He was able to free the girl, but in the exchange of fire with Brambani he took a bullet in the leg. He still bore the scar today, and during changes of season it throbbed with pain, reminding him of the whole unpleasant affair. He'd got what he wanted, but that same night Cerutti hanged himself in his holding cell, using strips of cloth he'd obtained by shredding his shirt. Perhaps he couldn't stand the idea that, despite the carabiniere's promises, someone might still learn of those photographs and think he was a pederast. Arcieri had never been able to accept this death, which surely could have been avoided. On top of everything else, the arrest of the maniac and the liberation of the little girl had earned him a promotion to the rank of captain, an idea that had already been in the air for a while. On other occasions, too, he'd acted more or less in the same way, though without such dire consequences. False evidence fabricated on the sly to entrap criminals who would otherwise have got off scot-free . . .

'And every time I was convinced I was doing what was best. As I got older, however, I began more and more to wonder whether serving Justice is something else altogether,' the colonel said in conclusion, looking through the trees at the distant horizon.

Bordelli was chewing the inside of his cheek, thinking that the murder of the three maniacs responsible for little Giacomo's death could likewise have been avoided. He could have done what the young Arcieri had done and fabricated false evidence to entrap the culprits. It might well have proved complicated and convoluted, but with effort and determination he could perhaps have pulled it off. Whereas he'd ended up making a grave mistake. Blinded by disgust, he'd goaded those perverts in the worst possible way, convinced that fear might lead them to do something careless and rash . . . But that's not what happened. It was Eleonora who had paid the price, sweet Eleonora, who was waiting for him in bed, to spend another night of lovemaking with him.

They both remained silent for a few minutes, and when their conversation resumed, they'd already changed subject, as though sharing a need to talk about something less grave.

Less than two hours later they were seated at the table, eating reheated leftovers from the night before.

An afternoon of rest, books and music. Followed by a light supper. Then, according to custom, the evening prolonged in front of the fire, with a glass of wine in hand and long journeys through the past.

At four in the afternoon Bordelli parked the Beetle outside the *collegio* at Poggio Imperiale and continued on foot. Driving into the centre of Florence on Christmas Eve would have been pure folly. It had been a sunny morning and the air seemed less chilly than in days past. Piras was probably in Sardinia by now, in his village.

Bordelli had an hour and a half before his appointment with the mystery woman, and he was nervous. After thinking about her for so long, it seemed almost impossible that he would finally meet her. Would it be another dead end? He would soon find out. However it might turn out, one thing was certain: Colonel Arcieri had given him a truly wonderful gift.

He walked past the restaurant where he had eaten with Eleonora for the first time, right after the flood, and he *tirò innanz*, as poet Francesco Redi would have said – that is, he pressed onwards, trying not to let himself be overwhelmed with memories. He didn't want to think about Eleonora, not right then. At the corner he glanced over at the Rosai crucifix, so coarse and earthly, surrounded by the three Mary figures, each contorted with grief. He had always appreciated that Christ for its ungodliness, at once awkward and delicate. The Lord looked like a poor peasant who had been tricked by the Fox and the Cat in 'Pinocchio'. Or like some poor bloke from a tough neighbourhood who had to do everything he could just to put a meal on the table. Bordelli nodded at Christ as if he was an old friend and turned onto Via San Leonardo, perhaps one of the most beautiful streets in Florence and, without a doubt, one of the narrowest.

He crossed the boulevard and continued on towards the city. One car after another passed by, and he had to press up against the wall as he walked in order not to slip off the extremely narrow pavement. As he went, he tried to picture Antonio's mysterious, elegant mistress . . . Would she really be so attractive? Would she let him see her face? What if she didn't show up? When he reached Forte Belvedere, daylight was already fading. For a second he considered turning down Costa San Giorgio, but then he thought about the bedlam at Ponte Vecchio and changed his mind. He turned right down Via di Belvedere, a narrow street that descended steeply towards the San Niccolò neighbourhood, with the fourteenth-century city walls on one side and a high stone wall on the other, which, in comparison to the former, looked fit for a doll's house. A long row of cars advanced at a snail's pace, spewing a stench of petrol into the air, each of the vehicles stuffed with big beribboned Christmas presents. Bordelli passed a doorway in the doll's-house wall that led to a garden, and when he looked up at the roof of the villa, he was thrown back in time, as often happened to him these days. Some twenty years earlier he had gone out with a girl who lived there, a young blonde who was to all appearances timid and defenceless, but who was actually as brave as a lioness, not to mention irascible and tormented. What was her name? Sara? Silvana? No, her name was Serena . . . never had there been a name less appropriate. Their almost-love story had lasted just a few weeks, through quarrels and unhealthy fits of passion, but then she disappeared, and his health improved . . . All in all it was a pleasurable memory, like the recollection of a danger averted.

Night had fallen. He kept walking down the narrow street, stepping carefully as he went. Ten minutes later he passed through Porta San Miniato and couldn't help but think again of Eleonora . . . that was where she lived when they first met, and where they had spoken for the first time, while shovelling the mud from the flood along with other people from the neighbourhood. He had to resign himself; if he wanted to stop thinking about her he would have to change city.

The traffic along the Lungarni was insane; there were, of course, a number of those classic geniuses who think they can part the waters of the Red Sea just by sounding their horns. Thick columns of exhaust rose up in the air and were dispersed by the wind.

He crossed the bridge and turned up Via dei Benci. It was hard to make one's way forward without constantly bumping into people.

He turned down Via dei Neri and was submerged by a river of people. He didn't dare imagine the situation in the streets even closer to the centre, where he had to meet the mystery woman. Never had he felt so pleased to live in the countryside, far from the chaos and noise.

Coming up on the fine palazzo where Rosa lived, he remembered that he had promised to stop by to pick up his present. Maybe on the way back from his rendezvous, when he hoped to have learnt something important from Antonio's mistress. When he reached the crossroads by her building he looked up and couldn't help but smile. He had never noticed it before. At first-floor height, almost at the corner of the building, there was a blue niche with an azure Madonna statuette . . . So this was the famous *Madonnina* that Rosa was always evoking in her curses, though she probably also just talked to her now and then.

He turned onto Via dei Rustici, where there were far fewer people, and managed to catch his breath. A few more half-empty alleys and he came out in Piazza San Firenze, and back into the chaos. At the base of the staircase that led to the courts, he saw an old man selling Christmas trees, ranging in size from small to two and a half metres tall. The vendor had struck gold with the late holiday shoppers. A stop there, too, on his way back might be in order. How long had it been since he had bought a Christmas tree?

He avoided heading into Piazza della Signoria and continued on, making his way past fur-clad ladies and crying children. He didn't dare walk up Via del Corso, preferring to take Via della Condotta. And he found himself in darkest hell. It felt like May 1938, when Hitler and Mussolini came to visit Florence. He remembered that day well. The whole city had been decorated like a great theatre, with banners and Nazi flags, and the streets were lined with cheering crowds. But back then the expression in people's eyes was entirely different from now . . .

On Via della Condotta the cars were practically at a standstill, as though afraid of crushing the ants. It was twelve minutes past five. The dark of night didn't affect those streets: shop windows were bursting with light, and garlands of electric lamps twinkled without restraint. It was getting harder and harder to walk. He only had two or three hundred more metres to go but didn't want to risk being late. Crowds exiting the stadium were nothing in comparison to that wall of people. So many faces passed before him that he couldn't tell them apart anymore, and his ears were bombarded by endless fragments of speech.

When he managed to turn into Via dei Cerchi it was already twenty minutes past five. It had taken him eight minutes just to advance a few steps. He glanced at his watch continuously. Now and then he saw a beautiful woman, but then she would disappear into the havoc. Five twenty-three, 5.24 . . . At 5.27 he reached the intersection with Via del Corso. He peered up at the white marble Red Cross tabernacle, which was walled into the corner. At the base it read *Amo chi mi ama*: I love them that love me.

He took his position under the tabernacle with an unlit cigarette in his mouth, as the mystery woman had requested. Passers-by jostled him every which way, but he held his ground. And now that he was there, the seconds seemed to stop passing. Five twenty-eight, 5.29 . . . *I love them that love me* . . . If he remembered correctly, it was a phrase from Proverbs, and it had been Divine Knowledge incarnate that had uttered it.

Suddenly a gloved hand took the cigarette out of his mouth. A blond woman with dark glasses and an azure foulard tied under her chin looked at him briefly, before moving off into the mob. Yes, she was beautiful. He hadn't seen her eyes but he could tell that she was beautiful. He followed her down the same alley he had taken to get there, without losing sight of her and yet without staying too close. He felt a strange sense of euphoria. The woman seemed to be much better than he was at making her way through a crowd, or perhaps people made room for this goddess of beauty. The fact was that he had to make a considerable effort to keep up with her.

The woman reached Piazza della Signoria and turned left. She walked along one side of Palazzo Vecchio, then turned and walked the length of the other side. Suddenly she crossed the street and disappeared under the arch of Via Vinegia. Bordelli followed her down the deserted alley, staying about twenty steps behind. In the twilight of the street lamps he could finally admire her elegant gait, the harmonious curves visible under her dark coat, and the perfect pair of legs sprouting from under her skirt. It wasn't hard to understand why Antonio had felt such passion for that woman. Even the sound of her heels on the cobblestones was fascinating.

The hum of the crowd began to recede in the distance. Then the woman suddenly vanished around the corner of Piazza San Remigio. The inspector stepped up his pace, just in time to see her enter the church without turning around to see whether he was behind her. Crossing the small piazza, he looked over his shoulder to see whether they had been followed. All this mystery had got his imagination going . . . And suddenly it seemed so very absurd that he wanted to smile. Wouldn't it just have been easier to meet in a bar?

He hesitated for an instant and then pushed open the door to the church. It was silent and barely illuminated by the light of a few candles. It smelled like incense and repentance. In a corner there was a modest crèche, with the manger still empty. He took a few steps forward. In the shadows he made out the dark, motionless shape of an old woman kneeling and praying in the first pew. But where was the mystery woman? He looked around for her, treading softly so as not to make any noise. And suddenly he saw her leaning against the wall. As he walked towards her she invited him to sit in the confessional in the place of the priest.

As soon as he saw her kneel down, Bordelli slipped into the confessional and pulled the curtain behind him, sinking into the darkness and its vague smell of antique wood. He hadn't expected to feel so emotional but the sense of doing something forbidden gave him butterflies in his stomach. He remembered with painful nostalgia how, as a child, his mother would drag him to Sunday mass and send him off to confess. On the other side of the iron grate he would hear the sound of a little door opening, and immediately afterwards the priest would whisper . . . *Tell me, my son.* He knew he would not tell the truth. It felt so good to have secrets. It made him feel grown up. And why on earth should he tell his secrets to someone he didn't even know? Now he was on the priest's side of the grate, he was the unknown figure, and all he wanted to know was the truth, the whole truth . . . While these thoughts were crossing his mind he fumbled about in the dark.

Finally he found the small pommel of a bolt. He slid it open, and as soon as he opened it he smelled a scent of face lotion.

'Good evening,' he said softly.

'I don't have much time,' the woman whispered anxiously, her lips close to the grate. Bordelli felt a pleasurable sensation in the near-total darkness of the confessional, as when, in childhood, he used to hide under the bed or in the broom closet.

'I have to ask you some indiscreet questions, and I want you to be completely sincere in your replies.'

'Ask me anything you like.'

'My sole purpose is to find out who killed Migliorini.'

'I agreed to meet with you for the same reason, but if I had known anything important I would not have hesitated to call the police,' the woman said, holding back her tears. She had a very light Sicilian accent.

'Pardon my bluntness, but were you Migliorini's mistress?'

'Yes . . .'

'And for how long?'

'About two months.'

'Where were you on the night he was killed?'

'I was at a dinner at a friend's house.'

'Where?'

'In Bellosguardo.'

'And your husband?'

'We were together.'

'Did your husband leave the dinner party at any point?'

'No . . .'

'At what time did you return home?'

'About two thirty or so.'

'Do you sleep in the same room?'

'Yes, but in separate beds.'

'At what time did you go to sleep?'

'I understand where you are going with this, but you are wrong. My husband cannot have killed Antonio.'

'Maybe he found out about your affair and wanted to—'

'Impossible!' she hissed decisively, interrupting him.

'How can you be so sure?'

'My husband would never be able to keep such a discovery to

himself; it would have been the end of the world . . . Not to mention that he would have taken it out on me and no one else. He's very jealous, but he's not a brute.'

'People are not always predictable.'

'In any case, it cannot have been him. I'm a light sleeper, and on the rare occasion that my husband gets up in the night, I wake up immediately. What's more, that night I couldn't fall asleep until dawn. Maybe I had a premonition . . .' She started to cry, sobbing softly, and Bordelli waited patiently for her to blow her nose.

'When did you find out about the murder?'

'The next morning, on the news . . . I thought I was going to die . . . those were the worst moments of my life . . .' She broke into tears again, but managed to stop at once. Bordelli had no way of verifying the woman's words. His only choice was to believe her, and he felt she was sincere.

'May I continue?'

'Yes . . . I'm sorry . . .'

'Were you alone when you heard the news?'

'My husband was right in front of me; we were having lunch.'

'He knew Migliorini too, I imagine . . .'

'He had seen him a few times but I don't think they had ever spoken.'

'How did he react to the news?'

'He was deeply saddened.'

'Did he realise how upset you were?'

'I don't think so.'

'How did you manage to hide what you were feeling?'

'It wasn't easy . . . for a bit I managed to keep it all in and appear normal, then I took to my bed, saying I had a terrible headache . . . I wanted to be alone. I couldn't even cry . . . I tried to recall our last few moments together, his last words . . . He was a very sweet man, with a sensitivity that I had never seen in anyone else.' She had probably never told anyone about her secret liaison and now she finally could. She needed to talk about Antonio and their love.

'When was the last time you saw him?' Bordelli continued.

'Saturday afternoon. We always met in the afternoon, for an hour or two. But only when I was certain that my husband wouldn't wonder where I was,' she said, her voice still cracking.

'Did you talk on the telephone after Saturday?'

'Yes, the same day he died, shortly before dinner. I called him from a bar in town.'

'Did he seem worried? Did he mention anything strange?'

'He was the same as ever, loving and affectionate.' This time she managed not to cry but sniffled like a child.

'Did he ever tell you about any disagreements he might have had with anyone?'

'No . . .'

'Did you have another appointment set up?'

'We were supposed to see each other on Friday, after lunch. My husband had a bridge game with his friends.'

Suddenly the dull thud of the church door closing echoed through the nave and aisles, and the mystery woman let slip a soft cry of concern. Bordelli moved the curtain aside to peer out and he saw that all the pews were empty, and that the elderly lady had left. He reassured the woman, but his heart was pounding, too. Who knew what would have happened if the priest had found him in the confessional. He waited a few more seconds to regain his composure, and then continued.

'Did you love Antonio?'

'He is the only man I have ever loved,' she said softly, with some effort.

'And did Antonio love you?'

'Yes,' she said without hesitating.

'I presume you're not very happy with your husband.'

'When I got married I was convinced that I loved him, and I continued to feel that way until I met Antonio. It's not easy to find the right words . . . It was like waking up after a long sleep,' the woman said, sniffling again.

'Did you think of leaving your husband when you fell in love with Antonio?'

'I wish I'd had the courage to talk to him sincerely . . . it was terrible having to hide my true feelings, like a thief . . . But I didn't feel guilty for loving Antonio . . . We wanted to get married . . . Sooner or later I would have had my marriage annulled by the Roman Rota, but I kept putting it off . . . I was afraid of the consequences . . . the scandal, my husband's reaction . . . Everyone would have been against me, his family and my own . . . I couldn't bear the idea of hearing people say wicked things about our love . . .' She'd finished saying what she wanted to say without crying, but it could not have been easy.

'Will you request an annulment now?' whispered Bordelli, even though it had nothing to do with the inquiry.

'What purpose would it serve? It would just make my husband suffer needlessly.'

'And are you able to live with a man you do not love?'

'Antonio is gone . . . I feel empty . . . It doesn't matter whether I am happy or not,' the woman said in resignation.

'Have you ever wondered who might have killed him?'

'I wonder about it constantly . . . I just can't . . . Antonio was . . .' She couldn't go on, and again Bordelli waited while she caught her breath.

'Did he ever mention Oberto, the gardener, to you?' he asked her, without any real reason.

'Yes, he was terribly fond of him. They were connected by a tragic event. Many years ago the boy's father . . .'

'I know the story . . .' the inspector interrupted her, running his hands over his face. He had learnt absolutely nothing from the meeting and was feeling discouraged. He'd come up empty handed. He sat there in silence, listening to the mystery woman breathing. He had hoped to find out so much, and instead . . .

'I have to go now,' she whispered.

'So, can't you think of anything which . . . ? I don't know . . . something strange he might have said, some allusion . . .'

'No, I can't think of anything.'

'Did Antonio ever talk about his past relationships? A love story that ended badly, a woman who didn't want to let him go, an angry husband . . . forgive me for being so blunt . . .'

'We never spoke about those kinds of things,' she replied in a whisper. Bordelli looked around in the dark like a beast in a cage. He didn't know what else he could ask, and in the end he threw in the towel.

'I don't want to steal any more of your time . . . I wish you a pleasant Christmas . . .' He pulled the curtain open, ready to leave the confessional.

'On second thoughts . . .' she muttered.

'What?'

'It may not be important, but certainly nobody knows about it.'

'What is that?'

'Well . . . Antonio had something of a problem with his sister-in-law.'

'Claretta?'

'Yes . . .'

'What kind of problem?' Bordelli asked, closing the curtain again.

'Well . . . Antonio told me that after the tragic death of her sister . . .'

The pretty sister-in-law started to buzz around the new widower, flirting with him, and one evening she confided in him that she had been in love with him ever since she was a little girl. Antonio had had no idea of how she felt and laughed it off. He liked Claretta, but didn't feel the same way about her. Not wanting to hurt her feelings, however, he gently tried to dissuade her. He also told her that it wouldn't be right, such things just weren't done . . . But Claretta wouldn't give up. She continued to stay close by, waiting for the right moment to climb into his bed. She often went to the villa to see him, and several times she stayed for dinner. Some women have a great deal of patience and know how to get what they want. One evening when Antonio felt particularly sad, Claretta tried to comfort him in the sweetest of ways. He had drunk a little too much, and was feeling lonely . . . In the end he let himself go and fell into his sister-in-law's arms. They spent the night together. Antonio knew he wasn't in love with her, but he liked Claretta. She was a pretty girl full of life, and her kisses managed to lessen some of the pain of his wife's passing. They continued to see each other, without anyone finding out. It was better if it stayed a secret; nobody would have approved of such an improper arrangement. Then Antonio started seeing another woman, and after a few tantrums, Claretta stepped aside. But she didn't want to give up on the man she desired, and so she told him openly that he could have her whenever he wanted. At first Antonio didn't take her offer seriously, but things changed over time. When he wasn't in a relationship he enjoyed being in Claretta's arms, and, truth be told, it sometimes happened even when he was seeing someone else. In essence she'd accepted becoming his woman in reserve. Things went on like this, and always in secret. Claretta noticed that he never fell in love too seriously, and she was willing to wait. She made do with those moments, and repressed her jealousy, and convinced herself that sooner or later she would have Antonio all to herself. She didn't mind remaining in the shadows, but only because she was sure that she was the most important woman to him . . . his favourite. To her alone Antonio confided his innermost feelings, his hopes, his disappointments . . . To her alone he spoke of his amorous adventures, his latest infatuations. With her alone he felt truly free to say anything he wished . . . No woman could ever take her place, and no woman could ever come between them . . . Every so often she would say this to Antonio, as though joking. And he would smile, thinking it was something to smile about. But when he met the mystery woman, Claretta understood right away that it was not just another affair, and she got frightened. She became unkind, envious, and over the phone often behaved like a jealous girlfriend. Antonio tried explaining to her that their little game was over, but she didn't want to accept it . . .

'I think I'm the only one who knows about this. Antonio told me about it a few days before he died, on Thursday afternoon, I think it was. I had just arrived at the villa when the phone rang. Antonio answered it and I saw him shake his head in dismay. I went up to him, trying to find out what was going on, and Antonio held the receiver away from his ear so that I could hear. I didn't know about Claretta yet; I only heard a desperate woman crying, ranting . . . She was saying between sobs that she would never let *a hussy* take her place. Then suddenly she changed her tone and began to apologise, whispering sweet nothings, saying that she would be happy just to remain in her secret corner, but when she realised she wasn't getting the desired result, she started crying again and threatening him. Antonio tried to reason with her for a long time, but when he saw that it was impossible he hung up. He was worried, and above all upset. The phone call had changed his mood, and he couldn't bring himself to smile. Then she started calling back, and Antonio unplugged the telephone. We sat down in the living room and he told me all about her. But the scene with Claretta wasn't over yet. Half an hour later she showed up at the villa and started ringing the bell. Antonio wouldn't open for her and didn't go out. He didn't want to put our intimacy, our dreams, at risk . . . No one must ever see me, no one must ever find out who I was,' the mystery woman concluded with a sigh.

After listening in silence, immobile, in complete darkness, Bordelli could see Claretta in his mind's eye, in a jealous rage, running her brother-in-law through with the foil.

'Did Antonio ever tell you he was afraid his sister-in-law might do something rash?'

'You don't think that Claretta . . .' whispered the woman, without finishing her sentence.

'I don't think anything,' Bordelli lied.

'Antonio said he felt a little guilty about her. He hadn't behaved well, he'd been selfish, he'd acted impulsively, and now he regretted it. Anyway, after that time we never talked about Claretta again, though I must say that it wasn't easy for me not to think about her. I have always been put off by women who lose their dignity over a man, and that telephone call had disturbed me.'

'I can well believe it.'

'My God, I really must go now,' she said fearfully.

'Thank you . . . Goodbye . . .' The inspector whispered, feeling sorry . . . for Migliorini, for Claretta, and above all for the young, resigned woman beside him.

'Please wait for a few minutes before leaving,' she whispered.

'All right.'

'Farewell . . .'

'Farewell,' Bordelli replied. He heard the elegant sound of her heels as she walked away. The door of the church opened with a creak and closed with a slight thud. The inspector rested his head against the wooden wall of the confessional and, despite the pitch dark, he closed his eyes . . . He thought about her, Claretta . . . The pretty sister-in-law, in a jealous rage . . . Who wasn't going to let a hussy . . . Had she killed Antonio in a moment of rage? Perhaps he had opened the safe with the intention of giving her a jewel to console her? Maybe even the very ring made by the Parisian jeweller that he had given to her sister many years before? At last he had a lead, a trail to follow, but he didn't want to throw himself in one sole direction simply because he had nothing else to go on. He plunged farther into the dark forest of the imagination, fluttering like a butterfly . . . And suddenly he felt tired, very tired . . . Perhaps it was due to the dark, or that smell of old wood and dusty vestments . . . He had never sat in the priest's section of the confessional before . . . Was it a sin? What would his mother have said? *So long since I've seen the stars* . . . When did his mother find time to write her poems? In the morning, while she was doing chores? Or maybe during her long sleepless nights? And why on earth hadn't she told him?

There were only a few hours until Christmas, and he didn't even have a lousy tree to put presents under . . . He had to remember to drop by Rosa's house . . . His mother had always made tortellini in broth for Christmas lunch, the best he had ever eaten . . . The crèche, the little shepherds made of coloured clay, the moss that he and his father would collect in the forest . . .

Suddenly he thought he heard a whisper, and he woke up, trying to determine whether he had been dreaming. He remained silent and held his breath, and after a few seconds he heard whispering again.

'Father, I must confess . . . I cheated on my husband . . .' the sinner started in right away, her voice trembling. But Bordelli didn't hear another word; he was already out of the confessional and walking quickly towards the door. There was some commotion behind him, and as he was leaving someone's shocked voice rang out loudly in the church, echoing all the way up into the truss-beams.

'Hey! That's not Don Giuliano!'

Bordelli ran off, his heart in his throat and shivers up his spine, just like when he was a youngster and someone was chasing him. He turned round to see whether the sinner was following him, but no one was there. After a bit he slowed down, smiling. Who would have known that one day he would interrogate someone in a confessional . . . and then fall asleep!

It was twenty minutes to seven. He calculated the amount of time that he had spent 'confessing' the mystery woman and realised that he had slept for more than half an hour. How embarrassing it would have been had the parish priest surprised him in the confessional . . .

Taking the less crowded roads, he reached Borgo de' Greci, which opened onto Piazza San Firenze, still crowded with people. He quickly purchased the smallest tree there was and escaped from the infernal crowds. He went back the same way he came, thinking about Claretta's jealous ways. This definitely constituted good news, especially because the cheeky sister-in-law hadn't told him about her relationship with Antonio.

When he reached Via dei Neri, he rang Rosa's doorbell, and with his tree under his arm he slowly climbed the staircase up to the top floor. Rosa was in slippers and had an apron wrapped around her, but she was already made up and perfumed. She was in a hurry; her friends were due to arrive and she still had to finish preparing dinner.

'The kitchen is a mess . . .' She was very excited and flustered.

'I bet you're expecting a man.'

'And what do you care?' she said, cackling. She put a present in his pocket, kissed him noisily on the lips, pushed him away, and wished him happy Christmas.

'No more roses . . .' sighed the inspector, making his way to the stairs.

'No more bordellos either,' Rosa said, making a pun on his surname, bursting into laughter and closing the door behind her. Going downstairs, Bordelli remembered how often his classmates – and teachers – used to make fun of his name, both before and after the March on Rome. Now they were all simply pleasurable, almost touching, memories, from a mythical era. The Christmas tree was also part of his family mythology and, after having ignored it for so many years, the desire to have one at home had returned. He would leave the presents underneath it all night, just as his father had done, and open them the following morning before having coffee.

As soon as he walked out of the building he was swallowed up by the crowd again. In half an hour the streets would be empty, with only stray cats left. He made his way with the tree under his arm, trying not to bump into anyone. He was fed up with being surrounded by people and hearing their constant chatter in his ears.

The sky was grey and seemed laden with snow. He couldn't wait to be at home in front of the fire, conversing with the colonel. He had almost reached the intersection with Via dei Benci when all of a sudden his jaw dropped and he stopped in his tracks, heart pounding in his ears. He didn't even notice how irritated the people behind him were. He had seen Eleonora walk by, leaning on someone's arm, and all of his fantasies and dreams had crumbled in a second.

Standing on tiptoe, he caught a glimpse of her walking off. She was arm in arm with a tall, thin, young man with longish hair . . . but Bordelli hadn't managed to see whether the lad was handsome or not. He continued to look for her among the bobbing heads but it was as if she had disappeared. For a moment he was tempted to follow her and find her, but immediately felt like a fool.

He continued walking, biting his lip. So Eleonora had a beau. He shook his head in dismay. What could he possibly expect, that she was waiting for her Prince Bordelli? Why shouldn't she have a beau? Actually, in a way it should have made him happy. It meant that she had started living again, that she had been able to forget about that terrible night . . . and this should have alleviated, a little, the sense of guilt he'd been carrying around for more than a year. Logically it made sense, but feelings often had little to do with logic.

He had often imagined finding himself face to face with her again, but obviously it had happened when he was least expecting it. He felt depressed and even a bit ridiculous. He couldn't even grant himself the luxury of feeling jealous. For months he'd been imagining the scene, telling himself stories, good ones, bad ones, and now he'd been forced to wake up. Destiny had given him a lousy gift for Christmas, damn it all, one of those you can't put under the tree. But why was he wasting time thinking about it? It was better just to let it go. All he needed was to go home and eat a good dish of pasta, drink a bottle of wine, and sit by the fire with the colonel, smoking a cigarette and travelling back in time. And let Eleonora live happily ever after with her tall, skinny beau.

He had almost reached the Lungarno and was feeling resigned

about the matter when he felt someone touch his shoulder. He turned and saw Eleonora, who was looking at him with her dark, dark eyes. She was alone and wearing a short jacket, her hands in her pockets.

'Ciao,' she said, without smiling.

'Ciao,' Bordelli stammered, his heart beating hard.

'I saw you walk by and . . .' She gave a little shrug with that beautiful shoulder that he had kissed so many times.

'How are you?' he asked, trying to smile.

'Fine, and you?'

'Not too bad . . . I'm going home to set up the tree . . .' He nodded towards the little fir tree in his arms. Was that all they had to say to each other? Had their great love not left any mark on them?

'It looks like snow tonight,' Eleonora said, glancing up at the sky. Bordelli felt that it was up to him to say something less banal. He wanted to ask her for forgiveness, and tell her that it was all his fault . . . but she looked happy, and he didn't want to remind her of those horrible moments.

'Where did your boyfriend go?'

'Who?'

'The lad who was with you . . .'

'Oh, so you saw me?'

'I didn't want to interrupt.'

'He's not a boyfriend,' she said, unruffled. Bordelli stared at her, knowing that he was about to ask her a difficult question. Maybe it was just to find out whether they still had the same level of confidence as before.

'Do you sleep with him?'

'What a question . . .' she said, amused. She was so beautiful when she smiled. He couldn't look at her lips without thinking of . . .

'Did anyone ever tell you that you are beautiful?' He might never see her again, and he didn't want to lose the chance to tell her that he . . .

'Is your house still such a mess?' she asked, ignoring the compliment. Maybe it was an elegant, discreet way of asking whether he had a woman.

'I don't live in San Frediano anymore.'

'Ah . . .'

'I live out in the country.' His heart was beating even faster, but he tried to seem natural.

'Far away?'

'Impruneta.'

'I went there once when I was a girl, for the Festa dell'Uva.'

'And where are you living?'

'For now I'm still with my parents, but in the spring I'd like to go back to my own little place,' she said happily.

'Why don't we have dinner together one of these evenings?' He was playing his last cards. It was all or nothing.

'Are you trying to woo me?' That smile again. Everything seemed to have gone back to the way it was at the start, even before their first kiss, when they would amuse themselves with verbal give-and-take.

'I couldn't possibly compete with your long-haired admirer.' He smiled too, and held back the desire to touch her face.

'Has anyone ever told you how silly you are?'

'There was a girl who used to tell me that a while back.'

'Not anymore?'

'Unfortunately not.'

'Did she die?' she said, cocking her head.

'She, no. But I may have.' This was a bit melodramatic, so he tried to temper it with a hint of a smile.

'So you're a ghost,' she said, touching him with a finger.

'A ghost in flesh and blood.' Feeling her touch him with that finger made him want very much to hug and kiss her.

'Mainly flesh,' she said, laughing.

'One does what one can . . .'

'Do you like living out in the country?'

'I couldn't live anywhere else.'

'Too quiet for my tastes,' she said. Suddenly Bordelli realised that the tall, skinny lad was standing at the corner of Via dei Neri, watching them nervously. He felt a certain joy at the thought of a young man being jealous of an old fuddy-duddy like him . . . but maybe the kid was just bored of being left alone.

'He's waiting for you,' Bordelli said, nodding towards the

long-haired chap. Eleonora turned to look, just for a second, and let out the briefest of sighs.

'I'd better go . . . Have a happy holiday . . .'

'Merry Christmas,' murmured Bordelli, his heart as small as a chickpea. He hoped she might deign to kiss him on the cheek, although it would probably be better if she didn't. And in fact, no kisses were forthcoming, not even a handshake.

''Bye,' Eleonora said, sadly, and before he could say anything she was already walking towards the lanky boy, who opened his arms in a gesture of relief.

Not wanting to see them with their arms around each other, Bordelli walked off with his tail between his legs and his tree under his arm. To cheer himself up he reminded himself that when he was young and strong he was shooting at Nazis. That beanpole could never have handled a forced march for twenty kilometres with a rucksack on his back . . . But that wasn't much consolation, was it? Eleonora was still walking about town with the youth, while the old inspector headed home alone.

Crossing the bridge, he glanced periodically at the muddy, swollen Arno, flowing fast and silent towards the sea. The mass of coursing water made him think about time, how the past can never return. He saw himself as a child, playing with his very modern Meccano set, creating fanciful objects, and it felt like just yesterday.

To reach the Beetle he had to climb Via di Belvedere and walk the length of Via San Leonardo in the dark, but he couldn't have asked for more. He wanted to walk, to move, to feel his heartbeat throughout his body. He tried to distract himself but in the end he gave in to the most useless occupation in the world: he started analysing every word that Eleonora had said, her tone of voice, her gaze, even the most insignificant movements, in the hope of understanding whether she, too . . .

A warm fire in the hearth, a glass of Balzini in hand, the first cigarette of the day, Coltrane's saxophone snaking through the house at low volume, a few snowflakes falling outside the window . . . If Bordelli hadn't run into the beautiful Eleonora, he would simply be spending another agreeable evening in the country. He tried not to think about her, but it wasn't easy. Even Jeremiah seemed a bit downcast, his shadowy gaze looking out at the living with a touch of sorrow.

For dinner they'd eaten sausages and beans, and amidst lively conversation they'd dispatched a whole bottle and opened a second. The inspector had just finished telling the colonel about his meeting with the mystery woman and their whispered exchange in the silence of the confessional.

'Claretta . . .' Arcieri said thoughtfully.

'I don't know . . . At that moment I felt the same way, but then . . . I certainly wouldn't want to be led astray by the easiest road.'

Or by the only road in the middle of the desert . . . or by the only faint flicker in the utter darkness . . .

They sat there in silence, listening to the music. The little tree looked nice in a corner of the kitchen. Bordelli had set it in a fine terracotta vase and then hung from the branches a few coloured glass ornaments he'd found in the still-unpacked boxes from his move. And they'd placed the presents under it. With Rosa's, that made five.

'Well, in two hours it'll be Christmas,' said the colonel, glancing at the clock on the wall.

'Feel like going for a walk to La Panca tomorrow morning?'

'That would be lovely.'

'Unless there is three feet of snow on the ground,' said Bordelli.

He tossed his cigarette butt into the fire and stood up to look out of the window. The flakes were very small, and an ever so light veil of white was forming on the ground.

'Is it settling?' asked the colonel.

'Not much.'

He went and sat back down and refilled their glasses. He was having trouble clearing his head. Before him he still saw the beanpole hugging Eleonora, who was now kissing him, undressing him and . . . and all the rest. It wasn't just a matter of jealousy; things just didn't seem in their proper places. It was probably silly of him, but after seeing her again he felt that she was *his* and no one else's. But it wasn't possessiveness – no, that had nothing to do with it. Eleonora could sleep with whoever she wanted; she would always remain his. It wasn't easy to explain. Something very deep was involved, and it had nothing to do with everyday matters. Unless it was all just the ravings of a lovesick fool without hope . . .

'Still thinking about that girl?' asked Arcieri, like a real mind-reader. The inspector looked at him in amazement.

'Well . . .'

'Sorry to intrude, I probably shouldn't have said anything.'

'It doesn't matter . . . You guessed right, in any case. I was indeed thinking about her. This evening I ran into her by chance, in the centre of Florence . . . But I'd rather not discuss it.'

'Of course. Sorry.'

'No need to apologise.'

The record had finished playing, but there was no palpable emptiness in the air. It was as though the music was still sticking to the walls.

'I think a lot about Elena myself, and sometimes I worry I may never see her again,' Arcieri said, smiling sadly.

'You're right. I'll stop now.'

'Not at all! It's all my fault . . .'

At that moment they heard a strange noise upstairs, like something being dragged across the floor. The colonel stiffened.

'What was that?' he whispered.

'I have no idea . . .' Bordelli said softly, turning round and glancing at the darkened staircase. They sat there listening, ears pricked, when they heard more rustling upstairs.

'Hear that?' whispered Arcieri.

'Yes . . .' said the inspector, holding his breath. He remembered the words of the peasant who'd sold him the olive oil . . . *Seems there's ghosts in there, too . . .*

'Shall we go and have a look?' asked the colonel, rising. Bordelli crossed the kitchen on tiptoe, grabbed the pistol he'd placed atop the hutch, and headed up the stairs, with Arcieri following behind.

They made the rounds of the rooms, throwing open the doors and turning on all the lights. They checked the windows, opened the shutters and looked outside. A light snow was falling softly. The moon glowed behind a blanket of clouds, casting long white shafts of light across the darkened countryside . . .

Bordelli's bedroom, the bathroom and the other bedrooms nobody ever entered, two nearly empty rooms, and lastly Arcieri's room. Everything was in order, nobody could have entered. The colonel calmed down, Bordelli activated the safety catch on his pistol, and they headed back towards the staircase. And yet that noise . . . Suddenly they heard it again; it was coming from above the ceiling over the hallway. A piece of plaster scraping, followed by a swift pattering of little feet running away.

'Mice,' said Bordelli.

'They sound pretty big,' the colonel concurred, with some relief.

They went back downstairs. Bordelli put the pistol back next to the death's-head, and both men resumed their positions in the armchairs and raised their glasses just a smidgen, as if to toast the false alarm.

'I was really thinking it was *them*, though I don't even know exactly who *they* are,' said Arcieri, taking another cigarette from the coffee table. Bordelli grabbed one as well.

'Sooner or later they're going to find me . . .'

'You should be safe here, in this house, as long as we're careful.'

'Whatever the case, I think it's best if I leave as soon as possible. I really wouldn't want you to have any trouble because of me.'

'Don't you worry about me. You can stay as long as you like.'

'I need to find a way to get some money from one of my bank accounts without leaving any record, but I don't know how. I'm probably too mistrusting, but ever since they tried to knock me off I'd rather not leave anything to chance.'

'I can lend you some money. You can pay me back later, when you're able.'

'If they kill me I won't be able to repay any debts.'

'I'll take the chance,' said Bordelli, shrugging.

'Maybe through a foreign bank . . .' Arcieri mumbled, thinking aloud. All it had taken was a couple of mice running across the ceiling to alarm him. As they sat comfortably by the fire, he was preparing himself for every possible sudden danger.

'There's something I've been wanting to tell you,' said the inspector, running a hand over his already stubbly face.

'Sounds like more than just mice,' said Arcieri, crossing his legs.

'I could have mentioned it to you earlier, but I thought it was better not to trouble you about it.'

'Are you going to keep me hanging?'

'Oh, it's nothing so dire as that. Actually, in a way it's good news. A few days ago I talked with a former colleague of yours from the Special Services, Admiral Agostinelli . . .'

'Actually, I know him, though I've never worked for him directly,' Arcieri interrupted, frowning.

'We've been friends since the war . . .'

He began telling him about his confidential conversations with Agostinelli, who'd asked him to help him in the search for a sheep who had strayed from the SID fold. Therefore they didn't know where Arcieri was hiding, that much was certain. The colonel listened with a deep furrow in his brow, as though trying to decipher the hidden meaning of it all. Bordelli concluded by assuring him that the admiral was a man of the highest integrity, absolutely trustworthy, and would never have willingly got entangled in anything the least bit shady. Arcieri nodded and started drumming his fingertips on the arm of his chair.

'I don't doubt it for a second, but he may not know just how shady a certain affair really is . . .'

'That's why I didn't tell him anything.'

'You were absolutely right not to,' said Arcieri, who knew the Special Services milieu far better than Bordelli did. It was absolutely normal for one sector of the Services not to know what another department was doing, especially when it involved less-than-transparent operations secretly guided by officially unacknowledged political forces. Those offices, in short, were bubbling with a heady stew of interests, every one of which wanted to turn public servants into a sort of secular arm of their own personal will.

'Another splash of wine?' asked the inspector, bottle in hand.

'Just one more, but only because it's Christmas,' Arcieri lied, holding out his glass.

'The Baby Jesus hasn't been born yet, and here we are already drinking his blood.'

They smiled, feeling relaxed again. The fire was getting hungry for wood, and Bordelli fed it a fine log that caught fire after a few seconds.

'A little toasted bread with oil might be nice,' said the colonel.

'Sure, we can make that sacrifice . . .'

'Please don't bother getting up, I'll get it myself.'

Arcieri went and cut three nice slices of bread, as Bordelli spread some embers outside the andirons and set up the grill. Division of labour, in short.

Minutes later they were already sinking their teeth into the bread, as their glasses were refilled several more very, very last times. All things considered, the mice had not succeeded in ruining their Christmas Eve.

Sprawling lazily on the armchairs, they ventured off into the borderless confines of memory, telling each other briefly about their most unforgettable Christmas holidays past . . . The best, the worst, the saddest, the oddest. Aside from those they'd experienced as children, which were touching to the point of tears, Bordelli nostalgically recalled Christmas night in '43, in Abruzzo near Torricella Peligna, when the front had stalled along the Gustav Line. It was snowing, and he found himself holed up in a stable with two strangers. The countryside was immersed in utter silence, which seemed unreal after two weeks of bombing. They each had something in their rucksacks and managed to put together a Christmas dinner worthy of a stray cat. That was the first time he'd ever suggested to his table companions that they each tell a story to close out the evening. He'd never seen those two again. One was a twenty-year-old officer in the San Marco Battalion, Florentine and as handsome as the sun. The other was . . . Curzio Malaparte.

'Malaparte?' Arcieri asked in amazement.

'None other. At the time I didn't know who he was.'

But at that moment Bordelli was too tired to go into the details, and let the colonel take over and recall other Christmasses past.

When the chimes rang midnight, the two men exchanged best wishes, and after downing their very last glasses, they went to bed. Bordelli slipped quickly under the covers and turned out the light at once. He felt drained. Face buried in the pillow, he started whispering a few of his mother's poems, which by now he knew by heart. He'd hoped to fall right asleep, but his thoughts kept somersaulting in his head. He tossed and turned in agitation, mind peopled with visions . . . Claretta's nervous hands, the long neck of the girl with the puppy, Juliette's jade-like eyes . . . Elenora's slightly open lips . . .

Bordelli slept fitfully and when he awoke it was still dark. Outside it was quiet. Not even any owls hooting or dogs barking.

He rolled over in bed, happy to have come to the end of a nightmare that he couldn't recall for the life of him. He wished he could get back to sleep, but his thoughts had already been set in motion . . . He saw Eleonora hugging her boyfriend, a hippy who surely went to all the anti-Vietnam protests. And that was good, because wars shouldn't exist. He knew a thing or two about that. Who knew where Juliette was. Was she sleeping in her bed or was she at a client's house? Did Claretta kill her brother-in-law? Sometimes homicide was a childish gesture . . . You are an obstacle to my desires and so I will get you out of the way, like a newborn who pushes aside a rival to get to the teat. In war, things were different: you were actually expected to kill.

Once Bordelli had come upon a wounded Nazi leaning against a tree, his uniform soaked with blood. He approached him with the intention of bringing him back to camp to get him help. The German raised his gun to shoot him, but Bordelli was faster and shot him instantly. He was blond, about twenty years old. He was the nineteenth Nazi that Bordelli had killed, and that meant another notch on the butt of his rifle. He wondered what life that boy would have led if he hadn't died in the war. Maybe he would have started a family, maybe he would have been a good father, maybe one of his children would have become a scientific genius, a Nobel prize winner . . . Who could know? The world was a pot boiling over with endless enigmas. Casual encounters could lead to love affairs, as with Eleonora, even if that one had ended badly . . . And to think that just a few hours earlier he had seen her embracing a boy. Should he consider it all dead and buried? On Christmas Day, no less? A fine present indeed . . .

All he ever did was complain . . . Good God, are we men or corporals? Bordelli thought to himself, quoting from a film of Totò. Eleonora was a beautiful memory, but the healthiest thing now would be to turn the page . . . He didn't want to think about her anymore. Another woman, that's what he needed. A fascinating creature, someone sweet, someone who would make him feel handsome. Someone like that girl with Arturo, the puppy, someone elegant and as haughty as a princess . . . Why not her? Or maybe Juliette, with her big green eyes and her angelic gaze . . . Or Claretta, the pretty sister-in-law who wore too much perfume . . . Ah, Claretta . . . Had she been the one to run Antonio through with the foil, in a jealous rage over the mystery woman? He needed to see her again, but there was no hurry. He would let Christmas go by and pay her a call the day after, with St Stephen's blessing. Maybe he would tell her point blank that he knew about her relationship with Antonio, and see how she reacted. She appeared, at least, to be a fragile woman, always on the verge of a breakdown. If Claretta really was the killer, putting her on the spot might achieve some good results. This would solve the murder case, of course, but in truth he hoped it wasn't her. It would be sad to have to arrest her . . .

How many killers had he managed to lock up in his twenty years on the force? A drop in the ocean of unpunished injustices polluting the world. He felt like a sailor sweeping the deck as the ship was sinking . . .

At that point he knew he wasn't going to get back to sleep so he decided to get up. He put on some clothes and went downstairs on tiptoe so as not to wake the colonel. Lighting a few candles in the kitchen in an attempt to revive the Christmas atmosphere, he remembered what it was like when his mother and father were still around. It was Christmas . . . children unwrapped presents as their noses ran, families gathered round the table, and churches were full of people celebrating the birth of the Saviour.

The embers in the fireplace still glowed; lighting the fire wasn't going to be hard. He could finally open his presents now, alone in the silence. He went and gathered the gifts from under the tree with the same thrill he had felt as a child, and lined them up on the table. He would leave Rosa's present for last. He got comfy and picked one up randomly. It was a long, narrow, rather heavy box. Ennio had written his name on the wrapping paper. Bordelli tugged at the ribbon and opened the packet. It was a beautiful knife with a bone handle and a folding blade, useful for peeling apples in the woods. There was also a note . . . *The next time we see each other I will prick your arm with the tip of the blade and you will have to give me a coin – even five lire is fine. That way we will never be enemies, Ennio.* Bordelli smiled to himself, thinking that it would be hard to become enemies with Botta. He opened the blade, and looked at it gleaming in the dark. He had used such a knife to pry German bullets out of his fellow soldiers' bodies, and it had not always been easy.

He closed the knife and picked up the second present. A little card attached to the ribbon read: *Merry Christmas, Pietrino.* He wondered what the Sardinian could have given him. He opened the package and found himself holding a miniature Volkswagen Beetle, exactly the same colour as his. He raised it in the air and thought back to how, as a child, he imagined being a giant, dominating Florence from above and controlling the destiny of the people moving about the streets like large ants. Back then, his parents slept in the room across the hall and, when he couldn't sleep, he used to listen to his father snoring . . . Distant memories which would disappear with him . . . It occurred to him how sad this thought was. This was why writers jotted down their thoughts, to trick themselves into believing that memories wouldn't disappear. Who knew, maybe one day he would write his own memoirs, but not just war stories, as Piras had suggested.

He put the little car down next to Botta's knife and started to open the third gift, which, judging from the shape, was a book. And in fact . . . it was two books. One was *Il Vero Sesto Cajo Bacelli, Guida per l'agricoltore, Lunario per l'anno 1968*, a farmer's almanac. But the giver had crossed through the name Baccelli on the cover and added Bordelli so that now it read . . . *Il vero Sesto Cajo Bordelli.* It could only be from Diotivede: lunar phases, when to sow, popular sayings, farmers' rhymes, proverbs, recipes . . . An amusing and interesting book to keep on hand. The other book was *The Albanian War*, by Giancarlo Fusco. He opened the cover and read the dedication: *I, too, trudged through the mud. Peppino.* War again. Bloody hell. War was ugly but there was nothing better for revealing human nature. War stripped men naked and showed them for what they really were. He thanked Diotivede the corpse-cutter and instinctively looked up at Jeremiah, who in the candlelight seemed to be happier than ever.

It was time to open the fourth gift, which had to be from Dante. He turned it over in his hands a few times, trying to guess what it was. He undid the ribbon and removed the paper. It was a small glass frog, which in the faint candlelight looked almost real. In the box was also a little piece of paper folded in two on which was written: *Don't kiss me, I don't want to become a prince.* Who knew whether those words alluded to something specific or were just a joke. But the frog was beautiful and he would put it on his bedside table. He knew that one day it would fall and break but he wouldn't throw it away. He would put it away in a box, until he could find time to glue it back together, and that was where it would remain until the end of his days. One day someone would find it, and without hesitation would throw it out with the rubbish . . . Amen.

He put the frog delicately down on the table, already sorry for its sad destiny, and found himself face to face with Rosa's gift, which was elegantly wrapped in thin, pink paper, and tied with a pink ribbon. It was more or less the shape of a pack of cigarettes, but heavier. He opened it slowly and discovered that it was a deck of cards illustrated with naked ladies. There was also a pink card and envelope inside, which read *I bet you'll fall in love with all of them. Merry Christmas, Monkey* . . . How silly, he thought with a smile. He started to go through the cards, and stopped when he saw a naked woman who resembled Eleonora. It was an ace of spades, and it made him none too happy.

It had been ages since he had last played poker, the time he had won so much that he had refused to cash in, so as not to leave his friend out on the pavement. He hadn't even seen a pack of cards since then. He had ignored the rigid laws of poker that said that the loser had to honour his debts and it wouldn't be right to continue playing. And then there was the fact that the game itself might seek revenge and make him lose infinitely, as the poker buffs said. So much time had passed since then, since that night, that the offence had certainly been forgotten. He would have to organise a game one evening at his home, in remembrance of times past.

He mentally thanked his friends for the beautiful gifts. He put away the deck of cards and got up with a yawn. The feeble, flickering light of the candles gave him a sense of peace he hadn't felt in a very long time. He sat down in the armchair in front of the fire and leaned his head back, eyes closed. He remained that way for a long time, without moving, thinking of nothing, merely letting confused images and distant memories pass back and forth through his mind. After a few minutes he slipped into a deep and pleasant sleep. Every so often he would wake up, perhaps from the sound of the wood popping in the hearth, and barely open his eyes and look out of the window to see whether the sun was up, but dawn was always far off. So he would close his eyes and go back to sleep.

Then all once he woke up, without knowing why, and saw that it was day. To judge from the light, it looked like a sunny day. It was almost nine . . . He heard a shout from upstairs. It could only be the colonel. He ran to the hutch to get his gun and dashed upstairs, Arcieri continuing to yell at someone. He reached the end of the hall, threw open the door and turned on the light, aiming his gun . . . The colonel was shouting and twisting and turning in bed as if he was trying to get away from a monster. Bordelli sighed with relief, put the gun in his pocket, and went up to the bed.

'Colonel . . . Colonel,' he said, shaking his shoulder. Arcieri eventually opened his eyes and looked around with a lost expression. He rubbed his face with his hands.

'They wanted to tie me up,' he murmured, as if he was talking about something that actually happened.

'They didn't succeed,' Bordelli said with a smile.

'I'm sorry if I woke you up.'

'I've been awake for a while . . .'

'What time is it?' the colonel asked, sitting up in bed.

'Nine o'clock.'

'Did it snow?'

'It's sunny out.'

'Happy Christmas.'

'Happy Christmas . . . I'll go and make some coffee . . .'

'I'll be right there.'

'Take your time,' the inspector said. He went back downstairs to the kitchen, prepared the moka pot and put it on the cooker. His presents were strewn on the table, amidst open boxes and coloured ribbons. He made a little room for two cups and the sugar bowl and stood there looking at Jeremiah, *the skull that keeps you company* . . .

As the coffee was bubbling up, Arcieri came downstairs, dark circles under his eyes and frowning like a child who had woken up in a bad mood. He sat down and stared at the fire. The nightmare had really disturbed him.

'Were you being chased by a monster?' Bordelli asked to deflate the drama.

'Ever since childhood I periodically have these dreams . . . that someone is chasing me, and that they want to kill me, but it's never the same scene.'

'Dr Fabiani, my psychoanalyst friend, would say that the monster is inside you.'

'Of that I am quite certain,' the colonel said, hinting at a smile. The inspector filled their coffee cups and was about to sit down when the phone rang. He shook his head and went to answer. It was Piras, long distance. He was sending his family's best wishes; there was static on the line. Bordelli wished them well in turn and thanked him for the Beetle. But Piras hadn't phoned for that . . .

'Do you remember the open window, Inspector?'

'Which window?'

'In Migliorini's study . . . Do you remember?'

'Ah yes, I had forgotten about it.'

'I think I've worked it out.'

'I'm all ears.'

'It's Columbus's egg, Inspector. Why do we open a window?'

'Usually to let in some air.'

'Exactly . . . maybe the killer didn't want us to smell a certain odour or perfume.'

'A perfume . . .' the inspector repeated with a shudder, thinking immediately of Claretta.

'I'm sure you noticed that Migliorini's sister-in-law practically bathes in the stuff.'

'It's impossible not to smell it.'

'It's not hard evidence, of course, but I think it's worth keeping in mind.'

'You're right,' Bordelli mumbled, without telling him what he had learned from the mystery woman. He didn't want to run up Piras's phone bill.

'Maybe Claretta was keen on her sister's husband and was jealous,' added the Sardinian, who had arrived at the same hypothesis by another route. If the killer really was Claretta, Piras deserved another bottle of olive oil.

'I see you're thinking about work,' the inspector said.

'This morning I woke up with that thought buzzing in my head. I don't know why I didn't think of it earlier.'

'Thank you, Pietrino. Have a good Christmas. Give my best wishes to Gavino and give your mother a kiss for me.'

'Thank you, Inspector. Have a g—'

'Piras? Hello? Can you hear me?' There was a buzzing sound. They had lost the connection. The inspector hung up the phone and sat back down, still thinking about the perfume and the open window. Arcieri had waited for him, fiddling with his presents, and they drank their now-tepid coffee together.

'Feel like taking a short walk?' asked the colonel, putting his cup in the sink.

'Even a long one.'

Now that the evidence against Claretta was starting to rack up, he wanted to see her more than ever. He felt anxious. It wasn't like other times when he had been trying to find a killer. Of course he wanted to find out what had really happened, but he hoped she hadn't done it, he hoped it with all his heart . . .

They returned home exhausted from a long trek through the hills of Cintoia, seasoned with interesting discussions on life, the past and, inevitably, women. While distractedly listening to the news on the radio, they learned of the death of Amerigo Dumini, the Fascist *squadrista* involved in the murder of Matteotti. After exchanging a meaningful glance, they chose not to comment on this.

Christmas Day lunch was a spaghetti feast worthy of Polyphemus and a pleasant swim in a wine-dark sea of Balzini. Utter simplicity, but wanting for nothing. Migliorini was right. *It doesn't matter what you do, but who you're with . . .*

They spent the afternoon reading and napping. Arcieri lying on the couch in the living room, listening to Coltrane. Bordelli sitting in the kitchen by the hearth, with Chekhov's stories falling into his lap from time to time. While reading he'd noticed that his vision was blurring a bit, and realised sadly that the moment had come to see an eye doctor. On the other hand, he'd managed not to think too much about Eleonora and was proud of the fact. A few more weeks and she would be all but forgotten, as was best for all involved. He had to look forward. The world was brimming with women . . . Blondes, brunettes, chestnut-haired, tall, short, slender, full-bodied, elegant, shy, brazen, naïve . . . An endless catalogue of wonders to be discovered.

'Franchino, when are you ever going to get your head on straight?' his mother asked sweetly. She was sitting opposite him, her knitting on her lap, looking at him with love.

'What do you mean, Mamma?' he muttered, trying to buy time.

'Come now, you know exactly what I mean . . .'

'But what can I do about it?'

'What are you waiting for to find a good woman and start raising a family?' she replied, a shadow of reproach in her eyes.

'I'd found myself a good girl, Mamma . . . But then the devil came between us . . .'

'That poor thing could be your daughter,' his mother chided him, waving her index finger as one does with naughty children.

'Did you know I found your poems, Mamma?'

'Oh, rubbish, the lot of them . . .' she said, embarrassed, looking down and resuming her knitting.

'What are you saying? They're beautiful.'

'Oh, go on, don't mock me.'

'I'm not mocking you, Mamma. I can't tell you how beautiful they are.'

'Ah, so it's as bad as that . . .' she said, laughing.

'Simple words, full of light . . . Poems that go straight to the heart . . .'

'You'd do better to throw them away,' his mother said softly, shrugging her shoulders. But he could see she was pleased.

'Every night I repeat a line or two to myself, before falling asleep.'

'Stop being silly,' she said, getting up.

'Where are you going, Mamma?'

'God bless you, Franco . . .' She bent over him and kissed him lightly on the forehead with a pair of gelid lips that made him shudder.

'Mamma . . .'

'I don't know if we'll ever see each other again . . . But you behave now, I mean it.'

Before he could think of anything to say, his mother stepped into the fireplace and vanished amid the flames.

'Mamma . . .' he said again, opening his eyes. The fire had died down to a pile of embers, and silence reigned throughout the house. All one could hear was the gloomy sound of the long gusts of wind whipping across the countryside. He remained seated, looking at the armchair in which his mother had been sitting. He felt both deep melancholy and infinite tenderness. What difference was there between lived experience and dreams? In the end there was no difference. What remained in memory were only images and emotions, all of them real, profoundly real. He would never lose his childhood memories, just as he could never forget this heart-warming visit from his mother. All forms of the past were made of the same matter, even the imagined ones. Nothing would ever be lost, except in death. And everyone had his or her own trunks of memories to drag along, some light, some terribly heavy . . .

He looked at the clock on the wall. Eight forty. Getting up to put some wood on the fire, he began preparing the kitchen for dinner. A bit of bread, a piece of pecorino, a few slices of prosciutto and, of course, a bottle of Balzini. By now he was used to that good wine and knew he would soon be back in Tavernelle to buy a few more cases of it.

He put everything on the table then went into the sitting room to wake the colonel, who had fallen asleep on the couch with Dostoevsky on his lap.

They dined in peace and quiet, sipping wine and chatting lightly. They told each other amusing anecdotes and funny family tales. It was as though they had decided, by tacit agreement, not to talk about anything painful.

After dinner they started playing draughts, with a lot of help from Bacchus but not much from tobaccus, and especially with no mention of Venus.[33] They hadn't moved any draughts for what seemed like forever, and every move was as involved as if they'd been playing chess.

'Do you know the legend of the invention of chess?' the colonel asked, gobbling up three draughts in a single move.

'I don't think so . . .'

'It's a lovely story. Would you like to hear it?'

'What more could I ask for?' said Bordelli, wishing he could listen to it curled up under the covers with the light off.

'Once upon a time there was an Indian prince . . .'

He was so rich he could fulfil his every desire, and for this very reason he ended up feeling bored to death. He would spend his days walking back and forth inside his magnificent palace, without ever feeling the slightest emotion. When his boredom reached its peak, he ordered his criers to announce throughout the realm that he would grant any wish to whoever was able to make him feel amused again. Every manner of person came to the court, from wizards to mountebanks, fakirs to fire-eaters, poets to dancers, but not one was able to elicit so much as a smile or a prick of emotion in the prince, who by this point in his life had seen and known everything under the sun. But then one day a merchant appeared, a man famous for his inventions. He showed the prince a wooden table divided into sixty-four squares, each alternately black or white. He placed thirty-two carved wooden figurines, in a variety of shapes and sizes, on the table, and told the prince that he called this invention the 'game of chess'. The prince asked him what the rules were, and the merchant told him. We can play, if you wish, he said; that way it will become clearer to you. The prince accepted. He lost the match, but immediately wanted revenge. But he lost again, and so it went the third and fourth times as well. At a certain point he realised he was enjoying himself more than he had done in a very long time. Indeed, the merchant had rescued him from his boredom. Ask me for whatever you want, and I will grant your wish, he said. The merchant shrugged and, as though asking for something insignificant, he said: All I want is a grain of wheat, doubled for every square on this chessboard. The prince found such modesty admirable, and immediately ordered his scribes to count how many grains of wheat the merchant had requested. When the sum had been calculated, the result was staggering: to produce the amount of wheat demanded, they would have to plant an area greater than the surface of the Earth itself, and for several years over! The prince was therefore unable to grant the merchant's outlandish request and, not wanting to fail to keep his word, he decided it was best to have the inventor of chess executed . . .

'There is a moral to this little story,' Arcieri added, taking another draught from Bordelli.

'And what would that be?' asked the inspector, glass in hand.

'If an Indian prince is dying of boredom, let him die.'

'Sacred words.'

'And here you go, you've lost another game . . .'

It was almost seven o'clock when Bordelli finally made up his mind to leave the office. The radiators, as usual, were blazing hot, at the expense of the citizenry, and he left the window open to let in some cool air. Passing by the guards' booth, he said goodbye to Mugnai, who looked as if he'd put on weight.

He headed out along Via San Gallo, fists clenched in his pockets. There was no one to be seen on the pavements, and even cars were rare. After the Christmas chaos, now the desert. The north wind bore into your face and wickedly worked its way into your bones, smelling as if it was carrying the scent of the Fiesole cemetery's cypresses . . .

He'd woken up late, after playing draughts until three in the morning. And while he'd lost a great many games, he'd had fun not thinking either of work or the woman he was trying to forget. Later in the morning he'd phoned Rosa to thank her for her present, and she'd started singing off-key, at risk of breaking the little speaker inside the receiver.

'*La chiamavano Bocca di Rosa metteva l'amore metteva l'amore* . . . It's a record somebody gave me for Christmas . . . *Dai diamanti non nasce niente, dal letame nascono i fior* . . .[34] It even talks about hookers . . . The singer has a beautiful voice, and he's very handsome too . . .'

'What's his name?'

'I don't remember right off hand, but I'll put the record on next time you come, so you can hear . . . Ohmygod, I have to run! I've got an appointment at the beauty salon in five minutes!'

For lunch he'd made some pasta with the colonel's help, following his precious advice . . . *To keep the onions from burning, you need only add a little water* . . . After coffee he'd sprawled out in the armchair and read until sunset, as if he had nothing important to do, sighing every so often at the inexorable passage of time. In the end he'd decided to go down into the city and spent more than an hour staring at the wall in his office.

Now he was strolling along, biting his lips, in a bitterly cold wind that tousled his hair. He was headed for Viale Don Minzoni, to pay a call on Claretta Biagiotti at home. He hadn't bothered to forewarn her, preferring a surprise visit. He'd put the moment off for an entire day, trying to fool himself into not thinking about what he needed to do. The fact was . . . In short, though he hoped he was wrong, he had a strong feeling that it was indeed Claretta who had murdered her brother-in-law. He would have given anything to discover that she hadn't done it. In that case he would, of course, have to start all over from square one, and Migliorini's murder might even go unpunished . . . But to see her end up in jail would be very sad . . .

He stopped right outside Claretta's front door, and after taking a deep breath he pressed the top doorbell. After a long, cold wait, just as he was about to ring again, he heard a metallic voice call from the intercom.

'Who is it?'

'Good evening, I am Inspector Bordelli, of Florence police . . . I apologise for bothering you on Boxing Day, but I need to speak with Signorina Claretta.'

'I'm sorry, but the signorina is not at home.' It must have been Fidalma, the housekeeper, speaking.

'When might I find her at home?'

'Try again in an hour or so. She left word that she would be home for dinner.'

'If it's not too much of a bother, I'd rather wait for her here . . . Could you please let me in?' He couldn't stand waiting in the cold any longer. The woman remained silent.

'It's a rather delicate matter,' Bordelli added. The woman let another few seconds pass before answering.

'Third floor,' was all she said, and a moment later the electrical lock on the door clicked open. Bordelli walked through the high-ceilinged entrance hall in semi-darkness and began climbing the great stone staircase, combing his hair with his fingers.

On the third floor he found the door ajar, though still chained.

He knocked discreetly, and moments later saw an eye appear in the chink.

'Good evening . . .' he said, bowing slightly. The door closed and a moment later reopened.

'Please come in,' the woman said, standing aside.

Bordelli crossed the threshold with a polite smile on his face, stepping into the warm air of the apartment, and behind a vague scent of roast beef he smelled Claretta's unmistakable perfume, which was downright pleasant in small doses. As the housekeeper was closing the door, he removed his overcoat and hung it from a lovely art nouveau coatrack.

'You must be Signora Fidalma . . .' he said, to break the ice. The woman nodded almost imperceptibly, without saying anything. Bordelli thought she looked like someone, but couldn't remember who. She must have been about forty years old, was tall and well-built and erect as a tree, with chiselled, almost masculine features. Despite the blue apron and slippers there was something elegant about her, a sort of innate pride.

Fidalma headed down the corridor's polished, crushed-stone flooring, with the confident step of someone who faced life fearlessly. The inspector followed behind her, looking around. Dark, low tables, female nude statuettes, a few paintings, a pendulum clock riddled with woodworm holes. They entered a small sitting room with a frescoed ceiling; the air smelled of furniture wax.

'I'll be going back to the kitchen now,' said Fidalma, about to leave.

'I'm sorry, but may I ask you a question?'

'Please go ahead.' She had penetrating eyes, with the gaze of someone who could look into your soul.

'Were you at home on the evening Migliorini was killed?

'Yes.'

'Do you remember whether Signorina Claretta went out or not?'

'I went to bed at half past nine, as always.'

'And you didn't hear the sound of the front door?'

'I never hear anything when I'm asleep.'

'Where do you sleep?'

'Upstairs, at the end of the hallway.' These were the same words Claretta had used.

'And what if Claretta's mother needs you for something?'

'The signora has a bell that rings in my bedroom.'

'Thank you.'

'Not at all.'

Fidalma headed off, closing the door behind her. She was a woman of few words, but seemed sensitive.

Bordelli started pacing about the room, studying his surroundings. The furnishings were austere, though with a few touches of fancy here and there, clearly Claretta's doing. A swan-shaped lamp, a glass soup tureen full of multicoloured marble eggs, the bronze bust of a man from the Risorgimento era rendered ridiculous by a feminine bonnet placed on his head. A number of other variously coloured objects scattered here and there lightened the nineteenth-century atmosphere a little.

He plopped into a small Empire-style armchair, wondering how long he would have to wait. In the silence he could hear the quiet ticking of a clock that he couldn't quite manage to see. To pass the time he started looking at the mythological scenes painted on the ceiling . . . A plump Venus emerging from the sea, a large white bull running with Europa on his back, lovesick Orpheus turning around to look at his Eurydice . . .

He suddenly heard the doorknob squeak, as the door slowly opened. Taking short steps, a rather stout old woman entered the room, helping herself along with cane of black wood. She was dressed the old-fashioned way, with a gold pin applied to her beige cardigan and a pearl necklace. Her resemblance to Claretta was striking. The inspector was already on his feet, ready to kiss her hand.

'Good evening, signora . . . Forgive the intrusion . . .' he said, a bit embarrassed.

The signora said nothing and, looking at him with curiosity, stopped in the middle of the room. At that moment a huge white cat with very long hair appeared and, trotting up to him, began to sniff the stranger's shoes. Bordelli bent down to pat it, then dodged a claws-bared swipe by just a hair's breadth.

'Adelmo! You naughty cat!' the lady shrieked.

'He's a watchcat,' the inspector joked.

'He doesn't like to be touched.'

'He makes that quite clear.'

The big cat hopped up onto a little sofa, sank into a sphinx-like crouch and started staring at Bordelli with very green, menacing eyes.

'Have the Germans left?' the old woman asked with concern, her chin trembling slightly.

'I'm sorry, what was that?'

'The Germans . . . Have they left?' she repeated, gesturing a military salute.

'Well, yes . . . Quite some time ago, actually . . .' said Bordelli.

'Ah, what a relief! At last I can take my ninety-nine bottles of Osborne out of their hiding place. I'd had them walled in, behind a false wall, so those boors wouldn't steal them from me . . . Have you ever tasted my Osborne?'

'No, I don't think so . . .'

'How can that be? By God, you absolutely must try some . . . Please don't leave, for heaven's sake . . .' the woman said, turning back towards the door, muttering all the while.

'Please don't bother for my sake . . .'

'You absolutely must taste my Osborne . . . And you will not leave this house until you have . . .'

She went out of the room, leaving the door open behind her. Bordelli sat back down. The cat was still watching him, immobile, emitting a strong scent of old carpets. His claws were as big as billhooks. Bordelli looked away, trying not to irritate the animal.

Minutes later from the corridor came a sound of tinkling glass drawing near, and Adelmo cocked one of his ears in the direction of the doorway. Claretta's mother entered without the help of her cane, carrying a wobbly little tray with two small glasses and a bottle on it. Refusing the inspector's offer to help, by some miracle she managed to set the tray down on the low table.

'Osborne, 1910,' she said with satisfaction, sitting down beside the massive pussycat.

'Same age as me,' said Bordelli.

The lady poured the port herself and raised two glasses, offering one to the inspector. They each took a sip . . . Good heavens . . . The nectar of the gods, by comparison, was Coca-Cola . . .

'No one in the world can boast of such a *promenade* of flavours,' the lady said proudly.

'Superb,' Bordelli commented, using a word he hardly ever uttered.

'I couldn't bear the thought of it ending up in the hands of those louts . . . Even though . . . truth be told . . . there was a young German lieutenant . . . So sweet . . . Everyone knows that love doesn't look at the uniform . . . It only takes a second to turn someone into a scamp . . . You look like a big old scamp yourself, in fact . . .'

'Me?' said Bordelli in self-defence, looking over at the cat. He felt as if he'd slipped back into the early days of the twentieth century, with horse-drawn carriages in the streets of Florence, men as well as women flaunting their hats, trains running on steam . . .

'You must promise me you'll behave like a gentleman,' the lady continued with a wink, alluding to who knew what.

'How could you ever doubt it, signora?' said the inspector, just to play along. But then the old woman started gesturing strangely, as though she was having trouble breathing and wanted to open a window. Bordelli shot to his feet and rushed to her aid, under the placid gaze of Adelmo.

'Are you unwell?' he asked, having her lean back on her little sofa. Then he went to look for the housekeeper, whom he found in the kitchen, chopping onions with a mezzaluna, eyes watering. He told her the signora didn't feel well.

'Is she having trouble breathing?' asked Fidalma, serenely continuing her chopping.

'Yes . . .'

'It's nothing. She thinks she's closed up inside a bottle.'

'Inside a bottle?'

'Just pretend to remove the cork, and she'll feel better instantly, you'll see.'

'Ah, all right, then . . .' said Bordelli, reassured.

Dashing back to the signora's side, he found her standing though still suffocating inside her bottle. With confident movements, he got busy removing the enormous cork, whereupon the signora emitted a long wail.

'Oooohh, my Lord . . . I nearly died . . .' she rasped, cheeks bright red, shaking her arms and stepping forward to exit the great bottle.

'I think another little splash might do you some good,' said Bordelli, sitting back down.

He refilled the glasses, thinking that stealing one of those bottles might not be such a bad idea . . . The divine Osborne had won him over. The signora settled back onto her little sofa and, stroking the cat, recovered her smile at last.

'There are certain things a woman must never say, but did you know that you are a very handsome man?' she whispered coquettishly.

'Let's not exaggerate . . .' said Bordelli, flattered.

At that moment they heard the front door opening and closing, followed by the sound of heels walking down the hallway. They both turned to face the sitting-room door, which was open. Claretta came in, peeled her gloves off distractedly and, upon seeing the inspector, gave a start. Followed by a smile. She didn't seem too cross with him.

'Good evening, Inspector . . .'

'Good evening. I took the liberty of waiting for you,' Bordelli said, rising to his feet.

'Have you come to beg forgiveness?'

It wasn't really a question, and Bordelli merely smiled. Claretta took off her coat and tossed it on the back of a chair along with her cap. She had her hair in a bun and was wearing a fine baby-blue dress that delicately sheathed her body. She came forward and let him kiss her hand. Her perfume had already invaded the room, and Bordelli couldn't help but think of what Piras had said over the phone.

'Mamma, you know you're not supposed to drink too much,' said Claretta, eyeing the bottle of Osborne. She snatched up her mother's glass and drank it down in one gulp. Her mother grabbed her arm.

'This fine gentleman wishes to invite you to dinner,' she declared solemnly.

'Mamma, what are you saying?' Claretta blushed and very nearly sat down on the cat.

'Don't you like romantic candlelight dinners?'

'Mamma, please . . .'

'Your mother is telling the truth. I've come here to you ask you out to dinner,' Bordelli lied, taking advantage of the situation.

'Ah . . .' said Claretta, blushing ever more deeply.

'Will you do me the honour?' asked Bordelli, adopting the language of the occasion.

'What are you waiting for to accept?' asked the old woman.

'Oh, please, Mamma . . .'

'It would make me so happy,' the inspector insisted, now convinced it would be the best way to talk to her calmly, without alarming her.

'Well, I don't know . . . Out of the blue, just like that . . . Oh, all right, why not? . . . But I'll need some time to get ready,' she said, rising. She actually seemed rather excited.

'Take as long as you like. I'll have to go back to headquarters to get my car,' said Bordelli, hoping Claretta wasn't thinking of putting on more perfume.

'And you, Mamma, stop talking rubbish . . . I mean it,' she said, heading out of the room with the air of a diva.

'Please take your time. I'll be waiting for you outside your front door.'

'*A tout à l'heure* . . .' said Claretta.

The moment she left the room, her mother went up to Bordelli and grabbed his arm.

'You know what?' she whispered.

'Tell me . . .'

'You remind me of someone . . . An actor . . .'

'People sometimes tell me I look like Lino Ventura.'

'Yes, quite right . . . He's the one . . .' she said, clapping with contentment.

'May I ask you something, signora?'

'Of course, I love being asked things . . . I love chocolates even more, but I love it when people ask me things.'

'So . . . Do you remember what you did on the evening . . . I imagine you've heard about Migliorini . . .'

'Who?'

'Antonio Migliorini, your daughter's husband.'

'Has Claretta got married? She hasn't told me anything about it . . . Claretta!!!'

'No, no, I didn't mean Claretta.'

'Where did you leave your car?' the signora asked, frowning.

'At the police station . . .'

'Ah . . . and do they wash it well?'

'They do an excellent job . . . But now I really must go, or I'll be late,' said Bordelli. As soon as he rose to his feet, the old woman grabbed his jacket.

'Please don't let her have too much to drink, I beg you.'

'Please don't worry.'

'She's a good girl, but when she drinks too much, she loses her head.'

'Set your mind at rest.'

'Do you intend to kiss her?'

'I don't know yet . . .'

'Please don't make her cry . . . You men are so fickle . . .'

'I really must go now, signora. I'm delighted to have met you,' said the inspector, gallantly bending forward to kiss her hand. The movement troubled the tomcat, who flattened his ears and hissed.

'Adelmo, you are such a boor! Can't you see this is Claretta's gentleman friend?'

'My very best wishes . . .'

'Will you come back soon to see me?' asked the old woman, refilling her little glass with port.

'Very soon . . . And have a very good night . . .'

Bowing slightly, he finally managed to take his leave. As he walked back down the long corridor, he turned round every so often to make sure Adelmo wasn't following him. When he was putting on his overcoat, Fidalma popped out of the kitchen, wiping her hands on her apron. Bordelli wondered again who she looked like, but it wouldn't come to him. The woman opened the door for him and, returning his goodbye with a mumble, closed it again behind him somewhat unceremoniously. Heading down the stairs, Bordelli tried to imagine what kind of evening lay ahead of him . . .

‘Where are we going?’ Claretta, now powdered and above all perfumed, asked excitedly as the Beetle set off down the boulevard.

‘I was thinking we might go to Fiesole . . .’

‘Oh yes, Fiesole!’ She was wearing a white fur coat and her black curls were gathered and hidden under a charming Davy Crockett-style hat. The car was so filled with the smell of her perfume that Bordelli had to open the side vent.

‘Your mother is charming.’

‘She loves to joke around . . .’

‘Has she been . . . that way . . . for a long time?’

‘What way?’

‘Well, every so often it seems that . . .’ Bordelli didn’t know quite how to put it.

‘Mummy is a real joker,’ Claretta said, bringing the subject to a close. Bordelli didn’t have the courage to continue. Past the flyover at Le Cure he turned up Viale dei Mille, avoiding Viale Volta on purpose. He didn’t want to drive past his childhood home, not that evening. He was worried he might see his mother at the window, rosary in hand . . . *Franchino, what are you doing? You’re not going to . . .*

‘I liked Fidalma, too.’

‘An exceptional woman,’ Claretta said, jiggling her knees.

‘She resembles someone but I can’t remember who.’

‘So you noticed it too? Well then, I’ll tell you a secret . . . Fidalma has never met her father, and her mother, a peasant from the Garfagnana area, never wanted to tell her who he was. But she was always convinced that her father was an important person and a few years ago I realised she was right.’

‘Really?’

‘Yes, a few years ago, when I was at the hairdresser and looking through some magazine, there was a picture of someone famous and it was exactly like looking at Fidalma! I am sure he was her father; they were identical.'

'Who was he?' Bordelli asked jokingly.

'You really want to know?' Claretta squealed with delight, keeping him on tenterhooks. Her brother-in-law's death seemed very remote indeed.

'I'm more curious than a concierge,' the inspector said.

'Ungaretti!'

'You're right! They're identical,' Bordelli said, mildly thrilled. He had talked to Ungaretti's daughter – and had only just now realised it.

'But I didn't tell her! I wouldn't want it to go to her head . . .' Claretta said, bursting out in laughter. She had a way of laughing that made Bordelli want to kiss her.

'Maybe Fidalma writes poems in secret,' the inspector hypothesised, thinking of the poems his mother wrote without anyone's knowing.

'Oh, I wouldn't be surprised,' Claretta said, shaking her pretty little head.

Bordelli turned onto Via Inghirami, thinking that the beautiful Juliette lived not far from there . . . Women were very much on his mind. He was in love with Eleonora, although he was trying to erase her from his memory. He was fascinated by Juliette and had even kissed her. But now he was in the car with Claretta, and who knew what might happen . . .

They reached Piazza Edison, and turned up the road that led to San Domenico. They drove in silence, but it didn't feel at all awkward. They arrived at the bend with the chestnut trees – actually two bends in the road – a place known as 'the chestnuts', the best curves in Florence for people who liked to drive fast. Two majestic, sweet bends flanked by immense chestnut trees. He had tackled those curves numerous times as a boy on his bike, always breathless, always feeling as if he were accomplishing some great feat, and before reaching the church of San Domenico he would turn to the left into Via della Piazzuola. Then, at the intersection, he would cruise down Via delle Forbici, and after a few kilometres, come out on Viale Volta, not far from his home. He had taken that long ride on the very day that the king, half out of fear and half hopeful, succumbed to the will of Mussolini and granted him the right to form a government. The entire country was in a state of ferment, you could see it in people's eyes. For many people it was as if a ship abandoned in a storm had finally found a captain, for others it was a dangerously stupid move . . .

'What are you thinking about?'

'Nothing . . .'

'It's impossible to think about nothing,' Claretta said, coyer than ever.

'What were you thinking?' the inspector asked, just to provoke her.

'I was wondering what you might be thinking.'

'That doesn't count.'

'There are certain thoughts one can't say out loud . . .'

'And yet, those might be the most interesting thoughts.'

'Ça va sans dire . . .'

'Do you like Paris?'

'That would be like asking a bee if it liked flowers,' Claretta said, in a silly tone that would have been more appropriate for a phrase like: *Why haven't you jumped on me yet?*

'I wonder if there's a woman alive who doesn't love Paris,' Bordelli said.

She laughed. 'It would be easier to find a chicken with four legs.' They continued joking around, as light hearted as two teenagers. Bordelli hadn't forgotten he was supposed to be finding out whether the woman beside him was the killer; but he didn't want to relinquish the pleasure of dining with her, either. Perhaps this was the best way to get Eleonora out of his mind . . .

When they got to Fiesole they parked the Beetle in the main square, which was full of cars. After trying at a few other places, they managed to get a table at a restaurant of a certain calibre. As soon as they sat down, the waiter lit a candle, the way they do for couples. At least he didn't think they were father and daughter, Bordelli thought, looking at her beautiful mouth, bright with red lipstick.

Claretta took off her hat, freeing the long black curls tied at the back of her neck. Under her fur she had on a black, low-cut dress that showed off her small but proud breasts. Her skin was smooth. Around her neck she wore a delicate, tiny owl with diamond eyes. She certainly was an attractive woman, who knew how to please men.

The restaurant was full of people, almost all couples. No one spoke too loudly, and soft classical music played in the background, allowing each table the right level of intimacy.

'What a nice place . . .' Claretta said, opening the menu.

'We were lucky.'

'I'm dying of hunger.'

'Are you always so beautiful when you're hungry?' Bordelli said with a Casanova look in his eye. She smiled slightly, pretending to pay little regard to the compliment.

'Mmmm . . . I'm undecided . . .' She was referring to the menu, but there was a mischievous tone in her answer.

'Follow your sixth sense,' Bordelli said in the same tone.

At last she found inspiration, and they were able to order. After a little more wordplay, their antipasti arrived. Bordelli ordered a bottle of good Chianti and made sure that Claretta's glass was never empty. Between one forkful and the next they continued to chat, jumping from one subject to another, guided by the pleasure of getting to know each other. Bordelli never missed a chance to flirt with her, and she was tickled pink. Murderess or not, she was a woman who needed to feel desired. She was a fragile woman, at least in appearance, and also very sensitive. The inspector was having fun, he couldn't deny it, and he continued to hope that Claretta was innocent. She might even be the right woman to help chase away the ghost of Eleonora . . .

'What is the first thing you look at in a woman?' she asked, with a childish smile.

'Her eyes.'

'From now on, I will call you Pinocchio.'

'You women like liars.'

'It's worse than that. We women like rascals,' Claretta said with a laugh. By now Bordelli was so used to her perfume that he didn't notice it anymore. Every so often the thought came into his mind that he could suddenly start jabbing her with embarrassing questions . . . *Did you have a relationship with your brother-in-law? Why did you hide it from me? Were you in love with him?* But he preferred to wait. He too had had a bit to drink and was enjoying being silly. Except for that unforgettable dinner with Juliette, how long had it been since he had flirted like this with a woman?

At the end of the meal, Claretta gave in to the temptation of custard cake, and Bordelli ordered two glasses of champagne.

'Are you trying to get me drunk?' she said coyly.

'It might be fun . . .'

'You're quite the ladies' man, aren't you.'

'Nothing could be less true.'

'Do you mean to say that you fall in love every time?'

'I'm a lost cause.'

When Bordelli asked for the bill it must have already been midnight. There was hardly anyone left in the restaurant. The waiters were putting away the tables, and long ribbons of smoke hung in the air. Even Claretta and Bordelli each had a cigarette. For him it was the first of the day; he was no longer in the monster's clutches.

Claretta got up to go to the ladies' room, taking her little purse with her, and the inspector couldn't help but admire her derrière. She was truly charming, and despite the wine, she moved with elegance in her patent leather, stiletto heels.

Bordelli hadn't forgotten the real reason for that dinner, but kept putting it off. He had to be on his toes and find just the right moment, he kept saying to himself; but he was also well aware that the pleasure of being in the company of a pretty woman was holding him back. He paid the bill, pretending not to find it too expensive, and even left a generous tip.

Claretta returned after what seemed like an eternity, walking through the restaurant like a fashion model. She had powdered her nose and reapplied her fiery red lipstick. Very seductive, damn it all, Bordelli thought. He stood to help her put on her fur, and a waiter escorted them to the exit. Once they were outside, Claretta took his arm quite naturally, as if it was the only proper thing to do.

'What a beautiful sky . . .' she sighed with a shiver, looking up at the celestial vault speckled with stars.

'That one is Sirius,' Bordelli said, indicating the brightest star.

'I've never understood a thing about the stars.'

'It's easier than you think . . . There you see the constellation of Orion, shaped like an hourglass . . . that one there is Taurus . . . those are Gemini . . . and there's Auriga . . .' He became her tour guide through the stars, exhuming everything he'd learned at the Naval Academy. They stopped in front of the Beetle with their noses in the air. Claretta listened, as attentive as a child, her arm firmly linked with his.

After their promenade through the stars, they got into the car and descended slowly towards Florence. The roar of the Beetle's German engine had something comforting about it. Once again they didn't talk, but the silence was different now. There was a sweet tension in the air, one that both knew well.

It's been so long since I'd seen the stars, I'd forgotten I was nothing, Bordelli thought, remembering one of his mother's most beautiful lines of poetry. Out of the corner of his eye he saw Claretta turning to look at him every so often, but he pretended not to notice.

'Poor Antonio . . .' she murmured all of a sudden, as if she felt guilty for having spent a pleasant evening only two weeks after her brother-in-law's death. The inspector didn't say a word, and waited in vain for her to say more.

When they arrived at Claretta's house, Bordelli walked her to the door. She had to rummage through her purse a long time for her keys, smiling all the while, but at last she found them.

'Goodnight,' she said, looking him straight in the eye. Her red mouth was slightly open.

'Sweet dreams, Claretta . . .' The inspector approached her, took her face in his hands and kissed her. She let herself be kissed. A long kiss, one that had been hanging in the air all evening. They said nothing, only looked at each other again, and then Claretta disappeared into the building.

Bordelli got back into his car with a sigh and drove off in the direction of Piazza San Gallo. There was still quite a bit of traffic on the avenues. He had a pleasant taste of lipstick on his lips. *The man who kissed women at the door* . . . that could be a good title for a novel. He had kissed Juliette at the door, but that had been a farewell. He wondered what Claretta was like in bed . . . Would she take the initiative or did she let herself be guided? And why did she bathe in perfume? Had she really killed Antonio? Had she been there now, he would have kissed her again. He would gladly have taken her home with him, got under the covers with her, and banished the ghosts of the past . . .

But unfortunately Claretta was also the only suspect, at least for the moment, and he had to find out how things really stood. Piecing together the little fragments he had available yielded a simple story, one he kept seeing unfold before his eyes . . . Claretta rushing over to her brother-in-law's house in the middle of the night, consumed with jealousy . . . She trying to win him back, he showing no interest and talking only about the woman he loved . . . she crying desperately, hurling abuse . . . Antonio attempting to calm her down, to console her; maybe opening the safe and offering her the ring that had belonged to her sister . . . she feeling humiliated, grabbing the foil and threatening him . . . Antonio approaching her without fear, ring in hand, certain she was just behaving like a spoilt child . . . But then, lo, she runs it through him, almost without realising it . . . Overcome with terror, she wipes everything she's touched clean with a handkerchief and then throws open the window to clear the air, knowing that her perfume might betray her, and to make the whole thing look like a robbery, she takes the jewellery box with her . . .

It all made perfect sense, but was that what really happened? He would think about it tomorrow; now he needed some sleep. Feeling anxious to get into bed, he stepped on the accelerator along the Imprunetana.

By the time he got home it was past one o'clock. The colonel had already gone to bed, and a last stump of oak was burning in the hearth. On the kitchen table he saw a note: *This house is beautiful. Goodnight.* He smiled and tiptoed up the stairs. Five minutes later he was in bed.

As soon as he turned off the light a phalanx of ghosts appeared. This wasn't anything new; every so often it happened. They came to him from every period of his life, crowding around his bed in disorderly fashion . . . but he had his way of keeping them away. He needed only to tell himself a story, as he used to do as a kid when he couldn't get to sleep. They were usually stories made up right on the spot, but sometimes they included real people, or even him as protagonist. The important thing was to let go and follow the thread of the story, and gradually the ghosts would vanish . . . *Once upon a time there was a man, who lived all alone in a big castle, and one night . . .*

He fell asleep almost immediately, hearing two owls hooting to each other in the distance.

'And the last time?'

'Right before midnight,' said Arcieri, pouring the espresso into the little cups. They were talking about the phone. It had rung various times the previous evening, until late into the night.

'Must be some princess who's in love with me . . .'

It was past nine o'clock. Bordelli had just got up and didn't feel at all like going to the office.

'Anything new with Claretta?' asked the colonel.

'Not yet, but I'm working on it.'

He didn't really want to talk about it . . . What was there to say? A flirtatious dinner, champagne, and a kiss outside her door?

'I'll go and get some wood,' said Arcieri, getting up.

'I'll give you a hand . . .'

After stacking the wood they started cleaning, armed with broom and mop, chatting all the while. A pair of housewives couldn't have done a better job. Doing one room after another, they ended up cleaning even the bathroom.

'What do you say, Colonel? Shall we have a nice dinner, just the two of us, on New Year's Eve?'

'Gladly, if I'm still here.'

'And why wouldn't you still be here?'

'One never knows . . .'

By half past one they were both starving, and so together they whipped up a fine dish of *penne alla carrettiera* with a generous dose of hot pepper. To put out the fire they used Balzini wine, raising their glasses to Jeremiah every so often. When they rose from the table it was almost three o'clock, and Bordelli went upstairs to his room to make a phone call he'd had on his mind since waking up.

'Claretta?'

'Oh, hello, Inspector . . .'

'Did you sleep well?'

'Like a baby.'

'May I be brazen with you?'

'Dear me, what do you want to tell me?' asked Claretta, giggling like a hen.

'May I invite you out to dinner again this evening?'

'Oh, you really *are* brazen . . .' They'd already kissed, but kept up the game of formalities. It was fun.

'May I take that to mean yes?'

'Well, I'm even more brazen than you . . . Why don't you take me first to see a movie?'

'It's a deal. At what time shall I pick you up?'

'Five o'clock?'

'All right. Do you already know what film you'd like to see?'

'Shall we choose one together?'

'Excellent idea. See you at five.'

'Perfect . . . See you soon . . .'

'Please give your mother a kiss for me, and Fidalma, too,' said Bordelli, making Claretta laugh.

They said goodbye, and Bordelli went into the bathroom to get ready. He opened the faucet in the tub, then turned his attentions to shaving while waiting for it to fill up. He lathered his face twice, manoeuvring the razor with unusual attention. Not a single hair must be spared, and so it was. Then he sprinkled his cheeks with Aqua Velva, enjoying the burning sensation, before sinking into the hot water and parboiling his body for a long spell. A sound of barely audible music rose up from downstairs, seeming at moments to vibrate with energy . . . Then he recognised Schubert's *Unfinished* . . . Yet again the *Unfinished*, as in Dante's laboratory a few nights before. His investigation, too, remained unfinished, though his visions were as finished as a movie . . . *Claretta in a rage . . . Claretta humiliated . . . Claretta running Migliorini through . . .* An Aeschylean trilogy . . .

Wrapped in his bathrobe, he dried what remained of his hair with care, consoling himself with the mythical *charm of the mature gentleman.* In her later years his mother often used to say to him, 'You used to have such beautiful hair as a boy, Franco . . .' It made him feel bad, but he didn't let on. Lino Ventura might indeed be more handsome, but he himself wasn't exactly fit to be thrown away.

He put on the finest clothes he could find in his wardrobe, but they were nothing special. At twenty past four he went downstairs to say goodbye to Arcieri, who was reading by the fire. Coltrane's follies were blaring from the living room.

'I shan't be home for dinner tonight either.'

'Don't you worry about me; I like being alone,' Arcieri declared, noticing the inspector's fancy clothes but saying nothing.

'Beware of ghosts,' said Bordelli.

'We're old friends by now . . . Could you perhaps leave me a cigarette, if you don't mind?'

'Shall I leave you the packet?'

'No, just one, thank you,' said Arcieri.

'I'll leave it on the table.'

'So kind of you.'

'See you in the morning. Have a pleasant evening,' said Bordelli, putting on his coat.

'Happy hunting . . .' said the colonel, who seemed to have understood everything.

Bordelli nodded, smiling, and after a last wave goodbye, went out of the house. Getting into the Beetle, he started her up and began the climb up the dirt road. The sun was setting over the horizon, and the sky over San Casciano had turned bloody red. He was only doing his job, he kept repeating to himself, and yet he still felt butterflies in his stomach.

He drove down to Florence at a leisurely pace, and pulled up outside Claretta's front door at two minutes past five. He rang the doorbell, and a few seconds later heard the click of the intercom.

'I'll be right down,' Claretta's voice chirped.

'No hurry.'

He waited outside the door, pacing back and forth for a bit, and with a little effort was able not to think too much about Eleonora. A few more days and . . .

Claretta came out about twenty minutes later, smiling but only a little, as was only proper for a woman of refinement. She was wearing an orange coat, a leopardskin busby, white gloves, and beige, low-heeled pumps. Cute as a button, eyes more effervescent than ever. Bordelli kissed her hand by way of greeting and had the impression she'd put on less perfume than usual. He circled round the Beetle to open the door for her, and when he got into the car himself, Claretta was already holding the cinema page she'd torn out of *La Nazione*.

'Have a look for yourself . . .' she said, handing him the crumpled page. One film had been circled with ballpoint pen: *The Graduate*, showing at the Cinema Ideale, on its second run. Bordelli quickly scanned the other titles, just out of curiosity. If it had been up to him, he would have gone to see *The Dirty Dozen*, with Ernest Borgnine and Lee Marvin, or the latest Bond movie, just for the fun of it.

'Find anything?' asked Claretta.

'I don't know . . . What do you think about seeing *The Graduate*?'

'Why not?' she said, smiling, hands on her purse.

'The next show starts at quarter to six.'

'Oh, it's as if they'd done it on purpose . . .'

'Heaven is on our side,' said Bordelli, starting up the car. The Cinema Ideale was barely a few hundred yards away, in Via Firenzuola, near the corner with Piazza delle Cure.

They crossed the flyover and parked near the movie house. Bordelli paid for the tickets; the newsreel was just ending as they went in.

'I love these little neighbourhood movie theatres,' Claretta whispered, sitting down.

The place was almost empty, and they laid their coats down on the seats next to them. A few minutes later the film began; the print was slightly damaged at the start. Behind the opening credits, a thoughtful-looking young man was landing in Los Angeles, then staring into space with a profoundly unhappy expression while riding the escalator to the baggage claim area . . . At first glance it seemed like a pretty good film. Nice images, sweet, melancholy music. A short while later Bordelli felt a small hand slide under his own, and he squeezed it ever so gently . . .

As soon as Bordelli left the house, the colonel placed a fresh log on the fire, wrapped a scarf around his neck, put on his overcoat, and went out the back door. It was terribly cold. He lit the cigarette his friend had left him, and smoked it while watching the sunset. The sky was slashed with a violent redness that reminded him of an abattoir.

Oddly enough, he felt good. In fact he may never have felt so at peace with himself as he did at that moment. Yes, he was in danger, someone was looking for him, indeed wanted him dead, and he couldn't even trust his old colleagues. But in spite of this, he no longer felt afraid. He exhaled the smoke into the darkened sky and thought about how he had been welcomed into this house by a person he barely knew. He and Bordelli had only met a few times before, and neither of them could say he knew the other well.

They belonged to two different generations, Bordelli and he. Bordelli was almost ten years his junior. They had grown up in two very different worlds. Their ways of thinking and their ways of facing things were very different. That wasn't too hard to see. And yet, Arcieri felt a strong affinity for Bordelli. Yes, that's what it was . . . He felt a genuine, deep affection for the generous inspector, and not only because he had welcomed him into his home without hesitation. Affection can't be earned with favours. He felt truly fond of the man, and of late this sentiment had become all too rare for him. Essentially, Arcieri considered Bordelli a true friend, someone he could tell his innermost thoughts to, someone with whom he could share his most private emotions and secrets. It had been a long time since he had felt affection for anyone, and he realised how much he missed this. Naturally it was all because of his line of work: he was part of an environment that was rife with suspicion and constantly fluctuating, often absurd, interpretations. His was a world where sentiments were often a burden, even useless. For years he had had merely cordial relations with just a few colleagues. At best he might meet some people during his brief summer travels. He always tried to be consistent, to keep his word, never to betray another's trust . . . these were his constants . . . as well as a strong sense of duty, dominated by a strict sense of aesthetics. But things were different with Bordelli, other considerations came into play. In short, he liked him. He felt free with him, was able to let himself go . . . How many people had he really liked in his life? He wasn't thinking about love or passion; that was another matter, even though affection played a part in those emotions as well.

He had felt strongly for Elena and loved his mother, his father and his brother. He had had a good friend when he was a child . . . and now he had the inspector. Who knew what kind of 'motives' governed the universe of feelings.

He smiled, tossed the cigarette butt aside, and stood looking at the horizon, the dark outline of the hill in the distance, black against the last red streaks in the sky. He let himself be carried off by these vaguely melancholy thoughts and the pleasure of exploring places unknown to him. He heard a dog bark in the distance, and every so often a gust of wind rustled the boughs of the cypresses . . . He wouldn't have minded living out the rest of his days in a big country house like Bordelli's, far from the disgust of his past life and the anguish of ageing. Taking this thought even farther, he imagined staying on as the inspector's guest until the end of time. He could farm, cook, become the caretaker.

He heard the phone ring inside the house. He started counting the rings but lost count. When silence returned he tried to collect his thoughts . . . he tried to imagine what it would be like to live in that house in different seasons. There would always be something to do: cut the grass, tend the vegetable garden, repair a shutter, change a roof tile. He could build a new, stronger fence for the vegetable garden or a tool shed. He was sure he'd make a good carpenter, and even a farmer. He would learn how to prune the olive trees, fertilise them, take care of them . . . *How absurd!* he thought to himself, realising he had to get out of there, and as soon as possible. Still, daydreaming helped him relax, just like listening to good jazz . . .

He walked around the house, taking in everything he saw. Even at dusk the view was magnificent. The dark, sad outline of the castle loomed atop the hill in front. It felt like another century. The moon had already set and the dark sky was filling with stars, millions of stars whose glow was just enough to make the contours of things faintly visible.

For no apparent reason, he suddenly started charging up the dirt road that led towards town. Maybe he wanted to prove to himself that he was entirely recovered and strong enough to confront the adventure that awaited him. It had been days since he'd last thought about the lad he met in the hospital, but he certainly hadn't forgotten his promise. He would find out what lay behind the whole nasty affair, even if it cost him his life . . . There he went again . . . Such bluster . . . Who did he think he was, a knight of the Round Table or something? But the hill before him looked indeed like an obstacle to be surmounted, like something out of a chivalric romance . . . What on earth? . . . Was he just a pathetic old man afflicted with a grave form of romanticism? But how could he turn back now? He might never forgive himself if he did. He would rather try and fail than give up. He was convinced his friend Bordelli felt the same way . . .

After marching briskly for a bit he had to stop. He was out of breath and felt a sharp pain in his left side. He was trying to do too much. It wasn't just because of his age; it was everything he had gone through before and after the hospital. It was a miracle that he had come out of his accident at Sant'Anna alive – he must not forget that. He stopped to catch his breath and then went on at a slower pace, pausing every thirty steps or so, letting his thoughts wander where they would . . . During the summer of '44 he had marched into Florence along the Via Cassia. The British had not been very nice to the late-arriving Italian allies under Badoglio's command. Not with Intelligence, nor with officers in the Service such as he. They had entered the city through Porta Romana, heading up a long column of infantry from the first British division. As soon as they passed through the immense stone gates, they were welcomed with celebrations. But the road, which was long and narrow, had some nasty surprises in store for them. Fascist snipers and German sharpshooters were perched on rooftops, presenting a mortal danger for soldiers and civilians alike. The marchers could take only a few steps at a time and then had to duck into buildings for safety. When they arrived within sight of Ponte Santa Trinita, a young English lieutenant stepped out into the middle of the road, fascinated by the Renaissance architecture, which he had probably studied at school and was seeing for the first time. Arcieri was a few metres ahead of him, hidden in an archway. He shouted at the soldier to get out of the street and take cover. Then he heard a sound like someone taking a bite of an apple, and saw the Englishman stand stock still, as though amazed by so much beauty . . . but only for a second, because then he crashed to the ground like a bag of potatoes, arms splayed. A stray bullet, either Fascist or German, probably fired from the other side of the river, had hit him square in the middle of the brow and passed through his skull, leaving it intact. His eyes remained open wide, still full of amazement, and the hole in his forehead, small and red, looked like a Hindu bindi. To avoid getting shot in turn, Arcieri had to run like a cat, zigzagging from one side of the street to the other, from doorway to doorway, together with four twenty-year-old boys.

Reaching the top of the hill, Arcieri planted a metaphorical flag and started back down. It hadn't been so bad after all. He was no longer limping, and the pain in his back was almost gone. Still, it felt good to be inside the house again. After hanging up his coat, he sat down in front of the fire to warm up.

It was still too early to make dinner. He put on some good music and sat back down in front of the fire, a book in hand – a Russian novel he had never read. He read for a long time, enjoying it enormously, and even forgot to put more wood on the fire.

When he looked at the time it was already half past eight. He stoked the fire, put a good-size log on the andirons and turned his attentions to dinner. He was very hungry, as if he had walked all day. After a friendly nod to the skull, he opened the cabinet. The plates and bowls came from three different services, one of which was very elegant, old, expensive stuff. Who knew where it came from . . . maybe Bordelli had inherited it from an old aunt. There was something sweet but also cruel in the fact that objects outlived humans. A piece of furniture, a lamp or even a simple plate carried images and memories of an ever more distant past until the last descendants capable of remembering that past had themselves quit this world . . . After which, a paperweight that for decades had been the heartbreaking symbol of a loved one, or another era, became an object with no value. There, he was doing it again. All it had taken was an old china plate and Arcieri had slipped back into the great lake of melancholy in which of late he'd often found himself swimming.

But now to dinner. The idea of cooking something gave him great pleasure. While trying to decide what to make, he thought back to the days he'd spent as a scullery boy in the lowest-level trattorias, trying to hide out in a small city like Florence. Now, on the other hand, he felt like a king: he had a full refrigerator, a pantry, a gas cooker, and all the time in the world. It was truly surprising to see how little it took to feel joyful.

Although he knew that he would be dining alone, he set the table with care, choosing the finest cutlery and dishes. There had been a time, some thirty years earlier, when he regularly ate off precious china plates and was served by waiters in livery. That was in the thirties, when Elena Contini was his fiancée and he frequented a milieu altogether foreign to him. His parents had been ordinary lower-middle-class folks. Elena, on the other hand, belonged to high society, to a world where the Florentine aristocracy and haute bourgeoisie used to go arm in arm with the most prominent members of the Jewish community . . . Often, at parties or receptions, he had felt like an intruder, a little like the young De Sica in *Signor Max*, a film that was released at the time: *If you don't know how to play bridge, just say so, Max, there's nothing wrong with that!* Arcieri smiled nostalgically, feeling benevolent compassion for the young man he once was, dark hair slicked down with pomade like a Cinecittà movie star. The actress in the film who had delivered those lines, whose *nom d'art* was Rubi Dalma, truly was of aristocratic stock, with a double- or even triple-barrelled surname . . . What was it again? Oh yes, Giusta Manca di Villahermosa. He shook his head, smoothing out the tablecloth with the palm of his hand. Rubi Dalma was very believable in that film, embodying perfectly one of those fascinating, bored women he had been forced to frequent with Elena. Who knew whether Elena ever realised how embarrassed he was. At times it seemed to him that even a fish out of water would have felt more at ease than he did. Then came 1938, and the racial laws, and everything changed for his beautiful Jewish fiancée . . .

He put a pot of water on the cooker to boil and forced himself to sever the connection with those memories, amazed at how clear they were in his mind . . .

'Now that's what I call love,' Claretta said as they were leaving the movie theatre. She seemed electrified, and with every step she lightly rubbed shoulders with her escort.

'A very fine film indeed,' Bordelli commented, genuinely impressed by the courage of the protagonist, who took on the world to save his dreams.

'The girl's mother is a real tart . . . if you'll excuse my language.'

'The right words are always the most effective.'

'Have you ever done anything so outlandish for a woman?'

'More than once.'

'Give me an example.'

'They're not the sorts of things one talks about.'

'Oh, you're just being mean . . .' Claretta said mincingly. She knew how to play the coquette well, and must have had men falling routinely into her hands like ripe pears.

They got into the car and headed back towards the centre of town. It was barely a quarter to eight, too early for dinner.

They left the car in Piazza San Marco and went for a walk along the main streets like a pair of tourists. There were few people out and about. The air was cold, but neither of them seemed to notice.

'Tell me something about yourself,' said Claretta.

'I'm afraid I'm not a very interesting person . . .'

'Others might not agree.'

'What about you? Have you ever done anything outrageous for a man?'

'That's not the sort of thing you ask a lady . . .' she said, repaying him in kind.

The mutual goading continued until they arrived at Piazza del Mercato Nuovo, and Bordelli pointed to a window on the second floor of a building.

'Know who once lived up there?'

'A girlfriend of yours?'

'Dostoevsky . . .'

'Really?'

'Yes, he always looked for corner flats, with windows looking out onto two streets.'

'How do you know these things?'

'A young man who works at Seeber's told me. He knows everything about the writers he loves best.'

'Love is always what makes the world go round,' she said cheerfully, taking his arm.

'People also commit atrocities in the name of love,' said Bordelli, pretending to enjoy playing the devil's advocate, when in fact he was making a veiled allusion. He thought he felt Claretta stiffen.

'But let's not talk about unpleasant things tonight. Please? Would you do that for me?' she said in the tone of a pouty little girl.

'I'm sorry, but when you're always hunting down killers as I do you tend to see evil everywhere.'

'Well, tonight you're with me, and you must forget you're a police inspector.'

'I'll try my best.'

'There's a good boy . . .'

Talking all the while, they crossed the Ponte Vecchio at a slow pace, then continued on up to Piazza Pitti. Bordelli pointed to another apartment the great Russian novelist had lived in, then they ducked into the side streets until they reached Via Maggio. He chose the itinerary, and Claretta let herself be guided.

They headed back towards the river, and after the Ponte Santa Trinita they turned right onto the Lungarno. Passing through a sort of tunnel, they came out in tiny Piazza del Limbo, where the smell of the flood was still in the air, and they stole a kiss in the darkness of the square. It lasted only a few seconds, after which they climbed the stairs and vanished into the ancient little streets, still arm in arm. Bordelli was still waiting for the right moment to lay his cards on the table, but kept putting it off. He couldn't help it. He truly liked Claretta, and this made the whole thing more thrilling . . .

'You're suddenly so quiet,' she said, pulling him gently closer.

'I was thinking . . .'

'I can imagine what . . . A woman?'

'You guessed it.' They'd just kissed for a second time, but still maintained the formal mode of address as though it were the most normal thing in the world.

'And who might she be?'

'I've got her right here beside me,' Bordelli said with his best lady-killer smile.

'Oh, look, your nose is getting longer!'

'That always happens when I tell the truth.'

'And what were you thinking about me?' she asked contentedly.

'Do you really expect me to tell you?'

'Is it really so indecent?'

'Depends on your point of view,' said Bordelli, more allusive than ever.

'You're very good at not answering questions,' Claretta reproached him.

'That may be an asset . . .'

It had been a long time since he'd last engaged in this sort of verbal tussling, and he was enjoying it immensely. When they reached Piazza della Repubblica, he suggested they go and eat at an old trattoria in San Lorenzo.

'Is that where you always take your women?'

'I haven't been back there for quite a while.'

'So, then, where do you take them?'

'You seem to think I'm some kind of Casanova.'

'I love Casanova. I feel so free when I think of Casanova . . .'

'All women melt when they think of Casanova, but if their husbands turn their heads to eye another woman, there's always trouble,' Bordelli said, smiling.

'Oh, not all women are alike,' Claretta protested.

'Are you trying to tell me you're not the jealous type?'

'That's not the kind of question one asks a lady . . .'

'I get it, to punish me, that's going to be your answer to everything tonight.'

'Well, you deserve it . . . What about you? Do you get jealous?'

'Extremely jealous, but I try not to let it show.'

'You still haven't told me if you're married . . .'

'Not yet,' he joked.

'Girlfriend?'

'Not even.'

Piazza San Lorenzo was deserted, buffeted as it was by a cold wind that made one's hair stand on end. Bordelli escorted Claretta to the trattoria of Sergio Gozzi, and they entered with a feeling of relief. Almost all the tables were taken, and the buzz of voices was quite audible.

'Hello, Inspector . . . How's it going?' said Sergio, shaking his hand.

'I'm getting by. How about yourself?'

'Could be worse . . . Good evening, signora . . . Please go and sit down at that table in the back. I'll send the boy over to you at once . . . Gino, as soon as you can, please go and take care of these people . . . Ciao, I'll see you later . . .'

They went over to their table, followed by the stares of the other customers. The inspector helped Claretta off with her coat, and they sat down.

'What a charming place . . .' Claretta whispered, leaning forward and looking around at the other people. Simple men and women, a bit coarse, the few coins in their pockets enabling them to eat out. The only exception was a well-dressed foreign couple, probably British, seated at the table beside them, dining in silence while occasionally casting an amused glance about the room at all those noisy Italians . . .

Colonel Arcieri finished setting the table, carefully arranging every item. He was better off not thinking about the past. Now he wanted to cook and enjoy his dinner. Maybe he would even turn on the telly and watch a good programme.

Every so often he heard the telephone ring, but each time the number of rings diminished. He couldn't answer; it simply wouldn't have been prudent, although he was very curious to know who was at the other end.

Opening the refrigerator, he chose the ingredients he would use for a spaghetti sauce. If nothing else, he had learned a few good recipes from those horrible places where he had worked for a pittance. While waiting for the pot of water to boil, he opened a bottle of wine, filled a glass, and took a sip.

The phone rang again. For a moment he was almost tempted to answer . . . But he knew he had better not, so he kept on cooking. He was thrilled to recall that after dinner he would finally have time to explore the large dusty rooms on the ground floor, rooms that were used more or less as storage areas not only for farming tools but for all kinds of things. Two trunks particularly piqued his curiosity, and while waiting for dinner he tried to imagine what they might contain.

When Arcieri was a child, his family would take him to his maternal grandmother's big, mysterious house, where he would dig through the junk in the attic and find all kinds of unforgettable things. His childhood memories were quite vivid and mainly connected to the period when he was four or five years old. His grandmother had lived in a small town not far away, and for their visits there his parents used to dress him up like a little sailor, as was the fashion back then. The steam engine would huff and puff at a standstill as the old station in Florence teemed with commotion, and he felt as though he was leaving for the mysterious Orient.

His grandmother's town, however, was always a disappointment. The little station had only one track. Peasants plodded along the road here and there. Sleepy houses dotted the flat grey countryside, which stretched outwards from a river.

After lunch his parents would sit and talk to his grandmother in the kitchen of the old house, while he was free to go off and explore the rooms. What attracted him most was the attic, full as it was of old objects and spiders' webs. A dusty old dormer window let in a little wan light. His grandmother had long been a widow, and had stored all her memories up there in the attic. Old furniture, broken chairs, headless statues, books and newspapers dating back forty years, various objects, a plaster bust with a broken nose, large dolls shut inside bell jars, trunks full of all sorts of odds and ends.

Sometimes he would take something home with him – nothing special, maybe an old rusty pen, a foreign coin, an animal tooth, which he would carry in his pocket like a trophy from a journey to a faraway land. These exercises of the imagination would then set him endlessly dreaming late into the night, back home in his own bed.

Bordelli's house, though very different in style, reminded him of his grandmother Aldagisa's house. Even the old trunks were similar: rough wooden crates with large, rusty hinges.

Once at his grandmother's house he had climbed up dangerously high on top of those coffers to reach a shelf where something colourful had caught his eye. At the top he extended a hand and gingerly gripped a sort of box with brightly painted figures on the outside. Inside he found a miniature theatre made of delicate plywood, partially covered with decorated paper and in places painted by hand, and only lightly covered with a layer of dust. He felt like a giant who had stuck his head inside a real theatre, like Gulliver, whose story his mother had read to help him fall asleep. Sticking his little hands behind the scenery, he felt something there; it was a tiny marionette of painted chalk that had been forgotten in the box, as if dead. He examined it closely, turning it towards the light behind him. It was an old Pantaloon, and his jaw was missing . . . That sinister grimace gave him a fright, making him lose his balance and fall, luckily onto a pile of old blankets. He broke out in tears, and when his parents and grandmother came running with concern, they found him with his legs in the air, clothes dirty with dust and the scary toy still in his hand . . .

He wondered whether he would find a miniature theatre in Bordelli's mysterious rooms. He was truly curious to go and have a look. There could be anything. Old books, old records of cardboard or Bakelite, magazines, stuffed animals, family photo albums, forgotten objects that spoke only to those who knew how to listen to the voices of the past. Over time, everybody had their own reason for abandoning certain objects to a place that was both so near and yet so far away. Attics and cellars were like rooms of memory, where one keeps the things that one doesn't want to throw away but doesn't want to see every day either . . .

When he realised that the water in the pot had been boiling for a while, he could only shake his head. Grabbing a hefty serving of spaghetti, he threw it into the boiling water and went to put another log on the fire. It was already past nine o'clock. He was ravenous, and after an enjoyable meal an adventurous evening awaited him, one that would surely also be very dusty. Who needed television? He could get used to this way of life . . .

'If I have even one more glass you'll have to carry me in your arms,' said Claretta, laughing, hand over her mouth.

'I couldn't ask for more.'

'Oh, my . . . And where would you take me?'

'Wherever you told me to take you,' said Bordelli, pouring her more wine. At Gozzi's they served it in flasks instead of bottles, and instead of fine tulip glasses on the tables, they had simple eatery glasses. But although it was already past ten, the trattoria was still packed.

'You know what? I never believed a man like you could exist,' said Claretta, bursting out in laughter.

'There's one born every hundred years,' Bordelli said ironically, to keep her laughing. They felt good together. They were having fun. It didn't matter what they talked about. Every statement seemed to mean something else. Bordelli was observing her, feeling quite sorry. Claretta was so fragile; he wished he could protect her.

'Do you believe in the supernatural?' she asked out of the blue.

'I don't know what to say.'

'Have you ever seen a ghost?'

'No, I'm sorry to say.'

'Then I'll tell you a story . . . A few years ago, a friend of mine's husband was driving down in southern Lazio. At a certain point he saw a friar at the side of the road, hitchhiking, a great big man with no hair on his head and a long white beard. My friend's husband was in a hurry and didn't stop. A few more miles down the road he saw another friar hitchhiking, and as he approached he noticed the man looked a lot like the first one. So he started imagining all sorts of strange things, just to pass the time, and after a few minutes he stopped thinking about it. But then, as he went on down the road, to his great surprise, lo and behold, he sees the same man, but this time he decided to stop. The man got into the car and asked whether he could be taken to a small town at the top of the hill farther on down the road. He had a large mole next to his left eye with a great many black hairs growing out of it. During the ride he didn't say a word, but only stared into space, as if he was looking at nothing. My friend's husband took him all the way to the town's little church, and before getting out of the car, the friar said: *Why hurry, when what awaits us at the end of the road is death?* And then, after thanking him, he left at once, allowing him no time to reply. He slipped into the church and vanished. The encounter left quite an impression on my friend's husband, and after some hesitation he decided to go and look for the friar, hoping, for no precise reason, to exchange a few words with him. To his surprise he found the church door locked. But he didn't want to give up. Just a few steps away was the little door to the presbytery, and he tapped the door knocker a few times. After a long wait, the priest's housekeeper came and opened the door. She told him the priest had gone out to give someone last rites, and she didn't know when he would be back. So my friend's husband said he was looking for a friar, to whom he'd given a lift in his car all the way to the church, which he'd just seen him enter. The housekeeper opened her eyes wide, as though she thought she was dealing with a madman. *You must believe me*, he said. *He's a big, stout friar with a beard so long and a mole next to his eye.* The woman took a step back and crossed herself. *But that*, she said in terror, *is Friar Orlando!* And she looked at him with big round eyes. *He's the one I'm looking for all right. Doesn't he live here?* The woman crossed herself again. *He used to come to say mass*, she said. *He no longer does?* he asked. The housekeeper kept staring at him. *He's dead*, she said. *It must be ten years now* . . . At that point my friend's husband got back in his car and sped away, foot on the accelerator, thinking he'd given a lift to a ghost . . .'

'I'd like to have been in his shoes,' said the inspector, and he told her about a medium they once had in the family, one of his father's aunts, who, among other things, had founded the Bologna chapter of the Fascist Party along with Mussolini . . . Claretta burst out laughing and said that when the war broke out, she was still just a little girl in braids . . . They kept on chatting, following the threads of memory, and at some point Claretta mentioned Antonio . . .

'I'm told your brother-in-law left you a nice little bequest,' Bordelli let drop with feigned nonchalance.

'Yes, I can't complain . . .' she said, as though slightly embarrassed.

'Were you expecting anything?'

'Of course! Antonio was very fond of me.'

Her eyes welled up with tears, but she forced herself to smile. The waiter arrived to remove their plates and asked whether they wanted to order anything else. Claretta said no, and Bordelli requested the bill. A few minutes later Sergio in person came over and whispered in his ear that he need only pay for the flask of wine. Bordelli tried to protest, but was forced to give in. He thanked Sergio and, after leaving a nice tip for the lad, helped Claretta with her coat. They went out into the cold, and she immediately took his arm.

Arcieri opened the creaky door and peered into the dark. He found the antique switch and turned it. A light bulb hanging from the beam lit up; it was so dusty that its light seemed grey. He went into the room, feeling the cold air on his face. He had done well to put on his coat. The old olive mill was full of things of every kind: cardboard boxes, old bricks, paint cans, a canister with *US Army* printed on it . . . Chaos reigned. Old pieces of furniture half broken and covered with spiders' webs, chairs stacked high, wooden crates filled with empty bottles, rusty farm tools, rolled carpets half eaten by mice, bicycle tyres hanging on the wall, disintegrating straw-covered flasks, doors leaning one against the other, a wrought-iron headboard, and a host of other things honouring times gone by. He felt as if he had walked into a sanctuary of the past, like the first time he had entered his grandmother's attic.

There were two large trunks pushed up against the wall which caught his attention. He opened one of them, but the light was too dim and he couldn't see a thing. He went down into the kitchen, returned with a torch and started looking inside the trunk. There was the headlamp of a motorbike, a home-made crystal radio, military boots, old shoes, broken frames, scrap iron of every sort, petrol lamps, spools of metal wire, bed warmers, blackened pots and pans . . . A cemetery of memories from a distant past. Every object was a whole novel, a string of stories of men and women, passion and suffering, the drama and tragedy it had witnessed at the time of its manufacture, sale, acquisition, use and eventual abandonment.

Arcieri closed the magic chest and went to the trunk next to it. It was different from the first, cruder, with a heavy wrought-iron lock. Terracotta pots had been stacked on top of it. He rested the torch on a chair and removed the pots. He opened the heavy lid, its hinges completely silent. A vague smell of mould rose up into the air, a smell dear to librarians. The trunk was full of paper and other objects. Arcieri was attracted by a small stack of 78s. He picked them up with excitement: Duke Ellington, Count Basie, Satchmo, and other music from the forties. The records were half broken or in bad condition; it was painful to see. He kept on digging. Travel guides in English from the twenties and thirties, a tattered map of Tuscany, a book of Renaissance art that had been heavily underlined in pencil . . .

He found a bunch of photos tied with a blue ribbon. They were small and had jagged edges. Mountain landscapes, medieval towns, famous monuments: Rome, Venice, Naples. A girl sitting on a plain sofa, wearing a large white hat.

In a small box were other photographs of an entirely different sort. He felt a wave of disgust run through him when he found himself looking at a charred corpse in the foreground, with the remainder of a German tank that had been blown up by a bazooka in the background. It must have been from North Africa. There were others, all of the same nature. Infinite desert, corpses, rocks . . . No palm trees or minarets, as in the movies. Just death. Other photos showed British officers in safari jackets and khaki shorts, smiling, cigarettes in their mouths. One photo showed two German prisoners from the Afrika Korps looking frightened and desperate.

He found an old accounts book, filled in in a perfect calligraphic hand. A tattered score of a piece by Ravel. Yellow and red wine labels with a coat of arms that resembled that of the Vatican. Old newspapers from the twenties. An elementary school report card with the coat of arms of the House of Savoy . . . The funny pages from some American newspapers. Propaganda postcards with the face of the Duce and famous slogans: Believe, Obey, Fight . . . *Boia chi molla* ('Cowards are Murderers').

He picked up a book that brought tears to his eyes: a pocket edition for soldiers of the *Human Comedy* by Saroyan, in English. He had read it many years earlier, right after the war, and could still remember a few of the scenes that had moved him deeply. He wanted to read it again and so slipped it into the pocket of his overcoat.

He found the odes of Catullus, in Latin, untranslated, but full of annotations in pencil done by someone with minute, perfect handwriting. There was also *The Golden Ass*, *Satyricon*, *De bello Gallico* and other classics of antiquity . . .

He continued searching through the trunk with great respect, knowing full well that he was violating the intimacy of someone no longer of this world. A harmonica lay in an old blue velvet case. He picked it up and tried to play it. An awkward sound came out of it, confirming his hunch that such a simple-looking instrument was not at all easy to play.

At the bottom of the trunk, hidden under a pile of old postcards, was a small notebook, wrapped in a piece of cloth that seemed to be from a military shirt. On the cover was a name: *Lieutenant James Jenkins*. He looked through it carefully. At the top of the first page was a date: *7 September 1943*, two days before the boats landed at Salerno. It was a war diary, written in a careful hand – angular, almost decorative. The officer had not written every single day, and sometimes there was a gap of one or two weeks between entries.

Within the pages of the diary was a letter folded in four, without an envelope. *Chelmsford, 2 October 1943. James, dear, my love, I dream about you every night* . . . He stopped reading, out of respect, but let himself read the last line . . . *I love you I love you I love you* . . . *God bless you* . . . *Constance.*

He put the letter back and continued to look through the diary. He knew English rather well and it wasn't hard for him to understand. Jenkins wrote about Naples, Cassino, the Gothic Line. Bombings, aircraft shot down, friends killed, towns freed. He often hinted at his state of mind. Jenkins had had his own Grand Tour up the Italian peninsula, from south to north. The last page of writing was three-quarters of the way through the diary. *Florence, 3 August 1944* . . . the last sentence was dramatic . . . *Constance, my love, I'm dying* . . . *I wish I could fall asleep and wake up in your arms* . . . Eight days later Florence was liberated, but apparently James Jenkins hadn't made it. And Constance? Arcieri felt his heart break with sadness at the thought that she had never read her James's last words. How many years would it have been now? Had she stayed true to her fiancé's memory? Or had she married someone else?

Bordelli parked in Viale Don Minzone, just outside Claretta's building, and got out of the car to walk her to the door. They'd had a bit to drink and were smiling. After a moment's hesitation, they kissed, this time embracing as well. A long, passionate kiss, filled with desire. When their mouths parted, she looked him in the eye.

'Would you like to come upstairs for a minute?' she said breathlessly.

'You don't think that might seem improper?' asked Bordelli, holding her in his arms.

'At the moment I'm not thinking at all . . .' she whispered. And she gently freed herself from his embrace to search for the keys in her handbag. She unlocked the door, seeming frantic and lost, then smiled as she invited him inside.

They climbed the stairs to the third floor in silence, and when they entered the apartment Claretta didn't bother trying to be quiet as she shut the door behind them. The staircase leading to the floor above disappeared in the darkness. The silence was total.

'Can I get you something to drink?' Claretta asked almost as breathlessly as before, as Bordelli was helping her off with her coat.

'Thank you, that would be lovely.'

The inspector removed his overcoat, laid it down on top of Claretta's and followed her down the corridor, pleasantly enjoying the scent of her perfume. They did not go into the sitting room Bordelli already knew, but continued on down the hall. Claretta opened the last door at the far end and turned on the light. A rather pleasant room, not too big, furnished somewhat differently from the rest of the house, with modern pieces of very high quality.

'Please sit down . . . I'll be right back . . .' Claretta whispered before fluttering away. The clicking of her heels faded into the distance. The inspector sank into a soft, navy-blue sofa, stretching his legs as he looked around . . . A rather originally shaped bookcase with several shelves lined with yellow-spined mystery novels of the Gialli Mondadori imprint, a low, crystal-topped coffee table, fanciful lamps, a record-playing console, a large wooden radio, a luxury television set, a small walnut cabinet, and a fine carpet covering most of the pink-marble floor . . . Only two paintings hung from the wall: an abstract work and a portrait in oils of a young girl holding a baby girl by the hand, both seated on a sofa from another age. To judge by the resemblance, the younger girl was certainly Claretta, and the other must have been her sister. The only antique in the room was a pendulum clock attached to the wall and ticking loudly.

Claretta returned a few minutes later, apologising for having left him alone. She'd put on a small aviator-blue dress a little shorter than the last one, highlighting her beautiful legs. Her hair was held back with a clip, and she'd applied fresh lipstick to her lips.

'What can I get for you? Some vermouth? A China?'[35]

'You wouldn't by any chance have more of that port your mother had me taste?'

'Oh, of course . . .'

'It's the best thing I've ever tasted,' said Bordelli, genuinely pleased to be able to enjoy a little more of the nectar. Claretta went and opened the little walnut cabinet, the inside of whose doors were lined with tiny rectangular mirrors; then, without bothering to reclose the doors, she returned with a nearly full bottle of Osborne. She filled two small glasses and remained standing.

'A little music?'

'Perhaps something soft . . .'

'Yes, of course . . .' she said, going over to the record player, light as a butterfly.

Turning it on, she placed a disc on the turntable, and the music began playing at very low volume. After the first notes Bordelli recognised Chopin and promptly sank into a pleasant melancholia. Claretta excused herself again and rushed out of the room. She was so joyous and excited that her childish frivolity was contagious. Bordelli had trouble imagining how, scarcely two weeks earlier, she could have . . . Or maybe she was just good at faking it, playing the silly girl, and was in reality racked with feelings of guilt . . . Or . . . Perhaps . . . But he couldn't think of any other hypotheses . . . Barely a minute later Claretta reappeared, holding a still-virgin bottle of Osborne, cork and seal still intact.

'This is for you,' she said, setting it down on the crystal table.

'Oh my, I'm not sure I'm worthy of it . . .'

'Consider it my Christmas present.'

She was as sparkly as a little girl awaiting a pre-announced surprise. Bordelli took the bottle and looked at Claretta with gratitude.

'Thank you ever so much . . . But who knows whether your mother would approve . . . I noticed she's very fond of the stuff . . .'

'Oh, we've got dozens of bottles,' said Claretta, sitting down on the sofa as far as possible from her guest.

'But is it true that they were hidden inside a wall during the war?'

'Yes, of course, ninety-nine bottles. Right after the Armistice, Mamma had them walled up along with a few paintings and family jewels. If she hadn't, the Germans would have taken it all away.'

'A toast to the stonemasons, then,' said Bordelli.

'Cheers,' Claretta twittered.

'Cheers . . .'

They clinked glasses and took a sip. If God liked to drink, thought Bordelli, then His cellar must be full of Osborne. Claretta's eyes were luminous and flashing, as she huddled more and more into her corner of the sofa. Chopin meanwhile delved farther and farther into the depths of the human soul with the lightness of a dragonfly, taking care of the two of them in the process.

'Don't you think the light's a bit too bright?' asked Claretta, getting up again. She couldn't hold still for an instant. Setting down a small white porcelain candlestick on the table, she lit all three candles and turned off the electric light.

'You're right. It's so much nicer this way . . .' said the inspector.

Finding her way through the dimness, she returned to her corner of the sofa, took off her shoes, and folded her delicate feet under her bottom, uncovering in the process far more than just her knees . . . Osborne was telling them that life could be beautiful, the candles created the illusion of being outside of time, and Chopin had by now entered their thoughts . . . It was a magical moment, one that seemed to partake of dreams. Claretta held out her little glass for a refill, which she then knocked back in a single gulp as though committing an act of disobedience.

'You'll never believe me, but the *Nocturnes* always put me in a good mood,' she said, undoing her hair. It was the first time Bordelli had seen her with her hair loose, and she looked even more beautiful to him.

'I'm sure Chopin would be very pleased.'

'Oh, if he were ever to come back to life I'm sure I would fall hopelessly in love with him.'

'He's buried in Paris, if I'm not mistaken.'

'At Père Lachaise . . . I once spent a whole afternoon reading in front of his grave . . .'

They'd kissed three times and were now pleasantly chatting as though nothing were happening. One more kiss would open the floodgates, and they both knew it. Bordelli was taking his time. He felt a little guilty, knowing that behind all his gallantry lay an ulterior motive. But by now it was too late to pull back, and on top of that he really did want to keep going. Every so often Claretta let out a sigh, nibbling her lips, as though before leaping into the void she needed still to think about it a little. Her hesitations didn't last very long, however . . . All at once, without saying a word, she came over to Bordelli and climbed on top of him, straddling his thighs. She took his face into her hands.

'Don't you like me anymore?'

'I thought you were in love with Chopin . . .'

At such a moment, the formalities merely added to the excitement . . . After a few more kisses they found themselves lying in each other's arms on the sofa, as their clothes began falling onto the carpet . . . Bordelli held her close, as if wanting to protect her from the wickedness of the world . . . Claretta let herself be conquered little by little, with a bit of gentle shilly-shallying, and every so often whispered a few obscene words . . .

At that very moment Rosa was at a girlfriend's house in Santo Spirito, on the top floor of an old palazzo. They were enjoying a drink of *nocino* and relaxing on the sofa, remembering the days when they used to work together in the villa on the Lungarno del Tempio. They laughed and laughed, recalling some of their more ridiculous customers, but also sharing more touching memories as well.

Botta had just finished making love to his new lady-friend, who perhaps was the most beautiful woman he had ever had. She was the daughter of a vegetable vendor who had a stall at the San Lorenzo market. He had spread a map of Europe out on their bed and was showing Anita exactly where he had been 'on holiday', and she was smiling . . . Had Ennio found the woman of his dreams?

Piras was already in bed. He had a book in his hands but couldn't follow what he was reading. He was thinking about the phone call he had made a few hours earlier from the Bonarcado bar to his lovely Sicilian girlfriend. He had tried to convince Sonia to come to Sardinia to spend New Year's Eve with him, but she wanted to spend more time with her parents, whom she had seen so little in the recent past.

Diotivede was snoozing in front of the telly, which at that moment was relaying information about the usual marches against the war in Vietnam, while his wife, sitting at a table, wrote a letter to Gisella, a childhood friend who had married an American and lived in Boston.

High in the hills of Mezzomonte, Dante the insomniac was pacing up and down the length of his underground laboratory in a spectral half-light, accompanied by puffs of smoke from his cigar. He was thinking about a piece of machinery he had been trying to build for a long time now: a machine to peel apples. Another part of his mind was busy trying to remember a nursery rhyme his mother had taught him when he was small, and he gradually remembered the words. But in all truth he was also thinking about some passages in Aristotle's *Poetics*.

They were still het up and panting, skin glistening with sweat in the wan light of the candles, Claretta turned towards the back of the sofa with her eyes closed. Bordelli was inside her, stuck to her like an adhesive bandage and caressing her belly. Every so often he would reach down to the hair on her mons veneris, and Claretta would twitter softly. It could have been the start of a beautiful love affair.

'I feel so good . . .' she murmured.

'Me too,' Bordelli said into her ear, feeling a twist in his gut at the thought that sooner or later he would have to resume the role of police detective. But he hadn't lied; he really did feel good. He wished he could prolong that moment forever, to keep it all from spoiling.

'I didn't expect you to be so sweet,' said Claretta. The inspector kissed her shoulder, smelling her true scent, which had made its way through the curtain of perfume. It was a nice scent, of young flesh. She was twisting a lock of hair around a finger, then letting it go, then starting over again.

'May I ask you an impertinent question?'

'I'll take the risk,' said Bordelli, thinking of the moment in which he would break the spell with just a few words. Claretta started rubbing against him.

'When was the last time you went to bed with a woman?'

'A few months ago.'

'Was she beautiful?'

'Very beautiful,' said the inspector, thinking of the pleasurable moments he'd spent with Adele.

'Were you together for a long time?'

'Just one night.'

'Oh! So why didn't it work out?'

'I'm afraid you'd have to ask her,' he whispered into her hair.

'Was she good in bed?'

'Those are things one doesn't talk about.'

'Oh, go on . . . Why are you so mean?' Claretta kept moving like a wave, inviting him to start all over again. Bordelli submitted to her will.

It was even better than the first time, and wilder.

Afterwards, they were sweaty, exhausted, and found themselves in the exact same position as before, stuck together like two sardines. They lay there in silence, immersed in a kind of half-sleep, and the rhythmical sound of the pendulum clock created a feeling of peace in the room. Bordelli would gladly have let himself sink into sleep, arms around Claretta's warm body . . .

Tick . . .

Tock . . .

Tick . . .

Tock . . .

Tick . . .

Tock . . .

'Now can you tell me what you're thinking?' she whispered, squeezing his hand, which was covering one of her breasts.

'I was thinking about fate,' said Bordelli, taking the opportunity to bring them one step closer to the final act.

'You mean . . . us?'

'If you . . .' He stopped, feeling like a cad. First he takes her to bed, and now . . .

'If I what?' Claretta whispered sweetly, consumed with curiosity. She had no idea what was about to come crashing down on her.

'If you hadn't killed your brother-in-law, we would never have met,' said Bordelli, as though saying the most obvious thing in the world.

She didn't move, and indeed seemed to have stopped breathing. All at once she started shaking with little starts, and at first the inspector couldn't tell whether she was laughing or crying. Then, after an isolated sob, barely suppressed, Claretta abandoned herself to sustained, bitter weeping, silent and desperate.

'You didn't mean to do it, am I right?' said Bordelli, to soften the blow.

She shook her head 'no', without ceasing her tears. With that gesture, she had as good as confessed to running Antonio through with the foil. Bordelli squeezed her tight and kissed her hair, waiting for the crying to stop.

Driving along the Imprunetana, he opened the vent window and lit his third cigarette of the day, overwhelmed by deep sadness. The bottle of Osborne was on the passenger seat; it represented the entire ordeal perfectly. Every so often he glanced up at the stars, remembering when he and Claretta had looked at them together.

It wasn't terribly late, just past one, but the past few hours had been a veritable odyssey. Too much had happened in too brief a span of time. He needed to make sense of everything. He had fallen for the woman he had just had arrested. He could still smell her on him, could still taste her lipstick on his lips. He couldn't get her confession out of his mind. It was all so terribly sad, devastating really, almost surreal. He would never forget those moments for as long as he lived . . .

Once Claretta stopped crying she delicately freed herself from his embrace and shifted her position so that she was huddled in the corner of the settee, arms around her knees. He got to his feet, put on his shorts, and sat back down at the other end of the little sofa. After filling their glasses with Osborne, Bordelli lit two cigarettes and passed one to Claretta. They sat next to each other: she nude, he in shorts, both smoking voraciously. Claretta leaned forward to reach her glass, unconcerned about covering herself. She emptied the glass in one go and put it back on the table. Even though it was warm in the room, she had goose bumps. Her expression was sad but still revealed something of the pleasure she had experienced not long before. In fact, her skin looked golden in the candlelight. Her mother and Fidalma were fast asleep upstairs, unaware of what was taking place on the floor below.

'Antonio was cruel to me . . .' Claretta started, with no hint of bitterness. She just wanted to tell him the truth, nothing but the truth. It had all happened rather as he had imagined . . .

Antonio had not only been unkind to Claretta, he had been downright wicked. Claretta, meanwhile, had been in love with him ever since she was a girl. When her sister died, she dreamed of becoming his wife. Antonio managed to keep her at bay for some time, mostly out of decency, but ultimately she managed to find her way into his bed, hoping for a love affair and then marriage. But things did not go as planned. Antonio kept her waiting and would use her for his own pleasure, secretly, like a clandestine mistress. Then he would ignore her. Basically, he called her over when it suited him. This situation came about gradually, after many tears and arguments, but ultimately she resigned herself to waiting for those rare moments when he would deign to invite her into his bed. She even put up with hearing about his amorous adventures, pretending not to suffer. What else could she do? She knew she was behaving like a slave but she truly hoped that one day he would realise that he loved her and that he wanted her by his side, always. It was an illusion, but she didn't know it at the time. Antonio had many lovers and periodically went out with high-class prostitutes. But she always waited her turn, happy to hold him in her arms when she could.

They spoke often on the telephone, but it was always she who called. One day he told her he was in love with a beautiful young woman and had never been happier. Antonio had often said such things in the past about other women, but this time she intuited that the situation was different. She felt lost and dejected. She stopped phoning him, vainly hoping that he would miss her and take the initiative himself. After three long weeks of silence she couldn't take it anymore, and she called him, begging for a meeting. He had the gall to say that he didn't see why they should meet. She cried and implored him to give her at least five minutes of his time. Antonio, somewhat annoyed, told her not to behave like a child . . . Why should they see each other? She didn't want to believe she had lost him forever, and that night she did nothing but cry.

Once, on the phone, she made a terrible scene and Antonio hung up on her. She tried to call back but the phone just rang and rang. She rushed over to the villa in desperation, but he wouldn't open the door for her. She continued to ring him every day, without ever getting an answer.

Then came that terrible Tuesday. The whole day she had done nothing but imagine the two lovebirds rolling around in bed together. She couldn't bear it anymore. Antonio was happy, but she wanted to die. She felt diminished, scorned. She understood that her pain had to do more with humiliation than with love, but at that precise moment she was certain that she was the most loving woman in the world. She had been abandoned, thrown away. She felt ugly, old, and couldn't stand to look at herself in the mirror. Antonio's hussy was a goddess but she felt as insignificant as a clam. No man would ever desire her again . . . She had never got married so that she could remain available for Antonio, and now he had thrown her away like a potato peel. How had this happened? Why was God so cruel? At some point past midnight, at the height of her desperation, she felt a twinge of pride. Enough whining. She wouldn't be that kind of woman. She put on a provocative outfit, made herself up with care, and went to see him. Driving there, she prayed to the Madonna that he would be at home and that she could see him. She wanted to look him in the eye one last time, tell him exactly what she thought, and then she would disappear from his life forever. When she got to the villa she rang the bell gently, so he wouldn't know how upset she was . . .

She waited for a long time, her legs trembling. When Antonio answered the intercom, she thanked the Madonna and felt a wave of warmth run through her body. She told him that something terrible had happened and that they absolutely needed to talk. He sighed as if he knew it was a lie but let her in just the same. He opened the door coldly, dressed in his bathrobe and slippers. He told her that he was very tired and was about to go to bed. She ran upstairs and rushed into his room, ready to face her rival. She found the bed empty, but just being in the bedroom hurt her terribly. She was reminded of the unforgettable nights she had spent in Antonio's arms, and now, instead, some stupid hussy . . . Why couldn't things go back to the way they used to be?

Weeping, she followed Antonio upstairs to his study. He

asked her ironically what she had to tell him that was so important. She couldn't stop crying and blowing her nose. Antonio sighed impatiently, eager to be alone again. Seeing that she wasn't saying anything, he said he had something to tell her . . . He wanted her to leave him alone. How could he get that through to her? He was in love with an amazing woman, he said, a woman with a noble soul and with whom he had a deep affinity. He had never felt this way before, and he couldn't wait to marry her.

Upon hearing these words, she felt utterly devastated and humiliated. As soon as she recovered her voice she asked him to keep her in a corner in his heart, not to abandon her, to let her sleep with him once in a while, as they had done in the past. Antonio shook his head . . . He seemed somewhat annoyed but couldn't entirely hide his masculine smugness at having a besotted woman beg for his attention. He kept telling her that she had to resign herself, that he didn't need certain things anymore . . . She broke down in tears and threatened to kill herself, and he just laughed. He didn't take her seriously; he treated her like a child. She opened the window and leaned out, hoping to scare him. But it didn't work. Antonio didn't move a muscle. Go ahead and jump, he had said. God, how humiliating! She wanted to throw herself into the emptiness just so he would feel guilty for the rest of his life! It was a desperate and childish thought, because she knew she would never do it. She felt dead inside, but didn't want to die. The idea of falling into nothingness terrified her. The worst part was that Antonio knew it better than she did. He knew she would never have the courage to jump. She bit her lip until it bled, disheartened, then stepped away from the window but left it open. She needed air. She leaned against the wall, her face in her hands. Somehow she had ended up in a nightmare and didn't know how to get out of it. Suddenly, he came up to her with a smile, took her in his arms, and kissed her. She knew that the kiss was fake, that Antonio was only trying to calm her down to get her to leave, but she couldn't push him away. She wanted to keep kissing him, again and again; she wanted more . . . And this, too, was humiliating. By now she had lost every trace of dignity. She would even have paid him to take her to bed, to have him treat her harshly . . . She became so despondent that being humiliated only increased her desire. Let me be your whore, she whispered to him, unbuttoning her shirt. He started laughing and told her not to be ridiculous . . . Now calm down, he said, patting her head like a puppy's. It was mortifying: she would rather have been slapped. She stood there, bra exposed, just waiting for another kiss . . .

Antonio shivered, walked over to the window and closed it, but then Claretta rushed over and opened it again, begging him to leave it as it was. The cool air gave her some relief, she said, but the truth was that when it was closed it only added to her sense of anguish. She buttoned her blouse, still whimpering. She didn't know how to get out of the prison in which she found herself. Now everything seemed black; she had not even the faintest ray of hope, and she no longer felt any desire at all. At a certain point, Antonio raised her face towards his so that she had to look him in the eye. He started by saying that he loved her very much and went on to say that she was one of the most important women in his life, and that he had enjoyed some unforgettable moments with her. Smiling, he called her 'my pretty sister-in-law'. She saw compassion and even disdain in his eyes. She imagined a catalogue of women, with her picture on one of the last pages . . .

Suddenly she felt a deep sense of embarrassment and shame and this tiny hint of pride gave her the strength to react. She broke out in tears again but pushed him away, calling him a liar and a monster . . . He had used her like a rag to clean the toilets . . . he had humiliated her . . . He wasn't worthy of her or her sister. He was a deceitful man, a horrible egotist, a womaniser who couldn't see past his nose . . . She was trying hard to offend and wound him, but he seemed untouchable . . . And so she went on . . . What do you think? That you make women happy? No! Not at all! On top of everything he was lousy in bed and didn't know how to satisfy a woman . . . He thought he was so fascinating, but really he was just a caveman . . . she never wanted to have anything to do with the likes of him ever again . . . Enough! She would never see him again! Never! She would leave and never come back! But not without her sister's jewels. She couldn't stand the idea of Carla's jewels being in the hands of such a disgusting man, she said, such a vulgar, uncouth man. He never even deserved to marry a woman like her . . .

At the end of her tirade she was out of breath, shaking and afraid, and she was expecting a good slap on the face. But Antonio didn't even blink. He went to the safe and pulled out the jewel box. He laid it on the desk, opened it, and said coldly that she could take anything she wanted. She didn't move. She was still shocked by everything she had said. Antonio picked out the beautiful ring that he had given Carla before their wedding and held it up in the air. This is the most precious object I have, he said, and in my will I left it to you, but you can have it now, if you want – just let me live in peace. Claretta felt confused and lost. Her eyes were so full of tears she couldn't see straight anymore. Antonio clenched his jaws, fuming. He was fed up. He couldn't stand seeing her cry anymore . . . All you can do is cry, like a spoilt child . . . I love a woman, and I will marry her whatever it takes, and there's nothing you can do but accept it . . . What do you think? That you can force someone to love you? Not even the stupidest woman alive would try to do that. Why don't you just grow up? You can't always get what you want! It takes two for there to be real love . . . Find a man and get married, start a family. After all, you're not a little girl anymore . . .

She felt like a piece of chewing gum that had been spat out. In a fit of rage she grabbed the antique foil from where it hung on the wall. This upset Antonio deeply; he didn't like people touching his things. It all happened very quickly. With a proprietary air he lunged at her to get it back. And the very moment she raised the unprotected foil to keep him at bay, he tripped on the carpet and fell forward, his chest falling straight onto the tip of the foil . . . And there it was . . . She hadn't wanted to kill him, and she never would have been able to. It had been an accident, a cruel joke of fate . . . If only she had never gone to the villa! She would be walking proud now! Instead she had followed her own weakness and stupidity and created a disaster that couldn't be fixed . . . When she saw Antonio fall to the ground with the foil between his ribs, she felt like dying. It was terrible to hear him take his last breaths, the sound of the death rattle, but at least it was fast. After a final shudder, Antonio stopped moving. A moment earlier he had looked her in the eye and spoken to her. Now he was dead. It was hard to believe. She had to sit down in order not to faint. She was terrified. No one would ever believe that it had been an accident, that she hadn't meant to kill him. The idea of ending up in prison frightened her to death. It would be better to die, she said to herself, thinking again about throwing herself out the window.

Little by little she regained a spark of lucidity. She tried to concentrate and not let herself be overwhelmed by fear. Calm, she had to stay calm. First of all she had to save herself, then she would take care of the rest. Recalling certain detective novels she had read, she took her handkerchief from her purse and started to wipe down everything she had touched. The worst moment was when she cleaned the handle of the foil, which was still sticking out of his chest. My God, what had she done? But prison, no. Never. She couldn't even imagine it. To make it look like a robbery she grabbed the jewel box and ran out of the villa, remembering to clean the handle of the door as she left. While she was getting into her car she remembered that she had left the window open as if it was the most normal thing in the world, but then it occurred to her that it was probably for the best: the smell of her perfume would vanish.

She got home in a terrible state. She didn't see anyone on the staircase of her building on her way back in, nor had she seen anyone when she was leaving. She shut herself in her room and hid the jewel box in the bottom drawer of her wardrobe, under her slips. Her alarm clock said forty minutes past two. When she left for Antonio's house, at about twenty to one, her mother and Fidalma had already been in bed for some time. In short, no one had seen her go out or come back. It was as if she had never left the house. She was safe. She cried for half the night and then slept. The next morning she woke up early, feeling somewhat better than the night before. She wasn't a murderess – but who would believe her? She had to get ready for a difficult day ahead. In a few hours someone would call her to tell her about Antonio's death and she had to be ready to feign complete surprise . . . She didn't want to be sent off to jail. She couldn't possibly . . . She wasn't a murderess, she kept repeating to herself. She would have done anything to save herself. To confuse things she even insinuated that Oberto had killed Antonio and now she was embarrassed about that. . . But whatever happened, she wouldn't let herself be unfairly convicted. . .. Yes, she had behaved terribly, but it was just because she didn't want to end up in prison . . .

'I don't expect you to believe me . . .' Claretta said, with a smile that wasn't really a smile. She seemed somewhat relieved, as if a weight had been lifted from her heart. She no longer seemed like a silly woman who just wanted to flirt with men, and this made her all the more fascinating. In the candlelight her face was beautiful.

Bordelli moved closer to her, put his arm around her shoulder, and pulled her gently close to him. Claretta let herself be embraced and rested her head on his chest. He stroked her hair.

'I believe you,' he said. This would be her last half-hour of freedom, he thought to himself. *Her* Antonio was not as immaculate as others made him out to be. Bordelli was certain that she was being honest; he would have bet on it. Ever since childhood, he had had a sort of sixth sense, and could always tell whether a person was lying.

'Will you let me go?' she whispered, without moving.

'Please don't ask me to do that.' He continued to run his fingers through her hair.

'Will they give me life in prison?'

'You have to tell the judge what you told me. When they call me in as a witness I will do everything I can to confirm that it was an accident, even if I have to lie.'

'Why would you do that?'

'Because I feel that you are telling the truth.'

'You trust me that much?'

'I trust my intuition.'

'That's more or less the same thing, isn't it?'

'I will try and convince the court of your good faith. A good lawyer can help you get manslaughter, or in the worst-case scenario, voluntary manslaughter. With good behaviour, you could be out in a few years. And with a little luck, you might even get a suspended sentence.'

For a couple that had just made love, this was truly an unusual conversation.

'Poor Antonio . . . What happened was terrible but I have to admit that his death has given me a sense of freedom.'

'Don't say that to the judge.'

'I wasn't in love with him, I was obsessed.'

'You also mustn't say anything about what happened between us: my testimony would mean next to nothing.'

'Don't worry, I'm used to having sex on the sly . . .' she said lovingly and in a sweet voice. He kissed her hair.

'And until the final sentence is pronounced I won't be able to come and see you in prison, for the same reason.'

'I understand . . .'

'Afterwards, though, it won't be a problem.'

'Would you really come and see me?'

'Yes . . .'

'Can I ask you a question?'

'Of course.'

'Did you sleep with me just to get me to confess?'

'Don't be ridiculous . . .'

'I've just had the most beautiful night of my life and soon I shall have the worst,' Claretta whispered with a hint of bitterness.

'It won't be as bad as you think,' he replied, without believing what he was saying.

'Shall we go?'

'Yes, let's . . .'

They got dressed in silence, without looking at each other. They were like two ghosts, getting ready to travel to the other side. The candles had burnt all the way down, and every so often they spluttered, their flickering flames making the shadows in the room dance.

'Don't forget that,' Claretta had said, indicating the bottle of Osborne.

'Thank you . . .' Bordelli picked up the bottle with false bonhomie.

'At least that way you will be forced to think of me.' Claretta managed to smile and he admired her for that. He accompanied her upstairs to help her put some clothes and other personal things in a suitcase, the two old ladies sleeping beatifically in their beds.

'Take the jewels,' she said, opening the bottom drawer of her wardrobe, and handing Bordelli the mother-of-pearl case with the initials in silver. He didn't even open it.

In the doorway they kissed tenderly and held each other tight. Then they started downstairs without a word. They got into the car and Bordelli drove to headquarters, the rumble of the Beetle's engine diffusing a sense of sadness. They entered through a back door to avoid being seen by the journalist for *La Nazione*, who was snoozing on a bench in the hallway, waiting for fresh news. Bordelli handed Claretta and the jewels over to the junior detective on duty, Chiodi, a young, recently arrived Calabrian. Bordelli took him aside and explained that the lady needed to sign a confession.

'Treat her with kid gloves . . . no handcuffs . . .'

'Yes, sir, Inspector,' Chiodi replied, standing almost at attention.

'You can tell the journalist once she has already been taken away . . . and be sure to help her with her suitcase . . .'

'Not to worry, sir.'

'Goodnight.'

Before leaving, he looked over at Claretta one last time. She gave him a wink.

He got home with his morale in tatters, still thinking about the day he'd just left behind. And when the others found out – Antonio's sister, his sons and friends – how hard was it going to be on them? And how would Oberto take it?

He went and put the Osborne away on a shelf in the broom closet, imagining he would open it when Claretta regained her freedom . . . He would invite her out to dinner, and perhaps they would resume the conversation they'd been forced to suspend . . .

The kitchen had never looked so clean. There was nothing in the sink to wash. On the table he found another note from the colonel . . . *Last night I did some exploring in your cellars and became a kid again. Today the telephone rang a great many times, until late. Goodnight . . .*

He tossed the note onto the embers in the fireplace, and a few seconds later the paper caught fire. A single burst, and then ash. Exactly like what he'd just been through. A burst of flame, then ash . . . *Dreams born in the morning, dead in the evening.*

He climbed the stairs noiselessly and noticed that the stove had already been filled. From the back of the hallway came the placid sound of the colonel snoring. Bordelli would tell him about Claretta in the morning, taking care to omit what had happened on the sofa.

Moments later he lay down in bed and turned off the light. He felt drained, but the Sandman was late in arriving. As he turned under the covers he thought he smelled Claretta's scent, the real one, the smell of her skin . . . *For my love to die like that, on a night of frost, was never my wish . . .*

He could hardly wait to sink into the dream world, but it wasn't coming easily, and he remembered again the remedy he'd used as a boy . . . He would tell himself a story in his mind, usually something he made up then and there . . . *A little boy was walking through the woods one night, when suddenly before him appeared an old hag with a gnarly nose* . . . Or he would start compiling lists of whatever subject came to mind . . . The names of his schoolmates, the roads he knew, or every kind of pudding he loved . . . At other times he would sing himself a song in his head, inserting the lyrics he was able to remember . . . *Sing a song of sixpence, a pocket full of rye, four and twenty blackbirds baked in a pie* . . .

While growing up he'd kept on using the same remedy, but for his stories he would borrow things from the novels of Salgari and Verne that he'd read and reread so many times . . . And then, little by little, the songs, too, began to change . . . *Il fiume scorre lento, /frusciando sotto i ponti,/la luna splende in cielo,/dorme tutta la città* . . .[36] But what really changed were the lists to memorise . . . Names of comrades who'd died in the war, women he'd loved, killers he'd arrested . . .

That evening he started cataloguing all the times he'd eluded death by a hair's breadth during the war . . . The German sniper who just missed him, grazing the cheek of one of his mates instead . . . The mortar shell that one morning laid to waste a small tree under which the previous evening he had almost decided to lie down to sleep . . . The red-hot shrapnel that punctured the wall of the submarine and passed a quarter-inch from his head . . . The iron cudgel that one night, shortly after the Armistice, in the centre of Brindisi, was coming straight for his head but which he'd managed to dodge, taking the blow in the shoulder instead . . . The time an SS officer . . .

At last he fell asleep, into troubled dreams in which he never stopped shooting his gun . . .

At the first ring of the telephone, he woke up with a start, scrambling madly for his machine gun, as he'd always done during the war. He wrenched himself painfully from sleep, heart racing. The phone was still ringing violently, piercing his ears. He turned on the light and looked at the clock. Quarter to three. Who could it be, in the middle of the night like that? The same person who'd been calling the past two days? He sat up in bed and picked up the receiver.

'Yes . . . ?'

'Franco?' said a very deep voice.

'Who is this?'

'Carnera . . .' said Agostinelli, using his *nom de guerre*.

'What's going on? Are you the one who's been trying to get me for the past two days?'

'No, that wasn't me . . . But now listen carefully, and don't ask me any questions . . . Concerning that person I mentioned to you, the one I asked you to look for . . . Don't ask me why, but I don't see the matter in the same way as before . . . Everything's been changing here, and I don't like it one bit . . . That man is in danger . . . Perhaps you could find out where he's been hiding . . . If you know what I mean . . . You must tell him to leave at once . . . His general whereabouts have been discovered . . . They're already looking for him . . . Over and out.'

Agostinelli hung up without saying goodbye, and Bordelli tried to regain his bearings . . . So it was indeed someone from Special Services who was looking for Arcieri . . . For what? And they'd really managed to track him down? And they already knew he was hiding out at his house? He heard a sound and turned round. The colonel was in the doorway, in slippers, and in trousers so oversized he had to hold them up with one hand.

'It was for me, wasn't it?'

'Yes . . .'

'Immediate departure?'

'That's what they advised.'

'Could you lend me a suitcase?'

'I should have some kind of travel bag somewhere.'

'It'll only take a second . . .' said Arcieri, disappearing down the hall.

The inspector got dressed as quickly as he could, staggering with fatigue, and went and grabbed a bag from above the armoire. As the colonel was gathering together his few possessions, Bordelli went quickly from room to room and peered out through the slats in the shutters. All looked calm. He hadn't quite grasped whether 'they' already knew Arcieri was hiding out at his house, or were simply searching the Impruneta area. He helped the colonel pack his bag, and then they went downstairs to the light of a torch. Bordelli looked out of the kitchen window, but could barely see beyond the threshing floor. Past the cypresses was total darkness.

'Don't forget to take some food,' he said, opening the refrigerator.

'Please don't bother . . .' said Arcieri, looking around sadly, like someone saying goodbye to a cherished place to which he would never return. Bordelli put a bag of food and a bottle of water in the colonel's bag, then added some Balzini wine.

'It's a little heavy, but it'll be worth it,' he said, trying to smile.

'Thank you . . . I guess I'm ready . . .'

'Let's go.'

Bordelli took the pistol from above the hutch and released the safety. A moment later they were outside and got into the Beetle without a word, peering into the darkness. Bordelli set out slowly on the unpaved route in the direction of Il Ferrone, constantly checking the rear-view mirror. There wasn't a breath of wind, and the sky looked like the black bottom of a lake scattered with diamonds. It was a good night for escaping.

'Who was that on the phone?' asked Arcieri.

'Admiral Agostinelli . . .' And he told him about the ever so brief phone call, trying to remember the exact words.

'It was bound to happen sooner or later,' the colonel commented.

'I'd like to know just how they managed it.'

'It's probably my fault . . .'

'How's that?'

'It's no longer important,' said Arcieri, thinking of his risky descent into Florence to talk to his friend Serenella. Bordelli remained curious, but it was not the moment for such discussions. At the bottom of the hill into Il Ferrone, he turned right, and a kilometre later he took a left onto a small dirt road that led to Mercatale. While deciding on a plan of action, he wanted to avoid the main roads as much as possible. There seemed to be nobody about, and the darkness on either side of the path was more total than in a cave.

'So, what do we do now?' asked Bordelli.

'That's what I'd like to know.'

'You wouldn't want to go back to the Hospice for the Poor?'

'I think it's best if I leave Florence altogether, at least for a while,' the colonel said softly.

'Any idea where you should go?'

'That'll take some thought.'

They racked their brains trying to think what place might be best, and in the end Bordelli suggested they go and talk to Ennio. He would ask him to do him a favour and drive Arcieri somewhere far from Florence in his beautiful Alfa Romeo.

'That seems the least risky, don't you think? If those fine gentlemen of the SID have found out you've been staying with me, they'll also already have my licence-plate number.'

Anyway, he wasn't exactly up to driving for very long that night; he was so tired he might fall asleep at the wheel.

'Sounds good to me, if your friend is willing,' said the colonel, who hadn't yet thought of anywhere to go.

'Let's hope he's at home.'

As they were leaving the Luiano farms behind them, Bordelli noticed a car's headlights in the rear-view mirror and, pistol in hand, slowed down to let it pass. It was a Fiat 600 spewing a lot of smoke, with four youths inside.

At the top of the climb he turned in the direction of San Casciano and suggested they have a smoke. It would be his fourth of the day, but after a day like that, it was only a venial sin. They opened the side vents and lit up.

'I had to arrest Claretta last night,' said Bordelli, sighing. He really felt like talking about her, even if it probably wasn't the right moment.

'I get the impression you're not exactly pleased.'

'No, not really.'

'Did she confess?'

'Yes . . .'

'Jealousy?'

'They'd been quarrelling, but it was an accident . . .'

He briefly recounted Claretta's version of events and felt a pang of anxiety as he saw again her small, naked body huddled on the sofa.

'Do you believe her?'

'I'd bet the house on it,' Bordelli exaggerated.

'Then I believe her too,' said the colonel.

'I'll never have proof, but I feel that she's telling the truth.'

By now Claretta was no doubt already in a cell at Santa Verdiana with who knew how many other unlucky women. Would she make friends with her new companions in misfortune, or would she close up like a hedgehog? He was wondering how she would feel, being unable to brush her teeth in her own clean little sink, in her own scented bathroom, in her luxurious apartment.

'She'll need a good lawyer,' said Arcieri, who had already embraced Claretta's cause.

'She can certainly afford one.'

'If she gets manslaughter she won't even go to prison.'

'That's what I'm hoping,' said the inspector.

Poor Migliorini. He certainly didn't deserve such an end . . . But Claretta wasn't a murderess. It was more or less as if she'd run over him with her car, perhaps while under the influence . . .

After San Casciano they headed down by way of Via degli Scoperti, and at the intersection turned onto Via di Faltignano. They passed a youth on a scooter singing who knew what song at the top of his lungs. He must have been very happy, or very angry.

'Before I forget . . .' said Arcieri, taking something out of his coat pocket.

'What is it?' asked Bordelli, keeping his eyes on the road.

'I found it at the bottom of a trunk, in your cellar. It's the war diary of a young British officer. His name was James Jenkins.'

'Did you read it?'

'I've read bits here and there. He talks of the Allied advance from Naples to Florence, starting around the Armistice . . . Monte Cassino, the Gustav Line, then north along the Cassia, and up into Tuscany . . . In late July he gets wounded in a firefight with the Germans, in the same woods at Cintoia that we went walking in . . . He must have died just a week before the liberation of Florence . . . There was also a letter from his fiancée between the pages . . .'

And he told him of Constance's loving words, and how she probably never saw her beloved again. Then he put the diary in the glove compartment and closed it.

'You can keep it if you like . . . You found it, after all,' said Bordelli.

'Better not. I wouldn't want it to get lost. The best thing would be to find a way to send it to Constance.'

'You're right . . . I'll see what I can do . . .' said Bordelli, knowing it wouldn't be easy.

'But there is one thing I'd like to keep. It's a British edition of a novel I'd like to reread.'

'What is it?' asked Bordelli.

'*The Human Comedy*.'

'I don't know it. Who's it by?'

'William Saroyan, an Armenian born and raised in the United States.'

'I'll look for it at Seeber's.'

'It's a wonderful novel. He's able to talk of the evils of the world with the utmost delicacy,' said the colonel, with a smile Bordelli couldn't see.

Past Chiesanuova they carried on along the Volterrana, and after a series of bends came down into Galluzzo.

'Ennio? Hey, Ennio!'

Crouching on the pavement of Via del Campuccio, Bordelli knocked on the window of the basement apartment, hoping to find Botta at home. The colonel was lying down on the back seat of the Beetle, parked not far away.

'Ennio, are you there?' he whispered loudly. At last the window opened, and Botta's sleepy face appeared from the shadows of the room.

'Inspector . . . what's going on?'

'You have to do me a favour, Ennio.'

'But it's four o'clock in the morning . . .' Botta said, rubbing his eyes, somewhat bewildered.

'Get dressed and come outside. Hurry,' the inspector said. His eyes glanced over at Ennio's bed, where he saw a mass of dark hair spread out against the pillow.

'That's Anita . . .' Botta said. A delicate foot peeped out from under the covers.

'Is she asleep?'

'She wouldn't wake up even if I slapped her.'

'Maybe you should leave her a note and tell her you don't know when you'll be back.'

'Seriously?'

'Come out as fast as you can.'

'I'm coming.'

'Wait. How much money do you have on you?'

'About forty thousand lire.'

'Bring it . . . Hurry . . .' Bordelli stepped away from the window, glanced up the deserted street and got back in the Beetle.

'He's coming,' Bordelli said to the colonel.

'I'm sorry to be such a bother.'

'You'll pay me back . . .' Bordelli joked. They sat in silence, waiting. Not five minutes later, Botta appeared, all bundled up in a jacket. The inspector got out of the car and walked towards him.

'General Fucilieri is in the car,' he whispered.

'What happened?'

'I can't explain now, I'll tell you another time. I need you to get him out of Florence.'

'Where to?'

'I don't know, he'll tell you. Take him wherever he wants. Do you have petrol in your tank?'

'Not a lot but I can get some on the highway.'

'Don't ask him a lot of questions. He can't say anything.'

'Don't worry, we'll talk about cooking.'

'Have you got your money?'

'Of course . . .' Botta dug into his pocket, pulled out thirty thousand lire and passed them to Bordelli.

'I'll pay you back.'

'I'd better keep ten thousand for the petrol.'

'Where's your car?'

'In Piazza Tasso.'

'I'll wait for you here,' the inspector said. He watched as Botta hurried off and vanished into the darkness of the piazza. He climbed back into the Beetle with a shiver and handed Ennio's money and his own ten thousand lire to the colonel.

'I couldn't scrape together any more than that.'

'I'm forced to accept it, but sooner or later I will return every last lira to you.'

'With interest, of course,' Bordelli said, to lighten the tone. A few minutes later, a red torpedo emerged from the darkness of Piazza Tasso, its engine rumbling softly. Ennio pulled up next to the Beetle and turned off the engine.

'We're all set,' the inspector said. The two men got out of the car. The street was completely silent. Ennio got out of his car, too, and nodded at the general. Bordelli put the suitcase in the boot of the Alfa Romeo and went to say goodbye to the colonel.

'Try to get in touch with me as soon as you can.' They shook hands, but it was as if they were embracing.

'Farewell, Inspector.'

'See you again soon . . .'

'Who knows,' said Arcieri with a smile.

'Be careful.'

'I'll do my best.' He got into the car with Botta and before he could close the door, Bordelli leaned in.

'Ennio, as soon as you get back, call me at home or at the office and invite me to come and play a game of billiards at Fosco's. See you there.'

'Will do.'

'Goodbye, General.'

'Go and get some rest,' Arcieri said, squeezing his arm. Botta turned the key in the ignition, now impatient to leave, and the inspector closed the door. He stood watching as the Alfa Romeo drove off, heart heavy with sadness. As soon as he saw it turn onto Via dei Serragli he got into his own car. First he'd had to say goodbye to Claretta, and now the colonel. It certainly had been a full night.

He headed slowly towards Via del Campuccio feeling utterly dejected. The urge for a cigarette was powerful, but he swore he would resist. When he reached Porta Romana, he turned up towards Poggio Imperiale. He was so tired he wished he could stop on the side of the road to sleep.

Driving along the Imprunetana, he struggled with the emptiness yawning inside him, but it was useless. Every so often he thought he saw an animal cross the road or jump into the grass, but he realised that it was just fatigue. The world of dreams was trying to break into reality, eager to take its place.

When his house came into view at the end of the dirt road, it was a quarter to five in the morning. From far off he thought he saw a mass of white fur lying in front of the house, and he smiled, thinking of Blisk, the white bear . . . Had Fate repented and was now begging forgiveness? Then he realised it was just the reflection from the light above the door, and he sighed in disappointment.

Entering the house, he wondered whether any SID agents had paid him a visit. The door seemed fine, but maybe they were better at opening locks than Botta. He stopped in the kitchen to drink a glass of water. The ashes in the fireplace were still those of the fire that the colonel had built. He wondered where Arcieri would go.

Would he succeed in discovering the truth about that young man's death? Would they ever see each other again?

He went upstairs, filled the pot-bellied stove with wood, and walked through each room, checking the windows. He could make all the noise he wanted now and would never wake anyone up. Everything looked to be in its proper place. He went into his bedroom, took off his clothes, threw them on a chair, and lay down. He barely had time to turn off the light before he fell fast asleep.

Botta's Alfa Romeo was racing along the trunk road, propelled by its hundred horses, and only now and then was forced to pass a lorry. The warm air of the heating system had a faint smell of burning petrol. Arcieri was dozing, lulled by the sound of the engine and the motions of the road, but was unable to turn his conscious mind off altogether. He'd been chatting with Ennio until minutes before, mostly about cooking and cars. Apparently Bordelli had asked Botta not to ask the colonel any questions as to the reasons for his flight. The destination had been chosen a while back. It would take them a few hours to get there, but Botta had merely shrugged, as if to say that it would be a piece of cake.

Arcieri could only think of his lost paradise, Bordelli's big house, in which he'd succeeded in finding a little peace for a few days. He felt as if he was leaving part of himself behind, as if he'd been living there for years. He remembered the time when he was a little boy and had a secret hiding place for his things, small knick-knacks of incalculable value to him. It was inside an old dry-stone wall, along the road to his house. One of the stones was easy to remove, and behind it he'd found a small niche. Then one day, with little warning, his family had upped sticks and moved house, and he hadn't had time to go and empty out his private nook. His secrets were all still there now, unless of course the wall had been demolished. When he was in the military, especially during the war, whenever he wanted to protect some secret thought of his he would go and hide it in that old wall in Milan in his mind . . . But now his secret nook was Bordelli's house. That was where he'd left his most secret thoughts. And no one would ever find them.

He realised he was chasing after pointless conjectures, but figured that was exactly what he needed just then. To let himself go . . . The rumble of the car's engine made him think of racing . . . The

Thousand Miles, Tazio Nuvolari, the crackling voice of the Giornale Luce . . . He found himself back at the wheel of his Alfa Giulia as it flew off the mountainside of Sant'Anna di Stazzema, and to interrupt this vision, he opened his eyes . . . The headlights lit up a road snaking along some cliffsides . . . To the left, beyond the darkness, he sensed the vastness of the sea . . . He closed his eyes again and saw a sunny beach from half a century before . . .

It was the middle of the night. Rolling over in bed, Bordelli slowly emerged from sleep, but more with his senses than with his mind. He curled up in a ball to stay warm, as he used to do as a child. Things felt timeless, and the sound of night birds hooting in the silence made it even more so. Suddenly he heard the sound of hooves approaching from a distance, and then a horse's nervous whinny. The clattering slowed and then stopped just under his window. He raised his head, now fully awake. The horse kept snorting, every so often pawing the ground with its hoof.

'Is anyone there, pray tell?' a virile voice called out. Bordelli staggered out of bed and peeked through the shutters. Sitting astride an enormous white stallion was a knight in armour, a large sword hanging by his side. Through the dark slit in his helmet burned two proud eyes.

'Is anyone awake at this hour of the night?' the knight insisted. Bordelli opened the window and looked out.

'What brings you?' he asked.

'I seek Count Francaccio de' Bordelli.'

'He stands before you . . .'

'May God bless you. My name is Duccio de' Marescalchi, duke of Borracciani. I have a missive to deliver to you.'

'Who sends it?'

'You shall know forthwith, but for now be so kind as to welcome me into your abode. I have been travelling since sunset from faraway Fiorenza. My horse wants water and rest and, in truth, I should not decline the same comforts myself, if offered.'

'I'll be right down to open for you,' said Count Francaccio, and he ventured down the stairs with torch in hand then removed the keys from the heavy door and lowered the drawbridge. The knight entered the castle with his helmet under his arm, armour jangling.

He was not tall, but had an imposing air. A great mane of black hair framed his dusty face.

'I've had your groom take Asturcone, the most valiant steed in the land, to the stables. For my part, I merely want fire and a goblet of wine.'

'You are most welcome here . . . please make yourself at home . . .'

Count de' Bordelli accompanied the knight to the warmest room in the castle, where a great fire roared in a majestic fireplace. The knight set his helmet down on the table manfully, and the two men sat down on straight-back chairs, close to the fire. Two goblets abrim with blood-red wine appeared in their hands. The knight had something animal about him, a fierce sort of pride, typical of the bold. He took a long draught of wine, unconcerned when it drizzled down his scraggly beard. He wiped his mouth with his hand, and after a sigh of relief, took a rolled parchment out of his haversack.

'Your missive, Count,' he said with a kind of solemnity. De' Bordelli took the parchment, broke the wax seal, and opened it with trepidation.

My beloved Franco,

What cruel wind has kept you away from me? What devilish influences have managed to dispel the magic of our kisses? It is as if Charon has ferried our good fortune away to the kingdom of the Hereafter, among the souls of the damned. But there is no force in the world that can defeat love, and you know this better than anyone. And so I ask, what keeps you? Do you want me to die? Must an angel descend from heaven to beseech you to return to me? My every thought is for you, for my heart belongs to you, and shall belong to you forever . . .

Eternally yours,
Eleonora

Francaccio de' Bordelli had tears in his eyes, and his heart beat like the drums that announce the beginning of a joust. He looked up at the duke of Borracciani, incapable of uttering a single word. The knight was gazing at the tongues of fire shooting out from a log of oak, but when he realised that the count was watching him, he cast him a harsh glance.

'Can you no longer speak, man?'

'No . . . I had no idea . . .' Count de' Bordelli stammered confusedly. The duke of Borracciani pointed a frighteningly long index finger and cast a dour eye upon him.

'To win a lady's favour, a real knight must face a thousand dangers, venture into dark forests, fight dragons and ghosts, do battle with werewolves and the demon's wiles . . . And you? What are you doing? You hide out in your castle like a baby rabbit in its burrow; you're not even capable of writing a few words to your beloved . . . How dare you consider yourself a knight! A worm has more courage than you! Your cowardice will be remembered for centuries to come!' he said with flames in his eyes, full of contempt.

'It's not true . . . I am not a coward . . .' Bordelli stood up, lost, holding the parchment to his chest.

'You know very well what you are!' said the duke. He tore the parchment out of the count's hands and threw it into the fire.

'What have you done?' Count de' Bordelli protested feebly, staring at his beloved's letter as it burned in the flames. The duke downed his goblet of wine in one gulp and threw it into the fire, smashing it into a thousand pieces.

'It is you who threw it into the fire, it is you who have burnt the sweet words of Milady Eleonora . . . Can't you see what is happening? I am you and you are me. We are one and one alone. But I am Duccio de' Marescalchi, duke of Borracciani, and you are a rabbit. Such is the mystery of man.'

'I don't understand . . . I don't understand . . .' Francaccio said, running a hand through his hair. The duke laughed mightily, amused by such childishness, and then, after a long, compassionate sigh, rested his hands on his thighs and stared pensively down at the ground.

'To know or not to know, this is the question . . .' he murmured melancholically. There was a long, sad silence, heavy with unasked questions, mitigated only by the gentle crackling of the logs on the fire. It seemed as if that moment would never end, that everything could remain suspended forever, and all mysteries would remain untouched. But then the knight shook his head.

'The night is still long . . . before returning to my manor I have one last task to fulfil. In the forest of Poneta there is a blood-starved ogre who deserves to taste the edge of my sword . . .'

Getting up slowly from the straight-backed chair, he gathered his helmet from the table and walked off towards the castle door, armour clanging. Count de' Bordelli followed him, feeling lost; he couldn't think of a single appropriate word to say for the occasion. They went outside into the frosty night, and the mysterious horseman rode away, vanishing into the dark like a ghost, never once looking back. The sky was black and endless. An immense moon hung between the stars, and the land was a great expanse of shadows . . .

As Francaccio was having the drawbridge lowered, the court jester started ringing a little bell next to the count's ears and laughing wildly . . . And Bordelli woke up with a start, heart beating fast in his chest. Once again it was the phone wrenching him from his sleep, but by the time he managed to pick up the receiver, the caller had already hung up. It was already past noon. Tongues of light beamed through the shutter slats. He fell back down, wondering who had rung. Perhaps Botta? Or were they calling him from the police station? He remained under the covers, to catch his breath. He was about to fall back asleep when the telephone rang again. He reached out with one arm and quickly picked up.

'Hello?'

'Did I wake you up?' asked a woman's voice, with a hint of irony in it. It took Bordelli a second to recognise it, since she was the last person he was expecting to ring him. His heart jumped into this throat, and he sat up, trying to sound completely awake.

'Hi . . . Was that you a few seconds ago?' The excitement was making his voice quaver a little.

'I've been trying to call you for the last three days,' said Eleonora.

'I haven't been at home much . . .'

'Are you in another woman's arms?'

'Unfortunately, no . . .'

'You sound sleepy.'

'I went to bed very late.'

'Would you like to have dinner with me?' she asked point blank.

'When?'

'Are you free tonight?'

'Yes . . .'

'Half eight in front of San Miniato?'

'All right . . .'

'And now I'll let you sleep,' she said with unexpected tenderness.

''Bye . . .'

'See you later.'

Eleonora hung up, and he fell back on the bed and lay there studying the ceiling rafters, feeling bewildered. He'd succeeded in getting her for the most part out of his mind, in convincing himself he had to forget her, and now he had to wait eight long hours before he could see her again . . . And where? Why, right in front of the Church of San Miniato, where they'd met for their first date. Why had Eleonora decided to get in touch with him? What did she have in mind? Was it merely because they'd run into each other on the street? Did she have a boyfriend? He didn't want to get his hopes up, but neither did he feel like spending the day asking himself pointless questions. He got out of bed and staggered downstairs, determined to put her out of his mind.

By now he'd become accustomed to the colonel's presence, and the deserted kitchen seemed too sad for words . . . Ennio hadn't rung yet . . . Who knew where Arcieri had made him go . . . Bordelli put the espresso pot on the stove and rang headquarters. Nobody'd called for him. He took advantage of the situation to say he wouldn't be coming in that day, either.

'I'll be at home if anyone calls . . .'

He knocked back his coffee, hoping to wake up a little. After sweeping the ashes out of the fireplace, he lit a nice big fire to last the afternoon. Exchanging a glance of understanding with Jeremiah, who was smiling at him benevolently, he was about to go back upstairs when the phone rang again. Maybe Eleonora had changed her mind? No, it had to be Ennio . . .

'Hello?'

'Why didn't you come in to work today?' asked Diotivede.

'I'll tell you another time.'

'I read in the paper that you arrested Migliorini's sister-in-law.'

'Did they say it was an accident?'

'I only saw the headline: MURDERESS CONFESSES.'

'She didn't mean to kill him.'

He told the doctor how it had all happened, leaving out the personal details.

'At any rate, that's not why I rang you,' said Diotivede.

'Then tell me.'

'I'd like your friend the general to give me a couple of recipes. Is he still staying with you?'

'Since when did you start cooking?'

'Since my wife started cooking . . .'

'Ah, I see.'

'Could you pass me the general?'

'He left just last night, for Japan, in fact, or maybe it was Brazil, but I wouldn't rule out Finland, either. . .' said Bordelli, in case anyone from Special Services might be listening.

'Too bad . . . When you hear from him next, could you ask him to give you the recipes from last Friday?'

'I most certainly shall.'

'Feel like dining at our place one of these evenings?'

'All right . . .'

'But now I have to go; there's a lovely lady here waiting for me.'

'Dead or alive?'

'I couldn't say, but she's lying on a stretcher with a sheet over her.'

'I'll leave you to your fun and games . . .'

They said goodbye, and Bordelli went upstairs and into the bathroom. While shaving he saw his mother in the mirror, sitting on the edge of the bathtub and wearing the light-blue dressing gown she'd worn for years when he was a little boy.

'Good morning, Francolino, you look a little tired . . .'

'I'm a wreck, Ma'.'

'Always chasing after women.'

'That's not true . . .'

'Well, at least the one you'll be seeing tonight is a nice girl.'

'I know, Mamma.'

'But she's too young for you, don't you think?'

'No, Mamma, it's me who's too old.'

'Still the same joker . . .' said his mother, smiling, and a moment later she was gone.

Bordelli rewarded himself with a long hot bath, and even managed not to ask himself too many questions about Eleonora. He was in no hurry. He had a long afternoon ahead of him and already imagined himself reading in his armchair, as he'd done during the period when he'd quit the force.

After dousing his hair with Bipantol, he got dressed and went downstairs. Being already out of the habit of cooking, he thought he would make a nice dish of penne with olive oil and hot pepper. He put the pasta water on to boil, and while waiting tried to ring Agostinelli. He wanted to ask him what the situation at the Services was concerning the fugitive, but was told that the admiral was out of the office. This made him worried, and more anxious than ever to hear from Botta.

Then he remembered the British officer's diary and went to the car to get it. He thumbed through it while eating, trying to decipher the words, but his knowledge of English was scant. The notebook's spine was blackened with dried blood, and one could see clearly that certain pages were written with blood-covered fingers. Here and there he recognised the names of cities he'd been through himself, coming up through Italy on the Germans' tail, and the hell of those months came back to him. Taking a look at the letter from the British man's girlfriend, he realised he didn't understand a thing other than the signature. Turning page after page, he found, at the back of the notebook, inside the cover, two strange little drawings with some incomprehensible writing under them. The first was a small circle with wavy lines radiating out from it in all directions. It looked a bit like a pane of glass punctured by a bullet, but it might also be a crater. The second drawing was shaped like a canoe. The writing said: N30 NW60 N57 and, under the 'canoe', NNW. What the hell did it mean? Four initials couldn't represent a geographical coordinate, could they? The combination to a safe, perhaps? A secret code? A magic formula? He closed the diary, postponing the solution of the enigma to another day.

After lunch he went into the sitting room to put on an old disc by the Trio Lescano, at low volume, and then finally sat down in the armchair with a book in his hand. Jack London . . . *The best storyteller in the world*, the young salesman at Seeber's had called him. But he'd said the same thing about Melville, Dickens, Balzac, Dostoevsky, and many others . . . He was probably right.

For the third time in a matter of hours Bordelli was woken up by the ringing of the phone. He peered over at the clock on the wall. Ten minutes to seven. He got up to answer, unsteady on his legs.

'What do you say to a game of pool, Inspector?' It was Botta. Finally.

'Are you ready to be humiliated?'

'I think you'll have a hard time doing that . . .'

'See you at half past seven at Fosco's?'

'Fine . . . shall we bet a drink?'

'You know that betting is illegal . . .'

'That's why I like it.'

'See you in a bit.' Bordelli hung up and went to the bathroom to brush his teeth. He didn't dare look at himself in the mirror, afraid of seeing an old man. His mother was right: Eleonora was too young for him . . .

To mix things up a bit, he took the Bagnolo road towards Florence. Keeping an eye on the clock, he parked in Piazza Tasso at exactly half past seven. It wasn't as cold as in the country. Upon entering, he nodded hello to Fosco and went directly to the billiards room, which smelled of stale smoke. Ennio was sitting on a bench. He looked tired and had dark circles under his eyes.

'Everything's all right . . .' he said.

'Don't tell me where you left him, I'd rather not know.'

'In case of torture?'

'Exactly. Shall we play?'

'You'd win. I'm a wreck. I drove for fourteen hours.'

'Could've been worse . . .'

'I slept for an hour on the motorway, and my ears are ringing.'

'Forget you ever made this journey. Don't mention it to anyone, not even your pretty girlfriend.'

'What journey?' Botta asked, with feigned surprise that seemed rather convincing. The inspector smiled and sat down beside him on the bench.

'When will I meet Anita?'

'I still don't know how I'm going to explain my sudden departure to her,' Ennio said with concern.

'Tell her the pope wanted to talk to you about the thirty pieces of silver.'

'I really don't know what I would do without you, Inspector.'

They sat on the bench and talked for another half an hour. At ten past eight, Bordelli said he had to go but then realised that he had given the colonel all his money. His wallet was as empty as a politician's words. Botta didn't have any cash either, so Bordelli had to ask Fosco for a quick loan.

Afraid of arriving late, he climbed into the Beetle in a hurry. By twenty-five past he was parked in front of San Miniato. It felt like a flashback to the days of the flood, when he had waited there for Eleonora.

She was only ten minutes late. She parked her clean, white Cinquecento and Bordelli went to greet her. They didn't shake hands: that would have been too formal. Neither did they kiss each other on the cheek, as two friends would have done. They just said *ciao* and got into the Beetle. Driving towards town, they exchanged just a few words, uncertain as to where they would go for dinner. There was no sense of embarrassment, but neither were they ready for any complicated conversations.

They found a little restaurant on Borgo Pinto which was new to them both. Candles, soft lighting, a nice bottle of wine: the right atmosphere for a special evening. The other guests were mainly couples, some with a furtive air about them. They, too, could have been secret lovers . . . He was older and dressed like an old man, she was young and wore a tight pair of jeans and an orange top that could have been painted on.

'So, what have you been up to?' she asked him while they were waiting for the starters.

'Oh, the usual things . . .' He couldn't tell her that he had killed three men in the name of justice.

'Bacchus, tobacco and Venus?'

'I've almost entirely stopped smoking,' Bordelli said.

'So just Bacchus and Venus?'

'Just Bacchus,' he lied with a smile. He thought about the night before and how he had dined with Claretta not too far away. Then the sequel, back at her house, on the sofa . . .

'Are you thinking about a woman?'

'Yes,' he said, amazed that she had been able to tell.

'Someone who wouldn't be happy to know that you are with me?'

'Someone whom I arrested last night.'

'Oh yes, I read about it in the paper . . . there was a photo. She looked quite pretty.'

'Yes, she is pretty.'

'Have you ever fallen in love with a killer?'

'That's a professional secret.'

'Shall we take turns asking embarrassing questions?'

She was truly beautiful. And how she loved to play. When the antipasti arrived, the wine bottle was already half empty.

'You go first,' Bordelli said. She thought for a moment, as though looking for an impertinent question.

'Have you ever slept with a man?'

'It has never even occurred to me . . . and you?'

'With a man?' she joked.

'With a woman . . .'

'Umm, yes.'

'Ah . . .'

'Once, just to see what it was like.'

'And what was it like?' he asked, slightly disturbed.

'It was fun. Women have much more imagination than men, and they are much sweeter. But to tell the truth, something was missing,' she said, laughing.

'Can I guess what that might have been?'

'I'm not sure . . .'

'It's your turn again.'

'Have you been thinking about me all these months?' she asked.

'A little . . . Now it's my turn,' Bordelli said quickly, to cover up his embarrassment.

'I'm ready,' she said with a smile, pretending that nothing had happened.

'The boy from the other night – does he know that you're with me?'

'My God, you're obsessed.'

'Isn't this a game of embarrassing questions?'

'Yes, but not stupid ones.'

'Okay, let me change my question: how many boyfriends have you had this year?'

'None.'

'I don't believe you.'

'I swear, not one boyfriend. But I've had a lot of affairs.'

'How many?'

'I've lost count.'

'So it was a kind of job,' Bordelli said jokingly, but he felt a pain in his stomach. Eleonora burst out laughing.

'I love seeing you so jealous.'

'I'm not jealous.'

'Anyway, there's no need – it's not as if we're a couple or anything.'

'I know . . . you're right . . . It's you who . . .' stammered Bordelli, blushing. She was gracious, though, and didn't tease him about it. She was thirty years younger than him . . . it was like a cat playing with a mouse before eating it. Well, he wouldn't mind being eaten by her, not at all . . .

They continued their game of embarrassing questions, enjoying themselves as they had in the early days. It was as if they had erased the past and started over. But Bordelli steered clear of asking her further about love affairs and boyfriends.

Eleonora polished off her apple cake and got up to go to the ladies' room. Bordelli followed her with his gaze; he was dying to kiss her. When she disappeared around the corner he finished his wine and sat there staring into space. It was strange to be with her, and yet it felt like the most natural thing in the world. He thought of how many times he had tried to write her a letter, or was on the verge of ringing her. Imagining this meeting, he had thought it would be packed with tension and remorse. He would never have imagined such a delightful evening, so light hearted. And what would happen afterwards? Well, it wasn't up to him to decide . . .

He gestured to the waiter to bring the bill and took his wallet out of his jacket. The waiter came up to him, smiling faintly.

'The young lady has already taken care of it,' he whispered.

'What?'

'Sorry . . .' the waiter said, seeing that Bordelli seemed displeased. At that moment Eleonora reappeared, and the waiter slipped away.

'Shall we go?' she asked, taking her seat.

'You shouldn't have,' Bordelli said, putting his wallet back in his jacket.

'Do you want to arrest me?'

'I wouldn't mind at all,' the inspector said, getting to his feet. Eleonora put on her coat by herself, and they made their way outside, shivering from the cold. They headed for the Beetle.

'I'm drunk . . .' she said.

'Do you want to take a little walk?'

'Didn't you want to show me your collection of toy soldiers?'

He was sitting on the beach at Marina di Massa, looking out at a stormy sea. Watching the high, white-capped billows crash against the shore, he enjoyed the feel of the tiny droplets of water wetting his face. The wind tossing his hair smelled of the sea and of ancient memories.

It was half past two. His friend Riccà's trattoria was closed for the holidays, and he'd just eaten a pizza at Baffo's. He'd come out to the seaside after buying a ticket at Santa Maria Novella station in Florence. The train for Paris left at eleven that evening. His suitcase was already in the car. Renewing his passport had taken only a couple of minutes, and he'd already changed two hundred thousand lire into francs at the bank. He'd given no indication at the office as to when he would be back. But it wasn't just Eleonora's fault. He felt he needed a period of rest, far from murders and killers. Too many things had happened in the past few days.

Watching the sea made him think of time. Not the time on one's watch or on the calendar, but the time of memory, which he was unable to seize hold of. He saw himself again as a child on that same sand, in summertime, with the sun burning his skin. The beach was exceptionally long, women's bathing suits barely revealed their knees, and the Colonia Torino didn't exist yet.[37] He would spend the whole morning splashing about in the water, and then, at a certain point, his mother would start calling him . . . *Francoooo . . . Francoooo . . . That's enough now* . . . He would ruefully obey, coming out of the water with blue lips, huffing and puffing in frustration, but his pique was always compensated by a piece of warm foccaccia sprinkled with large salt crystals. He would eat it while sitting on the scalding-hot sand, watching the motionless ships on the horizon, spellbound by the sound of the surf. Behind him his father's ancient aunts were chatting, sitting in deckchairs under great parasols, always dressed as though on their way to church . . . Vittorina . . . Cecilia . . . Ilda . . . Costanza . . . It was as if he could still see them, in their little caps with half-veils . . . Where had those moments gone? Did they now exist only in his memory? Or were they still unfolding somewhere? The Fascist Youth parades, the bicycle races with friends, the war, the comrades torn apart by mines, the Germans he'd killed . . .

And the evening he'd just spent with Eleonora, where had that gone? They'd started kissing in front of the fire, then made their way into the bedroom. The hardest part was getting her jeans off . . . They'd made love late into the night, without saying a single word, and had fallen asleep in each other's arms. When he'd opened his eyes the following morning, the bed was empty. Twenty past ten. He'd gone downstairs to look for her, even sticking his head out of the door, but she was gone. At what time had she left? Had she walked into Impruneta to catch the bus? Or had she hitched a ride?

On the bathroom mirror he'd found the lipsticked imprint of a kiss, and on the sink, a note:

Now don't go thinking that a quickie like that means we're together again. Please don't come looking for me. I'll be back when I feel I'm ready.
Ele

That was the moment when he'd decided to go away. Aside from the fact that he was dead tired, he didn't feel like losing himself yet again in a forest of questions, and he especially didn't want to spend all his days waiting, hoping and fantasising. Better Paris.

At any rate, he felt happy, deep down. Eleonora still had the same *joie de vivre*, the same passion for lovemaking, as before. Let the chips fall where they may. He didn't want to suffer for her any longer. Not for her, or for any other woman.

He'd got dressed in a hurry, and while packing his bag, he'd heard a horn outside. Rushing over to the window, he had a surprise. Eleonora might have left, but as a consolation, a small van full of cases of wine was waiting outside . . . Balzini wine. Three hundred bottles. Olinto Marinari had kept his promise.

'Tout s'est bien passé? Désirez-vous autre chose?'

'Another one of these, please,' Bordelli said, raising the empty glass. The Café Mont Cenis was crowded. It hadn't been easy finding a table next to the window.

'*Albert, un autre gamay pour monsieur.*'

The host looked like a character out of a Maigret novel: balding with sharp eyes, cordial but not servile.

'*Merci,*' said Bordelli. It was one of the few words he could recall, along with the usual *amour*, *merde* and *putain*. If Rosa ever learnt that he'd gone alone to Paris, she would never forgive him. But this time round, it couldn't have been any other way.

He had travelled all night on the train, jostled this way and that, sleeping not a wink, but he didn't feel tired. After leaving his suitcase in a pension near Abbesses, he'd spent the morning strolling through the neighbourhood, walking up and down stairs, admiring the women, and looking out at Paris below. The temperature was comparable to that in Impruneta. The sky was leaden grey; every so often it started to drizzle but it never wet his hair. He walked past the small vineyard of Montmartre, under the windmill of the Moulin Rouge, down the alleys of Marché Saint-Pierre, and even strolled a bit through the big Place de Clichy cemetery. But he didn't feel like a tourist. On the contrary, he felt as though he was revisiting places from his childhood. No two ways about it: he felt at home in Paris.

Around one o'clock he'd realised he was starving and sat down at the corner café at the top of rue de Mont Cenis, across from one of the staircases leading up to Montmartre. He enjoyed watching the people walking by, trying to imagine who they were, what sort of lives they led . . . Maybe that was what writers did . . .

'Pardon me, but have you got anything to write with?' he asked when Albert brought him the glass of wine, using gestures to make himself understood.

'*Oui, monsieur, je vous l'amène tout de suite.*' The young man leaned over the counter, grabbed a pen and pad, left it on the table, and rushed off. Bordelli thought for a moment, then wrote: *I am in Paris for at least two weeks. Stop. Every day from one to two I shall be at the café at the corner of rue de Mont Cenis and rue Custine. Stop. It would be nice to see you. Stop. Franco . . .*

He read it over a few times. Then, as always, he wadded up the paper and put the pen down. He took a sip of wine. He needed to stop imagining things. He was in Paris, the city was waiting for him; all he had to do was try to have fun. When he looked up he saw a pretty lady sitting by herself on the other side of the bar, a small dog in her lap. She was watching him tenderly, as if she had understood. He smiled at her, and she smiled back . . .

Notes

by Stephen Sartarelli and Ooonagh Stransky

1. –From September 1943 to August 1944, the Villa Triste ('House of Sadness') at 67 Via Bolognese in Florence lodged a unit of the German 'political police', the SD (*Sicherheitsdienst*), and a section of the Milizia Volontaria per la Sicurezza Nationale (the Voluntary Militia for National Security) of the pro-Nazi puppet government of the Republic of Salò, set up by the Germans in 1943 after they occupied Italy to fill the power void following the fall of the Fascist government and the 8 September armistice. The Villa Triste of Florence was one of several buildings so called in the Italy of the occupation, the others being in Rome, Milan, Trieste, Genoa and elsewhere.
2. –In colloquial Italian, exclaiming '*Madonna!*' is a mild form of curse. Thus, the statement that 'Madonnas are flying' is a play on words meaning that a great many people are cursing at that moment. Hence the amused reaction of the crowd. Florentines and Tuscans, moreover, are known for their cursing, which can get rather inventive at times.
3. –A nuraghe is an ancient conical megalith found in central Sardinia.
4. –The Bersaglieri are a division of light infantry created in 1836.
5. –Moplen is the registered trademark of a plastic material, isotactic polypropelene, useful for its resistant properties and strength.
6. –An important expedition in the Italian Risorgimento, led by patriot Giuseppe Garibaldi in 1860, who landed at Marsala, Sicily, with a small but determined force fighting to free the island from the Bourbon monarchy, with a view to its incorporation in the eventually unified Italian nation.
7. –During the twenty-odd years of Fascist rule in Italy, the country began to fill with sculpted effigies of Il Duce, who,

like many men of diminutive stature, appeared to have a head too big for his body. In addition, given the generally impressive nature of Mussolini's head, there were more than a few effigies of just his head in public places. These various factors led to his being called Il Testone, or 'Bighead', by the Italians.

8. –Ciacco is a historically unidentified character in Dante's *Inferno*, in hell for the sin of gluttony.
9. –The last line of 'L'infinito' (' . . . *e il naufragar m'è dolce in questo mare*'), perhaps the most famous poem of Italian Romantic Giacomo Leopardi (1798–1837).
10. –2 November is *il giorno dei morti*, the 'day of the dead', when many families throng to the cemeteries to visit their lost loved ones.
11. –Grilled bread with olive oil and sometimes garlic. Can also be served with a variety of toppings.
12. –The SID is the acronym for Servizio Informazioni Difesa, a sort of Italian equivalent of MI5 and MI6 rolled into one.
13. –It was through a breach at Porta Pia – a gate in the ancient Aurelian walls of Rome renovated by Michelangelo and others – that the *bersaglieri* of the national Unification army entered Rome in 1870, on their way to conquering the Eternal City, later to become the capital of unified Italy.
14. –'Champagne in cups, perfume in drops.'
15. –A Fiat all-terrain vehicle, a bit like the American jeep.
16. –'I am sure that . . . in this vast emptiness/someone is thinking a little of me . . .'
17. –Stenterello is a traditional character of the Florentine Carnival, clownish and often dressed in unmatching clothes.
18. –A sweet muscat wine.
19. –From a famous short poem, the 'Canzona di Bacco' (Song of Bacchus), a *carpe diem* rhyme by the great Renaissance patron Lorenzo de' Medici (1449–1492) 'Quant'è bella giovinezza,/Che si fugge tuttavia!/Chi vuol esser lieto, sia:/di doman non v'è certezza.'(How beautiful is youth/which yet flees withal!/Be happy, who would be so:/for uncertain is the morrow.)
20. –Members of the Nazi occupation government of Italy, which went under the name of the Repubblica di Salò.

21. –Tom Ponzi (1921-1997) was an Italian private and sometimes public investigator and criminologist. As a private investigator he frequently worked for some of the richest people in the world.
22. –The Case del Popolo were social centres established and run by the Italian Communist Party.
23. –Also called the Repubblica di Salò. See note, p. 197.
24. –In the third book in the Bordelli series, *Death in Sardinia* (orig. *Il nuovo venuto*), the inspector's investigation into the murder of a notorious loan shark leads him to the conclusion that Odoardo was the killer, but he refrains from arresting the young man, because the circumstances of the murder – in which Odoardo kills the loan shark out of revenge after the usurer's blackmail had driven his mother to suicide – lead him to sympathise more with the killer than with his victim.
25. –Literally, 'to show the miracle': a quote from a sonnet in Chapter XXVI of Dante's *Vita Nova*, in which the poet's beloved, Beatrice, is so gracious and beautiful in her manner that she appears descended from heaven to work miracles.
26. –In Italy, *la Befana* is a legendary 'good witch' who comes and fills the children's Christmas stockings on the feast of the Epiphany. For those who have been naughty, however, she gives coal instead of presents. The name *Befana* is simply a corruption of the Italian word for Epiphany, *Epifania*.
27. –See note on p269, *Death in Sardinia*, by Marco Vichi.
28. –'I'm not the right age to love you . . .' From a 1964 song, 'Non ho l'età', by Gigliola Cinquetti.
29. –Homer, *Odyssey*, Book I, line 185, tr. Robert Fitzgerald. New York: Vintage Classics, p. 6.
30. –8 September 1943 was the date of the official announcement of the so-called Armistice – in reality an unconditional surrender – whereby the nation of Italy would cease all hostilities against Allied forces. The country's armed forces were disbanded and the soldiers sent home. Just four days later, however, on 12 September, the Germans, who already controlled the northern half of the peninsula, sprang Mussolini and quickly set up the quisling Salò government, with the disgraced Mussolini as figurehead.

31. –'Remember always to dare'. A Latin dictum coined by the Italian nationalist poet Gabriele D'Annunzio (1863–1938).
32. –This is the red star of communism, indicating, like an insignia, the presence of a Casa del Popolo, one of the many social centres established and run by the Communist Party across Italy.
33. –In Italian there is a saying that *Bacco, tabacco e venere, riducono l'uomo in cenere*, which loses its sonority, and therefore its charm and purpose, in English translation ('Bacchus, tobacco, and Venus will reduce man to ashes').
34. –They called her Rosy Mouth, and she put her love/put her love . . . [. . .] Nothing is born from diamonds, while dung gives birth to flowers . . . From the song 'Bocca di Rosa', by Fabrizio De André (1940–1999).
35. –Liqueur made from cinchona bark.
36. –'The river slowly flows,/splashing 'neath the bridges,/the moon shines in the sky,/the entire city sleeps . . .' from 'Vecchio frak' (Old Tuxedo), by Domenico Modugno (1928–1994).
37. –A large, modest resort complex built by the Mussolini regime in the mid-1930s at Marina di Massa for Turinese youth, the unsightly building later became a school but has now fallen into disuse.

Author's Note

The writing of *Ghosts of the Past* followed a rather unusual procedure. The actions, thoughts, dreams and fantasies of Bruno Arcieri were 'provided' by Leonardo Gori and then rewritten and adapted by me.

The character of Bruno Arcieri, by Leonardo Gori.

The stories of Bruno Arcieri and Franco Bordelli have periodically crossed in the past, particularly in the novel *L'angelo del fango* [The Angel of the Mud], in which the same scene as figures in my *Death in Florence* (Guanda, 2009) appears as told from the opposite point of view.

Carabinieri Captain (later Colonel) Bruno Arcieri, secret agent for the SIM (and later for the SIFAR and finally the SID), is the protagonist of seven novels by Leonardo Gori, set in the time span from the 1930s to the 1960s. His initial story is told in *Nero di Maggio* (Hobby & Work, 2000), which was followed by *Il passaggio* (Hobby & Work, 2002); *La finale* (Hobby & Work, 2003); *Lo specchio Nero* (Hobby & Work, 2004, with Franco Cardini); *L'angelo del fango* (Rizzoli, 2005); *Il fiore d'oro* (with Franco Cardini, Hobby & Work, 2006); and *Musica nera* (Hobby & Work, 2008).

The story of Arcieri and the young man in the hospital at Viareggio has its roots in *Musica nera* and will be concluded in Leonardo Gori's next novel.

All the poems quoted in this novel are by my mother, Paola Cannas, and drawn from *Respiri e sospiri* (Felici Editore, 2013). Some of the proceeds of this great little book of poetry go to finance the work of the Filo di juta association (www.filodijuta.it), which is devoted to primary school education in Bangladesh. Whoever would like to know more about the book and the association can consult my website, www.marcovichi.it.

Acknowledgements

Enneli Poli, peerless huntress of typographical errors.

Michele Giusti, who gave me the gift of a war story from his family history.

Vincenzo Infantino, who gave me the gift of a war story from his adolescence.

Divier Nelli, for some useful suggestions.

Francesco Castanini, for some historical confirmations concerning the period of the liberation.

The mysterious Laura, who knows why.

Laura Tangherlini, who, without knowing it, helped me give life to a character in the novel.

My mother, for appearing to me in a dream.

Briciola the kitten, and Dago the puppy, for having busted my chops during the writing of the novel.

Death in Florence

Marco Vichi

Florence, October 1966. The rain is never-ending. When a young boy vanishes on his way home from school the police fear the worst, and Inspector Bordelli begins an increasingly desperate investigation.

Then the flood hits. During the night of 4th November the swollen River Arno, already lapping the arches of the Ponte Vecchio, breaks its banks and overwhelms the city. Streets become rushing torrents, the force of the water sweeping away cars and trees, doors, shutters and anything else in its wake.

In the aftermath of this unimaginable tragedy the mystery of the child's disappearance seems destined to go unsolved. But obstinate as ever, Bordelli is not prepared to give up.

Out now in paperback and ebook

Death and the Olive Grove

Marco Vichi

April 1964, but spring hasn't quite sprung. The bad weather seems suited to nothing but bad news. And bad news is coming to the police station.

First, Bordelli's friend Casimiro, who insists he's discovered the body of a man in a field above Fiesole. Bordelli races to the scene, but doesn't find any sign of a corpse.

Only a couple of days later, a little girl is found at Villa Ventaglio. She has been strangled, and there is a horrible bite mark on her belly. Then another little girl is found murdered, with the same macabre signature.

And meanwhile Casimiro has disappeared without a trace.

The investigation marks the start of one of the darkest periods of Bordelli's life: a nightmare without end, as black as the sky above Florence.

Out now in paperback and ebook